Beneath the Stands

EMILY MCINTIRE

Beneath the Stands
(Sugarlake Series, Book Two)
By: Emily McIntire

Copyright © 2020 by Emily McIntire

Cover Design: Clarise Tan—CT Cover Creations
Editing: My Brother's Editor
Proofreading: My Brother's Editor

Ebook ISBN 978-1-7349994-2-6
Paperback ISBN 978-1-7349994-3-3

❀ Created with Vellum

For anyone who has ever felt unworthy. You are perfect just the way you are.

Being deeply loved by someone gives you strength,
while loving someone deeply gives you courage.

1

BECCA

My palms are sweating. It's not because of the weather, although Florida in August is hot and humid as hell. It's because I'm fixing to Face-Time my old man and let him know I'm not coming home after senior year. I'm not sure when I made the decision, although if pressed to think back, I'd guess it was sometime *before* getting accepted into Florida Coast University, and sometime *after* I walked in on him screwing the youth leader of our church on his big oak desk. But I digress. The point is that although my hometown, Sugarlake, Tennessee, will always hold a special place in my heart, it won't hold me. Florida suits me just fine. I've fallen in love with the nonexistent winters and the palm trees. And maybe a little bit with the fact I'm not in a town where everyone knows me as Preacher Sanger's daughter.

The apple that fell too far from the tree.

So, here I sit, on the front steps to my apartment complex. I've just finished moving in with my dorm mate of the past three years, Sabrina. After Papa found out I was spending more time going to dorm parties instead of classes, he decided to foot the bill for a place off campus. A place where I can "focus" and get my degree "as quickly as possible." Probably so he can have a daughter with something to be proud of. Momma, on the other hand, is just hoping I'll come home —back to the church that's been strangling me my whole life, and into her clutches where she can mold me to perfection. Maybe if I give in, she'd stop with the incessant nagging over all the ways I make her look bad.

I drop the ends of my frizzy red hair when my phone screen lights up with Papa's name for a FaceTime call. *I may love Florida heat, but it does not love my curls.* Wiping my clammy hands on my sun-kissed thighs, I swipe to answer.

"Hi, Papa." The smile I plaster on my face strains the muscles in my cheeks.

"Rebecca. You get moved in alright?" His face is stern, and those jade green eyes, identical to mine, chill me with their icy gaze.

"You betcha. Sabrina got here before me and picked the better room, but I'm thankful for any extra space. It's all a mansion compared to the dorms."

"Good, good. I'll let your momma know you made it safe. She can't come to the phone, she's makin' roast for supper and we're expectin' company."

I fight the urge to roll my eyes. *Of course, Momma's busy entertainin' his guests.*

"That's alright." My fingers twist my split ends. "But hey, Papa… before you go, there's somethin' I've been meanin' to tell ya."

His eyebrow cocks, the only indication he's listening.

My stomach pinches and I hesitate, wanting to hang up the phone instead of saying what needs to be said.

"Spit it out, Rebecca Jean, I'm a busy man."

A nervous laugh bubbles up my throat, but I bite it down.

"I'm gonna stay out here for a while after graduation. Sabrina's stayin', too, so it's not like it will be a big change."

He's silent.

A part of me thrills at the thought of his blood pressure rising from what I'm saying. Serves him right, thinking he can control everything.

"I think it'll be good for me, ya know? Plus, it'll give you and Momma a place to visit when you're wantin' to go on vacation."

Maybe appealing to how it could benefit him will make him more amiable to the idea. I like to push his buttons, but at the end of the day, he's the one that holds the reins to everything in my life, and I haven't figured out how to cut the rope.

"The heat gone to your head and made you lose it, girl? I didn't fork out four years of college in that sinful place just for you to spit in my face when it's time to come home."

My heart sinks.

"Your life is here in Sugarlake. With the church. With your family."

Church. Even from thousands of miles away, it clamps its claws into every orifice and makes me feel like I'm suffocating from its presence.

I suck in a deep breath, pushing out the words on my exhale—afraid if I don't say it now, I never will. "My life is where I make it, and I'm choosin' to make it here."

His jaw sets, even more rigid than it was when he first called. My chest twinges, aching for the naivete I had when I was a kid. Back when I thought Papa was the closest thing to God. To me, he walked on water. But he was the one who woke me up from that dream, even if he doesn't know it. He showed me the nightmare of empty words preached from the pulpit and pulled the curtain on the illusion of love.

So he can hate my choices all he wants. I hate his choices, too.

"Rebecca Jean. I am not payin' for you to start a new life. You already have one. You're comin' home and that's final."

"No. It's not." I try to make my voice sound firm, but I'm sure to him it comes across ungrateful. *Like it always does.*

"Then I guess you're on your own."

I jerk, my hair snagging on my ring. The root pulls, making me wince. "What's that supposed to mean?"

"You're not plannin' on comin' home? Then I'm not payin' your way."

He doesn't mean it. He already paid for my schooling, he can't just take it back. Besides, he wants my name on a diploma more than I ever have. The only difference is, I'd like to actually do something with it, and he wants it hung on a wall to look pretty. Another trophy he can add to his case.

"Yeah, okay, old man. Whatever you say." My eyeballs strain as I roll them.

"You think I'm jokin'? See how far that attitude gets you when you can't pay your rent. Call me when you get some sense in that head."

Click.

Papa's a thief of joy.

His last words steal the satisfaction pissing him off usually brings. I hadn't thought being cut off was truly a possibility, and now that it's happened, I'm not sure how to feel. Part of me revels in the opportunity for freedom, which is the one thing I've craved for as long as I can remember. But then my mind races, thinking of everything he controls, both with his money and his iron fist.

Rent. Food. Basic living necessities.

My breaths start coming shorter as I scramble to think of a way out of this situation. I have no backup plan, but I can't give in. Going back to Sugarlake is akin to the lowest levels of

Hell. I refuse to live trapped under the will of a false deity and a man who thinks his word is law. I see how that life pans out every time I look in Momma's eyes.

No fuckin' thanks.

"So, what are you gonna do?" Sabrina runs her fingers through her pink-streaked brunette hair.

I shrug, throwing my half-eaten pizza back in the box. I know I should eat more, but my stomach rolls every time I think about how Papa cut me off.

I just filled her and my friend Jeremy in on the conversation with my old man. They're as supportive as they can be, but they don't know too much about Sugarlake. It's nice not having people judge me for things I've done—and the family I have—so I like to keep my Florida life separate.

There's only one time I let it bleed over and that's when I talk to my soul-sister. My best friend, Alina May Carson, aka, Lee. I've known her since birth and we've been inseparable ever since. I would crawl across broken, burning glass for that girl. But even she isn't enough to keep me there.

I've tried to convince her to move to Florida a million times. All she's got in Sugarlake is a depressed Daddy and the memory of her brother—one who abandoned them before their momma hit six feet in her grave. But she's stuck in her ways and I reckon she'll stay in Sugarlake until she takes her last breath. Thoughts of the same thing happening to me tighten like a noose around my throat.

"I don't know," I say to Sabrina. "Get a job, I guess. Not that I have time with my courses this semester. But I'll make it work." I grimace, thinking about my class schedule.

"Why don't you just find a job at FCU?" Jeremy pipes in.

I look at him from where I'm leaning back on the couch.

His brows are drawn in as he ponders my looming destitution, and I'm hit with gratitude for his friendship. We met when I was a freshman, at one of the many parties I used to drag Sabrina to. One look at his almond colored eyes and dark brown hair and I was a goner. I spent half the night trying to climb all six feet of him. It was the first time I've ever been turned down for a one-night stand.

When I walked into my Psych 101 course that Monday and saw him sitting in the back row, I plopped my happy ass next to him and demanded he apologize for making me masturbate all weekend. He laughed and told me I wasn't his type. Turns out, he spent that night climbing a six-foot man of his own. I didn't find that out until later, of course—once he trusted me enough to spill his soul. Or maybe he got tired of me trying to jump on his dick. Either way, he swore me to secrecy. He's a basketball player on scholarship and terrified of the fallout if people find out he's gay. I know what it's like to feel trapped in expectations, so I swore my loyalty and we've been close ever since.

"What kinda job could I get at FCU before I even have a degree?" I scoff.

Jeremy shrugs. "They always have students as team managers on the basketball teams, and I know they get paid."

I scrunch my nose. "Don't you have to *like* basketball to do somethin' like that?"

He chuckles. "Probably."

"It's not a bad idea, though," Sabrina chimes in.

"Sounds like a shit one to me," I mutter. "I don't know the first thing about basketball."

"Do you have any better ideas?" Her eyes widen. "At least if you get a job on campus, you won't have to worry about gas money. The pay probably won't be great, but it might be enough to get by."

I sigh, realizing I don't really have a choice. It's either that

or finding something off campus and hoping they'll be flexi-
ble. I begrudgingly log on to my computer and pull up my
advisor's email, asking to set up a meeting.

Having to balance work and school might suck, but it's
much better than going home.

2

ELI

I wake up in a cold sweat. It's that damn dream again, the one I'm convinced is my subconscious coming through to haunt the hell out of me. I never remember the details, only the whisper of Ma's voice and the look on my baby sister's face the last time I saw her. Which was subsequently at Ma's funeral, after she died in a car crash, three years ago.

I shake off the nightmare, glancing at my clock. Three-thirty in the morning. Not exactly what I had in mind as the "good night's rest" before my first day. I know sleep is a lost cause, so I grab my phone off the nightstand and trudge past the white walls of my house, making my way to the kitchen for a glass of water.

Glancing down at my phone, I read through the missed texts from earlier tonight.

Connor: You in Florida yet? I need my wingman! This weekend, we're going out. Pretty up that face, so I can use those blue eyes and golden hair of yours.

Connor's messages always make me smile. We played

college ball together in Ohio, and he was the only one there for me through Ma's death, and then again when my dream slipped through my fingers. It's luck my new job as the Assistant Coach to the Florida Coast Stingrays coincides with his contract with the Florida Suns. He's the best damn shooting guard in the NBA.

And I'd be the best point guard if fate wasn't such a fickle bitch.

I bat away the thought before it can take root and wrap itself around me. I try not to think on the harsh things in life. Easier to push it back and focus on the here and now.

Exiting out of Connor's text, I pull up the one from my baby sister, Lee.

Sis: You gonna make it home for Daddy's birthday this year?

I grimace as I close the window, tossing my phone. I wish she'd stop sending me messages like this when she already knows the answer. They don't really need me there, anyway. I doubt Pops is in a celebratory mood—he never is these days, and I don't know what to do with this new version of him.

My entire life he's always been the one at my back, pushing me to go harder, dig deeper, succeed *better*. Hell, he's half the reason I wanted to get out of Sugarlake in the first place. I love Pops, but the pressure he mounted on my back had me struggling for breaths every damn day. But I'd take that version over the ghost of who he is now.

After losing Ma, he changed.

When I went number one in the NBA draft, there was no one there to celebrate. When I tore my ACL two months into my rookie contract with New York, no one came to my bedside. Not my Pops. Not my sister. *No one.* So forgive me for not wanting to rush back to a home that harbors nothing but memories of Ma—who I didn't spend enough time with —and the family who forgot to include me in the aftermath.

But it's just like Lee to guilt-trip me. Growing up, she didn't appreciate how different our folks were with her. She wasn't pushed to her breaking point. Never forced to give up any semblance of a normal life to be the best. She has no idea what it feels like to have an entire town tout you as their superstar before you've even made it through high school. No clue how the shame threatens to swallow me whole anytime I think about showing my face there, now that I'm not able to play. The gash is barely healed in my heart, I'm not sure I'd survive having three-thousand folks pouring salt in the wound.

I'll make something of myself here in Florida, though. I may not be on the court anymore, but I'll work my way through the ranks—make a different kind of name for myself. Maybe then, the thought of facing my hometown won't make me feel like I'm drowning.

Heading to the couch, I flip on the TV, hoping I'll be able to fall back asleep. I ignore the way the halls of my new house mock me with their emptiness.

A couple of hours and a gallon of coffee later, I make my way to the shower. I don't think there's enough caffeine in the world to make me feel rested enough for the day, but luckily, the jitters in my gut make up for my brain's lack of enthusiasm. Besides, I doubt today will be anything too intense. Preseason isn't for a month, and the NCAA is strict on how many practices you're allowed before the season starts. It's not time to meet with the players, and I already know Coach Andrews. He's the reason I got the job in the first place. It was barely an interview, to be honest. Andrews sang my praises. Told me how lucky he'd feel to have me on his staff after following my college career.

I'm flattered, of course, but I don't feel the greatness seeping out of me the way he seems to think it does. I just feel like a missed opportunity. A seed that was watered to a bud, then left in the sun to fend for itself. But even though I wasn't meant for the spotlight, some of these players will be. I'll do everything in my power to help them blossom into the best damn baller they can be.

If I can't live out my dream, the least I can do is help them live out theirs.

3

BECCA

The meeting with my advisor doesn't go as well as I hoped, even though I spent all morning visualizing the outcome I wanted. Sabrina tells me when you speak to the universe, the universe listens. So I closed my eyes and imagined Dr. Tooley saying there was an open position in the admissions office. Instead, he told me I'm shit out of luck. Said I'll be lucky to find anything since the semester's already started. My stomach sunk to the floor with every word he spoke, until I remembered what Jeremy said about the basketball managers, which is why I'm in Waycor Arena, ready to beg on my knees to work with the women's team.

My knowledge of basketball is close to nil. The only experience I've ever had is courtesy of Lee's older brother, Eli. He was known as the next big thing around Sugarlake, and always had a ball in his hands... unless he was throwing it at me. *Dick.*

But then he left for college and never looked back. Not even when Lee cried, begging him to come home. I'm not sure I'll ever forgive him for the way he abandoned her.

A large woman walks by me in the hallway. She's wearing

a green and white tracksuit, her blonde hair pulled back in a tight ponytail, a whistle hanging around her neck. *Is she the coach?* She stops in her tracks, turning around to face me.

"You the girl Tooley sent my way?"

"Sure am. I'm Becca. Nice to meet you." I stand from my spot on the floor, straightening my tank top before grasping her hand in a firm shake.

She waves her arm. "Come on, let's see what we can find for you."

I follow into her office and sit down. There're mounds of paper all over her desk, and I wonder how she finds anything in the mess.

I hope she doesn't want me to sort through all that.

She sighs, the chair creaking as she leans back, steepling her fingers. "I'll be honest, Becca. I know you're here looking for some type of team management position, but all the spots have already been filled."

My stomach sinks, matching the droop of my face. "Oh. Okay, I understand."

Her lips turn down in the corner and she eyes the curls on my head down to the heels on my feet.

"Do you know anything about basketball?"

I cringe. "Not really."

"Why'd you want to work with the team, then?"

"Honestly, I'm lookin' for a job on campus so I don't have to spend all my paycheck on gas money, and beg someone to work around my schedule." I lock my gaze on hers. "I just need my foot in the door... to be given a chance."

I'm feeling like I just made a mistake in admitting that, but after a few moments of tense silence, she surprises me. "You know what? Let me make a call to Coach Andrews. He usually waits until the start of the season to bring on students, so he may have something for you. It's a little unorthodox, because you're female, but there's no rule against it." She shrugs.

I perk up in my seat, my knee bouncing as I watch her pick up the phone. While she talks, I think about how I didn't even realize basketball *had* a season, let alone that it hadn't started yet.

What the hell am I gettin' myself into?

She hangs up, her lips stretching in a thin curve across her face. "You may be in luck. He said you could stop by on your way out. I can't promise anything, but I hope it helps."

My stomach knots as I walk to Coach Andrews's office, my heels clicking on the concrete floors and echoing off the walls. This is a gigantic building, but there's no way to miss when you enter the men's part of the arena. Where the women's was modest and small, tucked away in a back corner, the men's is damn near ostentatious. Rows of trophy filled cases line the halls, jerseys hanging proud above them. There are a few offices with their doors open, showcasing the floor-to-ceiling windows that look to the outside. Clearly, men's basketball is where the money is.

I find Coach Andrews's office and knock.

"Come in," a gruff voice says.

The office itself, while extremely large, isn't too fancy. It has a conference table with a projection screen at the head, and Coach Andrews's desk sits on the other side of the room. He's behind it, glasses on top of his buzzed brown hair, hunching over a stack of papers.

He snaps his head up when I take a seat.

"You Becca?"

"At your service." I grin. "Nice to meet you."

He straightens in his chair, peering at me from his muddy brown eyes. I hold his gaze. If I've learned one thing from Papa, it's that not holding eye contact is the first sign of weakness.

"Luanne says you're looking to be a student manager for the team."

"That's right, I sure am." I nod.

His lips twitch and he drops his pen on the desk. "Southern girl, huh?"

"Born and raised in Tennessee, sir."

He sighs, rubbing a palm over his face. "We've never had a female team manager before. It's just not really done." His hand drops from his forehead down to his chin, his fingers scratching at his jaw. "You know anything about basketball?"

My eyes grow wide and I straighten my spine, uncrossing my legs. "Yessir. I know the season hasn't started yet. And I know there's a hoop… and a net. I reckon there's a ball somewhere in there, too."

His head juts back from his loud, boisterous laugh. "So that's a no, then."

I grin, my cheeks tingeing with heat. "That's a no. But I grew up workin' for my old man in his church. I know how to focus in and learn quick."

"Well, that's something, at least. You even know what a student manager does?"

"I figure I'll find out once you give me the opportunity, sir."

He chuckles. "Sure of yourself, huh?"

"Just hopin' to nudge you into the right decision." My smile grows.

"It doesn't pay much."

I lift my shoulders. "If it's enough for rent and ramen, I'll survive."

His chair squeaks as he leans back, clearly assessing me. "Okay, here's the deal. I usually have three student managers on staff. You can't be in the locker room with the guys, except for before games, because frankly, you'll be a distraction. But

you can help with practices and anything else the coaching
staff may need."

I'm nodding my head, eyes wide and ears open. I'm
grateful for the opportunity and I don't intend to waste it.

He clicks the keyboard on his computer, his printer
whirring to life. Swinging his chair around, he grabs the
freshly printed papers, laying them in front of me.

"You still need to fill out the paperwork and turn it in so
you're official." His knuckle taps the forms. "Practice doesn't
start for a month. In the meantime, I want you here, learning
the basics. I can't have someone working for me that doesn't
respect the game."

"Got it." I bob my head. "Thank you, sir."

"And quit calling me sir. Coach will do just fine."

"Okay, Coach." I stand up, grabbing the papers and
saluting him like a jackass. But I don't care. *I did it.* It feels
good to accomplish something without Papa in the background pulling the strings.

"Oh, and Becca?"

I swing around, my hand grabbing the doorframe.

"Get yourself some better shoes, yeah?" He looks down at
my heels, raising his brows.

The grin cracks my face, and I feel it all the way to my
toes. "Sure thing, Coach."

I spin around, eager to get home and call Lee with the
good news when my face smashes into a hard wall of muscle.

Sonnofabitch.

I back up, my hand rushing to cover my now throbbing
nose.

"Whoa, you okay?" a deep voice rumbles. His breath
whooshes over the strands of my hair.

My eyes are watering because seriously—*ouch*—so I don't
look up as I respond. "Other than a bruised nose and a
broken ego, I'm fine. Sorry about that. Watchin' and walkin' is

a learned trait I haven't mastered." Lifting my head, I attempt a grin.

My smile drops with a quickness when I see whose chest I greeted with my face.

Elliot Carson.

The man. The myth. The legend.

But to me... he's just the asshole who got too big for his britches and abandoned my best friend.

4

BECCA

"You," I gasp.

Eli's eyes bulge and he stumbles back a step. "Becca. How... what..." His hand runs through those honey-blond locks, so similar to his sister's.

I hope he thinks of her every time his stupid ass looks in the mirror.

"What are you doing here? In Florida? I mean... in Coach Andrews's office?"

I snort, both at his audacity to question me and at his posh, decidedly un-southern accent. "What am *I* doin' here? What are *you* doin' here?"

"I work here."

Nausea punches my gut. Coach Andrews walks from behind me, slapping Eli on the shoulder with a gigantic smile on his face. The sick feeling grows, my breakfast teasing my throat.

Fuck my life.

"Becca, you know Eli? Our team's been needing someone like him for a long time," Coach Andrews preens. My eyes swing just in time to see Eli wince at his words.

My sharp tongue lashes out before I can stop it. "Oh, really? Might wanna hold on tight there, Coach. Eli has a nasty habit of runnin' from the people who need him most."

Eli tenses, his eyes narrowing as they darken to a stormy blue.

Coach clears his throat, shifting on his feet. "Right. Well… how do you two know each other?"

"She's my little sister's best friend," Eli provides.

I snort. "Surprised you remember her."

Coach's brows raise. "You guys are from the same town? I never would have guessed."

My thoughts exactly, Coach. I cock my head, fingers tapping my hip. "Yeah, Eli. What happened to that nice, southern drawl you used to beat my eardrums with?"

Eli shrugs, a painful smile gracing his face as he speaks through his teeth. "Time away from home makes you lose the dialect, I guess. I haven't really thought about it."

I purse my lips as I watch him lie out of his ass. No chance in hell his accent just up and disappeared. I'm sure it's buried underneath the thousands of other lies he tells himself so he can sleep at night.

Coach claps his hands, rubbing them together. "This works well. Since you're already acquainted, I'll have her report to you for basic training."

Eli turns his head, the line between his eyes creasing. "Basic training?"

"Becca's our new student manager, and in order to *keep* that title, she needs to learn the love of the game."

I force a grin, trying to hide the straight-up disgust that's creeping through my insides when I think of having to spend hours with Eli. "I'm lovin' it more every second, Coach."

Eli chuckles, and I squint my eyes in his direction. "What's so funny about that?"

He rubs his hand over his mouth, shaking his head

slightly. "You might want to find a different girl, Coach. Becca here is *known* for a lot of things, but her loving nature isn't one of them."

Heat rises from my chest, scorching my cheeks. I imagine junk-punching him then watching him writhe beneath me in pain. The thought makes me smile.

Coach chortles. "Come on now, Eli. Let's give the girl a chance to prove you wrong." He points at me. "You got Monday morning classes?"

I shake my head. "Not until ten-thirty."

"Be here Monday at eight then, and we'll get you started."

I nod, biting the inside of my cheek. Eli's head turns to watch me as I walk by, and when I'm sure Coach can't see, I throw my middle fingers up, waving them in the air.

Driving home, my thoughts race. I don't know the best way to process what the hell just happened. One thing's for sure, I plan on having a stern talking to with Sabrina about her "universe" bullshit because this is not what I signed up for. I can't believe Eli is at FCU. As a coach.

Oh my God, does that make him my boss?

I'm sick to my stomach, and a bit pissed off at Lee. What the hell is she thinking not telling me something like this? *Maybe she didn't know?*

Once I hit my complex, I throw my car in park, ripping my phone from the charger and forcefully pressing send when I reach Lee's name. She doesn't pick up and I don't leave a message. Instead, I send a text.

Me: You gots some 'splainin to do!

Lee has a bad habit of avoiding confrontation, so I don't expect a response. I sit in my car for a few more seconds, reflecting on my morning. The positives? At least I got a job. And for every ounce of asshole residing in Eli's cold, dead heart—there's double that of good genes. He's a fine specimen to look at if there ever was one. I just wish I didn't *have* to look at him.

It's Friday night and I'm on the prowl. After a grueling first week of classes, Sabrina and I meet up with some friends and grace the downtown bars with our presence. I'm a shot of tequila in and a perusal away from picking my flavor of the night. I could really use a nice guy to dick me down and relieve the stress from the past week.

Our group is huddled around a table in the corner, and everyone's lost in conversation except for me.

Standing up, I run my hands over my black bodycon dress. It's tight, and with its plunging neckline, it does amazing things for my tits. I motion to Sabrina that I'm heading to the bar, but she's deep in some philosophical conversation about women's rights, and barely acknowledges me.

Fortunately, the bar isn't too packed. *Un*fortunately, the bartender is ignoring me. I plop down on a stool and rest my chin in my hands, waiting to get some service.

"Odd to be sitting at a bar without a drink, don't you think?"

I spin toward the voice, my eyes meeting the broad chest of a green-eyed devil. A smile creeps on my face as I assess the beauty before me. He's tall and fit. Tousled dark hair and a black button-down that does nothing to hide his muscles. A tingle runs through my lady bits.

Damn, he's fine.

I twist a strand of hair around my finger. "Odd you would think that's a clever pickup line."

The right side of his mouth lifts, showcasing a perfect

dimple. "Yeah, well... my wingman's supposed to be here to smooth out my edges, but I think he may be standing me up."

"How awful," I deadpan.

"Yeah. It's a shame."

"For you," I say.

"For both of us," he corrects.

"Is that right?"

"It is. My wingman's a bit of a dick. An attractive dick, but a dick, nonetheless. If he were here, you'd realize just how charming I actually am."

I lick my lips, leaning toward him. "Maybe I like dicks."

He steps closer, resting an arm on the bar. "Oh, I'm counting on it."

The bartender finally makes her way over, interrupting our moment. I order a shot of tequila and a glass of water— my mystery man slapping a twenty on the bar before I have a chance to pay.

I grin, running my finger around the rim of the shot glass. "What's your name, charmer?"

"Connor. And you, my sweet southern belle?"

I tsk. "I may be southern, sugar, but I'm not sweet."

His eyes spark. "I'll be the judge of that."

My pussy clenches as I picture his head between my legs, his tongue diving into my folds to find the only *sweet* spot on me.

"Hey, man. Sorry I'm late." A hand grips Connor's shoulder and my heart stalls in my chest.

If God exists, he hates me.

Connor smiles, turning to Eli, his teeth gleaming under the lights of the bar. "Hey, I was just talking about you."

Sharp blue eyes lock on to mine, widening a fraction as they glide up and down my body. "Becca."

"Fuckface." I raise my shot, tilting it toward him before

slamming it back, the burn distracting me from the heat of his gaze.

"You two know each other?" Connor points between us.

I roll my eyes, wiping the corner of my mouth and standing up. "I'm tired of answerin' this question." I point to Eli. "This your wingman?"

Connor's brow quirks. "That depends. Do I still need one?"

"I doubt he'd help your chances."

Eli is leaning against the bar, eyes volleying between us. "I definitely would *not* help your chances, Connor. You're not fucking Rebecca."

"Dude." Connor groans, turning toward him.

"Excuse me?" I push past Connor and step into Eli's space. He straightens, and I have to crane my neck to maintain eye contact. "He'll fuck me six ways from Sunday if I want him to, and there's not a damn thing you can do about it. God, when did you turn into such a prick?"

Eli's perfect jaw tics. "I'd imagine it was around the time you turned into a raging bitch."

"*Dude,*" Connor hisses again.

Anger bubbles in my veins as I huff out a laugh. "Oh, that's rich. I only see one *bitch* here, Eli, and it ain't me."

Eli straightens, his chest pressing into me, clean laundry and cinnamon assaulting my senses. "You wanna try me, Becca? Keep fuckin' pushin'."

There's that accent.

My heart bangs against my chest so hard it vibrates my entire body.

It's only when Connor grips my shoulders, pulling me back that I realize how close Eli and I were standing—how harsh my breaths are coming.

"Okay, firecracker. Let's calm down," Connor says,

rubbing my shoulders. "And for the record, Eli, you are the worst wingman ever."

If he's trying to lighten the mood, it doesn't work. I can't even look at him now without thinking of Eli. I shrug out of Connor's grip and turn around, storming to my table. Dragging a chair out, I slam myself in it, crossing my arms over my chest. I'm upset that Eli's here and I'm pissed he just ruined a sure thing for me. *Cockblock.*

Sabrina tilts her head, narrowing her eyes.

"I don't wanna talk about it." And I don't. Not to her, at least. But if Lee would call me back instead of playing her favorite game of avoidance, that'd be great. I dig my phone out of my purse and fire off a text.

Me: I swear to all that's holy, Lee, if you don't call me by tomorrow I will fly back home and tell the entire town about the time in fifth grade you pissed your pants because Ms. Johnson wouldn't let you use the bathroom. THE. WHOLE. TOWN.

I throw my phone down and glance at the bar. Connor's already moved onto greener pastures, a girl pressed in between his and Eli's side. But Eli's not paying attention to that.

No, his eyes are busy boring a hole into me. I glare back and now we're locked in this weird stare-off that I refuse to lose. Right when I'm about to scream from how infuriating he is just by *existing*, he smirks and looks away.

Asshole.

5

ELI

"You wanna tell me what the hell that was about?"
I hear Connor's voice, but my eyes have trailed back to the insufferable redhead at the far table. *What the hell is her problem?*

Becca was always a little too loud and a little too bratty, but I don't remember her being this obnoxious. Really, Connor should be thanking me for saving him the headache. I don't blame him for trying to get it in, though—she's easily the hottest woman in the bar. Too bad that shit personality ruins it.

"Hello. Earth to douchebag."

I snap my head over, tearing my eyes from Becca. Time has clearly turned her into a bitter bitch, but she's sadly mistaken if she thinks I'll lay down and let her steamroll over me. That sharp tongue does nothing but stoke a fire in me to snuff hers out. If she wants to start this game, I'm in. She must have forgotten I play to win.

My eyes slide back, gliding up those legs that never end, over her tiny waist and dipping into the ample cleavage that ridiculous dress shows off. My dick twitches and irritation simmers in my gut.

The nerve of this chick.

She doesn't know the first thing about me or what I've been through, yet she's so quick to pass judgment.

"Eli." Connor smacks the side of my head.

I break my gaze from Becca *again*, pasting a lazy smile on my face as I meet Connor's eyes. "What?"

"First." He throws up his finger. "You royally screwed me on the redhead."

"Becca."

"Right." He nods. "Which I would have found out for myself if you hadn't waltzed in with your asshole on display."

I laugh. "What's that even mean?"

"It doesn't matter. What matters is she was a sure thing, dude. I was *this close* to having those mile-long legs wrapped around my head."

The girl next to him huffs, and he grins down at her. "It is what it is, girl. You knew who I was when you walked over."

I take a sip of my beer while he placates his pussy of the night.

"Truly, from the bottom of my heart, fuck you for ruining that, Eli." He glances over toward Becca's table. "She's so, *so* sexy. I mean… have you looked at her?"

I open my mouth to respond, but he swipes his hand through the air. "Never mind. Clearly, you have. Your eyes have been glued to her since you walked in the bar."

I scoff. "Because she pisses me off."

Connor raises his chin. "So, staring at her is supposed to somehow… alleviate your anger?"

I shrug because I don't have an answer. Not one I want to admit out loud, anyway. The truth is, Becca makes me feel like I'm losing my goddamn mind, and I don't particularly enjoy the loss of control. When her slender body pressed to mine in that tight as hell dress and those hot as fuck heels, my cock strained against my zipper, and that's unacceptable. Baby sister's best friend is a definite no-go. So is her being a student. And if all those things weren't enough to stamp a giant red x on that tight little body then that belligerent mouth of hers definitely is. No matter how much my dick disagrees.

I glance at her one last time before forcing myself to look away.

Get some damn control, Eli.

I lean over, throwing my arm around the blonde that was just tucked into Connor's side. "Got any friends?"

The blonde nods and Connor smirks, slapping his hand on the bar. "There he is! About time you showed up, brother."

I smile, ignoring the way my mind begs me to steal one last look at the redhead in the corner.

It's September first. It also happens to be the first Saturday of the month, which is why I'm sitting at my kitchen counter, staring at my phone, willing it to disappear. If it does, I don't have to make the call I'm desperate to avoid, but know I'll never miss. At least this time I'll have some good news to share. Maybe Pops will see the prestige in coaching, and it'll help bring a little bit of his spark back. But I doubt it.

I blow out a breath, pinching the bridge of my nose, steeling myself for the guilt that's about to rise up like a tidal wave and capsize me for not going home. There are not many times I let it in, but during these calls it's unavoidable.

I grab my phone and dial.

"Hey, Eli," my sister answers.

She used to be the happiest—if not the most naive—kid

on the block. Somewhere along the way, that changed. Now when we talk, it's lined with a melancholy I wouldn't know the first thing about fixing, even if I could.

"Hey, baby sis. How are you and Pops?"

"Same as last time you called. Eli... he's not doin' good, you know? He drinks. A lot. I think he needs help."

"Did you get the check I sent?"

She sighs. "Yeah. I wish you'd stop sendin' 'em. We can't have money lyin' around here like that. Daddy can't be trusted with it."

I laugh. "Come on, Lee. Pops is a grown man. If he's not working, you two should use all the help you can get. Let me take care of you."

She's so dramatic when it comes to Pops. Always spouting off about his drinking and trying to guilt me into coming back home. I'm not worried. He's the most controlled man in the universe.

Where's she think I learned it from?

"What else is going on? You still working both jobs? How are things with your dancing?"

"Yep, still both. And I'll have you know we do just fine without your guilt money."

I swallow, my throat suddenly thick. *Guilt money.* I don't know what she wants from me. She begs me to help then bitches when I try. "It's to help, sis. So you don't have to work so hard. So Pops doesn't have to go back to construction since you say he's in no shape."

"Fine, Eli." She sighs again. "Listen, Daddy's up. You wanna talk to him?"

The little bit of hope I had going into this call drains away. My stomach sinks, the knot in my throat growing when I realize she's not planning to ask about me. I'm not even sure she knows I'm in Florida. Last she asked, I had only been interviewed. Maybe she just doesn't care. She never really has. I wish with everything in me I could just not care too.

"Sure. Hey... you doing okay? You sound tired."

She exhales. "Yeah, Eli. I'm doin' alright. Just gettin' by one day at a time. Here's Daddy."

Pops comes down the line, but we never talk for long. Quite the twist from growing up when he'd lecture me for hours. He tells me all about his fishing, and how he's enjoying his "retired" life. I ask how things are with Lee, and he complains about her mothering him.

He doesn't ask what I'm up to.

Like father, like daughter.

I'm not surprised. If it doesn't involve my name in bright lights or bringing Ma back from the dead, he's not interested.

I hang up after an excruciating ten minutes of small talk and glance at the clock on the stove. *Five minutes.* That's how long I'll give myself to feel this... ache that reaches through my stomach and splits open my chest, gripping my heart and squeezing. But only five minutes. After that, I'll push it to the corner of my mind and lock it up tight.

Back where it belongs.

6

ELI

I'm standing in the middle of the basketball court, eyeing my setup. It's not perfect, but it'll do. My job today is to teach Becca the basics. Introduce her to the love of my life. That is, if she even shows up. I'm pretty sure Coach told her to get here at eight a.m., but it's ten 'til and she still hasn't arrived.

Doesn't she know "on time" is late?

I kneel, smoothing the painter's tape I put on the mid-court line. I spent all of Sunday figuring out my game plan. I'm not sure it will work, but I figured visual representation and teaching her to play is better than her listening to me talk for hours on end.

The squeak of sneakers on the polished maple floor has me looking toward the noise. Becca struts in, bookbag slung over a shoulder, barely-there shorts, and a skin-tight tee that says "FCU" across her tits.

Jesus.

At least she's wearing better shoes today.

"Cutting it a little close, aren't you?" I stand.

Emeralds slice through me with her glare. She tosses her

bag to the floor and stomps over. "It's not even eight yet. I've got..." She grabs my wrist, peering at my watch. "Four minutes to spare."

I jerk my arm back, my skin prickling from where her fingers wrapped around it. "I don't need the attitude, Rebecca. I need you to take this seriously."

She throws her hair into a ponytail, drawing my eyes to the smooth, pale expanse of her neck.

"Don't call me Rebecca. Ugh, just when I think I can't hate you more, you go and sound like my old man."

"I don't really give a damn if you like me."

"You should."

"And why's that?"

"Because you're stuck with me for the foreseeable future. It'd be a shame to make your life a livin' hell while I'm here." She smiles as if the thought pleases her.

"I'm pretty sure being around you is the definition of a living hell."

"Then I'll be sure to live up to my reputation," she quips. "Can we just get today over with?"

I point to myself and grin. "I'm running this. Not you."

Her lips purse as she eyes me up and down. "Hasn't it been a few years since you could even play? I'm surprised you remember how to run anything."

My smile drops, teeth gritting as my blood heats.

Fuck her.

I lean in close. I want to grip her feisty little throat. Feel her heartbeat quicken under my fingers while I lay out how this will go. My fists clench to quell the urge. "Let's get one thing straight. Every single thing that happens when it comes to you and this court? I control it. You can run that *fuckin'* mouth of yours all day long. It'll only make your submission that much sweeter." My voice drops. "You want this job, Becca? You better learn to play my way, baby girl."

My gaze swings to her lips as they part.

"I ain't your baby."

"No?" I smirk. "That's fine. I'll settle for you being my *bitch*."

Her eyes flare, and satisfaction digs its way through my system, burrowing in my chest.

"Becca! Good, you're here," Coach interrupts.

I clear my throat, realizing how close we're standing, my lips a centimeter away from hers. I take two large steps back. Becca's eyes shutter, the heat dying as she looks toward Coach and smiles.

"Here and ready to learn, Coach." She taps her head.

"Atta girl." He stops next to me and surveys the court I've destroyed with painter's tape. "Inventive. Looks like you've got this under control." He faces Becca. "I got your class schedule, so after you're done here, stop by my office and we can work out your hours."

Becca bobs her head. Coach claps me on the back, walking away.

I sigh, turning to Becca. "How long do I get you for?"

She grabs a strand of hair from her ponytail and tugs. "I have class at ten-thirty."

"Okay." I walk to the sideline, grabbing a ball. "Let's start with what you know. See if you remember anything I taught you and Lee back in the day." I grin as I dribble.

She guffaws. "Clearly, you don't remember our childhood. The only thing you ever taught me is how to successfully avoid basketball players."

She's wrong, I do remember. Out of all my sister's friends, she was the one I enjoyed teasing the most. Even back then she was a loudmouth, and I found a sick sense of pleasure in figuring out the best ways to get her to shut the hell up. Plus, there's just something about watching that blush spread from her neck to her hairline. My dribbling slows as I think about what it would take to make that happen now.

"If I recall, your perky freshman face was at plenty of games and after-parties, hanging off a player or two."

While Lee was never one to go to a party—at least while I was still in town—Becca was at every one, front and center. I rarely went to any, too invested in making ball my life. But the rumors grew rampant around school, and the locker room talk wasn't exactly quiet. In the short time of our shared tenure at Sugarlake High, she made quite the name for herself. The slutty preacher's girl—wild and unruly.

I'm sure her folks have been so proud.

That thought gives me pause, stomach rolling from my judgment. It never crossed my mind what she may have gone through at home because of her reputation. If it's anything like what I feel with Pops, I wouldn't wish it on anyone. Failing to live up to people's expectations is a hell of a bruise.

I dribble between my legs, my eyes seeing her in a new light.

She waves me off. "That's beside the point. Those boys served a purpose and that's all they were good for. Kinda like you."

My brows lift, a smile teasing my lips. "What purpose do I serve?"

"Teachin' me the 'love of the game.' After that, I'll toss you to the side just like the rest of 'em."

I chuckle at the fact she thinks I'll need to be tossed. *Like I would give her that kind of power.*

"Okay, well *this*" —I hold the basketball in the air— "is a bas-ket-ball."

She widens her eyes. "Wow. That's amazin'."

"It is." I nod. "Just wait until you learn about shooting."

"Like a pistol?" she gasps, throwing a hand to her heart.

I make a finger gun, pointing it at her. "Bingo, little lady."

She snorts. "You're ridiculous. Can we be serious? I need this job, Eli."

I stifle a grin. "I've *been* serious. It's you who needs to be ready."

She nods, walking closer. "I'm ready. I hear you're the best to learn from. Besides, you know what they say."

I stare down at her, our eyes locking. If she can keep things civil like they have been for the past couple minutes, we'll get through this just fine.

"What do they say?" I ask.

"Those who can't do… teach." She winks, swiping the ball from my hands and sauntering to the basket.

Bitch.

7

BECCA

A m I flirting with Eli right now?

What the hell is wrong with me?

I woke up with a singular goal in mind. Show up and get this "basic training" shit over with as quickly as possible. Instead, I'm holding a basketball underneath a ten-foot hoop—which I only know because of the giant hand-written sign taped to it—trying to stop my stomach from flipping.

I have no clue why my reaction to him is so strong. I don't *want* to react to him at all. But, good Lord, seeing him handle that ball in his gigantic hands makes me wonder how he could handle *me*. Which is an issue within itself because I don't like to get handled. Ever.

I peek over my shoulder. Eli's eyes are slits as he stalks toward me, and I cringe at how pissed he looks. Regardless of how I feel about him personally, I should probably rein it in so we can get through these lessons without killing each other. But damn, he makes it difficult.

I spin around, hugging the ball to my chest. "So, what are we learnin' today, Coach?"

Eli stops in his tracks, the right side of his mouth lifting. "No need to call me Coach. Sir will work just fine."

I roll my eyes. "In your dreams. It's either Coach or asshole. Take your pick."

He chuckles, shaking his head. "Okay, I laid out painter's tape to signify the important areas of the court. We'll start with the basics. You already know you're holding a basketball."

"Only because of your superb teachin' skills."

"Don't you forget it." He winks.

A tingle rushes through me. *Shit.*

He points to the net. "That's the hoop. The goal is to get the ball *into* the hoop."

"Fascinatin', but I already know this. I used to kick Lee's ass playin' HORSE in y'all's driveway."

"Basketball is not like HORSE," he scoffs. "It's a team sport."

I nod. "Okay. Well, how many players are on a team?"

He squats down in front of me, hands dangling between his thighs, pants pulling tight across his hips.

Don't look at his dick. Don't look at his dick.

I look. I can't help it, he's just hovering. Spread eagle. And he's got big feet, so I really can't be blamed for wanting to know if the saying holds true.

"It differs depending on the league. But in general, fifteen players on the roster. Thirteen of which dress for games. Ten players on the court, five from each team. The main goal is to score more points than your opponent." He quirks a brow, standing back up. "You with me so far?"

My head bobs to his words, but my mind isn't soaking in anything. Talk about an info dump.

Maybe I should take notes.

Holding up a finger, I run to my bag, grabbing the first notebook I can find. I rush back, plopping down with my legs crossed, and look up at him. His nostrils flare as he peers down at me. I shift in place, his gaze making me antsy. With the way he's staring, you'd think I just dropped to my knees and offered to suck his dick. The thought brings a very much *unwanted* image to my mind, and even though I try to stop it, my pussy throbs.

The air grows thick as it crackles through the silence, and I don't like the way it feels. I point my pen at him. "Don't think 'cause you're lookin' down on me this means you're in a position of power. I just wanna be comfortable while I have to listen to that voice of yours drone on."

He clears his throat and looks away. "Got it."

"Okay, so five players on each side and the goal is to score." I'm writing down feverishly, trying to hide the flush on my cheeks.

What just happened?

"How many points if they get it in the hoop?"

"Two points if they score. Unless—" He puts up a finger and walks to an area marked with painter's tape. "Unless they're outside of this area, right here. You see this painted arch?" His arm stretches as he gestures, and I force myself not to inventory every dip and curve of his bicep.

I divert my gaze. "Mmhm."

"That's the three-point arc. If they shoot from outside this arch then the basket's three points, not two."

"Uh-huh." I frown, chewing on the end of my pen.

He blows out a breath and runs his fingers through his hair. "Yeah, I didn't mean to go into any of that today. I really just want to focus on the actual court itself. Once you get that down, we'll get into owning the paint."

My face scrunches. "Own the paint? That doesn't even make sense."

He smiles. "It will."

Class is over for the day. It's six p.m. and I am so ready for a long bath and a night of binge-watching *The Real Housewives*. My hand is cramping from all the notes I've taken, most of them from my lesson with Eli. My brain is still jumbled from all the "lines." Mid-court lines, free-throw lines, sidelines, baselines, and center circles.

Who knew those shapes on the high school gym floor actually meant somethin'?

I'll never admit it out loud, but Eli's a great teacher and he'll be a phenomenal coach. The Florida Coast Stingrays are lucky to have him. I can't imagine loving anything the way he loves the game. It bleeds through in every word he speaks, every action he takes, making it impossible not to feel his passion.

Plus, he'll be a nice decoration to the sidelines during the games. He is an exceptional specimen.

I send up a quick thanks to Mrs. Carson—may she rest in peace—for creating such a masterpiece. Now if only his personality could match that perfect face.

I'm snapped out of my thoughts when my phone vibrates with a text from Lee. *About damn time.* Lee will put off calling me for weeks if it means she doesn't have to hear me bitch about her choices.

Like not tellin' me her brother was at FCU.

She grew up living a pretty charmed, sheltered life. Innocent in comparison to mine, but we balanced each other out. Still do. The yin to my yang. She was always full of sparkle and sunshine, until a douchebag boy moved to town and stole her light. Life slapped her silly and she still hasn't fully recovered.

But I'll take a sad Lee over a catatonic one.

My anger at Eli re-emerges as I think about everything

Lee's had to go through without him.

Lee: It's been more than a day and I don't see your big booty anywhere in town. Guess you're all talk, huh?

Me: Oh, the threat is still good. I've just been busy dealing with YOUR DAMN BROTHER at my school. What the hell, Lee?

Lee: Oh, did he get the job there? Last I heard, he was only interviewing. Sorry, I didn't think you'd care!

My eyebrows furrow, wondering why she doesn't know. It seems like a big piece of information, and while I know Eli hasn't been back in years, I *also* know they talk on the phone once a month.

I roll my eyes, reminding myself that I don't actually care, and toss my phone on my nightstand. Laughter trickles in from the hallway, so I go to investigate, finding Sabrina and Jeremy sitting on the couch, giggling.

I put my hands on my hips. "What's so funny, y'all? And how come I wasn't invited to the party?"

Jeremy shrugs. "You stormed through here like hellfire and damnation were chasin' after you."

My lips twitch at his poor attempt at a southern accent. "Cute."

"How'd your first day go?" Sabrina asks.

I walk over, nudging Jeremy's leg to scooch him over. He doesn't move, so I plop down on his lap. His arms come around my waist and I sigh, leaning into him. "It went surprisingly well, all things considered."

"I still can't believe you know Elliot Carson. That's so wild." Jeremy's chomping at the bit to meet him. He's a little starstruck, which is annoying.

"He's an asshole."

"He's one of the best point guards I've ever seen play the game. It's a shame what happened to him." Jeremy sighs.

I push his arm off me, standing up and scrunching my

nose. "Try to tone down that hero-worship some before you meet him. I can't have people thinkin' I keep company with ass kissers."

Jeremy laughs. "I'm just happy I'll have my best girl at my games. I need that sweet ass on the sideline cheering." He smacks my ass cheek, making me jump. "You gonna wear my number? Or is that like... against the rules?"

"Rules never stopped me before." I smile. "When does practice even start for y'all? Coach didn't go over any of that, just gave me my hours."

"October. But you'll probably see some of us around before then for conditioning."

I blink. "I have no idea what that means."

"Me neither," Sabrina chimes in.

"Lucky for you, you've got a fine as hell, talented, assistant coach to help you study up." Jeremy's brows wiggle.

Irritation nags at my gut when I picture Eli's arrogant face. But under the irritation, a spark simmers, flushing my cheeks and heating my veins.

8

BECCA

It's been days of monotonous classes and grueling basketball lessons. Somewhere in the middle of all that, Eli and I have come to an unspoken truce. One where I don't antagonize him half to death, and he doesn't piss me off just by breathing. I'm not sure it will last, but I'm going to roll with it as long as I can.

On Sunday, I gave in to the urge to check on Momma, but she didn't answer. I haven't talked to my folks since I got to Florida and Papa cut me off, but it's not for lack of trying on my part. I should write them off completely like they seem to have done with me, but I've got a soft spot for Momma and I always will. I can't just leave her in the snake pit without making sure she's not bit.

I tried to tell her once—about Papa sleeping with the twenty-two-year-old youth leader. I was just trying to help, and I thought she deserved to know. In my mind, if Papa had the nerve to pretend he was a man of God who upheld his vows, then Momma deserved to know she married a viper.

I expected tears, and maybe sympathy that my eyes had to

see what they did, being that I was just a thirteen-year-old girl. Instead, she told me it was high time I learned that all men are liars. That love was a fairy tale told to children, and fairy tales don't exist. She told me to never disrespect her again by bringing it up.

I lost a lot that day. Respect for both my folks *and* my faith in God. If I couldn't trust my folks' love, how could I trust a man up in the sky who supposedly loved me the most?

Up until that point, I spent every day of my life loving God more than anything. I prayed every night at supper and then again by my bed. I looked at my folks' marriage with hearts in my stupid eyes, and soaked up Papa's sermons like a sponge. So when Momma sent me to the church, and I walked in on Sally Sanderson spread out on Papa's desk while he rutted on top of her, shock froze my heart and dropped my stomach to the floor. They were so lost in their sin they didn't even hear me at the door.

I still don't think he realizes I know. But I do. I'll never forget the grief of learning the man I thought raised me didn't exist.

Love is a fairy tale.

I'm sitting in the stands of Waycor Arena when Momma's name lights up my phone. Half of me doesn't want to answer. Especially since she didn't reach out to make sure I was okay after Papa cut me off. But the other side of me—the one that prods my insides to make sure she's okay—gives in and picks up the phone.

"Hi, Momma," I answer just as Eli strolls onto the court. He's dressed down today, in black basketball shorts and a white undershirt that pulls tight across his chest and abs. *Good Lord.* He sets down his gym bag and smiles, making his way over. I muster up a half-grin, too pissed off he's still affecting me to give him a full one.

"Rebecca Jean." Momma's voice cuts through my thoughts. "I waited a good long time before makin' this phone call, thinkin' maybe you would come to your senses and smooth things over with your father."

"Momma, it's amazin' how you can defend him. Why do I need to be the one to smooth things over? I didn't do anything wrong."

She scoffs. "He said you'd say that."

"God forbid you realize Papa's word ain't the gospel," I snark.

"You watch your mouth, young lady. Now, I want you to stop this nonsense and tell me you'll be comin' home at the end of the school year."

Irritation boils in my stomach, rising up my throat and coating my words. "I would, Momma, but you and Papa always taught me lyin' was a sin, and I don't wanna end up burnin' in the fiery pits of Hell just to appease y'all."

Eli's eavesdropping, and not even trying to hide it. He runs his hand over his mouth, clearly stifling his smile. I beam back at him, unable to stop myself, my heart quickening while Momma's voice screeches in the background.

"One day, you're gonna need to grow up, Rebecca. It's shameful the way you act."

Her words slice through my moment of happiness.

I swallow and nod, my eyes closing briefly against the sting. "Well, I figure at this point you expect it. I'm just tryin' to live up to your expectations."

Eli's lips turn down, his eyes boring a hole in the side of my head. I fidget, feeling too vulnerable under his gaze.

"Anyway, Momma. Thanks for callin'. School's goin' great, by the way, thanks for askin'. I'm actually at work, so I've gotta go."

I hang up before she responds, sucking in air through my

teeth. I don't know why I let her words affect me the way they do. I should be used to them, I've been hearing them since I was thirteen. Time lessens the burn, but at the heart of it all, I'm just a girl who wants my folks to accept me for *me*. Not for who they want me to be.

I glance at Eli. His arms are crossed, sinewy muscles on full display, his eyes honing in on my face.

"What?" I snap.

"You okay?"

"I'm fine." I take the wild hair Momma gave me out of its ponytail and retie it up.

Eli's still standing there, hovering like a damn gnat.

I throw my arms in the air. "We just gonna stand here, or are we gonna do this?"

Those blue irises trail up and down, assessing me. The ache from Momma's shame drains away, replaced with the heat from his pensive gaze. I thought being around him would desensitize me, but instead it's gotten worse.

I gotta get myself under control.

I can't entertain thoughts of him for so many reasons. One, he's technically my boss. Pretty sure we'd both get in heaps of trouble if I let him dive into my honey pot. Two, and most importantly, I can't stand his stupid ass. Which leads me to believe my body is only reacting because I've never had a hate fuck before. Plus, it's going on three weeks since my last orgasm, which is a goddamn tragedy, so I'm a ball of pent-up hormones.

"You hungry?" Eli's voice snaps me out of my lustful thoughts.

"What?"

"Food. Do you wanna get something to eat?"

I look around. "Uhh... aren't we supposed to be 'trainin'?'"

He shrugs. "Seems like you could use a day off."

His words shock me into silence. I'm not sure anyone has ever given a damn about what I could use, and even though I hate him, my chest warms at his thoughtfulness. "Okay. But you're buyin'."

9

ELI

We've been sitting at my favorite diner for thirty minutes and Becca's barely said three words. The quiet is different than what I've come to expect, and I don't like it.

The spark in her eyes dimmed every second she spent on her phone, a heaviness sinking in my gut as I watched. Which is funny because I thought I hated that fire. It's annoying as hell. *She's* annoying as hell, but I still find myself wanting to smooth away her frown and pluck the sadness from her eyes.

I lean back in the booth, taking her in. She's sipping on her Coke, looking at her surroundings, those damn curls threading through her fingers. She does that a lot, I've noticed —play with her hair.

I break the silence. "So, was that your ma on the phone?"

"Yep. The one and only." She nods.

"Things okay at home?" I don't know why I'm bothering to ask, it's not like she'll tell me.

"What is this, an after-school special? The coach takin' out the player to bond and learn life lessons?"

I point at her. "You should learn how to shoot the ball before calling yourself a player."

"I can shoot the damn ball." She crosses her arms. "I've been doin' it for days now."

"You're shit at it." My mouth tilts up. "Maybe you should try harder. You'd never make the team."

My heart skips when I see a flash in her eyes.

"Maybe I need a better coach." She chews on a fry, cocking her head. "You really wanna get into how things are with our families? Out of the two of us, I'm the one who's better off."

That shuts me up quick. In all the time we've spent together, we haven't mentioned my sister. It feels almost taboo, especially with the thoughts I have of Becca when I'm alone.

She drives me fucking crazy.

Besides, thinking of how close they are just highlights the fact that if Becca hates me the way she does, Lee must feel a thousand times worse. Sadness slithers its way up my spine, reaching around my neck and strangling me. I rub at my throat, trying to ebb the sting.

"You're right."

Her jaw drops. "I am?"

"Yeah." I blow out a breath, leaning back. "When it comes to my family, we're all pretty fucked."

"Hmm." She grabs the straw from her drink, plugging one end with her finger as she sucks liquid from the other. *Is she doing that on purpose?* I watch how her lips close around the straw, my cock growing as I adjust in my seat.

"You really are fucked," she agrees. "How come you never go home, Eli?"

"What is this, an after-school special?" I mock. "It really isn't your business, Rebecca."

Her eyes narrow, cheeks flushing as she purses her lips. My stomach flips, excitement rushing through me at the reemergence of my little spitfire. I was worried she wouldn't come back out to play.

"Not my *business*? You are such a prick. Let me tell you somethin', asshole. I'm the one who held your sister up day after day when she couldn't do it herself. She didn't have anyone there, Eli. No one except me and Jax."

My forehead creases. "Is Jax that kid who lived behind us?"

"The one and only." She pauses. "Truly, he's a better friend to her than I am, and you best believe that's a bitch for me to admit."

"I doubt that's true." I can't imagine someone more loyal than Becca.

"No, it is." She waves me off. "But he's stupid in love with her, and while I love your sister, I don't want to spend my life eatin' at her buffet."

I choke on my Coke, coughing while I try to stop my laughter.

She grins, shaking her head. "But it doesn't matter whether she had a thousand mes or a thousand Jaxs. She needed *you* there. She still does."

I rub the back of my neck, her words muddling up my perception of my baby sister. I don't feel needed. Never have. The only thing Lee talks about is Pops and how I need to help *him*, but whenever I try to dig deeper, Pops assures me it's just Lee struggling with the loss of Ma. That she's projecting her worries onto him.

I love my sister, but I'm more inclined to believe Pops.

"I don't wanna go back there, Becca. I don't think I can," I whisper, my voice raspy.

The line in between Becca's eyes deepens as she studies my face.

I wish she'd stop looking at me like that.

After a few moments, she runs her hand through her hair,

blowing out a breath. "I get it... not wantin' to be in Sugarlake."

"You do?"

"Yeah. It's what Momma was screamin' at me for today, actually."

Surprise trickles through my system. "You don't wanna be in Sugarlake?"

She huffs out a laugh. "Hell no. That town judges you quicker than a duck on a june bug."

"No shit." I chuckle.

I catch her eyes with mine. There's a softness there I've never noticed—or maybe it's never been directed my way—but now, it's hard not to get lost in its warmth. I clear my throat, glancing at my plate. "Thank you. For just... getting it. I don't think anyone ever has before."

She tugs on that curly hair, twirling it around her fingers. My heart bangs against my chest, my leg bouncing to its rhythm under the table. The air swirls and changes, appreciation for her words and my attraction mixing until I swear it can reach out and touch her.

She exhales and drops her gaze. "Yeah... well, I still think you're a pussy for not mannin' up and goin' back."

I smile, stretching my arm against the back of the booth. "Well, you know what they say."

Her brow lifts. "What do they say?"

"You are what you eat."

10

BECCA

I'm running late to meet Eli. Ever since he razzed me on the first day about cutting it close, I've made it my mission to show up before him, but last night I stayed up finishing a twenty-page paper that I procrastinated. So between that and my brain dissecting the "lunch date" from yesterday, I didn't get much sleep.

I saw a different side of Eli at that diner. My loyalty has always—and will always—be with Lee, but I guess I never realized how things might have been for him back home. And now that I've started thinking about it, I can't stop.

The longer it rolls around in my brain, the more frustrated I get, my heart twinging at the fact I can't remember Lee ever talking about how Eli handled their momma's death, or how he was dealing with not playing ball.

I have to wonder if she even knows, or if she's been so lost in her misery that she never asked.

But someone ought to.

I saw the shadow of the ghost that haunts him. It causes an odd sensation in my chest, seeing him look so lost—a familiarity that fills the space between us, one that makes me want to dive inside his darkness and find the cracks of light.

And then I snap myself the hell out of it because I don't want *anything* to do with Elliot Carson. The lack of sleep has clearly gone to my head. I will steel myself against whatever is malfunctioning in my body and brain when it comes to him.

I'll find myself a big, fat dick to ride this weekend and I'll fuck the thought of him away.

I walk into the arena with a new resolve, but all of that goes to complete shit when I drink in the scene in front of me. Eli's shooting hoops, and he's shirtless. Honest to God, he's not wearing a stitch of clothing other than his basketball shorts and shoes. There's nothing but the sound of his sneakers and the bounce of the ball.

Just him, the free-throw line and the focus of his craft.

My brain short-circuits, heart pumping blood so fast my body can't keep up. I put my hand on the concrete wall to keep upright. A light sheen of sweat glistens over his chest and abs, making him look ethereal under the fluorescent lights. He's clearly been practicing a while.

I stand stock still, my eyes devouring every line of his body, the control in his stance, the precision in his movement. It's a thing of beauty. *He's a thing of beauty.* My bag slips from my shoulder and drops to the ground, the sound harsh against the quiet of the air. Eli spins toward the noise, his posture relaxing once he sees me.

"Hey, figured I'd warm up while I waited." He runs his fingers through his hair, his abs flexing with the movement.

I'd respond, but my mouth is suddenly parched and I'm afraid my voice won't work.

His smile slowly drops while I stand there gaping. His eyes darken, the current of our energies dancing off each other, making the air grow heady.

I clear my throat, trying to snap out of it. "Yep. Hi. Sorry I'm late. I overslept."

He smiles and *fuck* the butterflies in my stomach for daring to flutter from his grin.

"What are we doin' today?"

He waves his arm at the cart of basketballs and the few stragglers on the floor. "Take a guess."

"Hmm. You decide you want me on your team after all?" My mouth curls up.

He smirks, bouncing a basketball between his legs. "Baby girl, you've been on my team since you walked on this court. I've just had you benched."

My eyes narrow even though my stomach flips at his words. I stretch my arms above my head, cracking my neck. I don't miss how his eyes follow the hem of my shirt as it rises, or how his Adam's apple bobs with his swallow.

I grin, my hands going to my hips. "Put me in, Coach."

"I seem to remember that gigantic head of yours going on about HORSE. Let's see what ya got, big talker." He tosses the basketball toward my chest, making my breath whoosh out of me when I catch it.

And so we play.

I throw from about two feet away and squeal when it goes in.

He easily mimics the move.

He shoots from the free-throw line, jogging backward after he makes it. "Nothin' but net, baby."

"Kobe!" I yell, attempting the same shot. The ball bounces off the rim and rolls to Eli's feet. He's keeled over laughing as he picks it up. I flip him off.

He does some fancy move where he runs up to the rim and jumps, twisting his body to toss the ball through the net with one hand.

I scoff. "Hardly fair. I barely know how to shoot. You're just showin' off now."

He chuckles and swaggers over, placing the ball in my hands and walking around until he's behind me. He's so close I feel the tingles of electricity radiating off his body as they snap at my back. I grip the ball tighter.

"First..." His fingers thread through my curls as he angles my face toward the rim. "You need to eye the target." He pulls slightly before releasing the strands, causing a shiver to race down my spine. His rough hands ghost over my sides, goose bumps sprouting as his fingers grip my hips. He adjusts me, squeezing once, and continues his trek.

My legs tremble and I bite my lip to keep from moaning at his touch.

"Next, you need to have an open stance." He kneels behind me, his palms sliding along the inside of my thighs until he reaches my knees, pushing them open. The light caress of his fingertips on my bare skin sends a tendril of arousal spiraling through my body, heating me from the inside and making my cheeks flush.

"Point your feet toward the left side of the basket."

I angle them. "Like this?" I ask, breathlessly.

He raises back up, his breath blowing on my neck as he leans in close. "Perfect." His voice is raspy and low. I suck in a breath.

His palms glide over my shoulders and down my arms until his big hands dwarf my small ones. I'm transfixed at the sight of them contrasting against the basketball's leather.

"Now this part is the most important. Are you payin' attention?"

His accent slips through, making my stomach tighten. I nod, the back of my head rubbing against his slick chest.

"Move the ball into the shot pocket." He moves our arms until the ball is situated several inches above my waist and aiming directly at the basket. I'm panting, my breasts heaving from the inability to catch my breath.

His fingers weave through mine, manipulating them until they're positioned the way he wants. He lifts our arms until they're raised level to my head. "Hand positioning is important."

His palms disappear and my fingers twitch at the loss. But soon enough they're back, one pressing into my stomach, while the other rests on my right arm. "Make sure you use your legs, core, and arm strength to shoot." He pushes into me and propels us forward. The heat of his body wraps around me and my ass pushes into his very prominent, stiff erection.

Oh my God.

I blow out a heavy breath, afraid that if I move an inch—a fucking centimeter—that my control will snap and I'll maul him right here in the middle of the court.

His hand leaves my stomach, moving up my body until it rests on my left arm.

"Now shoot." His whisper tickles my ear, shockwaves rippling through me. My body obeys his command before my mind can even process what he said. I let the ball fly and it swooshes through the net.

I don't even care. I twist my upper body in his arms, my eyes clashing with baby blues.

It's a second...

Two seconds...

Before I can take another breath, Eli's lips are on mine, his tongue ravaging my mouth. Our breaths meld and I moan at his taste. My hand tangles in his hair, his thick bulge pushing into me from behind. My panties are soaked through, my body vibrating from how bad I want to feel him plunging inside me. I'm lost. In his taste. His smell. His aura. In everything that is Elliot Carson.

Elliot Carson.

I jerk away, lips burning and heart screaming in protest.
What the hell am I doin'?

"Becca." Eli's voice is cautious, his arms still outstretched.

I shake my head, fingers touching my swollen lips. "No.
No. That did *not* just happen."

Eli's arms drop along with his head, his jaw clenching.
"Shit. You're right. That shouldn't have happened."

"Ya think, genius? What the hell were you thinkin'?"

"What was *I* thinking? You kissed *me.*"

I huff out a laugh, my arms waving wildly. "Oh, please.
You seduced me with your... your basketball voodoo."

He stares at me, his mouth twitching. "Basketball
voodoo?"

I groan, my hands wrenching my roots. "You know what I
mean. This—" I point between us. "Can't happen."

"I agree."

"For so many reasons. You're the damn coach of the
basketball team. Your sister is my *best friend,* for God's sake.
This cannot happen. I just..."

Eli's in front of me now, his hand pushing against my lips.
"*Christ,* do you ever listen? I said I agree."

"Oh," I mumble against his fingers.

He smirks. "Yeah. *Oh.*"

Relief floods through my veins, even as my heart twinges
at the thought of it never happening again.

That kiss was a mistake. One that we will not be repeating
ever again.

But damn, it was a great one.

11

BECCA

Hours later and I can't stop thinking about that kiss. I'm usually not a fan of lip to lip action. It's too personal, and my momentary lapse of judgment with Eli has reminded me of all the reasons I avoid it in the first place. I'm afraid the feel of his lips will be burned into mine for the rest of eternity.

But I'll try like hell to erase it.

I grab my phone and shoot a text to Jeremy.

Me: Please, please say you'll drop whatever you're doing this weekend and help me find a stallion to ride. I am in desperate need of a good fuck.

Jeremy: God, your lines are corny as hell.

Me: Is that a yes?

Jeremy: What's in it for me?

I roll my eyes.

Me: Are you seriously holding our friendship hostage right now? What kind of a dick does that?!

Jeremy: It's a simple question.

Me: ... what do you want?

His response is immediate.

**Jeremy: Introduce me to Elliot Carson personally...
before the season starts. And maybe get him to sign something, but don't tell him it's for me.**

My stomach jumps to my throat when I read Eli's name. I
slam myself back on my bed, groaning.

Me: Fine.

As if the world isn't torturing me enough, the phone rings
in my hand. Lee's name mocks me from the screen.

"Hey, girl." I sit up as I answer.

"Hiya, stranger. How's life in Florida?"

I swallow. *I doubt you wanna know.* "Huh? Oh... things are
fine here. Great. How's everything with you? Jax still actin'
like a lost puppy lappin' up your scraps?"

She laughs. "Jax is not a lost puppy, Becca. And he's just
fine. I was with him last night until he went home with Suzy
Abbott, of all people. Can you believe that? I swear, I hate
her."

"You could always just let Jax take *you* home, which we
both know is what he really wants. Then you wouldn't need
to worry about girls like Suzy Abbott."

Lee sighs. "You know I can't do that."

"And why the hell not? That boy would worship you like
a goddess."

"It would complicate things."

"Nothin' complicated about it, sister. Strip him down and
let those mechanic hands go to work on that sweet little body
of yours."

"Jax is my *friend*, Becca."

Jax is a fool for her, and he always has been. Even back
when she belonged to his best friend. There's nothing he
wouldn't do for a chance to be with her, and she knows it.

I nod even though she can't see. "Just think of how *friendly*
he'd be with your vagina."

She snorts. "You are so dang crass."

"So you always tell me." I smile. Damn, I miss her.

"You seen any more of Eli down there at that fancy school?"

My stomach rolls with her question, but my veins heat. A flash of our earlier kiss blinds me, infusing my cheeks with the flush of my guilt. "Nope. Not really. Why would I have seen him?"

I smack my forehead, squeezing my eyes. *Idiot.*

She blows out a breath. "I guess you wouldn't have. But I won't lie, the thought of you givin' him a good tongue lashin' is mighty appealin'."

I choke on my inhale, eyes watering as I try to stop the burning cough.

"You alright?"

"Yeah," I rasp. I clear my throat, my hand rubbing my chest. "I'm fine."

"Hey, maybe you can do me a favor though? Hunt him down and convince him to come home with you for Christmas?"

I purse my lips. "Ugh. Lee, my folks are bein' assholes. I don't know if *I'm* even comin' home for the holidays."

"What? What are they doin' now?"

I sigh, not wanting to think about yet another thing that's spiraled out of my control. Plus, if I go into it then I'll have to tell her about my new job, and I just told her I hadn't seen Eli. *Why did I do that?* My stomach sinks when I realize that I just walked myself into an extremely shitty situation. One where I can't tell my best friend the truth about my life, all because my mouth spoke before my brain could catch up. But if I go back on it now, she'll wonder why I lied.

Lee *hates* liars.

"Just the usual stuff. Wantin' me to chain myself down to the church and pop out a hundred kids."

She chuckles. "One day they'll realize you're a wild horse that can't be tamed."

I grin. "That's right, girlfriend. You're the only one who gets me."

"Well, I *don't* get why you won't just come home. Your folks are nothin' new. We miss you around here."

I snort. "Lee, you're the only one who misses me. And as much as you know me, this is one thing you just won't understand. Sugarlake runs through your veins deep. You're meant for that life. I'm not. Every second there feels like torture."

She doesn't press further, and I don't try to explain. This is something I know she'll never get.

I'm suddenly hit with the urge to talk to Eli... because *he* would.

My stomach is in my throat as I make my way to the basketball court. I had one blessed day off from having to meet with Eli, and I spent the entire time dreading having to face him again. Then I realized that I'm Becca goddamn Sanger. I do not cower in the face of a man. They kneel at *my* feet, not the other way around. Besides, it's not like I want anything to happen even if it could. He's an ocean of complication I am not interested in dipping into.

I told Jeremy to meet me here this morning so I could introduce them, even though I'd rather not. I'd say screw it and invite Sabrina this weekend instead, but she'll scare off all my potential one-night stands when she asks their name, followed closely by whether they're a feminist.

I walk into the arena and drop my bag in the stands, slinking down beside it. It hasn't been three minutes when Eli strolls in.

"Hey." I wave, jumping from the bleachers and making my way to the court floor.

He tips his chin in greeting and turns, walking toward the cart of balls against the far wall.

Well, alright then.

I follow him, my hands running through my hair. I'm halfway across the court when arms come around my waist, picking me up and swinging me around. I scream from the ambush, blood rushing to my head as I'm flipped over Jeremy's shoulder. *Ass.*

"Put me down, you giant oaf!" I beat my fists on his lower back.

He lets out a boisterous laugh and smacks my ass. "Say please."

"Fuck you."

Jeremy tsks. "You kiss your momma with that mouth?"

"Jeremy, I swear to God if you don't put me down—"

"Alright, alright. Calm your tits."

He gently slides me down his front. I reach out and grab his nipple through his shirt, twisting.

"Ow, *fuck*, Becca."

I smile. "That's what you get."

A throat clears, making us turn toward the sound. Eli is glaring, his arms crossed over his chest. *Damn, he's hot even when he's broody.* My core throbs as I get lost in visions of what it would be like to have his tongue dip between my legs the way it did my mouth.

An elbow in my side snaps me out of my daze.

"Right. Sorry." I nod. "Eli, this is Jeremy. Jeremy, Eli." I wave my hand between them.

Eli's brow lifts, his eyes lasering into Jeremy.

Jeremy rushes forward, hand outstretched. "I know who you are, of course. Huge fan. I watched *all* of your college games."

Eli's jaw tics, scowl firmly in place. "Fan of basketball then?"

I laugh. "He's more than a fan, he's one of your players."

Eli stands straighter, pointing to his chest. "My player? What position?"

Jeremy beams. "Point guard. I hope I do you proud."

"Little tall for a point guard." Eli rubs his chin. "I think I *do* remember your face from the roster." My heart skips when Eli's eyes meet mine. "How do you two know each other?"

Jeremy reaches behind himself and interlocks our fingers, pulling me into his side. Eli's stare snaps to our hands, his eyes glinting.

"Becca's been the other half of me since freshman year," Jeremy says. I grin up at him because it's true. He's the only person besides Lee who's burrowed his way into my soul, stealing a little piece for himself.

Eli's shoulders stiffen. "I see. Well, hopefully, she won't be a distraction. I'd hate to have to remove her because you two can't keep your hands in check."

My grin drops, my veins bubbling with anger. *Did he just threaten my job?*

I thought we'd moved forward. That the days of Eli being a complete prick were behind us, but clearly I was wrong.

He's still nothing but an asshole.

I 've only experienced this particular emotion one other time in my life. It was when I was twelve. Pops entered me into a hoops competition over in Nashville, so I was supposed to practice all that week. It was summer break and Pops told me I needed to stay sharp. But there was a new video game all my friends were playing, and for once in my life, I wanted to just be a kid, so I convinced Ma to buy it and not tell Pops. Whenever he was at work that week, I'd hole up in my room, playing that game instead of practicing. Needless to say, I didn't win the tournament. Some kid beat me by two damn points.

Pops has this way of cutting you with his disappointment —his words sharp as they slice into your skin. He wielded his weapon the entire drive home that day, droning on about how amazing the other kid was. How his parents must be so proud.

That's when I felt it. The bitter taste of jealousy. But even that doesn't compare to the lava searing my body at the sight of Becca being manhandled by someone other than me.

I shouldn't have touched her.

But I couldn't breathe from *not* touching her. My precious control snapped into a thousand pieces, shattering on the glossy, maple floor. But it doesn't matter. I could lose my job if FCU found out.

Has she had a boyfriend this entire time?

It wasn't like the kiss was planned. We both agreed it was a mistake, so what do I care if she's with this guy? It's better this way. Maybe knowing she's taken will help me keep my distance.

I watch the two of them together, envy punching my stomach and stealing my breath. I grit my teeth against the loss.

Why is he still here?

"You plannin' on actually workin' with me today, or are you gettin' paid to make eyes with your boyfriend?" I snap.

Becca spins toward me, her brows raising for a split second before her face smooths. She runs her palm up Jeremy's arm.

I grip the basketball in my hands so tight my knuckles turn white. Leaning on her tiptoes, she slides her hands around his neck—those same hands that were in my hair—tugging like she couldn't get close enough.

I bite my cheek, the tang of blood distracting me from ripping her out of his arms.

Jeremy glances my way, a smile splitting his face. "See ya later, Coach. Again, it's an honor. I can't wait to soak in everything you'll teach me."

Normally, I wouldn't be so thrilled with someone shouting my accolades from the rooftops—thinking I'm something I no longer am—but I can't find it in me to mind this guy's hero-worship. I can tell it makes Becca uncomfortable, which makes it delightful for me. I smirk as he leaves the court.

Her eyes narrow, the grin she had for *him* dropping off her face. "What's so funny?"

"Nothing's funny. I like him. He clearly has fantastic taste." I gesture to myself.

She flips her hair, smoothing down her tank. "I agree. He has an eye for beauty."

"Wow. Humble."

"Who said I was talkin' about me?"

I step closer, passing her the ball. Our fingers brush, and mine flex to keep from reaching out. I dip my head to catch those jade green eyes. "Come on now, Becca. You know you're beautiful."

I didn't mean to say that out loud, but I don't want to take it back. It's true. She's a siren. Once she steps into the room, there's no looking away. I *wish* I could look the hell away.

Her cheeks bloom the prettiest shade of pink and my inner beast roars. Jeremy may have gotten her smile, but he didn't get her blush. She steps closer, the basketball pressing into my stomach. Her tongue jets out, wetting those sinful lips. My mouth waters as it remembers the taste.

"Eli," she whispers, leaning in closer, her lashes fluttering. For the first time, I notice the light dusting of freckles along the ridge of her nose. I have the strangest urge to count every one.

"Eli." Her breath teases my lips, my mouth parting in response. "Jeremy isn't—"

His name is a splash of icy water on my heated body. I wince, stepping back. "Right." I slide my hand through my hair. "He's a lucky guy."

"No, I..." She stops mid-sentence, shaking her head. "Yeah. He is."

I nod, trying to appear unfazed. Calm, cool, and collected. Inside, I'm a mess. The thought of never touching her rips through my chest cavity, slapping my heart. It's not enough to break, but the bruise hurts all the same.

Somehow, I regain control and make it through Becca's lesson. I spend the rest of the day counting down the minutes until preseason, when these one-on-ones with her will end.

I call Connor on my way home. "What up? You doing anything tonight?"

"I was planning on taking it easy. My workout killed today, I can barely move. Why, what'd you have in mind?"

"I was just thinking you could come over and chill. Maybe... bring a couple girls?"

He chuckles. "Your hand not cutting it anymore?"

He's joking, but his words hit a little too close to home. "Something like that."

"Oh, you know I'm always down to help you out in that area. I have my sometimes chick on call. I'm sure she has a friend she can grab."

"Your *sometimes* chick?" I laugh. "God, you're disgusting. It's a miracle you get laid."

"All my ladies know the deal. Besides, I treat them with the utmost respect. I've never had a complaint."

"Maybe not to your face."

"The only thing they give my face is their pussy."

"Whatever you say, man. I just got home, so text me when you're heading over." I chuckle, hanging up my phone.

He shows up an hour later with his "sometimes chick" Ally, and her friend Sarah, who I get along with surprisingly well.

Sarah's gorgeous with her long, strawberry-blonde hair and sweet smile. My usual type, which is probably why Connor brought her. But I'm not into it, no matter how much I try to be.

"So, what do you do for a living?" I ask.

She smiles, taking a sip of wine and crossing her legs. "I'm a physical therapist. Specializing in sports therapy, actually."

My eyebrows raise. "No shit? I could have used you back when I got injured. My therapist was an asshole. You'd be much easier to work with."

She giggles and the sound makes me smile.

"Well, maybe you can give me some pointers on how to keep my clients happy." Her cheeks flush with her words.

Is she flirting?

I take a sip of my beer, considering whether I want to encourage her. She's sweet. Docile, even. And while that should be a breath of fresh air, I find myself wishing she'd have just a little bit of bite. But she gets my mind off the redheaded curls that cloud my vision, and that's enough for now.

I shouldn't lust for things I can't have. Sarah is right in front of me, and she doesn't make me feel like my soul is crawling out of my skin whenever she's near. It's nice, feeling in control again.

So when she leaves at the end of the night, I take her number. I convince myself she might be just what I need, even if my heart isn't in it.

13

BECCA

I haven't seen Eli since Wednesday. Coach Andrews has had me in the office helping him prepare for next week's preseason, so our "basketball lessons" have been cut prematurely. I'm relieved. Eli makes me want to *know* him, and that is not something I'll entertain.

Emotional connections are fleeting. They whisper like the devil in your ear, telling you to take a bite of apple. I have no interest in falling for the lies. Better to keep our interaction in public places where entire teams surround us.

I'm thankful it's Friday night, and I don't have to worry about running into him at all. I'm finally dragging Jeremy to a club—payment for introducing him to Eli before the season starts. My plan is to relieve this *tension* that's been twisting inside me since the moment I face-planted into Eli's chest.

When we walk inside the club, we head straight to the bar. The music is loud and the crowd is thick, so it's useless to try and hold a conversation. I order us a round of tequila shots, we throw them back and then head to the dance floor.

I'm not much of a dancer, but the liquor loosens my limbs enough to move with the bass as it thumps. I should probably care that Jeremy's up against my back—it's not like I can have *him* take me home, but I'm having too much fun to tell him to stop, so instead, I reach my arms back and around his neck, swinging my hips harder.

His head dips. "If I were into girls, you'd be giving me a hell of a show right now."

I smirk. "Just doin' my duty of bein' your beard."

He chuckles, his hands wrapping my hips, helping us move to the beat. My eyes scan the area, and suddenly my body jerks out of rhythm, heart stuttering in my chest.

Eli and Connor are standing across the room. Eli's leaning against the bar, his attention on some strawberry-blonde girl next to him. My stomach squeezes tight when she throws her head back, laughing at something he said.

He ain't that funny.

My movements are out of sync with Jeremy's, but he doesn't notice. There's an unfamiliar feeling rising inside me. I can't stand Eli giving that girl his attention. I know how it feels to have those baby blues locked on you like you're the only thing that matters, and irritation licks up my spine that someone else is getting to feel it. But for the life of me, I can't look away.

Like he can sense my stare, Eli's gaze searches the room until it locks with mine, his eyes widening as they burn a trail along my body. The girl next to him says something, but he pays her no mind.

My stomach flutters.

His posture stiffens as he spots Jeremy, his gaze growing cold. The ice in his eyes does nothing but spark a fire in mine. My body moves with intent, wanting, *needing* him to feel the same stifling grip that chokes my insides knowing he's here with someone else.

Knowing I shouldn't give a damn.

Jeremy plays his part without realizing, spinning me

around, dipping us down and bringing our bodies flush as we rise back up. I glance over my shoulder, unable to keep my eyes away, but Eli's not looking anymore. His focus is back on the strawberry-blonde.

The fire sizzles out, and I'm left feeling cold.

I pull out of Jeremy's arms, motioning to the bar. I order a shot as soon as I get there, the burn helping to numb the ache in my chest. Slamming the empty shot glass on the bar, I head down a long hallway to find the ladies' room. There's no line, which is surprising, since it's a one-person bathroom.

I've just turned around to close the door when a hand slips between the crack and shoves it open. I gasp, the force pushing me away. Eli stalks in the small room and reaches behind him, shutting the door and flipping the lock.

"This is the *ladies'* room, asshole."

His mouth quirks, but he doesn't speak, just continues his trek toward me. My ass bumps the sink. He steps into me, his chest rubbing against my braless nipples through the thin material of my dress. Thick arms encase me, those big hands grabbing on to the edge of the counter. Leaning in, his nose trails down the length of my neck, and I swear he's inhaling my scent. My entire body clenches, and a knot forms in my stomach.

"What—what are you doin'?"

"Do you enjoy torturing me, Rebecca?" His voice is low. It rumbles against my skin and sends goose bumps blazing down my body.

"I don't know what you mean."

"I think you do."

Each breath is a tease, his lips skimming my skin on every exhale. A moan slips out, unbidden.

His arms flex. "Does it feel this way with him?"

"What way?" My stomach rises and drops so fast it makes me lose my breath.

"Like I'll die if I can't touch you."

My heart quickens, blood singing through my veins, begging me to just *give in.*

I push into his body, surrendering to the feeling. "So touch me."

His head shakes against me, his jaw tense. "You aren't mine to touch."

"I'm not Jeremy's either."

His head snaps back.

"What about that girl you're with?" I ask.

"Just a friend."

My fingers trace the veins in his forearms as I slide my hands up, reaching to cup his face in my palms. "Eli. *Touch* me."

His nostrils flare, his body rigid against mine. I wait but he doesn't make a move.

My stomach sinks at the rejection and I take a step away, but I don't get far. His arms leap from the sink, wrapping around my waist and jerking me against him.

My breath whooshes out of me, every nerve ending lit up from his touch. My hands go back to palming his jaw. His arms tense around me while he lifts me off the ground, bringing my face to his.

"Don't tell me what to do," he growls as our lips meet.

I should care that this is happening. I *should* stop it. But I don't. The memory of his taste has been all I've thought of since the moment it hit my tongue.

I'll be damned if I give it up again.

14

ELI

I see Becca and my mind is lost. Like usual, everything fades away but her until I can't think straight. She's been dancing on that kid Jeremy when she should be dancing on *me*.

I tried to ignore her and put my focus on the girl who's within my reach. But looking at Sarah after soaking in Becca is like trying to see after staring into the sun.

When I see her storm off from the bar, I follow her down the hallway. I know it's wrong. I know what will happen the second I get her alone, but I'm so far past the point of caring. My need for her is absolute. Screw the consequences.

It doesn't matter that we're in a dirty restroom in the back of a club. I couldn't care less about the people we both have waiting for us.

She's fire. Absolutely insane. But I love the way she burns.

I grip her waist tight, her tongue caressing mine with a softness I didn't expect. I turn us slightly, slamming her against the wall, kissing her deeper. Those mile-long legs wrap around my waist, and I groan, pressing into her center. She rotates her hips, grinding against me, working my erection through the fabric and *goddamn* it feels amazing. My lips break away from hers, trailing kisses down her cheek.

"I didn't take you for the soft and sweet type," she pants.

Annoyance flickers at that *fucking* mouth, stoking the flames of my desire. My hand grasps her throat. "You'll take it any way I decide to give it to you, baby girl."

She tries to respond but my grip tightens, squeezing hard enough to feel her heart race under my palm. Her head tilts back as she lets out a moan.

"You don't like soft and sweet? How do you want me then? Do you want me here?" My thumb presses into her lip. "Want me to choke you with my cock until tears stream down that pretty, porcelain face?" Her legs tighten around my waist, eyes flaring.

I move my free hand lower, tracing her collarbone, fingers dipping into her sinful cleavage. "Or maybe here? Want to get on your knees like a good girl, and let me paint these perfect tits with my cum?"

"I don't get on my knees for anyone," she breathes.

I chuckle, my hand cupping her breast before continuing my path down. Reaching under her dress, I slip into her panties, dragging my fingers through her folds. "Here?"

She sucks in a breath, her wild curls mashing against the wall as she pushes into my hand. My dick is leaking like crazy, pulsing with every word I say.

I need to fuck her so bad.

I dip my fingertips inside her, just slightly, before sweeping up to rub against her clit. She's soaked, drenching my hand. "Is this all for me?"

"God, Eli. Just fuck me already."

Her plea makes my lips curl and my length grow. "Damn, you're pretty when you beg."

Smirking, her legs unwind from around me, her hand

diving into my pants, fingers circling my cock. "Not as pretty as you'll be."

She works me with one hand while the other unzips my slacks, pushing them down along with my boxers until my thick erection bobs between us. I glance down, growing dizzy from want at the sight of Becca's hand on me. Lifting my face to the ceiling, I try to think of something to calm me down. I need to regain some damn control.

"What's the matter, *baby*, cat got your tongue?"

My nostrils flare as she twists her hand around my tip. "Just letting you have your fun."

"Seems to me like you're all talk. What happened to the big, bad Eli from a few seconds ago?"

Her words stoke the flames in the pit of my stomach and I shove her back, my hands gripping under her ass and lifting, setting her on the edge of the counter. She spreads her legs, moving her panties to the side, her pretty, pink pussy exposed for my viewing pleasure. I grip myself, stroking lewdly, sparks igniting in my pelvis from having her eyes on me. From knowing she likes it.

She opens her mouth to speak but my hand slaps over it, muffling her words. "I've had about enough of that mouth of yours."

I line myself up and slam inside her. She moans, the sound vibrating my palm.

There is no tenderness here. No taking our time. This isn't making love.

My thrusts are deep and hard, our hips smacking on each forward movement. Sweat beads along my brow and I watch as it drips onto her skin.

"You like the way I feel inside you?"

She wraps her hands around my wrist and pulls, placing my fingers back on her throat. My balls tighten.

My girl likes it rough.

My other hand tangles in that fiery hair, elongating her neck as I pull. Her eyes roll back and my cock jerks inside her. My movement stutters as she clenches around me.

I suck her earlobe in between my teeth. "Tell me how you want it."

She leans up, her tongue licking the sweat off my neck. "With you desperate and needy."

My thrusts increase in speed, tightness coiling deep in my gut. "I've been desperate since the moment I saw you, baby girl."

She pushes me back, hopping off the counter. My dick weeps at the loss of her warmth. Flipping around, she bends over, sliding her panties down her legs. "Then maybe you should show me what it feels like."

Seeing her ass bare and her legs spread sends a shot of desire spiking through me. I step into her, my tip sliding through her lips, torturing us both.

"Not until you tell me," I whisper.

Our eyes lock in the mirror. My chest swells at the knowledge that in this moment, she's mine.

"I want you to fuck me hard and make me come." She hesitates. "And then I don't want it to ever happen again."

My heart squeezes, but I ignore the ache. She's right, after all. This can't go on after tonight.

I slide back inside her, picking up the same deep, fast pace. My palm lands harshly on her cheek, her ass jiggling, the smack resounding in the air.

"God. Yes. Do it again," she moans.

"You need to be punished, Rebecca? For that insolent *fuckin'* mouth of yours?"

I smack her harder. Heat simmers in my groin as I stare at the pink imprint of my hand.

She mewls, her pussy fluttering. I reach around, palming her tit, my lips next to her ear. "Come for me, baby girl."

She does. Immediately. Like she was waiting for me to say the words. My eyes snap to her face in the mirror, needing to see my effect on her. It's a thing of beauty, watching her fall apart on my dick. She bites her hand to stifle her scream, and the sight of her in the throes of orgasm pushes me over the edge. My balls draw up tight, my cock exploding violently, pumping my load deep inside her.

I collapse on top of her, panting, the aftershocks of my orgasm tingling through my body.

Knock. Knock.

"Hey, hurry the fuck up! You've been in there forever!"

Becca's eyes widen as they meet my reflection, her hands coming up to cover her mouth. She giggles. It's infectious and I can't help but laugh, my forehead resting against the small of her back.

Christ. This girl makes me crazy.

I wish I could keep her.

15

ELI

I have no idea what the hell to say as we get redressed, so I say nothing. I just lean against the cold concrete wall—knocks still pounding outside the door—watching as Becca tries to unsmear her makeup. Our eyes meet in the mirror.

"You know… you're lucky I'm on birth control." She wipes a finger under her lip.

My stomach drops. I was so lost in the moment of finally being with her that it wasn't even a thought in my mind.

I grimace. "Yeah, logical thought wasn't really happening. I'm sorry."

She stares at me for a second, rubbing her lips together. "It's okay."

Heaving a sigh, she spins, leaning against the counter I just fucked her on. My dick twitches at the memory.

The door bangs again from someone's fist, only this time we don't laugh. My chest wrings tight knowing when we walk out of this room things will go back to how they were. Becca twirls her hair around her hand and starts to leave. I step in front of her before she can twist the handle.

"Wait. Are you… are things—" I blow out a breath.

She gives me a small smile, shaking her head. "Eli, don't."

My jaw clenches and I nod. "Yeah. Okay."

She pushes past me. My stomach twists. I grab her wrist, her pulse jumping under my fingers.

She stops, sucking in a breath. "Let me go."

"Shit." I drop her arm. "I just… can we try and be friends? There's no rule against that, is there?" I'm grasping at straws and I'm confident we both know it, but I can't go back to the way things were. Not now. Not after this.

She gazes at me, chewing on her lip, those fingers playing in her strands of hair. I shove my hands in my pockets to keep from grabbing her face and kissing her.

She finally nods, a small grin peeking out. "You wouldn't be the first asshole I've been friends with."

Something that feels a lot like relief pours through my veins, loosening the knot in my stomach and dousing the lump in my throat.

"I'll see ya later." She cracks the door and slips into the crowd.

A girl bursts through, scoffing when she sees me. Maybe I should be embarrassed. It's obvious what we were up to. But I can't find it in me to care, so I give her a big smile and squeeze by.

Connor and Sarah are in the same spot I left them. Both of their heads snap in my direction as I walk up.

Connor's eyes widen as he looks me up and down, a smirk lining his face. "Hey, buddy. Where ya been?" His voice is loud, straining over the sound of the music.

I paste on a grin, not caring how obvious it is that my hair is damp from sweat and my clothes are wrinkled. "Just needed some air."

Sarah leans over, resting her hand on my arm and speaking into my ear. "I ordered you another drink."

"Thanks." My nerve endings are sensitive from being burned by Becca's touch, and I grit my teeth to keep from jerking away from Sarah's.

I thought fucking Becca would get this *need* out of my system. Let me regain some damn sense.

It wasn't like this back when we were kids. Or maybe it was and I was too focused on the ball to notice. Either way, it doesn't matter. I indulged in the temptation, and now I need to take whatever this feeling is and tamp it down. I've worked hard to get to where I am. Being involved with a student will *definitely* mess that up. Only... she doesn't feel like a student to me. She feels like more. I shake off the thought, reminding myself that she's out of reach.

But it doesn't stop my eyes from scanning the room, searching for a hint of fire.

It's finally practice season. *Thank God.* I've been busy preparing drills all day, and I'm looking forward to my schedule being busier. No downtime to focus on impossible things. D1 basketball is no joke, the crème de la crème in both coaching and players. There's no time for distractions.

I'm repeating that fact like it's a damn mantra when I see her. I'm in my office, the glass windows looking to the outside, and she's walking by with Jeremy. She's grinning wide—a genuine, toothy smile. My chest twinges, wishing that smile was mine. I watch them until they disappear, the green slime of jealousy dripping down my heart.

Shaking it off, I try to focus. It works for a few minutes, but before long, my mind strays back to the couple on the sidewalk. Tossing my pencil onto the desk, I sigh, searching my computer until I find his profile.

Jeremy Higgins
Senior

I stop reading. *What the hell am I doing?*

My exhale puffs out my cheeks. I need to get over my issue with him. He's the point guard. The "floor general." The de facto leader of the whole damn team. I won't let my petty feelings get in the way of coaching him to his full potential.

I walk onto the court floor thirty minutes later and the nerves take over, washing away the remnants of my jealousy. Players are spread out, some stretching, others shooting hoops. The smell of basketball is in the air.

Coach is standing off to the side talking to Becca. My stomach jumps as I make my way toward them.

"Eli, how ya doing?" Coach asks.

My eyes glance at Becca. I was worried things would be awkward after my dick had been living its best life inside her, but she doesn't seem phased by my presence. "Feeling great, Coach. Ready to get this season started."

He slaps my back, bobbing his head. "I'll introduce you to the team then let you do a little speech. Get the boys ready to go. Let the freshmen know this isn't high school ball."

I nod, my clipboard at my side. Adrenaline pumps through my veins and I bounce on my feet, my whistle jostling against my chest.

I'm ready.

Becca snorts and my head whips in her direction. "What's so funny?"

Her hand covers her mouth, her green eyes sparkling. "Nothin' funny. You're just cute. Bouncin' around like a little boy on Christmas mornin'."

My lips curl up and I take a step toward her. "Cute, huh?"

Her eyes roll. "Don't let it fill your ego, big head."

I tap my clipboard against my leg as I stand there like an

idiot, smiling at her. She fidgets under my gaze, looking around the room. "So this is it, huh? Time for me to shine with all this newfound ballin' knowledge I got." She taps her head.

"That's right. Don't let me down," I tease.

"Wouldn't dream of it… *sir.*" She smiles, walking away.

My cock jumps and my head spins.

For the first time in my life, I want to say fuck basketball. I'd rather steal her away and show her all the ways she makes me feel.

But not everything in life goes the way you want. So, instead of chasing after her, I lock it up tight—just like everything else—and head to greet my players.

16

BECCA

I 've been praying like a whore in church, which ironically is what my hometown thinks of me. All weekend, I've been hoping this feeling that tugs me toward Eli would disappear now that I've given in, but it hasn't. And Lord, did I give in. I knew I would the second he stormed through the bathroom door and gripped my throat like he owned me. His filthy words whispering in my ear, and the way his strong hand pressed on my pulse was intoxicating.

I thought sex would be the water to our fire, but turns out it was gasoline. I realized I was in trouble the second I laid in bed, reaching my hand up to my neck, desperate to recreate the feel of being under his palm. Even worse, he wants to be friends, and like a dumbass, I agreed, still dick-drunk and not able to think through the orgasm fog.

My thoughts are only reaffirmed as I stand with the other student managers while Eli talks. The rest of the team is huddled, sitting on the cold wood floor, eyes rapt on the man in front of them. He has this way of grabbing the energy in the room and controlling it without any effort. Almost like it can't help but want to sink into his skin and stay there for a while. Unfortunately, I can relate.

His hands are on his hips, and his gaze moves over every player while he talks.

I came prepared for the excitement at seeing the team come together and practice. I am *not* prepared for how my heart swells while Eli stands in front of them, his passion pouring out on the floor.

"Let's get this out of the way so we never have to bring it up again. I'm Elliot Carson, for those of you who don't know me."

"Everyone knows you, Coach," a player calls out.

Eli rubs a hand on the back of his neck. My skin prickles with jealousy that he's feeling the touch I crave.

"Maybe so." He chuckles. "In any case, I played ball in Ohio then was drafted to New York. I was hurt, and unfortunately, it ended my career. I don't really have much to say about it other than things happen for a reason. If I wasn't injured, I wouldn't be here to coach you guys, and I'm damn thankful I have the opportunity to be at your back."

"It wasn't your dream to play?" another player asks.

Eli nods. "It was. But..." He blows out a breath, his gaze locking on to mine. "You can't always have the thing you want most. Sometimes, no matter how bad you want it... it's just not meant to be."

I suck in a breath, my heart pinching so tight and my stomach flipping so fast I'm worried I'll pass out.

His eyes linger before he finally breaks our stare. "Anyway, that's enough about me. I'd rather focus on you. Some of you have been here. You've put your blood, sweat, and tears onto this court every day. You've earned your spot on this team, and the respect of your peers. I want you to know I'll do the same. Respect is earned, and I'll work every day to prove I'm worthy of it. For the new kids—look to your upper-

classmen and get ready. Division One is where the big boys
eat. We don't care if you have a paper due the next day, and
we don't fuck around with excuses. When you're here, you
need to be focused. There's no downtime. No life of glitz and
glamour. It's just you, the hardwood, and your
determination."

The players nod along. They look eager. Like they're
soaking up his words and wanting to prove to him they can
be what he's asking. He may want to earn their respect, but to
me, it looks like he already has it.

"Coach Andrews and I will ask a lot of you, and sometimes you'll hate us. You'll want to give in to that voice in
your mind, spinning lies to make your failures sound sweet."
He shakes his head. "Don't do it. I promise if you put your
head down and grind every day, push through the pain and
the doubts, then we'll do all we can to help you reach your
full potential. Together, we'll bring home the championship,
and it will be my honor to watch you grow into your
greatness."

The players hoot and holler, and Coach Andrews claps
him on the back as he takes over. A hint of a grin graces Eli's
face as he walks to the side. I watch him, mesmerized,
wondering what it would feel like to be loved as much as
Elliot Carson loves the game.

The rest of practice is intense. One player throws up and
goes back to drills like it's *normal*. Another pulls a hamstring
and continues to practice through it. But watching Eli in his
element is something else. He's fierce.

Sadness flows from my head to my heart, squeezing my
chest at the thought I never took the time to watch him play. I
bet he was a thing of beauty.

I'm still lost in thoughts of *why* I never saw him play long
after everyone has left. I've got my earbuds in, placing the
basketballs back in the rolling cart, and honestly, this gig is

better than I expected. So far, most of my job is just ticking things off a list.

Bending to pick up the last ball, I jump out of my skin when large hands reach down beside me and grab it before I can. I jerk up, coming face to chest with Eli. That damn cinnamon smell slams into me, making my stomach clench. I move my gaze upward, taking out my earbuds as I meet his eyes. They sparkle with something sinful and I have to bite back the urge to beg for his tongue in my pussy. It doesn't seem fair I haven't experienced it.

"Almost done?" He quirks a brow.

My palms go to my hips. "I was, until some big head came in and tried to distract me."

He smirks, tossing the ball into the cart with one hand, his eyes never leaving mine. *Show-off.* "You hungry?"

My stomach flips at his question. You'd think I've never hung out with a man before. I *do* want to, but I know I shouldn't.

"I don't know…"

"Come on. I don't bite."

"I beg to differ," I quip before I can stop myself.

Eli's eyes darken, the smirk sliding off his face. "Only one way to find out."

His voice is deeper. Huskier. A thrill zips down my spine and settles in between my legs.

I reach for my hair, grabbing my neck instead when I realize it's in a bun. "Ain't there some rule against it, anyway? Won't it look bad for you to be seen with me?"

He shrugs, running a hand through his locks. "Probably. I don't know, I guess I didn't think of it that way. I just thought maybe we could talk about how today went. How you thought I did with them. That's all." His jaw clenches as he slightly shakes his head. "It's stupid. I'll just call Connor."

I cock my head as I watch him ramble. *Is he nervous?* He

seems almost vulnerable. Or maybe I'm just reflecting the emotions I try to hide. Either way, I can't find it in me to say no, even though we both know I should.

"Okay."

His posture relaxes, and he bites his lip as he grins. A thousand fireflies light up my stomach. This is not a smart decision.

But it's never felt so good to act so dumb.

17

ELI

A sking Becca to go to dinner with me is the stupidest decision I can make, but the words spill out before I can suck them back in.

Friends.

If I can keep it to just that, then I'll consider it a win. The truth is there's a nagging insecurity scratching at my insides, threatening to swallow me whole. My heart pumps faster at the thought that I wasn't good enough—didn't live up to everyone's expectations. *Again.* There's no ulterior motive to my offer, I really do want to talk about the first day of practice. How I handled my first day as a coach.

It's stupid.

I should just call and meet up with Connor. *Or Sarah.* But they weren't there, and I'm not interested in another person who will just tell me what I want to hear. Becca's the only one who won't.

"Where you wanna go?" she asks.

I shrug. "Wherever is fine with me."

"There's a good spot about ten minutes from here that has

the *best* burritos." She pats her stomach and grins. Sparks burst through my chest at her smile.

"Sounds good."

I park next to her when we get there, watching as she hops out of her car and prances over to my driver side window, miming for me to roll it down.

"Lotta people here," I say.

She nods, her eyes scanning the groups filling the patio tables. "Yep. Lotta students, too. I recognize some of 'em from my classes."

I palm the back of my neck. This wasn't the best idea. She's probably right, I shouldn't be seen with her. Especially since I've already bent her over a sink and fucked her until she couldn't speak. If whispers started, there wouldn't be a way to keep my guilt under wraps. I've always had a shit poker face.

She leans into the window of my car, her arms resting along the frame, fingers dangling inside the door. From this angle, I'm level with her chest and I can't help where my eyes go. Her tits are just right *there*.

I swallow hard, visions of those same tits in my hands as I impale her from behind filling my mind. My mouth runs dry and I shift in my seat.

"Eyes up here, friend."

My gaze snaps to Becca's face.

Her eyes glint. "Maybe we should get the burritos to go? I don't think it's a good idea for us to be eatin' together at places crawlin' with students."

"Sure."

"Okay." She smiles. "I'll go in and grab the food. But I get to pick, and you'll just have to suffer through whatever I choose for you. I'll follow you back to your place?"

She sashays away before I can protest and my gut jolts at the thought of her being in my house. Alone. With me. *This is a terrible idea.* My mind knows it and repeats it to the rest of my body on a loop, but it doesn't stop the thrill of anticipation at the thought of having her all to myself.

She comes out with a bag of food and I start my car, reversing out of the lot and driving home, my nerves making my stomach jostle, my foot jerky on the gas pedal. I glance in the rearview mirror as I turn on my street, making sure she's following me.

Once I'm in my driveway, I blow out a breath, my knuckles tightening around the steering wheel as I give myself a pep talk. *You can do this, Eli. There's nothing wrong with being friends.*

I step out of my car and lean against the side, watching as Becca stares at my house with wide eyes.

"Whew, buddy." She whistles. "This is quite the place you got here. I didn't realize assistant coaches had such a nice salary."

I shrug. "NBA pays well."

Her eyes squint. "You didn't play in it very long."

"Doesn't matter. Contract was guaranteed, regardless of injury." I wave my arm toward the door. "Let's go inside before the food gets cold."

I'm not uncomfortable with the amount of money I have. I was paid out my forty-four million dollar contract from New York. I'm set for life. Which is just one of the reasons why I wish Lee wouldn't fight me so damn hard when I send them money every month.

Becca makes it sound like she's been struggling. Lee even makes it sound like they've been struggling, so I don't know why she's being so hardheaded. I can help. I *want* to help. I wish she'd understand that. But I guess that would involve her looking outside the bubble where only her issues matter.

Becca and I eat our burritos on the living room floor, our backs against the couch.

"I know you've been dyin' to ask me. So go for it." Becca pats her mouth with a napkin.

"Ask you what?"

She squints her eyes. "Don't you wanna know what I thought about your supreme coachin' skills? Stroke that ego of yours a bit, and make your head swell ten times its normal size?"

My cock jerks, stiffening instantly at her words. That mouth of hers makes words sound so damn *filthy*.

"If you insist." I smirk.

She rolls her eyes, reaching over and pushing me playfully. "And your sister calls *me* crass. Come on, Eli. You bleed basketball, it's the only thing runnin' through those veins. Don't need me to say how obvious it is to everyone around you."

The smile drops off my face, self-doubt wringing my insides tight. I used to think that, but now... how can I be sure?

She stares at me, her lips turning down. "You really don't see yourself right, do you?"

I shrug. "I see myself as anyone else."

"What are you worried about then?"

"Who says I'm worried about anything?"

She tsks. "You don't have to *say* it, Eli. It's clear as day on that pretty face of yours."

A grin tugs my lips. "Pretty?"

She groans. "You just gonna repeat everything I say all night, or can we have an actual conversation for once?"

I lean my back against the foot of the couch, running a hand through my hair. "I don't know, Becca. I guess I just want to hear it didn't seem like I was an imposter. Basketball is all I've known. It's all I've lived and breathed since Pops found out I could dribble the ball. But... I'm only a few years older than the guys on the team. And when it comes down to it, in the big leagues, I couldn't hack it."

Her brows draw in. "You got hurt, Eli. That's hardly a failure."

I huff out a laugh. "Yeah? Tell that to the expectations lingering on my back."

She scoots next to me, placing her hand on mine and squeezing. Tingles race up my arm, my heart slamming against my ribs at her touch.

"Eli, those boys don't care about your injury or your age. They *worship* you. If you could have seen the way their eyes lit up with every word you spoke..." She trails off, shaking her head.

A bit of my doubt chips away with her words. "You really think so?"

"I know so. If *I* could feel your passion, there's no way they didn't."

My eyes flick over her face. From the freckles on her nose to the sharp gaze of her emerald eyes. She's so close I can feel the heat of her energy zapping along my side, trying to lure me into its embrace. *Christ*, I want to kiss her.

Friends.

I clear my throat and scoot back. "Well, thanks. I hope I can live up to how you think they see me."

Her eyes dim as I say it, nodding her head as she jumps up, gathering the trash from our meal. I let her, not knowing what to say. Not daring to act on the things I want. Because what I want is to pull her into my arms. Apologize for not realizing the way she's always lit me up inside. For not voicing how damn beautiful she's always been, and not doing something about it when I had the chance. For not being able to do anything about it now.

What I *want* is to dive deep inside her and stay there, until she admits she feels this just as much as I do.

But I can't.

So I let her clean up as I open a bottle of wine and take it to the patio, overlooking the coast. I'll sink into a make-believe world where every fiber of my being doesn't reach out to fuse with hers.

I'll settle for her friendship, and pretend that it's enough.

18

BECCA

T ime moves differently after a few glasses of wine. I thought we were just grabbing a quick meal. Convinced myself I would leave right after eating, not wanting to torture myself by staying next to Eli for long periods of time. I hate how much I like him. I feel like my loyalty to Lee is slipping away with every second in his presence.

But I can't help it.

So here I am a few hours later. The sun has long since dipped behind the sea—which you can see from his million-dollar deck. Holy crap, how did I not know Eli was loaded? Talk about a smack in the face when I pulled up to his mansion with a view.

"How many rooms does this place have, anyway?" I sip my glass of wine, relaxing on a lounge chair.

"Six."

"*Six?* For what? Who's gonna be takin' up the space? Not like your family's gonna visit anytime soon." My hand slaps over my mouth immediately, the wine loosening my tongue beyond what I meant to say.

Eli sighs. "No shit, right? They wouldn't come out even if I asked." He hangs his head, peering into the liquid swirling in his glass.

"Have you?... asked, that is."

"Naw, why set myself up for the letdown, you know?"

My heart pinches at his words, but I'm not sure why he thinks that way. There's nothing that Lee would want more than to see him.

"Eli, Lee wants to see you. You know that, right? She misses you. She loves you. She *needs* you."

He scoffs, setting his glass on the wicker table and facing me, his elbows on his knees. "Please, spare me the theatrics, Becca. Lee doesn't miss me. Lee doesn't even *know* me. All she wants is someone there to help carry the weight of her life."

I sit forward, anger piercing my chest for my best friend. *How dare he act like she doesn't care.* "And that's a bad thing because...?"

"Because nobody was there to help me carry mine!" he explodes, his hands flying out to his sides.

"You wouldn't let them be!" I yell back. "Lee tells me how she tries with you. How she begs every time y'all talk for you to come home, and you just ignore her pleas. They fall on deaf ears... just like they always have."

His spine stiffens, his eyes narrowing. "This comin' from the girl who says she 'gets it.' You're runnin' so fast from your family, you can't even catch your breath. You have no clue what you're talkin' about."

That accent again. It's his biggest tell. He can try to hide it all he wants, but his emotions show the truth of his roots, no matter how many layers of dirt he tries to bury them under.

He's not wrong, though. His words cut into my skin, showing the hypocrisy underneath, but I won't let him know I feel it. "The only clue I need is that you're sittin' pretty in a multi-million dollar mansion while your family can barely make ends meet. Now *why* is that?"

"You think I don't try to help them?" he hisses through clenched teeth.

"Obviously not enough."

He chuckles, but it's an empty sound. "Must be nice on that pedestal, Rebecca. Does it ever get lonely up there?"

Irritation flares, making my cheeks hot. "Probably as lonely as is it is down there with the people who abandon their family."

"Well, make sure you ask Lee all about it when you talk to her next," he bites back.

I suck in a breath, the twang in his voice and the glassy sheen in his eyes twisting my stomach. Is he insinuating that Lee abandoned *him*?

"What are you talkin' about?"

He shakes his head, dusting off his pant legs as he stands. "It doesn't matter. You're right. I'm an asshole. Lee can do no wrong... and you should go."

I move to sit on the edge of my lounger, reaching out and grasping his wrist. "Hold on. I'm... I'm sorry, alright? I spent a lotta years wipin' Lee's tears that came attached to your name. It's hard for me to see past that to hear you."

He nods sharply. "It's late."

I don't move from my spot. My mind is telling me to pull myself away, to stand strong in my loyalty to Lee. But I swear I can see anguish swirling in Eli's eyes, and it calls to the part of me that aches for understanding. The part that wishes someone in that godforsaken town would open their eyes and just *see* me for me. Accept me the way I am.

"You're right," I whisper. "I don't know what I'm talkin' about."

His eyes lock on to mine and my stomach jumps so high I

swear it's trying to leave my body. It must know I'm a traitor for feeling about him the way I do.

I swallow, making the choice before my logical side can catch up to my mouth. "I don't wanna go."

His nostrils flare. "Pretty sure I didn't give you the option."

I blow out a breath, regret from my outburst inching through my body and squeezing my throat. Didn't I *just* tell him the other day I understood?

I'm no better than my folks.

Nodding, I set down my wine glass and stand up. I try to ignore the way his smell makes my heart ache as I brush by him.

"Wait." His hand grasps my wrist.

The word thickens the air, wrapping itself around my body and jerking me to a stop. I close my eyes, willing my heart to stop pounding so hard, afraid he'll be able to hear. I don't want him to know how much he affects me.

I wish he didn't affect me at all.

His hand leaves my wrist, sliding up my arm until he tangles his fingers in my hair, exposing the side of my neck. I feel his breath as he exhales, blowing lightly as his nose skims along my skin.

"Why do you drive me so goddamn crazy?" he rasps.

"I don't mean to," I whisper.

He hums. The sound, low and gravelly, is a match to the pit in my belly, sparking a blaze so deep I worry I'll burn alive.

"You make me want things I shouldn't. Things I can't have."

My heart races, my arms trembling against his fingers. "What do you want?"

The heat of his body flickers against my back, and his

hands grip my shoulders like he's afraid I'll run from his words.

I can't be sure I won't.

"I want *you*. Riding me against the backdrop of the sky until your body becomes my horizon. On my face, so I can revel in your taste. In my bed, so I can bury myself deep inside you instead of settling for my dreams."

His hips press into me.

"I want to say fuck the rules. Fuck my sister. Fuck anybody who says we shouldn't be together. How come they all get a say? They don't have to live with the torment of not being able to touch you."

My breath hitches.

"I want you to *admit* you feel this the same way I do."

My heart bangs against my ribs, and I bite my tongue to keep from spilling the truth.

"Say it."

I shake my head, my eyes squeezing tight. *I can't.*

His hand grasps my jaw, twisting my face toward him. His grip is strong, and my breathing grows heavy from the sting of his touch. His lips brush against mine.

"Say it." His voice is sharp, deep. *Authoritative.* It should piss me off, but all it does is turn me on. The hold on my restraint slackens, the need to please him rushing through my system and pouring out of my mouth.

"I feel it," I whisper.

His mouth crashes into mine. My body sings from his taste, and his words linger on my skin.

Why should they get a say?

I spin in his arms, allowing our kiss to deepen. He groans, his other hand moving to frame my face, cupping both sides of my jaw, and I'm lost. Totally and completely lost in him.

I can't fight it anymore. I don't want to.

So I won't.

I'll give in to whatever this is between us and pray to God it doesn't take us both down in its fury.

I'm addicted to the taste of Becca's mouth. Who knew it was possible to fall in love with something you hate?

She never knows when to shut the hell up, but every barb she throws is fuel on the fire, making my temper rage until I snap, wanting to fuck the attitude out of her.

She's judgmental. Crass. *Off-limits.* I want her in spite of all that. Hell, probably because of it. She calls to the deepest parts of me, pulling out the pieces that no one else can touch.

My hands reach down to grab her ass as my tongue tangles with hers. Her lithe body rubs against my dick in the most delicious way, and my hips involuntarily thrust, begging for more friction.

"We should stop," she mumbles against my lips.

My fingers grip tighter, anchoring her to me. "Probably."

One hand slides up her back, teasing the hem of her shirt. I'd like to take my time but the raw need I feel drives me into a frenzy. I break our kiss, tearing the fabric over her head, and tossing it to the side. She isn't wearing a bra.

Goddamn.

My eyes are greedy for her flesh, my mouth watering at

the sight of her exposed for me. Her stare reaches into my chest and squeezes, urging my blood to pump faster.

Her hands reach out and grasp the top of my pants, pulling me with her as she drops onto the lounge chair and leans back.

My body hovers, mind racing as fast as my heart, lost in the chaos of everything I want to do to her.

I lean down, my mouth molding to hers, tasting the berries of the wine and the headiness of her breath. I groan, breaking the kiss to trail my lips along her jaw, down her neck, until I make it to the pink of her nipples.

My fingers tease them into peaks. "Gorgeous."

"You gonna keep talkin', or are you gonna show your appreciation?" She arches, her breast grazing against my mouth.

I smirk against her skin. "Cute."

She pushes harder, her nipple breaking past the seam of my lips. I open wider and suck, reveling in her taste. She moans, the sound a straight shot to my dick, making it jerk and swell, straining for some relief.

With one last swipe of my tongue, I release her breast, working my way down further, my hands grabbing greedily at every inch of skin I can touch.

There's a chill in the air, but I've surrendered to our heat.

She bucks against me and mewls. My hand shoots up to her stomach, pinning her in place.

I tsk. "Patience, baby."

Her eyes blaze as she stares down at me, but she sucks in her lips and doesn't argue. *Good girl.*

My palm rises with her heavy breaths as I unbutton her pants. She lifts her hips, and my hands move to slide the jeans off her legs, exposing her perfect flesh to me one sinful inch at a time. Her panties follow shortly after until she's completely naked, laid out on my deck. The pounding of my heart drowns out the crash of waves against the shore, and I stare at her, transfixed by the vision.

Her thighs spread, her pussy glistening with arousal. I suck in a breath, ripping my shirt over my head and leaning back over her.

"Eli," she breathes.

The side of my mouth lifts. "Begging for me already, Rebecca?"

She huffs out a breath, her dainty fingers reaching between her legs, daring to touch what's mine.

I smack her hand out of the way. "Baby girl, you can touch me all you want, but *this*," I slide my fingers through her lips, her wetness coating my fingers. "This is all mine."

She scoffs. "You don't own my pussy."

I smile. "I look forward to proving you wrong."

My fingers slip inside her, my thumb pressing against her engorged clit. She gasps, her head slamming against the lounger.

I lean in, licking the shell of her ear. "Let me show you how good I treat my belongings."

I dip down, my mouth replacing my thumb on her clit, sucking to the rhythm of my fingers pumping inside her. A gush of liquid coats my hand, her walls clenching around me.

Fingers dive into my hair, twisting around my strands and sending a shiver down my spine. My cock throbs, and I pull back.

She grips my hair tighter. "Don't stop. Don't stop. Please."

"I want you to come on my dick, not my face." I sit back, the clang of my belt buckle ringing through the silence. The heaviness of her stare makes me dizzy, and my stomach clenches with want.

I push my pants and boxers down in one motion, my cock bobbing free, stiff as hell and leaking at the promise of sinking inside her.

Her legs wrap around my hips. I line myself up and slide into her pussy, my eyes rolling at the feeling.

She moans, lifting her pelvis to drag me in further. Heat rises in my chest and tightens my throat. *How the hell does she feel this good?*

My hips pull back. Her body follows mine like she can't bear the thought of us not touching. I thrust back in, working up a rhythm. Her fingernails dig into my skin and tingles prickle from the sting.

"Tell me how good it feels," I demand.

"So–so good. I need—"

"I know what you need, baby girl."

My hand slides along her torso, between her breasts, past her collarbone and around the back of her head, gripping her curls in my hand and pulling, *hard.*

She moans, her back arching and pussy quivering around me. My chest rubs against hers as I move, frissons of electricity lancing through my veins.

"Whose pussy is this?" I growl.

Her eyes snap to mine, a glint passing through them. My fingers tighten in her hair, my other hand angling her hips so I can drive in deeper.

She shakes her head and my hand moves to grip her jaw tight. "Say it."

"Yours," she gasps.

My balls tighten, lightning scorching through me, but I hold off, wanting to feel her come undone around me before I let go. I plunge back inside, seating my cock as deep as it will go, our hips flush. I grind against her, giving her clit the friction I know she craves. I pull back and glance down at my cock, soaked from her pussy and pulsing with the need to come.

"Oh, fuck, Eli, do that again." Her hands reach down and

grasp my ass, urging me into her and rubbing against my groin, getting herself off on my dick.

Fuck, it's the hottest thing I've ever seen.

Her body tenses, legs tightening and breaths wavering. I tug on her hair again, baring her neck as her body conforms to my pull.

I lean down, whispering in her ear. "Give it to me, Rebecca."

She does.

She screams, the sound harsh against the calm of the sea. Her pussy tightens around me, and the intensity of her orgasm makes me lose the hold on my control. My balls draw up and my cock lengthens. I speed up my thrusts, drawing out her orgasm and chasing my own.

Heat coils low in my gut, spiraling up and bursting through me. I pull out and stroke myself, groaning deep as I paint her body with my pleasure.

She takes a finger and drags it through the mess, sucking my cum into her mouth. I'm panting above her, my dick still in my hand, stars dotting my vision as I stare.

Christ.

She's perfect.

I pick up my shirt, running it over her skin and cleaning her up. She doesn't say a word, and neither do I, afraid to ruin the moment.

Scooping her in my arms, I walk us inside, taking her straight to my room, and plopping her in my bed. She giggles, and I lay down next to her, smiling.

The beat of my lonely heart strengthens, battering against my chest, urging me to lay it at her feet, hoping she picks it up and keeps it forever.

20

BECCA

I t's been a month since Eli and I started whatever this *thing* is that we're doing. A month of rendezvous at his house, longing looks on the court, and secret touches in the halls.

We're not together. We couldn't be even if I wanted—which I don't. The guilt threatens to swallow me whole as it is. I'm fucking him, then calling his sister and acting like I don't know his face from Adam.

I'm a terrible friend.

But I sure as hell can't tell Lee. She's pissed off at him enough, no need for me to widen their divide. Not when I can tell they both wish it would disappear.

Tonight is the first official game of the basketball season, and the arena is packed. Eli's been working around the clock, so I haven't seen him outside of practice all week, and even now as I stand in the back of the locker room, I'm relegated to watching him from a distance. He's calm, cool and collected, like usual, but I see the tension in his posture. After so many nights of feeling every dip and ridge of his body, I can tell when it's not his normal gait. I'd bet my bottom dollar he's nervous.

He's leaning against the far wall with his feet crossed, staring at whatever is written on his clipboard. His dark-blond hair is messier than usual, a sure sign he's been tugging on it. A thought of how much *I'd* like to tug on it flashes through my mind.

His face snaps up, roaming the room until he finds me, and I'm sucked into his gaze. My stomach lights up like pop rocks, heart swelling in my chest. I break our stare, uncomfortable with whatever this feeling is.

We smoke the team we're playing. One-hundred-forty to eighty-nine. Jeremy is a fantastic ballplayer, and the way Eli puts aside his animosity, embracing him after they win has my chest bubbling with warmth. A pang of guilt hits my gut knowing it's Jeremy's fourth year playing, and this is the first time I've actually seen him in action.

Tack another one on the shit friend tally.

I haven't told him about Eli, and even if I wanted to, he's been missing from my life a lot this semester. If I wasn't so busy hiding secrets of my own, I'd probably be badgering him about where he's been. As it is, it's probably for the best he hasn't been around, I already feel shitty enough not telling Lee, I'd rather not add my other best friend to that list. Plus, I'm worried Eli will lose his job if word gets out. It's a dangerous game we're playing, and if either of us had a lick of sense, we'd put a stop to it. Cut our losses and call it a day.

But no matter how many times I think it, I know I won't.

I'm in the locker room after everyone has left, picking up the discarded towels, and throwing them in the laundry bin to be washed. I hear the door open, straightening from where I'm bent, looking to see who it is.

Eli walks toward me.

"Hi, big head." I smile, my stomach flipping at the sight of him.

He smirks, stepping into me, pushing until my back hits the lockers, my hair catching on the metal. His chest presses against mine, and his hands cup my face, thumbs brushing against my cheeks.

"I've come to claim my victory kiss."

I quirk a brow. "Mighty presumptuous of you."

"I don't presume anything when it comes to you."

I huff out a laugh. "Oh, I beg to differ, you—"

He steals the rest of the words from my mouth. My eyes flutter closed, losing myself to the bliss that is Eli's lips. A deep-seated joy settles in my chest until every part of me is encased in the feeling.

What is he doin' to me?

He breaks the kiss, leaning his forehead against mine. "Will you stay with me tonight?"

I nod, breathless from the emotion coursing through my body. It's been happening more often lately—this *feeling*. Thinking about what it means makes nausea churn in my stomach, so I ignore it, content to be in the moment.

A door slams and Eli jumps back, leaning against the opposite lockers, his hands in his pockets. I hurry to pick up a towel from the floor.

"Anyone seen a sweet ass attached to a fiery redhead around here?" Jeremy's voice rings across the room.

Eli's eyes turn glacial and I cringe, a guilty rock sinking in my gut. I want to tell him about Jeremy. Let him know there's *nothing* to be jealous of. But I can't betray Jeremy's trust. So, I'm stuck on this teeter-totter with no way off—one where Jeremy doesn't know not to flirt, and the man I'm with has to stand back and think the worst.

"Hey, Jer." I sigh.

"Hey, girl." He picks me up off the floor in a bear hug. I

look past his shoulder to see Eli's fists clenching tight. My chest constricts around my lungs, a knot forming in my throat. I try to convey my apology through my eyes, but he breaks our stare, his face turning to the side.

Jeremy sets me down, and I back up immediately, throwing the dirty towel in the laundry bin.

"You coming out with me tonight to celebrate?" Jeremy wags his brows. I swallow, not sure what to say. I hadn't thought of a reason why I *couldn't,* and now that I'm standing in front of him, I'm worried it will look suspect if I think of something on the spot. Eli's eyes laser into me, and I know he's waiting to hear my answer.

Jeremy hasn't even noticed him yet.

"I don't know, Jer. I'm tired. I might just go home and sleep."

"That's cool. I'll come crash at yours then." He smiles and when I don't immediately smile back, his grin lessens. A creak sounds from Eli straightening off the lockers, and Jeremy turns, noticing him for the first time.

"Coach! You're like a ninja. I didn't even know you were here." He looks at Eli then back at me, his eyes narrowing the longer they bounce between us. "What *are* you doing in here?"

Eli's jaw clenches and I see the coldness trickle through his irises. "Thought I'd check and make sure the locker room was cleared out before heading home."

Jeremy's chin lifts as he looks at me. I fidget under his stare, trying to blanket all my secrets and hide them from his view. But I've always been a shit liar, and Jeremy reads me better than almost anyone, so I'm not sure it works.

I glance at Eli one more time before focusing my gaze on Jeremy. "Yeah, Jer. That's fine. Just let me finish up here, and I'll meet you at my place."

"Sweet." Jeremy grins, leaning in and smacking my ass.

Eli's nostrils flare. Jeremy nods to him, waltzing out the door.

The door clicks shut, echoing off the concrete walls. The silence that follows slices through my skin like a thousand knives, gripping my heart and holding it hostage. I'm afraid for it to beat.

My hand shoots up, twisting the ends of my hair.

"So that's it then, huh?" Eli asks.

My chest squeezes, but the intensity of my emotions throws me off-kilter. Why do I feel like I have something to apologize for? *We're not even in a relationship. This is ridiculous.*

"What's *it*? What did you expect me to do, Eli?"

"I don't know, Becca. Maybe *not* bail on me to sleep with the guy who claims you're his 'other half,'" he snaps.

"What was I supposed to say?" My hands hit my thighs. "Sorry, Jer, can't hang out with you. I have plans with my best friend's estranged older brother. Oh, he also happens to be your coach and my damn boss. You know, faculty at the school where I attend as a student!" My voice rises with each word.

Eli's eyes narrow and he stalks toward me, clamping a palm over my mouth, stifling my voice and stuttering my breath. "Shut the hell up. You want the whole buildin' to hear?"

I shake my head, heat flooding my core at his aggressive stance and tone.

What is wrong with me?

His eyes bore into mine, his hand pressing harder against my mouth. We're frozen for long moments, until he finally sighs, drops his hand and backs up.

I dart forward, gripping his jaw in my hands. "Eli, listen to me. Jeremy is *just* a friend."

He scoffs, but he grips my wrists, leaning into my touch.

"I hate this," he whispers. "I want him to know you're mine. I want *everyone* to know you're mine."

My heart slams against my ribs with fervor, but my stomach flips and twists, dropping to the floor. I lean my forehead against his chest. He blows out a breath and kisses the top of my head, wrapping his arms around me.

My body buzzes from his touch, but it doesn't bring me comfort. The echo of his words wrap themselves around my neck and tighten like a noose.

I clear my throat and push the feeling down.

21

BECCA

"**W**hat are you doing for Christmas break?"

I grimace in Sabrina's direction, taking a bite of sushi instead of answering her.

She sighs, dropping her chopsticks, leaning forward on our couch. "Are you planning to ignore me all night?"

"I'm not ignorin' you, I just don't have anything to say about it, is all."

Sabrina stares, her gaze searing into the side of my face. I avoid eye contact—something I've found myself doing more of lately, ever since I've been with Eli.

It's exhausting, keeping this secret, and I'm sick of hiding it. Over the past month, I've slowly come to terms with the fact that I want to be with him. I like him, no matter how many times I try to convince myself I don't.

Still, that noose around my neck dangles, threatening to pull tight with every twitch of my heart.

"Are you going home?" Sabrina prods.

I shrug. "Momma keeps callin' every other day, tryin' to strong-arm me. It's not gonna happen, though. Once I go back, I reckon they'll never let me leave again. Diploma be damned."

Sabrina scoffs. "They can't hold you hostage."

My lips turn down. "You'd be surprised at what my old man can do."

She looks down, fiddling with the wooden chopsticks on her sushi tray. "Well, I think it's ridiculous. You're a grown woman. You have rights." She crosses her arms.

I smile at her. "Oh, girl. It's adorable you think Sugarlake, Tennessee gives a damn about my 'rights.'"

Her forehead scrunches. "Your dad's one of the biggest assholes I've ever met."

Confusion tilts my head. "Technically, you never *have* met him. But… can't really argue your point."

"Yeah…" She takes another bite of sushi. "I guess you'll have the place to yourself if you decide to stay. I'll be in Colorado with the fam. They rented a cabin so we could ski."

My stomach clenches at her words. My mind wanders, thinking of what it would be like to spend it with Eli. No interruptions. No friends to steal me away. In a spur of the moment decision, I grab my phone and send a text.

Me: Whatcha doing for Xmas, big head?

Eli: You, hopefully.

I bite my lip, a tingle pricking between my legs.

He texts again.

Eli: You're not going home?

Me: That depends. If I stay with you, can we get a tree?

Why the hell did I say that? It's dumb, and I feel stupid for asking.

Last week, he told me Christmas was his favorite holiday even though he usually spends it alone. We got into a debate because I strongly disagree with that statement.

The truth is, I don't think there's a holiday I hate more. Growing up, all my friends spent the time loving on their families and spreading Christmas cheer. Mine was spent listening about our savior, Jesus Christ, and reading scripture. Our tree was set up before I even had a chance to know it was in the house—tucked in the corner, and pristine in its glory.

Sometimes, I'd try to touch it, marveling in the twinkly white lights and crystal ornaments. That was always a quick way to get a wooden spoon on the butt. After all, Christmas isn't for the children. It's for celebrating Jesus. No reason to indulge in silly traditions like Santa, or throwing on cheesy Christmas songs while we decorate the tree. No hot chocolate by the fire while we read a story, or cozy cuddles in front of the TV. I had presents, of course. Usually a new Bible or a nice Sunday outfit. Something to honor God, and the fact he sent us his most precious gift—his only son.

My phone vibrates, bringing me out of my thoughts.

Eli: Baby girl, if you stay with me for the holidays, I'll get you the world.

My stomach flutters, and I bite my cheek to stifle the grin. I know he doesn't mean it. We can't even be seen together. But the thought of spending Christmas with him already feels like the best part of any world I've ever had.

To say my folks were unhappy with my decision would be an understatement. Not that Papa told me himself, I still haven't heard from him since my first day in Florida.

Momma, on the other hand, has been screeching in my ear ever since I told her, talking about how bad it will look for me to not come home for the holidays. I let her words roll off my shoulders. I've gotten used to the disappointment that comes along with making my own decisions.

Just as I pull into Eli's driveway, my phone rings. I look

down, aching to see my folks' name flashing across the screen, calling to wish me a Merry Christmas.

I should know better than to hope.

Lee.

I swear that girl has a sixth sense, calling and texting every time I'm sneaking around with her brother.

"Hey, girl!" I cringe at how high-pitched my voice comes across. I pray she doesn't notice.

"Becca! Merry Christmas! We miss you around here."

"I miss you too, sister. What ya got planned for tonight?"

"Not much. Just wranglin' together a Christmas dinner for Daddy and me."

My brows furrow. "Y'all aren't gonna go to the service?"

"No, Daddy's not feelin' too well, so we're stayin' in tonight."

"That sucks. Just you and your old man then?"

"Yeah," she sighs. "Just got off the phone with Eli, but it was quick. He's not here, so I don't really care to talk."

The blood ices over in my veins, freezing me in place. I glance at Eli's house. Guilt slams into my chest, cracking it open and pouring over my insides.

"Anyway, I gotta go check on the ham, just wanted to wish you a Merry Christmas and say how much I love you. I wish you were home."

I blow out a breath, bile climbing my throat because while she's busy mourning the absence of her brother, I'm about to walk in and revel in his time. "I love you, too. Give your daddy and Jax a kiss from me, alright?"

The line goes silent, and I toss my phone in my bag, banging my head against the steering wheel. I hate myself for the secrets. I look up, staring at Eli's garage door. I should just start my car, and reverse the hell out of his neighborhood. Go home while I still can.

When I raise my head, the front door is open—Eli resting

against the frame, watching me. I take in his dark jeans, black polo, and messy blond hair, a fire striking low in my abdomen. The guilt withers away, perishing in the flames.

I jump out of my car, making my way to him.

"Hi, big head." I smile.

He grins, gesturing me inside. I walk by him, but before I get far, I'm hauled back against his broad chest. His arms wrap around my waist, every hard inch of his body plastered to mine. I close my eyes, melting into him.

"Merry Christmas, baby girl." His breath whispers along the wisps of my hair, goose bumps running down my arms.

I look over my shoulder and grin, pushing off him, and walking into his living room. I only make it a few feet before stopping in my tracks. There's a gigantic tree standing tall, perfectly showcased in front of his floor-to-ceiling windows that overlook the ocean. Christmas music floats softly through the air.

My hands brace against my chest.

Eli comes next to me, hands in his pockets, rocking back on his heels while he gazes at the tree. "Do you like it?"

My lips twitch. "Little plain."

He smirks, lacing our fingers and pulling me behind him until I can smell the pine. I scan the area, surveying the boxes and bags stacked neatly in the corner of the room, right in front of the fireplace. Stepping closer, I peer into them. Lights, ornaments, candy canes, stockings. It's all here. Everything to make a perfect Christmas. I spin around, my gaze searching for Eli's. *He did all this for me?*

"I thought we could decorate it together."

I blink back the sting in my eyes. Walking over, I grasp his neck, pulling his lips down to meet mine.

One of the chains around my heart snaps and breaks.

I don't bother trying to catch it as it falls.

22

ELI

I t's conference tournament time. Which means March Madness is right around the corner and the regular season is almost over. I had forgotten how quickly time goes when you're submerged in everything basketball. I'm finally starting to feel like I'm slotting a place in the hearts and the minds of these players. These halls. This court.

Rebecca.

She hates it when I call her that, so I do it as often as I can. I love drawing that little bit of extra attitude, so I can fuck it out of her when she sneaks to my house at night. It's been five months since we gave in to the energy pulling us together, and even though we're "keeping things casual" it feels anything but.

In two months, everything changes. She graduates. There won't be a need for us to lurk in darkened locker rooms and hide behind closed doors. No reason for more pieces of my heart to chip every time she ditches our plans to hang with her friends. No more feeling like an absolute piece of shit when my baby sister calls and Becca answers, her eyes dimming while she avoids mentioning my name.

I want everything with her. The laughter and tears, the yelling and the make-up sex. I want to go to bed with her every night, and wake up tangled in fiery curls each morning. I want her cheering at my games, and telling me how proud she is with each win. I just have to make sure that's something *she* wants too.

I think she does.

She stirs in bed next to me, throwing an arm and a leg over my body. I've never been a "girlfriend" kind of guy before. No need when basketball was my job, my wife, and my mistress all wrapped up in one. But lying here with Becca wrapped in my arms, I can't help thinking I would have picked her over everything, even back then.

I grasp her hand, lightly tracing her fingers with mine, wondering what Ma would think of us being together if she were still around. The last conversation we had was her wishing for me to find a nice girl and settle down. *Come home.* My stomach churns as the phone call plays in my head, and my arms squeeze Becca on reflex.

She wakes, blinking at me. I brush the hair out of her face, letting my fingers trail down her cheek. The softness in her eyes dulls the ache of Ma's memory.

"Hi." She smiles.

"Morning, baby girl." I peck her lips. She kisses me back but breaks it off quick, grabbing the sheet and bringing it to cover the lower half of her face.

"Eli, you know mornin' breath is a hard limit for me. Why do you insist on startin' the day off this way?"

I grin. "Are you insinuating that I *smell*?"

"You stink and you know it." Her eyes crinkle.

"Take it back."

"I can't. That would make me a liar."

She tries to scoot back, but my arm shoots out, wrapping around her waist and anchoring her to me.

"Take. It. Back."

She stares into my eyes and slowly lowers the sheet. "No," she whispers.

I sigh. "Then you leave me no choice."

My arm tightens on her waist, my other hand rising to her side, fingers digging in deep as I attack. One of the things I've learned while discovering every inch of Becca's body is she's *extremely* ticklish.

She screams, throwing her head back and laughing, her body wiggling against mine, trying to break free.

"Eli! Sto–stop it… ple–please!" she chokes out between giggles.

The smile threatens to crack my face as I slow down my torture. She collapses against the mattress, her body worn out from fighting my fingers. She's panting, her chest heaving as she tries to catch her breath.

I'm hovering, my eyes perusing every inch of her. She's so damn beautiful. So perfect here in my bed, wearing nothing but my shirt.

Her laughter dies down. She cups my jaw, her fingers scratching against my stubble. "What ya thinkin' about so hard up there, handsome?"

"You."

"What about me?"

How much I love you. "How much I wish I could take you out. Show you off."

Her smile dims. "Once I graduate, that won't be an issue. We can go wherever we please."

"Yeah, I know." I steal another kiss before she can turn, and she shrieks, pushing me away and hopping out of bed. I chuckle, leaning against my headboard, watching as she walks to the bathroom.

Her phone rings on the nightstand.

"Who is it?" she hollers.

I pick it up and look at the screen.

"It's your mom." I grimace, setting her phone back on the table. I already know she's not going to answer it.

Becca stomps back in the room, grabbing her phone and silencing the ringer before plopping in bed, staring at me.

I raise a brow. "What?"

She crosses her arms. "Are you just gonna sit there or will you go brush your teeth so I can kiss you the way I want?"

I lean forward, gripping the nape of her neck and drawing her to me, fusing our mouths together. She gives in, her body relaxing as she kisses me back. My hands frame her face and I pull away to look at her. Happiness climbs through my chest, expanding until I feel like I might burst. I trail my lips down to her collarbone and kiss along the necklace I bought her for Christmas. It's simple. A platinum basketball charm with 'My #1 Player' engraved on the back. I bought it on a whim, and almost didn't go through with it, afraid she would laugh in my face. But she hasn't taken it off a single time since I put it on her.

My mind wanders back to Ma. For some reason, she's on my mind a lot lately, not that she ever really leaves. Her memory is a constant twinge—a broken bone that never reset. But I don't like to dwell on the pain.

I don't realize I've paused in my ministrations until Becca pushes me back into a lying position and cuddles into my side. "What's wrong, big head?"

I blow out a breath. "Just thinking about Ma."

Her body tenses against mine. As much as I feel for Becca, I'm surprised I said that without a second thought. I've never talked to *anyone* about Ma. But Becca was there. She grew up with her. She lost her too.

Her fingers trace random shapes on my chest, the touch making the hair on my arms stand on end.

"I miss her," she sighs.

My stomach clenches. "Me too."

"She always had the best advice. When my momma was too busy makin' sure our family looked picture-perfect, yours was there to wipe my tears and teach me all about becomin' a woman. She always made me feel like I was somethin' special."

I swallow around the sudden lump in my throat. "I talked to her that day, did you know that?"

Becca's head tilts, her glassy eyes searing into mine.

"Her and Pops were driving back from Chattanooga, trying to make it home to some show of Lee's. Pops called to talk about my game, but Ma took over, like she was prone to do. Started preaching about finding a nice girl, settling down. One who would look past the basketball star and see the real me." I chuckle, shaking my head. "She was always so worried about 'my lonely heart.' Was dead set on me finding a girl who'd convince me to come back home... pop out a couple of kids."

Becca doesn't speak, just continues to run her fingers against my skin.

"'Find yourself a true beauty,' she told me. 'One whose soul shines so bright even the sun can't compare.'" I close my eyes, the regret sluicing through my veins. "I rushed her off the phone. I was sick of hearin' her talk about it. I don't—" My voice breaks, and I clear my throat, inhaling deep before trying again. "I don't even think I told her I loved her."

"Eli..." Becca whispers.

"If I would have known it was the last time I'd ever hear her voice..." I shake my head.

Reaching my hand down, I grip Becca's fingers tight against my chest, the stitching of my tattered soul pulling at the seams.

Becca doesn't say anything, but she doesn't have to. Just

her presence is a comfort I never knew I was missing. After a few minutes, she reaches up, pecking my lips and grinning.

I bask in her glow.

She blinds me to the sun.

Two more months, and everything will change.

23

BECCA

My phone is taunting me. It's vibrating across my desk, daring me to pick it up. *Papa* flashes across the screen on repeat, and I swear I can feel his glare from here.

What on Earth is he callin' for?

I haven't talked to him in months, and I'm not sure I want to break that streak now. Regardless, I swipe my screen and answer.

"Hi, Papa."

"Rebecca." Nails on a chalkboard rake down my insides. Just like that, he's tainted the name again.

"Long time no talk," I can't help but quip.

"And whose fault is that? I'm callin' to make sure you know we're comin' into town for your graduation. Your momma thought it would be good for you to hear it from me."

My stomach jolts at his words. I assumed they'd still show up. "Okay." I nod, even though he can't see me. "I figured y'all would be headin' down."

"Have you given up this foolish talk about not comin' back home?"

I sigh, my fingers tangling in my curls. "Papa, I wish you would understand. I need to be free of that place. Need to spread my wings and learn to fly on my own."

He huffs. "Here's your momma."

There's a quick moment where I ruminate on the fact he didn't even say goodbye, just dropped his words down the line and disappeared. Momma's voice rings in my ear, breaking the silence.

"Rebecca Jean, I wish you'd stop upsettin' your father the way you do. Liable to give him an ulcer, and Lord knows you don't need any more sins taintin' that soul."

"Momma, drop it will you? I don't even know why y'all want me home so bad. What difference does it make? All I do is embarrass you."

"You belong at home, helpin' us run the church, bein' a part of this family."

My face scrunches, dread filling up my bones at the thought of being chained to the church for the rest of my life. At being chained to my folks who wouldn't know what a family is supposed to be if it hit them upside the head. "Agree to disagree."

Momma tsks. "You prayin' every night?"

The tension in my chest draws tight. "Yes, Momma. I'm still prayin'."

It's not technically a lie. Eli makes me praise God almost every night. I smirk at the thought.

"Good. That's good. You talked to Alina May lately?"

My forehead wrinkles. "All the time, why?"

"Haven't seen her at Sunday service in a while. It's not a good look, you know. That whole family already has so much gossip goin' around the town, they need all the Jesus they can get."

A knock on my bedroom door steals my attention and Sabrina pokes her head in, tapping her finger to her wrist, reminding me it's almost time for the game.

"Momma, I gotta go. I'll see y'all when you get here."

I hang up the phone, nerves jumbling up my belly as I hop off my desk chair and follow Sabrina into our living room. It's the SEC Conference tournament this weekend in Nashville, and tonight is the final game. I'm supposed to be there, but I had a bit of a cold earlier this week so Coach made me stay home, afraid I'd get the players sick. But I've been glued to my TV every day. We're the number one seed, and we won our game on Thursday. Won again on Friday. Now it's Saturday, and this is the big one. *The title.*

I'm invested. Not only because I feel like part of the team, but because this is important to Eli. He deserves this. They all do.

I told him not to worry about us talking after the games, but it doesn't stop me from waiting by my phone like a lovesick girl. And every night, like clockwork, he calls. I almost wish he wouldn't. It's a dangerous thing, having faith in someone.

Sabrina plops on the couch, passing me a Coke, and putting a bowl of popcorn between us.

"I can't believe you talked me into watching this," she says.

"Well, we've gotta support Jeremy. Plus, I'm kinda into it after so many months of bein' with the team."

The camera pans across the arena and lands on Eli. My fingers dig into my knees, wishing I could reach through the screen and touch him. I grab the remote, turning up the volume when the announcers say his name.

"You know, Jeff, I never thought I'd be the one to say it, but I'm impressed with Elliot Carson. I'll be the first to admit I was firmly in the 'he's too young' camp. But the FCU Stingrays record speaks

for itself. It's like a different team out there, and between Coach Andrews and Carson, they've really done something special with these players."

"Talent, Carl. That's what it is. Some people are just born for the game and Carson is one of them."

My heart swells as they heap on the praise.

"Weren't you calling the game that ended his career?"

"I couldn't forget it if I tried. I've never seen an arena go so quiet. The nation heard twenty-thousand hearts break that night when he didn't get back up. New York's hopes and dreams were centered around that young man, and to see it all ripped away so fast... Devastating."

Their words travel across the room and slam against my lungs, making me lose my breath. I knew he was hurt—knew it ended his career, but I didn't know it was like *that*. I think back, trying to remember Lee or her old man leaving town, but I come up empty. In fact, other than Lee mentioning what happened in passing, it wasn't ever talked about again. Anytime folks in town brought it up, she'd shut it down, annoyed. My heart quickens, sickness climbing up my throat when I think of what it must have been like for him. I wonder if anyone was by his side, or if it's yet another thing he's had to go through all alone.

My head throbs, the sudden change of perspective making me dizzy.

FCU Stingrays win the game, and I should be thrilled, but I'm distracted. Instead of staying in the living room and celebrating with Sabrina—not that she gives a damn—I rush to my room and pull up Google.

Elliot Carson career-ending injury

My eyes widen as I scroll through hundreds of articles and images. I click on videos and watch it replay a thousand different ways. *How have I never seen this?* Seems like the entire college and NBA fandom mourned the loss, but I can't remember a single tear shed from his family.

For the first time, some of my anger shifts onto Lee. *Didn't she give a damn?*

Eli calls a few hours later while I'm lying in bed, pretending like I wasn't waiting to hear his voice. To him, the injury happened years ago, but for me, it's fresh. And so is this feeling of unease whenever I think about all the ways Lee *didn't* bring him up over the years. I bite back the tears, inhaling deep before I pick up.

"Hiya."

"Baby girl. Did you watch the game?"

I smile. "Why, did y'all win?"

"Like there was any doubt," he scoffs.

I laugh. "You sure do live up to your nickname, big head. Not surprisin' I suppose, with the way those announcers wouldn't shut up about you."

He sighs. "I wish they'd focus on the team, not me."

"Well, like it or not, you're part of the team too. They're impressed. Be proud of yourself, Eli."

"Yeah, I guess..."

The silence stretches, and even through the phone, thousands of miles away, it wraps itself around me and reaches inside my chest, drawing the words out. "I looked up the videos of your injury."

He sucks in a breath. "Why?"

I shrug even though he can't see, my heart battering against the wall of sadness that's infused itself around my edges. "The announcers talked about it and I..." I tug on the ends of a curl. "I got curious. Lee never talked about it much, and I realized I never even thought about what it must have been like for you."

He clears his throat. "It sucked."

"Yeah." I chew on my lip. "I'm sorry no one was with you. If I... I wish I coulda been there," I whisper. "I wish I woulda known to make sure Lee was, too."

"Me too, baby girl." His voice is pinched and low. "But that was a long time ago, and you're here now."

I wait for him to elaborate, but he never does. Instead, he sighs. "I miss you."

My stomach clenches at how his words strain against the things he obviously isn't saying. But I won't push him to talk about something if he doesn't want to. I just needed him to know that I *see* him, and that I'm sorry I didn't for so long.

"I miss you, too." I twirl the ends of my hair. "When do you get back?"

"If I tell you, will you be waiting in my bed?"

"I think I'd need a key for that." I choke on the words as they come out. *What the hell?* I don't want a key to his place. I have no idea why I just said that.

He chuckles. "I'll give you the code, and get you one made when I get back in town."

I cringe. "Alright then. Great."

It isn't great. In fact, it makes my stomach squeeze so tight I think I may pass out. Things are perfect the way they are, there's zero reason to change it.

Anxiety bangs against the walls of my heart, trying to break free.

As usual, I ignore it.

24

ELI

We're headed to Atlanta for the final four games in the championship. March Madness definitely lives up to its name, and after being on the road for the past few weeks, I can't wait to get home and relax. To be with Becca again. She traveled with us for some of the games, but one of her professors threatened to fail her if she didn't give a presentation on Monday. Since we aren't getting back until Tuesday, she ended up having to stay behind.

I'm sending her a text and getting comfortable in the back of the plane when a body plops in the seat next to me.

"Hi, friend."

I glance up, pocketing my phone. My brows shoot to my hairline when I see who it is. "Sarah. What are you doing here?"

She smiles, tucking a strand of her strawberry-blonde hair behind her ears. "I was planning to give you some warning, but Connor thought I should surprise you. I was just hired on as a physical therapist for FCU, and as luck would have it, assigned to the basketball team for the last of the games."

"Wow, what are the odds? Congratulations." I mean what

I say. From what she told me when we met, she's been trying to get her foot in the door for a while.

A light dusting of pink coats her cheekbones. "You aren't mad I didn't tell you?"

"Why would I be mad? It's not like we talk."

Her grin drops. "Yeah, I guess you're right."

I lean my head back, closing my eyes, trying to force away the nagging feeling that's prodding my gut. I'm a little uncomfortable with her here, sitting in the spot where I want Becca to be.

"Why is that again?" Sarah asks.

I swivel my head toward her and crack open an eye. "Why is what?"

"Why don't we talk? I thought..." She bites her lip, glancing at her hands resting in her lap. "I thought we hit it off. You took my number, and I really liked you, then out of nowhere you just disappeared."

I grit my teeth, suddenly feeling like an asshole. It's not her fault Becca shaded everyone else from my view. But I don't know what to say. I want to tell her the truth—that I'm taken. *In love with the craziest, most amazing woman in the world.* But I can't. Not yet.

I rub my jaw and blow out a breath. "We did hit it off. I'm just... not in that place right now. I don't want to lead you on, and have you expect something I'm not capable of giving."

She nods, biting on her lower lip. "I get it. But you don't have to ghost me. We can be friends, at least, right?"

I grin. "Sure, friends sounds good."

We make small talk for the rest of the flight, but I don't see her often after that. As the team's physical therapist, she doesn't really have direct contact with the coaching staff. She's on the outskirts, dealing with the players as needed.

The days go quick, and we make it through semi-finals without too much fanfare. But every spare second is tinged with the ache to have Becca here celebrating the wins. Talking to her on the phone is better than nothing, but it doesn't satisfy the need.

We won.

I'm standing in the middle of the arena, screaming fans drowning out the pounding of my heart. Players crowd around us, the Gatorade spilling down Coach Andrews's back. *This feels so damn good.* Almost like there's nothing in the world that can beat it. Except my joy is muted because the one person I really want to celebrate with isn't here.

I look at the reporters surrounding us and the cameramen holding equipment above our heads. I tap my heart, then kiss my fingers, pointing toward one of the cameras. I'm not sure if Becca will see, but if she does, I'm hopeful she'll know it's for her.

I'm still staring into the lens when someone tugs on my arm. I pivot, expecting a player to bring me in for a hug, but before I can stop her, Sarah jumps into my arms, wrapping herself around me. I hug her back, laughing at her excitement.

"We did it! Can I say 'we' when I'm new to the team?" She beams.

Her happiness is contagious and I feel the smile spreading on my face.

We did it.

I make it back to my room and shower, changing into something more comfortable before finally pulling out my phone. I haven't looked at it since before the game, and I'm antsy to talk to my girl. There's four unread messages, all from Becca.

#1 Player: Damn, big head. You're looking mighty fly out there on that court. Good luck, not that y'all will need it.

#1 Player: What is that ref THINKING?! That was clearly a foul.

My lips quirk up.

#1 Player: Just so you know, I only fuck winners. Here's hoping you make the cut.

#1 Player: CHAMPIONS BABY! I'm so proud of y'all. I wish I was there.

My heart swells with her last words because having her proud of me feels damn good. I bring up her name and press call.

"Hiya, Champ." Her voice is more subdued than I expect.

"Hey, baby girl. Did you watch the game?"

"Why, did y'all win?"

I smirk. "You gonna play that with me every time you're not here?"

"Maybe." There's a pause. "Doesn't seem like you need me at your games anyway."

My brow furrows. "You can't feel me pining all the way from here? I'm practically broken on the floor without you. Winning doesn't mean half as much without you here to stroke my ego."

She snorts. "The day you're broken on the floor is the day pigs fly. Ain't nothin' that can bring the great Elliot Carson down."

"I'll gladly go down on you… I mean for you."

She giggles and something loosens in my chest, my smile growing.

"At least you had that sweet little strawberry-blondie to help you celebrate."

My forehead scrunches. "Who, Sarah?"

She scoffs. "Like I'm supposed to know her name?"

I chuckle. "She was just hired on as a physical therapist

for the school, and we're friends. That's all. She was excited we won."

I hear Becca's heavy exhale. "It's fine, big head. I don't care who you spend your time with."

My stomach churns, something in her voice making my gut twist. I *want* her to care. "You should."

"You're a big boy. Not my problem. When do you get back in town?"

A tingle of warning pricks at my thoughts with the way she changes the topic. "Becca, it *is* your problem."

"Oh? So you're sayin' there's a problem for me to worry about?"

My head rolls back with my eyes. *This woman.* "What? No. I'm saying it's okay for you to give a fuck. I sure as hell care when it's you and Jeremy."

"I'm not the jealous type, Eli."

I tug on the ends of my hair, frustration boiling through my veins with the way she won't admit she cares. That she *is* jealous. "Yeah. Okay."

"You gonna tell me when you're comin' home?"

"That depends. You gonna admit you're jealous?"

"Nothin' to admit."

"No witty comeback, Rebecca?" My voice lowers. "Is it because you're imagining what it's gonna feel like when I force the truth out of those pretty, lying lips?"

She huffs. "Easy to act high and mighty when you're not here. And to think I was gonna offer you phone sex."

I sit up straighter against my headboard, my cock thickening. "Well, don't let me stop you."

"Where are you right now? On your bed?"

"Yes."

"What are you wearin'?" she purrs.

I look down at my clothes. "Basketball shorts and a tee."

"Hmm... Do you want me to make you come, Eli? Do you *deserve* it?"

Christ, I wish she was here. My palm tingles with the need to put my hands on her and remind her who *deserves* what, but I'll give her this little bit of control. I'll enjoy taking it back once I get home.

"I deserve anything you wanna do to me, baby girl."

"Good. Take your right hand and touch yourself, over your shorts." Her voice is sultry. Blood rushes to my groin, arousal spiraling through me.

My hand reaches down, palm gliding over my growing erection.

"I want you to imagine it's me workin' you through the fabric... teasin' you until you beg me to give you what you need."

I picture her next to me, her fingers rubbing against me as she tortures me with her words. My abs tighten.

"Are you stiff for me, baby?"

"Always," I growl.

"Good. That's how I like you. Take it out for me and work that thick cock... slowly."

I do what she says, my hips lifting as I rip off my clothes and toss them to the side. My dick springs into the air, precum bubbling at the tip. I use it to lubricate my hand, sliding it down until I'm gripping the base of my shaft.

"Are you touching my pussy, baby girl?" I rasp, stroking myself.

"What are you gonna do about it if I am? You aren't here to stop me. I'll use *my* pussy any way I want."

"*Fuck.*"

"Does that turn you on? Thinkin' about me rubbin' my clit to the sound of your pleasure?"

My muscles tense, my cock leaking steadily, making my hand skim easily along the length.

"Close your eyes," she whispers. "Imagine it's my mouth slidin' up and down, beggin' you to come down my throat."

I groan, throwing my head back as I follow her instruction. *Damn, this is hot.*

"I need you to tell me when you get close."

"I'm there, baby girl." My cock pulses as I say the words, a shot of desire spreading through my body.

"Where do you wanna give it to me, Eli? What was it you once said? 'On my knees so you can paint my porcelain skin?'"

My hips jerk into my fist at the vision. I *do* want to paint her with my cum. I love doing that. Marking her. Claiming her.

"On second thought," she continues. "I don't think so. I want you deep inside me, so I can feel every spasm as you fill me up."

A tingling burn starts at the base of my spine, racing up my back and around my hips, shooting euphoria through my limbs. I jerk in my hand, groaning as my cock throbs, spraying my release all over my knuckles and stomach. My head slams against my pillows as I stroke through my orgasm, squeezing out every drop.

"Good boy," she coos. "Goodnight, Eli. I'll see you when you get home."

Click.

I lay on my bed, out of breath. I'm confused by why she hung up so quick, but too hazy and blown away by everything she is to overthink it.

One more month and I can give her the world.

25

BECCA

I lied.

Add it to my list of sins.

But how can I admit the sight of that girl in Eli's arms caused my heart to stutter out a painful rhythm?

There's still wounds on my soul—caused by a church who wields a blade, and a papa who slices deep. I don't care much for the throbbing that's shown up, reminding me the scars are there.

My bedroom door creaks open, Sabrina's pink-tipped head peeking around the corner.

"Hey, girl. You got a second?"

"Of course." I spin in my desk chair. "What's up?"

She plops on my bed, wringing her hands together. "I've been offered a job."

My face cracks into a smile. "That's amazin'! I didn't even know you started applyin' to places."

"Yeah." She cringes and looks down. "It is amazing. They've offered me the Junior Assistant Specialist in Ecological Research at the Marine Science Institute."

I nod my head, my chest swelling with pride. "Look at you, miss thang."

My grin fades when I see she isn't jumping for joy like I expected. "What's up? You should be thrilled and we should be celebratin'."

"I just..." she sighs, rubbing a hand over her face. "The job is in California."

My chest tightens, my breath whooshing out at the squeeze. "Oh."

"I know we had plans of getting a place together after graduation, but honestly, Becca, it's my dream job. I'd be a fool to turn it down."

"No, no." I shake my head, wringing the ends of my hair in my fist. "I get it. Of course you have to take it. It's an amazin' opportunity."

I force a small smile, but inside I'm reeling. I can't afford rent on my own. I'm barely scraping by as it is, and without the campus job I have no clue what I'm planning to do for money. I don't even know what I want to do with my *life*.

I'm not brought out of my worry until long after Sabrina leaves and Eli texts, asking where I am. I was planning on surprising him when he got back home, but obviously that's shot to shit now since I've been sitting in my room for who knows how long, lost in my thoughts. But I'm excited he's back, so I rush to my car and head over, pushing down the dread marinating in my gut.

Walking to his front doorstep feels like coming home, and entering his code on the keypad has my heart banging against my ribs, anxiety pumping into my bloodstream.

Maybe I shouldn't be gettin' this comfortable.

I barely make it through the front door when I'm grabbed from behind, and spun into the hallway wall.

Eli's lips are on me before I can speak, and just like that, my worries disappear. All that matters is how good it feels in his arms. How *right* it feels.

"Damn, I missed you." He growls against my lips.

His tongue twists around mine, fingers trailing down my sides, slipping under the waistband of my panties as he slides two fingers deep inside me.

I gasp at the intrusion, my pussy clenching around his hand.

His fingers curl forward, massaging my inner walls until it feels so good it hurts. He presses on my throbbing clit, rolling it under the pad of his thumb. I try to push forward into his palm, but his grip tightens, keeping me in place.

Kisses trail down my neck while he strips off my clothes. He crouches, his touch burning a path for his tongue to follow.

My hands grasp his hair, trying to push his face into me. "Lick it, Eli. Please."

"So damn pretty when you beg," he growls.

His tongue swipes out, circling my clit, frissons of electricity sparking through my core and down my thighs. His fingers double their efforts, maintaining a steady rhythm that compliments his mouth. I tighten my grip around the strands of his hair, legs shaking from the effort to stay standing.

My nerves coil tight, making my breath catch in my throat.

Suddenly, he stops.

"Wha–what... why," I pant. My hands try to push his head back into me, desperate for release.

Leaving his fingers as deep as they'll go inside me, he slowly stands until his towering form dwarfs me in his shadow. He leans in, his breath hot against my ear.

"Admit you were jealous." His voice is a deep rumble.

My stomach flips.

He curls his fingers and pumps them once, his palm grazing my throbbing clit.

My body burns in its need, but I bite my lips to keep from saying the words.

"Three little words, Rebecca, and I'll make you come so hard you can't think." His fingers press deeper.

I moan, my eyes rolling back.

He moves, starting to retreat from my body, but my hands wrap around his wrist, holding him inside me. He chuckles, palming the back of my neck, leaning in and trailing his tongue from my throat to my ear.

My body trembles against him.

"Give me what I want, baby girl, and I'll give you what you *need*."

I blow out a breath as his head moves back, our eyes locking.

"I was jealous," I whisper.

His face blooms into a blinding smile. "I know."

It's a simple flick of his thumb, and I shatter into a thousand pieces around him, shockwaves of pleasure rippling through my body. My walls tense and release until I black out from the sensation.

I collapse against him, my breath coming in pants and my brain in a fog. He cradles me in his arms, his big hand smoothing down my curls and bringing me in tighter.

"Never be afraid to tell me how you feel, Becca." He kisses the top of my head. "I'll always be here to catch you in the end."

My chest swells with warmth, and I smile up at him. His eyes are deep and crystal blue, begging my heart to surrender. And I almost do. But a flash of strawberry-blonde in his arms, and the whisper of Momma's words make me pause.

All men are liars.

Reality crashes through my body, my soul free falling to the floor.

It's a long drop, reminding me of how bad things can break when they land.

Love is a fairy tale, and fairy tales don't exist.

26

BECCA

Three weeks. Twenty-one days. Five-hundred and four hours. That's how long it's been since I found out Sabrina wasn't staying in Florida, throwing all of my carefully laid plans out the window.

I haven't figured anything out. I haven't told anyone, either. I don't need them trying to swoop in and solve my problems, and it will be a dark day in Hell before I admit to Papa I'm not sure I can hack it on my own.

I'll figure somethin' out.

But whatever it is, I need to figure it out quick because my folks get in town this weekend for graduation. I envisioned the joy I'd feel watching defeat settle into Papa's eyes when he realized I have all my ducks in a row. Now, the reality is bleak. No jobs, even though I've been looking. No renewal of a lease. No money even if I *wanted* to renew it. And absolutely no sense of direction. In fact, the only thing that does feel right is being with Eli, which is another issue in itself because I promised myself a long time ago I'd never depend on a man to make me happy. It only leads to disappointment in the end.

"What are you thinking about so hard over there?" Jeremy asks.

I peek at him from the couch. He's inhaling two foot-long subs like it's his last meal.

"You gonna take a breath between bites? You're lucky you're not chokin' to death."

He sets down his sub, wiping a speck of mayo from the corner of his mouth, and points at me. "Don't change the subject. You're mopey, and I want to know why."

I bite my lip, my fingers reaching up to tug on my split ends. "I'm not a robot, Jer. I'm allowed to feel different emotions. Sorry I'm not as peppy and carefree as you like."

"Quit deflecting."

Irritation spreads through my chest. My hands fly to my hips. "And what about you, huh? You're the one pullin' a disappearin' act for the last semester. You don't see me over here askin' about your whereabouts. So leave my 'mopey' alone."

He props his chin on his hand, a grin pulling at his cheeks. "You done?"

"Maybe." I cross my arms. "What are you smilin' about?"

"You. You're so obvious. And I'm not as dumb as I look."

My stomach jumps. "What's that supposed to mean?"

"It means you and Elliot Carson are shit at hiding the *fuck me* eyes you give each other. You're also terrible at sneaking into his hotel room when we're on the road. You're lucky it was me that saw you and not someone else."

I groan, my palms rubbing my eyes. "*Shit.*"

"Yeah. *Shit.*" Jeremy sits next to me, grabbing a hand from my face and linking our fingers.

"Talk to me, girl. And also, tell me the dirty details. That man is F-I-N-E."

The tangle in my chest loosens now that he knows, and a weight I didn't realize was pressing down lifts from my shoulders. "There's not much to tell. We shouldn't be a thing, but somehow... it happened. And I can't seem to stop, no matter how much I try."

His brows furrow. "Why should you? You two aren't hurting anybody. In fact, you've been a hell of a lot more amicable. I think he must be fucking the sass right out of you."

His grin fades when he sees I'm not laughing. "Oh, hell. He really is a sex god, isn't he?"

I lean back against the couch, sighing. "He really is."

"So, what's the problem?"

"It's just... complicated. He's faculty. I'm a student."

Jeremy rolls his eyes. "For like two more days. Next issue, please."

"He's Lee's brother."

"And you think she'd care?"

I chew on my lip as I ponder his question because the truth is, I'm not sure if she would.

"It just feels... disloyal. You know, we had a friend growin' up, Lily." I pause, swallowing down the anxiety that gnaws on my insides whenever I think too long about Lily. She fell into a bad way when we were in high school and ran away, leaving everyone and everything behind. Thinking about her for too long is just another glaring reminder that everyone falls off the pedestal they're placed on eventually. "She had this absolute *dick* of a brother. Lee fell hard for him, and Lily didn't take too kindly to it. At all. Totally ruined their friendship. It makes me sick to think of the same thing happenin' to us."

Jeremy sighs, rubbing his palms down his jean-clad thighs. "Seems to me like she'd understand, since she's been in your position."

My nose scrunches. I hadn't thought of it that way.

"Is it just sex?"

My heart skips at his question. I don't want to put a label on my feelings for Eli. If I say it, then it's real. "It's not just sex," I mumble.

His arms lift to the sides. "Then what's the real issue here, Becca? Because your excuses are weak as hell."

"What makes you think there's an issue? Things are fine. Easy. They'll probably fizzle out once summer starts, anyway."

"Is that what you want?"

No. "I don't mind it either way."

Jeremy's phone vibrates on the coffee table and he sighs, picking it up to look at the screen. He types out a text and sets it back down, his gaze swinging back to me.

"Look, I'm gonna say this, and then I'm gonna go." His fingers tap on the top of his knee. "You asked where I've been."

I nod.

"I met someone. Someone I'd—" He runs his hand through his hair, exhaling heavily. "Someone I'd be willing to risk everything for."

I gasp, my hand reaching out to grip his. "Holy shit, Jer. That's amazin', who is it?"

He shakes his head. "I won't tell you that. He doesn't want anyone to know. Won't even admit it to himself, other than the times he's in my bed. Which I guess I can't blame him for." His lips twist. "But I'll tell you this, Becca. That feeling? The one where someone holds themselves back, even though you're giving them everything you are? That feeling fucking sucks. It's a disease. It sneaks in undetected and attaches to your cells, siphoning all the joy, and all the love, until you're a worthless shell." He smacks his chest. "Until you start to *hate* yourself, because how could you love someone who doesn't want to love you back?"

His voice cracks, and he rubs a hand over his mouth, tears

teasing his lower lids. "Don't be the reason that man loses his heart. Not unless you plan to keep it safe."

My throat tightens painfully around the sudden knot. I'm biting my cheek so hard I taste blood.

Jeremy cups my face in his hands, kissing my forehead. "You hear me, Becca? You're better than that. Either be all in or let him go."

Sucking in a stuttered breath, I nod.

Jeremy leaves a few minutes later, but the heaviness of our conversation lingers.

I don't want to be Eli's disease.

The next morning, my chest is tight—the weight of responsibility pushing down in a way I didn't know it could. I've taken Jeremy's words to heart. Slept on them, dreamed of them and woke up with a new outlook.

I'm going to try.

I'm all in.

The decision makes me antsy, impatience thrumming in my thoughts, wondering when I'll be able to see Eli again. I'm headed to Coach Andrews's office to pick up my final paycheck, and I'm hoping I run into him there.

I knock on the office door, a melancholy vibe weaving its way through my chest at the knowledge that after today, I won't be here anymore. I've grown to love the atmosphere, the people and even the game itself. It's sad knowing I won't have it at my fingertips in the same way.

"It's open."

I turn the knob, walking in and almost tripping over my heels. Coach is behind his desk, a remote in his hand pointed at the projection screen. Eli is perched on the corner of the desk, and there's a flash of strawberry-blonde in my peripheral.

Great.

"Hi, y'all." I wave.

Eli smirks at me, fire flashing through his eyes as he stares, unashamed. The heat from his gaze races across the room and slams into my cheeks, singeing them pink.

"Becca, good to see you. Miss you around here." Coach smiles.

I clear my throat, focusing in on Coach. "I miss it too. Hope I'm not interruptin' anything. I didn't know when the best time to come by would be."

I glance at the woman sitting to the side and do a double-take. When she was busy rubbing against my man, I only saw her back, so this is the first chance I've had to take her in fully. She's beautiful. *And familiar.* My eyes narrow as I try to place her.

"You're never an interruption," Eli's voice pipes in.

I look toward him, smiling. He winks and my core clenches.

"Alright." I nod, turning back to the woman. She's nagging at my brain.

"Do I know you from somewhere?" I can't help myself, it'll drive me crazy if I don't find out.

Her frown pulls down the corner of her eyes. "I don't think so. I'm Sarah."

"Huh. You just look so familiar, is all." I tap my heel on the ground and shrug. "No matter."

I graze my body on Eli's arm as I walk by, reaching to grab the check from Coach's hands. My nipples pebble against my shirt at the touch, and I feel Eli's arm tense.

"It's been a pleasure, y'all."

"You did good this year, Becca. You love the game yet?" Coach leans back in his chair.

Eli's eyes twinkle as he straightens off the edge of the desk. "I think she loves everything about it."

I smirk. "Keep dreamin', big head."

He chuckles.

With one last wave, I swing around, walking out of Coach's office for the last time.

It's not until I'm driving home that I remember Sarah's the girl from the bar. My solar plexus sours with jealousy, my knuckles turning white from my grip on the steering wheel. *Eli didn't tell me that.* I blow out a breath, attempting to talk myself down. Believe in my man.

But faith, once lost, is hard to find.

"**E**lliot Carson, what on Earth are you doin' here?"

I'm frozen, my fist wrapped around the knob of Becca's front door. I came over to wish her congratulations before her graduation ceremony. She said it was safe, that Sabrina was out with her parents, so no one else was there. Clearly, it was a stupid idea. That fact is being pile driven into my brain right now, since I'm staring into the eyes of Becca's father.

Preacher Sanger.

I clear my throat, unclenching from around the handle and straightening. "Preacher Sanger. It's good to see you, sir."

"It's bewilderin' to see you. I'm gonna ask you again, what are you doin' in the apartment I pay for?"

My brows dip because I'm pretty certain he doesn't pay for shit.

What the hell is he talking about?

"You didn't know? I coach at FCU. I was dropping by to wish Becca congratulations, on behalf of my little sister, since she couldn't be here in person."

My mouth waters from the bitter taste of the lie.

"Coachin', huh? Not quite the bright lights and fame you expected, is it boy?" He chuckles, smacking me on the back as he moves to walk inside. Becca's mom trails behind him, stopping in front of me and grasping my jaw in her hands.

"Elliot Carson." Her voice is low, and she glances toward her husband. "Who knew we'd find the towns' pride and joy hidin' away in our daughter's apartment."

She holds my gaze, her eyes flickering as they stare into mine.

"Momma, Papa, what are you two doin' here?" Becca's voice cuts through the tension as she walks into the living room.

Her father scoffs. "We're here to see you, of course."

"I thought I was meetin' y'all at the hotel." Becca fidgets, her eyes peeking at me before locking on to her mom's.

"Hi, Momma."

"Rebecca Jean. Is that what you're wearin'?"

My jaw tics at the way they haven't even embraced their daughter. Haven't said congratulations, haven't even smiled. Graduation is supposed to be a celebration, but the room is drenched in obligation.

Becca runs her hands over her tight, black dress. Personally, I think it looks fucking sexy, but no one has asked for my opinion. I'm not even sure why I'm still standing here, but I can't bring myself to leave when it feels like Becca needs someone on her side.

"Momma, please," she sighs. "You won't be able to see it under the god awful gown we all have to wear."

"Well, thank goodness for small miracles." Her mom brushes away a curl from her face. "And you should know better than to take the Lord's name in vain."

"This is exactly the reason why you need to come back

home," Preacher Sanger pipes in. "Too much freedom makes your tongue loose and your morals shaky, Rebecca."

"I think you look great." The words slip out before I can drag them back in.

All three of them shift their bodies toward me. Becca's eyes are wide. Preacher Sanger wears a frown, and Mrs. Sanger... her gaze is busy bouncing back and forth between Becca and me, her lips pinching more with each pass.

"Can we not talk about this right now?" Becca crosses her arms, defiance locking her jaw tight.

"We'll talk about whatever we want in the apartment I pay for," Preacher Sanger states.

Becca's posture straightens. "You *haven't* paid for a damn thing. Or did you forget that you wrote me off for wantin' to live my life?"

He chuckles, brushing the nonexistent lint off his suit jacket. "You really think your meager joke of a paycheck was coverin' all your expenses?"

My stomach drops with the dread that's settling on top of it.

Becca's eyebrows pull in. "Well, I... I mean..."

I'm not used to seeing her unsure in her words, and I don't like it. Part of me wonders if this is how it's always been between them—the oppressive nature of her father slumping her shoulders and dousing her fire.

My body burns with the need to reassure her of her strength.

"What are you talkin' about?" she finally manages. "I put everything I make directly into Sabrina's hands every month."

He nods, his brow rising. "And where do you think she gets the rest of it?"

Becca's hand pulls at one of her curls. "No, I... the rest of *what?*"

"A measly five-hundred dollars isn't enough to pay for the bed you sleep in, let alone everything that comes with it."

My stomach rolls. *Why didn't she tell me she needed money?*

Becca's lower lip trembles as she shakes her head. "Sabrina wouldn't take money from you without tellin' me."

Mrs. Sanger sighs, walking over and patting Becca's arm. "Oh, honey. When will you learn that people aren't always who you expect them to be?"

Becca's cheeks redden. I watch as realization filters into the irises of her eyes, whipping around and lighting them ablaze.

Preacher Sanger shakes his head. "Makes me wonder what type of education I've even been payin' for the past four years."

My heart pinches with the urge to walk over and stand at her back. Steal away the heaviness in her stance and let it rest on my shoulders, instead.

"But I..." Becca's voice trails off.

Her father walks closer, his hands coming to lay on her shoulders. "Do you truly believe I would let my daughter live broke and destitute? I'll always be holdin' the strings to tie you back together."

Does he really think his daughter is so weak?

My nostrils flare with the strength it's taking me to hold back my thoughts. I need to leave before I say something I'll regret, the last thing I want to do is make things worse for her.

"Anyway, now that I've sent my sister's congrats in person, I should head out." I lock my eyes on Becca. "Congratulations, Becca. Ma would be so proud." My voice catches on the last word.

Becca's lips part on a gasp, her eyes growing glassy as she mumbles out her thanks.

I want to drag her out of the apartment. Wrap her in my

arms, and shield her from her parents' ugly truths. But it's hard to use your limbs when they're tied behind your back.

So I leave alone, reassuring myself the constraints are temporary.

She's graduating. *Finally.*

And tonight, everything will change.

28

BECCA

T here's something desensitizing when you finally welcome in your demons.

I'm a fool.

Truly the dumbest woman on the planet, thinking I could hack it on my own. I can't even be pressed to check into the logistics of where I hand my money. *Or who I hand it to.*

I've known betrayal. Felt it slamming into the depths of my soul and spreading like ivy. Turns out, it never really leaves. Just remains stagnant until something pours water on its seeds, allowing it to grow.

I didn't know Sabrina held the watering can. But now I do.

How could she?

I make it through the graduation ceremony, but while most celebrate the breaking of their chains, wings spread and ready to soar, I feel mine clamping down and stuttering my flight. Strange, how the same experience can affect people so differently.

Sabrina tries to talk to me, tries to tell me congratulations, but I find only silence to offer. I can't even look at her. Can't stand what I'll see.

I'm quiet as my family walks into the upscale restaurant to "celebrate." Despondent as we sit at the table. Papa orders for all of us, just like he always does. He has to be in control of everything. I'm sure he's thrilled at my new subdued personality.

I was so close. At least, I thought I was, but everything I *thought* I knew was an illusion, put together by the ones I'm supposed to trust.

I've been outplayed in a game I didn't even know I was in. The realization is a bitch-slap to my psyche, reaffirming the truths my mind has always whispered, but I've tried so hard to ignore.

I ache to leave here and go to Eli's. Lay in his arms, and feel the comfort of his embrace. Beg him to fuck me unconscious, so my thoughts don't torture me in my dreams.

We're halfway through the meal before conversation is attempted. I've been playing with the food on my plate, my appetite lost after realizing I've been living in a cage with a view.

"I assume you'll be comin' home with us?" Papa asks.

My chest pulls tight. "No, Papa. I'm not comin' home."

He dabs his mouth with a red cloth napkin, then throws it on the table. "Enough, Rebecca. I let you live your life this semester. You have *responsibilities* in Sugarlake. I want you home where I can make sure you don't sully our name."

I pick up my glass, taking a sip while I mull his words. I lick my lips as I set the water down. "A little late for all that, don't you think?"

Papa's face grows as red as my hair, and a spike of satisfaction splits my face into a grin. "Besides, I don't think I *do* have responsibilities there. The church is your legacy, not mine."

He scoffs, his chair scratching against the floor as he jerks to stand. Pointing to me, his mouth straightens into a firm line, before he turns toward Momma. "Talk to your daughter. Maybe you can get it in her thick head I'm not givin' her a choice."

He storms away, moving to walk past the bar and then suddenly stopping. Momma and I watch as he sidles next to a curvy brunette. He doesn't even try to hide it. *Pig.* Nausea curdles my stomach when I think about how I used to look up to that man—used to think he was my everything.

I never see things the way they really are.

"How can you just let him disrespect you like that, Momma?" I wave my arm toward the bar, my nose scrunched.

She sighs, sipping on her water. *Wishing it was liquor, I'm sure.* She's always been a closet drinker. There were many nights growing up where Lee, Lily, and I would raid her secret stash.

"I made an oath in front of God to honor and cherish him all the days of my life, and I'll hold true to my word."

"Even when he doesn't?"

Her gaze spears me with its sadness, and there's a familiarity, beyond our genes, tugging me into its depth.

"He means well, you know. He loves you—"

I huff out a laugh.

"He does. Somewhere along the way, I think he just forgot he was supposed to show it."

My throat thickens.

"I had many good years with that man." She glances toward the bar, shaking her head, her eyes darkening.

Papa is laughing, his head thrown back, while he chats with the brunette who clearly doesn't mind the ring on his finger. I've known Papa was a cheat, but I've never seen him flaunt it this way. I guess when he's out of town, he can't be bothered to keep on the religious cloak that hides the snake underneath.

"There was a time..." She clears her throat, swallowing back whatever emotion was trying to break through her poised stature. "There was a time I thought he would move mountains to be with me. Looked at me like I was all he could see."

Momma's head angles down as she meets my stare. "He looked at me the way Elliot Carson looks at you."

My heart slams so hard against my ribs I'm surprised they don't break. "I'm not sure what you mean, Momma."

She chuckles, reaching out to pat my hand. "You do. But you won't admit it, to me or to yourself, I reckon. You're so like me, Rebecca Jean. In so many ways."

I tamp down the bile rising up my esophagus. There are a lot of things I aspire to be. Kind. Loving. *Free.* Turning into Momma is not on that list.

"Men are skilled at weavin' their words. Makin' them pretty. Puttin' dumb ideas in your head and promisin' you the world."

Bitterness coats her words, slicing into my ears like a blade.

My stomach twists. "But all men are liars, right?"

She nods. "If you remember anything I've ever taught you, Rebecca Jean, remember that."

"What happens when the woman's a liar too?" My elbows rest on the table.

Her fingernails tap against her glass. "I'm not quite sure what you're insinuatin'."

I should stop talking. Cut my losses and try to salvage what's an already ruined dinner. But years of resentment billow in my chest, pumping from my heart, and pouring into my veins.

"Momma, come on. You prance around in public for Papa,

actin' like the perfect little preacher's wife. But there's a reason your liquor is clear, and your water glass is always full."

Momma's eyes narrow, her lips pursing. "When did you become so *disrespectful*?"

"When did you become so *weak*?"

Her wince pulls at the seams of my heart, but I don't apologize. I'm so exhausted. Tired from a lifetime of watching a strong woman wither away into this doormat.

"Givin' my life to Jesus does *not* make me weak, young lady."

"No, but givin' your life to Papa sure does."

Her hand slaps the table. "I've accepted the twists and turns that brought me to where I am in life. I've learned to be at peace with the way things turned out. With the decisions I've made. You hate how *weak* I seem? Well you better get ready, because twenty years ago I *was* you. Thinkin' I had the world at my fingertips, and the love of a perfect man."

I suck in a breath, my insides churning from the torrential downpour of her words.

No. I will not be my momma.

She leans in, her voice low. "But while you get lost in your illusion of love, the world keeps spinnin'. It'll spin right outta your grasp. And all those years you spent tryin' to break free? *Wasted.* You'll be tied down and stuck anyway." Weariness paints her features. "Don't say I didn't warn you."

I roll my eyes to try and stem the tears, turning my head to the side and crossing my arms over my chest. But her words dig through the cavity in my chest, knocking against the cage that holds my heart, seeking to destroy.

29

BECCA

"You okay?"

Eli's voice floats through the air, caressing my dilapidated soul, but the wounds are too deep, and even his balm doesn't curb the sting.

I nod my head, sinking into the nook of his arm as we lie on his bed.

Eli has this way of knowing what I need before I can verbalize it. Took one look at me when I showed up, and walked me to his room, pushed me on the bed, and fucked me so hard he left bruises.

His fingers ghost up and down my arms, goose bumps sprouting to mark the places he's touched.

"Have your folks always been such assholes?"

"Not always," I murmur. "When I was little, they used to be like any other folk, I guess. Or, maybe I was just blind to what was really goin' on."

Looking back, it seems more likely I was an unknowing participant of a carefully crafted show. Probably would have played my part forever, if I hadn't stumbled behind the scenes and ruined the whole damn storyline.

"It doesn't matter anyway," I sigh. "I'm used to them bein'
who they are. I just don't know what I'm gonna do."

I taste salt on my lips, and realize tears have been trickling
down my face, soaking into Eli's skin. He doesn't acknowledge
the proof of my pain, and a gooey warmth spreads through
my chest—so damn thankful he knows not to bring it up.

"What do you *want* to do?" Eli's palm grazes against my
jaw as he angles my head toward him.

"I wanna stay here, in Florida. Figure out what the hell
I'm gonna do with my life. But I don't know how to make
that happen when I've got nothin'." My eyes close and I lean
into his touch, reveling in the comfort.

"You've got me," he whispers.

My eyes snap open, latching on to his. A tsunami of this...
feeling rises up and crashes against the edges of my soul,
sweeping me away in its wake. Desperation claws at my
insides, and I dive into him, molding our lips, needing him to
steal away the sensation before it drowns me with its power.

My hands cup his face, melding us together.

I need him closer.

His arms tighten around my waist and he rolls us, his
large frame settling over me. I moan into his mouth, his thickness pressing into the junction between my thighs. We're still
naked from earlier, and I thank God there's nothing to slow
this down. Not when my need is so all-consuming.

He breaks our kiss, his head leaning back, thumbs
sweeping across my cheeks as he cradles my face. The intensity of his gaze sizzles in my stomach, and my breath snags
on the feeling.

He swallows, his grip tightening along my jaw. "Becca,
I lo—"

My heart crashes against my sternum. My finger trembles
as I push it against his lips. "Don't."

The lines between his brows crease.

Reaching down, I wrap my fingers around his thick cock, feeling it jump against the palm of my hand.

I push my upper body off the bed, stroking him, our breaths mixing in the space between us. My hips start a slow grind, his tip dragging through my folds as my hand works his length. He pants, his teeth grazing my bottom lip.

I move him to my entrance. "I don't want your words. I need you to *show* me."

His eyes darken. I pull him in at the same time he drops down, and I cry out from being so full.

He's seated deep inside me, hip to hip. There isn't an inch of our bodies not connected, but I don't feel confined from his touch. I feel *free.*

He grasps my arms, pushing them above my head. His fingertips skim along my skin, prickles of electricity sinking into my pores. My blood is a conductor, spreading the current, striking my heart into a faster cadence.

Our fingers link, and his palms push my hands deeper into the mattress as he finally, *finally,* moves.

I moan as he pulls out and drives back in.

Heat lances into my core, my pussy walls pulsing around him. He keeps a steady rhythm, his eyes never leaving mine, our lips brushing with each thrust, his touch showing me what I won't let him say.

This isn't a power play. It's not about control.

This is a confession.

Sweat beads along his brow, and glistens on his neck. I lean in, licking his salty skin. His Adam's apple bobs under my tongue, and his hips jerk, the rhythm faltering.

"Christ, Becca," he breathes, his forehead resting on mine. "I can't…"

I squeeze our hands, still locked above my head, and I

place my mouth on his, unable to resist the call of his lips. His body. *His soul.*

His taste is heady. My muscles cinch and release, tension looping and tangling until I'm twisted so tight I can barely breathe.

I break away, gasping in air, careening over the cliff of my pleasure.

My vision goes white.

My ears go numb.

My stomach soars then sinks, and I cling to Eli's frame to keep from disintegrating to dust.

I surrender to the fall.

I'm vaguely aware of Eli's body shaking as he comes deep inside me. He collapses, breathing hard. After a few moments, he rolls to the side.

"Damn." He chuckles. Facing me, he props his head in his hand, a carefree smile lighting up his face. "Move in with me."

"Wh… what?" I stutter.

"Yeah." He grabs my hand, bringing it to his chest. Moving closer, he palms my jaw. "I want to be with you, baby girl." He pecks my lips. "See you every morning." Another peck. "Kiss you every night."

Imagining him by my side each night has my heart floundering in my chest.

"Besides, you need a place to stay anyway, yeah?" He lifts a brow.

I giggle. "You tryin' to be my white knight, Eli?"

He smirks. "Of course. Don't you know by now I would move mountains for you?"

My grin stays plastered on my face, but my blood turns glacial, freezing in my veins.

His smile drops. "What just happened? What's wrong?"

I shake my head, touching my lips to his, trying to kiss

away the acrid taste creeping onto the back of my tongue. "Nothin's wrong. I'll think about it, okay?"

His grip on my jaw tightens. "Becca... I love you."

No.

My eyes squeeze tight, my head turning to the side.

His hand pulls me back. "You know that, right? I'm so damn lost in my love for you."

I nod sharply at his words, my fingers tugging on my curls.

"Becca?" His voice is soft, pleading.

I don't open my eyes.

With a deep sigh, he kisses my forehead and leaves the bed.

My eyes snap open, my gut burning with the need to call him back, but the screams in my head stop the words on my tongue.

It's late when Eli finally comes back and falls asleep.

Silence blankets the ground, but the quiet is a fraud. Momma's voice drains from my mind to my heart, piercing holes through the tissue, leaching away the serenity I've worked so hard to find. My body fights the intrusion, desperate to stay whole. Anguished in its plea to forget that Eli spoke pretty words I begged him not to say.

But I can't forget.

I don't want to be Eli's disease.

Sliding out of the bed, I'm careful not to wake him as I pick up my clothes. Halfway through putting on my jeans, realization of what I'm doing hits and my heart splinters, the shards prodding against my lungs. My hand covers my mouth to muffle the cry.

I pause at the bedroom door. My hand shakes against the metal knob, causing a sharp rattle to puncture the calm air. My blurry eyes close, and I focus on the noise. Anything to keep me from turning around.

It doesn't work. I look anyway.

Eli's sleeping peacefully. Beautifully. *Perfectly.* My heart sputters and falls, diving into my stomach and laying there to bleed.

"There was a time I thought that man would move mountains for me."

I will *not* become my momma.

With a deep breath, I turn the handle and slip out the door.

30

ELI

It's the glare of the sun that wakes me. It beams through the curtains, my eyes squeezing tight against the shine. I roll to my side, arms reaching to pull Becca in. Only... I grasp a ghost, my fingers meeting Egyptian cotton instead of her supple skin.

My eyes crack open, forehead scrunching as I gain a bearing on my surroundings. I look around, but don't see Becca in the room.

Maybe she's already up?

I stretch before getting out of bed, throwing on a pair of boxer briefs, and stumbling to the bathroom. It's empty. Grabbing my phone, I head downstairs, the flipping of my stomach urging my feet to move fast.

"Becca?" Her name echoes off the walls I *still* haven't filled, and a prickle creeps up my spine.

I reach the kitchen.

Empty.

Dropping onto a barstool, I light up my phone screen. No missed calls. No messages.

I dial her number, not bothering to bring the phone to my

ear—straining to hear it ring somewhere in the house. My insides cramp when there's nothing but silence. I hang up and try again. Straight to voicemail this time.

Something's off.

Becca's missing, and the air feels different. Like it's been shocked into silence from the loss of her soul.

I set down my phone only to pick it up again as I stand. My movement is stilted. It's hard trying to maneuver around the lead weight that's dropped in my stomach.

Because I already feel it in my gut.

She's gone.

The burn in my chest rolls through my system, bursting through my limbs. I throw my phone, watching it ricochet off the marble countertop, landing on the floor. My fingers rip through my disheveled strands, and I puff out a breath, trying to calm my racing heart.

"This is ridiculous," I mumble, bending to pick up the broken screen.

I shouldn't have told her I loved her, but I didn't realize she wouldn't love me back.

The thought barrels into my stomach and up my throat, expanding until I have to swallow against the pain.

The words she didn't say slammed into my chest like a fist, my heart fracturing from her silence. I let the quiet linger because I didn't want to push. Left the bed and gave her space so I wouldn't break apart at her feet. So I wouldn't beg her to just *say the goddamn words* and keep me glued together.

But to wake up and find her gone?

Fuck. That.

She doesn't get to run from this. From me.

I hop off the barstool, my heart pumping determination through my veins, the adrenaline more potent than a hundred cups of coffee. Stumbling to my room, I rip open my dresser, throwing on the first thing I can find.

Then I'm out the door, on a mission.

My heart thunks against my sternum on the way to her apartment, my fingers tapping out a jittery rhythm on the wheel.

Why would she leave?

Slamming my car into park, I hop out, tripping over my shoes to get to her front door. Desperate in my need to see her. For her to soothe away this *ache*.

No one answers when I knock, and I bounce on the balls of my feet. Every second adds another brick to the layer of my anxiety.

As the door swings open, something loosens in my chest, a smile teasing the corner of my mouth. *She's here.* Only, the relief doesn't last, because it isn't Becca's beautiful face peeking at me. It's Sabrina.

Her eyes narrow and I realize how awkward it is for me to be here. No one knows about us, after all.

"Hey." My voice comes out gruff. I rock back on my heels, attempting to soften my tone. "Sabrina, right?"

Her brows draw together. "Yeah. Coach Carson, right? What are you doing here?"

I clear my throat. "I'm here to talk to Rebecca. Is she home?"

Her brows pull in further with the downturn of her lips. "Becca? No. I haven't seen her since yesterday at graduation, and I barely saw her then."

My heart stutters, the sickness of my thoughts infecting every beat. "Okay. Well, if you see her, let her know I stopped by, would you?"

Sabrina's hand slides against the doorframe as she cocks her head. "Why do you need to see her anyway?"

Irritation flares in my chest. "That's not really your business."

She purses her lips. "I think it is. She's *my* friend, and I'm not sure I should tell her you were here, unless I know your intentions."

I chuckle, my teeth gritting at this girl's audacity. "My *intention* is to find Becca and keep her away from people like you. Ones who parade around like her friend while holding a knife to her back. One her *father* provides."

Her eyes grow wide, her face draining of color.

"Bee, who's at the door?"

I peer around her, hearing Jeremy's voice. He comes to the door, standing next to Sabrina. "Coach." He tips his chin. "Nice to see you, you looking for Becca?"

I nod, suddenly unable to say the words.

Where is she?

He rubs Sabrina's shoulder, whispering in her ear. She gives a curt nod, and he walks out, closing the door. Jerking his head to follow, he walks around the corner of the building, leaning against the brick wall, one leg perched behind him.

My chest pulls tight and my fists clench at the show he's putting on. Like I have time to leisurely take a stroll. Like every second we spend walking isn't a second further away from wherever she is.

"She's gone." His voice is as flat as his face.

The words form an arrow straight through my heart, damaging the already cracked pieces.

"What do you mean '*she's gone?*'" I hiss, jealousy licking at my veins.

Of course, he already knows.

"She left me a voicemail this morning." He rubs a hand over his mouth, blowing out a breath. "She asked me not to tell you anything, but she's stock full of shit ideas, so screw what she wants right now."

He pulls out his phone, pressing a few buttons. Becca's

voice floats to my ears, my soul tearing through the wounds in my chest to reach her.

"Hi, Jer." Her voice is choked—soft, like she's holding back a sob.

My nostrils flare at the sound, my breath whooshing out from the urge to soothe her sadness.

"I'm leavin', Jer. I…" She sniffles. "I can't stay here. Goin' back with my folks. I know it won't make much sense to you, and honestly, it don't make much sense to me either, but it's just what needs to happen. I need to.. To ge-g-…" Her voice breaks.

My hand comes up to rub my chest, trying to ease the pressure that's building with every word.

"I need to get away fr–from everything here. I hope you understand. I'll miss you so much, Jer. I love you, you know?"

My stomach heaves at her words, my head growing dizzy. *What about me?*

"You were right. Everything you said." She sighs. "You know, about that guy you love? Don't… don't settle for a man who won't tell the world you're his, Jer. *Everyone* deserves to b-be loved by someone who ain't afraid of what it means." She sucks in a stuttered breath.

My stomach flips and my eyes snap to Jeremy's. The implication of her words are heavy in his stance. His face is wet, glistening from tear tracks that line his face, but he holds my gaze, his jaw tense and posture straight.

Jeremy's gay.

I should feel relief, but with her gone, I find I don't care.

"I love you, Jer. I'll try to keep in touch. And don't… don't tell Eli, okay? I don't want him to know."

A piece of my crumpled heart breaks, the jagged edge splitting my insides as it falls.

Jeremy doesn't speak, just slips his phone back into his pocket.

"She's gone." The words surprise me as I say them. Who knew a corpse could speak?

Jeremy nods, wiping his cheeks. "You gonna go after her?"

I huff out a laugh, shaking my head as I stare at the ground. I consider his words. I *could* track her ass down. Fuck an apology out of her, and force her to admit she feels this. *Feels us.*

But the thought of going back to Sugarlake chokes my throat until I'm gasping for air.

"I can't," I whisper.

Jeremy sighs. "Probably for the best. She's not ready for you, Coach. I hate to say it... but it's the truth. Maybe one day, she will be."

His words pierce the space between us, slicing my chest and wrangling the mangled flesh left behind.

She *was* ready. I felt it in every touch. Saw it in every look.

She just didn't care enough to stay.

I don't drive home when I leave. The thought of walking into a place that still reeks of her betrayal makes my stomach roil with nausea. So I drive to Waycor Arena instead.

Walking onto the empty court, my heart spasms, pinching so tight my knees give out. Every inch of this place is soaked in a memory. I touch my face, then stare at my hand, my fingers glistening from my tears.

I'm not sure what I expected. Maybe a sense of relief? The court is the only place where I've ever felt at peace.

But now there's just this *burn* singeing through my veins, turning everything to ash.

Fuck her for ruining the one thing I had left.

And fuck her for leaving. Doesn't she know she's taking a

piece of me with her? Doesn't she care that she's ruining my fucking soul?

Black rage surges through my gut, blasting a hole in my chest and mixing into my bloodstream.

I glance down at my watch. *Five minutes.* That's what I'll give myself. *Just five minutes.* And then... I'll lock it up tight in the corner of my mind where it belongs.

With everything else.

31

BECCA

FIVE YEARS LATER

Becca
Swipe left. Swipe left. Swipe left.

My finger hovers over the face of an attractive dark-haired, green-eyed man. He's the first one I've seen on this damn dating app that doesn't have characteristics I do everything in my power to avoid.

I don't use this app to "date" per se. More like a nice, free, uncomplicated way to find a nice out-of-town dick to ride, without having to deal with the town gossip, or the messy complications of someone wanting strings.

This guy, *John,* lives in Chattanooga and looks like he'd be a good distraction.

Swipe right.

I toss my phone to the side, leaning back on my lounger, soaking up the Saturday morning rays. It's summer here in Sugarlake, and the Tennessee sun is hot and delicious on my skin. I'm not a fan of many things in this town, but I *do* love relaxing on the back porch of my little one-bed, one-bath cottage. I rent, of course. Don't want to be too tied down in case I actually get the balls to leave.

I have about an hour before meeting Lee for brunch at Patty's Diner.

It's a thing—our Saturday morning brunches. It has been ever since I moved back five years ago, and realized Lee wasn't any better mentally than she was when I left for college. Somewhere between me being in Florida, and her other best friend, Jax, being on the road all the time, she's regressed into this melancholy state where we have to force her to be among the land of the living. I think she'd rather slip away to be with her momma's ghost.

I don't mind focusing on keeping Lee afloat. If I submerge myself in other people's problems, then I don't have to focus on my own.

Probably why I became a social worker for the high school.

Never mind the fact I'm twenty-six and back in the town I always dreamed of escaping. Or how I'm still under my old man's thumb, worse now than I ever was back then, because now, I don't put up a fight.

Better the devil you know.

Sabotaging your own future is something I excel in. Too bad there wasn't a major in that. I would have passed with flying colors, and taken over the world. Until I inevitably fucked it up, of course.

But I have my little cottage, my own money, and my career. All things Papa can never take from me. I've learned to stay afloat through compromise, wading slowly toward a life of independence. I don't know if I'll ever get there, but at least now I know better than to dream.

I glance at my phone to check the time. I want to get to the diner before Lee. She's been avoiding me again. *No surprise there.* Chase Adams is back in town. The boy who broke her heart and hung her out to dry, just like I always said he would. She doesn't have a clue I know, so she doesn't realize her energy at avoiding me is wasted. But I don't blame her.

I've been firmly in the 'hating Chase camp' since the moment he blew into town when we were eleven years old, making Lee's naive little heart swoon in curiosity and wonder.

I know at brunch she'll spill the beans. She's shit at holding in secrets, and if I ask her point blank, she won't hide from the truth. There's nothing Lee hates more in the world than a liar.

My stomach turns at the thought of things I keep from her. Things I've *been* keeping from her. Things I have no plan to ever tell her.

Omission is not a lie, Becca.

Maybe if I say it enough times, I'll start to believe it.

An hour later and I'm sitting on the patio at Patty's Diner, texting Lee. She's running late, and I'm wondering if she's even planning on showing the hell up. Normally, Jax would be here, but he's in high demand out in California being the car guru on movie sets, so he leaves a lot. It's a shame he's gone now, because he's the one that usually wrangles Lee, making sure she actually comes.

"Hey, girl."

I glance up at my long-haired, honey-blonde best friend as she plops in the seat across from me. Despite the dark circles that line her eyes, and the sorrow swirling in her baby blue gaze, she's gorgeous.

"She lives," I deadpan.

Lee grins, waving my snark off and diving into a story about her new job at some dance studio in Sweetwater. I let her ramble, knowing her filter is nonexistent and sooner or later she'll vomit out the truth. Her body is practically vibrating, and I'm sure it's from her nerves of telling me what I already know.

The air around us quiets as she sips from her mimosa, fidgeting in her seat.

I arch my brow.

"Chase is back," she blurts.

"I know."

She groans, throwing her head in her hands. "Dang it, how'd you know about that already?"

"Ran into him the other day. He let it slip you knew he was back."

She sighs. "I just didn't know how to bring it up."

Her shoulders relax like all she needed to relieve the weight was to speak it out loud.

A spark lights her eyes as she talks about him, and my chest warms at the sight. It's something that's been missing ever since her momma died. Ever since Chase tore her up and disappeared in the first place.

Is it that easy to forgive her heartbreak?

Hope that has no place living inside me makes a home, digging in deep and planting its roots. Ideas perch on my shoulder, whispering that maybe my mistakes aren't a permanent tarnish. That maybe forgiveness is a family trait.

"I get it, I guess. We all have secrets." I shrug, attempting to shake off the notion. But the thoughts are always there, lingering like a song stuck in my head, driving me insane even though no one else can hear. They scrape against my scars, the sting reminding me they haven't fully healed.

I doubt they ever will.

Up until this point, I've been a master of avoidance, the years having only strengthened my ability to push things down to the darkest corners of my soul.

"Oh, and you'll never guess what else," Lee says, while I pick from the breadbasket.

"Does it have to do with you, Logan, and a bottle of lube?" I grin, wiggling my eyebrows. Logan is her fling of the moment, and a fine specimen if there ever was one. I never miss a chance to try and get her to dish the dirt on his *abilities*.

Lee's cheeks flush pink and I tamp down a laugh. She's so

easy to rile up. So innocent in her acts, even as an adult. As sweet as cherry pie and as shiny as a whistle. I'm sure when Papa prays, he tacks on a favor from God, asking to make me more like her.

She rolls her eyes. "No, you deviant. Eli's comin' home."

My heart stammers so violently in my chest my body physically jerks, causing my fingers to fumble my champagne flute. I watch in despair as the alcohol-infused orange juice sloshes over the sides. If I heard her right, I'll need all the drink I can get.

"What?"

Lee's lips move, but I can't hear a thing over the blood whooshing through my ears, or the bang of my heart slamming against the icy cage it's been frozen in.

"What?" I repeat.

She nods, her nose scrunching while she sips from her glass. "I know. Get this, he's gettin' *married.*"

The knot forming in my chest surges up, lodging itself in my throat, my stomach spiraling against the turbulence of my body.

"What?" I rasp.

Her eyebrows draw in. "Are you broken? Is that all you can say?"

I'm surprised I can even manage that. A knife to the gut would hurt less than her words. Years of shoddy patchwork burst apart at the seams, the wounds I've tried to cover bleeding out.

My hands fly to my stomach, and I fold in on myself. The agony so deep, so *visceral*, I don't know if I'll survive the pain.

Married. Eli's gettin' married.

He's moved on.

He's loved again.

Thick, green jealousy oozes through the cracks of my heart, coating my lungs, and weighing down every breath.

I'm a coward. Too afraid of ending up chained down and miserable. Scared of being the spitting image of my momma. Only... I ended up in that life anyway. Shackled to my old man instead of being with the one who wanted nothing more than to love me. The one who only wanted to give me a piece of his soul.

And now he's giving that piece away. Letting someone else stake their claim.

I did it to myself. A fact I remind myself of as I lay in my bed that night, speaking to a God I don't believe in.

For the first time since I was thirteen years old, I pray.

I pray that whoever she is, she's able to love him the way he deserves. The way he's supposed to be loved. *The way I can't.*

I take solace in those simple truths. But before I fall asleep —my pillow damp from my regrets—the darkness creeps in, and I've never felt so alone.

32

ELI

"**A**re you sure this is what you want?" I ask for the
thousandth time.

"Yep."

I blow out a breath, my hands hanging between my knees
as I try to keep from cringing at Sarah's answer. Not that it
would matter anyway, we're already on the plane to the one
place I never wanted to be.

Sugarlake, Tennessee.

It's been eight years since I've been there, and even longer
since I've spent more than a weekend. Now, I'm headed back
for the foreseeable future—courtesy of my fiancée, who just
had to have our wedding there. Said it would lend "small-
town charm" to the big day.

"Charm" isn't exactly the word I would use. More like a
glimpse into an alternate reality, one I'm not sure I want to
see. With every tick on the altitude, my chest squeezes tight,
and my hands grow damp at the thought of what's waiting
once we step off the plane.

It won't be a welcoming committee.

Even worse, we'll be there the next two months. All of

summer break, planning the wedding of Sarah's dreams before going back to Florida as Mr. and Mrs. Carson. Problem is, there's only one place in Sugarlake to get married. And besides the high school—which is the glaring reminder of my broken dreams—it's the one place I'd like to avoid.

I should know by now I rarely get what I want.

Sarah thinks the fact my little sister has an "in" with the preacher's family just means it's meant to be. I'm still holding out hope that two months isn't enough notice. But I know it will be. There's only so many people clambering to get married in a small town.

"Don't you want to have it in Florida? Somewhere closer to where you grew up?" I try again.

Sarah sighs, patting my hand with her perfectly shaped, pink nails. "No, Eli. I want it in Tennessee, and I want to meet your family. Let's at least go and look at the options. Besides, you already talked to Lee about helping with the church, didn't you?"

I nod, my jaw tensing when I think about how the conversation went. My baby sister was *not* a fan of finding out I was getting married. Bitched in my ear for a good twenty minutes about having to hear it from Pops instead of from me.

She's right. I should have been the one to tell her, but I didn't know how. Every time I tried, an invisible hand smacked over my mouth, stopping the words from passing my lips. Maybe I didn't speak up because I'm still not sure of it myself. Or maybe it's because I know that once Lee finds out about something, Becca finds out too.

Not that it matters.

She wouldn't care anyway. She never did.

I sigh, rubbing the back of my neck, trying to ease the tension that's pulsing behind my ear and piercing my skull. I don't want to step foot back in Sugarlake. Don't want to face the ghosts that I left behind, or the ones that left me. But it's what Sarah wants and I can't find it in me to say no.

I can't give her all of me, I don't even know where my broken pieces lay, but at least I can give her this.

It's not even close to what she actually deserves.

Sarah's love is a constant warmth. It slides on top of my skin and blankets me in her comfort, sheltering me from the icy, frozen tundra of the cold, cruel world. Being with her is as easy as breathing. And maybe that's what love is supposed to feel like. Effortless. Steady. Calm.

But she doesn't consume me.

Thank fucking God.

Still, her presence in my life kept me out of my own head when there was nothing but bad memories and painful heartbreak there to greet me. Connor was the one to take me out, and Sarah was the one who brought me home. Somewhere in the middle of all that, we ended up together.

I proposed once I found out Coach Andrews is retiring at the end of next year, and that I'm up for head coach. This is the next logical step in my life. I'll have the career. The home. The wife. Everything Ma always wanted for me. All the things I didn't give her while I had the chance. Hopefully, I can appease her in death.

Maybe then the nightmares will stop.

Pops is the one who picks us up, and I'm shocked when I first see him. Granted, it's been years, but the difference from what I remember is striking. He looks worn down, almost emaciated in appearance. Deep grooves line his once handsome face, and purple bags sink into his dull blue eyes. This is not the man who raised me.

I can't say I really blame him. When Ma died, he lost the

other half of his soul—the match to his flame. There's no getting over that. There's just surviving.

My chest grows tight with each mile, every bump in the road flipping my stomach. Coming home is rife with things I'd rather leave buried, and I can't help the sinking feeling in my gut as we get closer to town, warning me there's a shovel with my name on it, waiting to dig.

Nostalgia hits me like a train, but it's not the gorgeous rise and fall of the smoky mountain range in the distance, or the smell of the yellow birch trees that get me. It's standing outside of my childhood home.

I can't believe I'm here.

Sarah gushes to Pops about the charm of the place—her favorite word, apparently—but I'm glued to my spot in the middle of the driveway, trying to ignore the absence of Ma's presence in everything I see. The blue shutters lining the front windows are faded and worn. The garden that sprouted tulips, Ma's favorite, are now overflowing with weeds.

A sickness fills my stomach, tossing around the whiskey I drank on the plane ride here.

Hands creep from behind me, wrapping around my chest while I stare at the basketball hoop still affixed to the side-walk lining our drive. Sarah lays her head against my shoulder blade, speaking into the fabric of my shirt, the heat from her breath soaking through to my skin.

It isn't enough to take away the sudden chill.

"You okay?" she asks.

I turn, pasting a smile on my face as I grab her hand, linking our fingers and swinging them between us.

"Yeah, I'm good. Just weird to be back."

She grins, her teeth blinding, matching the sparkle of her eyes. "Exciting, right?"

"Super." I draw out the word, my brows rising, and she smacks my chest with a giggle.

Once we're inside, Pops goes straight to the fridge, cracking open two Budweisers and handing me one. He quirks a brow, pointing the neck of his bottle toward Sarah. "You want one, lil' lady?"

She sits at the table, shaking her head no and asking for a water instead. I sit next to her, the heaviness of my heart making my legs too weak to stand. If I look hard enough, I swear I can see Ma baking her banana bread. I half expect Pops to sneak up behind her to press kisses on her neck. Tension pulls tight across my chest and I gulp down my beer, focusing on the cold as it slips down my throat. "Where's Lee, Pops?"

He lifts his shoulder, sinking into the seat across from me and tapping his fingers on the worn oak of the table. "Who knows where that girl is."

My forehead scrunches, his answer surprising me. Pops has always been extremely protective when it comes to Lee. Probably *too* protective, not wanting to see his little girl grow up before his eyes. His cold, detached demeanor makes my stomach sour.

The front door opens and shuts before I can respond, and my gut churns, the carbonation of the beer threatening to burn my throat on its way back up.

That must be her.

While seeing Pops was hard, I'm more nervous to come face to face with the baby sister who's hated me for most of my adult life. But it isn't her who walks into the kitchen.

My lungs expand as I suck in a deep breath of relief, but I can't deny the slight disappointment.

"Mr. Carson, I've got stuff to make fajitas tonight, hope you're hungry." The man's voice is deep and there's something about him that's familiar. He drops the grocery bags on the counter, spinning around and freezing in place, his hand halfway to his tousled dark hair. His eyes widen as they lock on me.

"Holy fuck, Eli?"

My brows furrow as I try to place him.

His posture is tense, his eyes scanning my face. "You have no clue who I am, do you?"

"Should I?"

"Depends. Do you normally forget the boy who grew up three houses down and dated your sister for years?"

I suck in a breath. "Chase?"

"The one and only." He smirks, his hands rising to his sides.

I know him, of course. His little sister and him were both attached to Lee's hip since they were kids. But he does *not* look like the gangly boy I remember. It makes me wonder what Lee looks like now, and if I saw her on the street, would I even know to stop? The thought clamps around my heart, spreading a deep ache through my chest.

"Does Goldi know you're here?" Chase asks, his face growing serious.

"Who's Goldi?" Sarah blurts. "I'm Sarah, by the way. Eli's fiancée."

"Hi," Chase responds, his eyes still locked on mine. "Does she? Or is she about to be blindsided when she walks in?"

"She knows," Pops grumbles. "She's been knowin' he was comin' home. No one invited *you* over though, boy."

Chase smirks, patting him on the shoulder before walking to the stove and getting out pots and pans like he's lived here his whole life. Hell, maybe he has. How would I know?

Pops grabs another beer for us both, and I accept it on autopilot, still foggy from the cocktail of emotions that have taken over since arriving back in town. It's barely a passing thought that while I'm just finishing my first drink, Pops is about to be on his fourth.

"So, Sarah..." Pops begins. "How'd Eli land a gal like you? He woo you by relivin' the good ol' days when he was king of this town?"

My stomach whips into my throat at his words because I *knew* he would bring this up. It's just like him. He's never been able to help himself from reliving the glory days. Used to be his own, now it's always mine. But there is nothing I want to talk about less than how things *used* to be.

Still, I force out a laugh like his words aren't a heated blade searing old wounds.

I turn my head and lose my breath. Lee is gawking in the doorway to the kitchen. My heart presses against my ribs with every beat, my throat thick with emotion at seeing my baby sister.

She's so damn grown up.

I clear my throat, smiling so wide, I almost convince myself I'm not scared half to death. "Baby sis! About time you got here. Pops and I were about to start in on all of your embarrassing stories."

It's not true. In fact, Pops hasn't brought her up a single time, other than when Chase mentioned her. Something dark and foreboding tingles across the back of my neck, making the hairs stand on end.

Lee jerks out of her frozen state, eyes flicking toward Chase before she sinks into a chair at the head of the table.

"Eli," she breathes. "I thought y'all weren't gettin' here until Friday."

"We decided to come early. Not excited to see me?" I chuckle to hide the confusion of my thoughts. *I thought Pops said he told her.*

"Just surprised is all." She nods toward Sarah. "Big city life make you forget your manners, Eli? You plannin' on makin' any introductions?"

The smile drops off my face, the guilt tossing my stomach

because honestly, I forgot Sarah was even there. Too caught up in my own shit to remember she's the reason I'm here in the first place.

To get married.

And to, hopefully, close this chapter of my life once and for all.

Sarah introduces herself, but I don't listen to what she's saying. I'm too busy trying to take in Lee. Her posture is slumped like there's a heavy weight on her back, and I wonder how long she's been carrying it.

Lee's eyes shift to me. "Speakin' of weddin' details, I'm just gonna give y'all Becca's number so you can call her yourself."

My shoulders stiffen. Her name is a shot of adrenaline, my heart slamming against my insides. I had asked Lee to see if Becca could pull some strings, guarantee the church for us in time for the ceremony. I had hoped if she did it for me, I wouldn't have to face Becca in the flesh. "What? I don't want to do that, why can't you just talk to her for me like I asked you to?"

"For one thing, Eli, I'm not your dang slave. For another, I *did* ask her and she wasn't exactly responsive." Lee's face scrunches, her head cocking to the side. "What happened with you two, anyway?"

My stomach twists and turns, her words knocking against the chained up parts of my soul—the parts I keep shrouded in darkness—trying to set them free.

My hand reaches out, squeezing Sarah's thigh, hoping her presence can anchor me enough to keep me in control. She's always there, silent but steady. Surface level and just what I need.

"Nothing important." My words are sharp, and I feel them all the way to my bones. It's true. No matter how important I *thought* it was, she proved me wrong the second she ran away.

Fuck her.

She's nothing to me now. And if I see her, I'll make sure she knows it.

They say parents aren't supposed to have a favorite, but I've known that was bullshit since the day Alina May Carson was born and I was pushed to the side. I was three at the time, so I don't remember the moment it happened, but the feeling snuck its way inside me and never left. Hard to forget something when you endure it every day.

Pops's eyes would light up at the mere mention of Lee's name, his cheeks growing rosy, and a smile splitting his face while he gushed about his girl. Maybe if I were a better brother—a better man—it would be easier to ignore the bitterness that festers as a result. What I wouldn't have given for Pops to look at *me* that way, just once.

Suffice to say, I'm a bit in shock after witnessing the way their relationship has eroded.

Dinner's long since ended, the dishes soaking in the sink, the smell of freshly brewed coffee in the air. It's strong enough to invade my senses, but not enough to mask the animosity pouring from across the table as my sister penetrates me with her steely glare.

We never had much of a relationship, even as kids. I was

a shit brother, I'll be the first to admit it. The only thing I could see was ball. Every second of my life was commandeered by the love of the game, and the need for Pops's approval.

"You want to go with us tomorrow, Lee? Help me show Sarah the town?" I smile at her, hoping she'll see the olive branch for what it is.

Lee chokes on her coffee, sputtering. "I can't. I have to work."

My heart pinches at her refusal, but I don't show it. Tapping my head, I force a lopsided grin. "Right. It's so strange to see you grown. Sometimes I forget."

"Maybe it wouldn't be so strange if you'd been around for all the years in between." Her smile is wide as she slings her words across the table, and I flinch when they hit.

"Alina. Mind your manners. We got... we got company." Pops's voice is low, his words molasses as they slur off his tongue.

"I'm just speakin' truth, Daddy," Lee huffs.

Irritation darts through my veins. "You don't know what you're talking about, Alina."

"Oh no? Why don't you enlighten me then, big brother?"

"I would have, if you had ever taken the time to ask," I seethe, cringing at the drawl that sneaks in my words.

I'm so *sick* of everyone thinking I'm the one who needs to shoulder the blame. Like I haven't tried every month for years to build a bridge across the distance. Even the strongest bridges collapse with no support.

I'm not the only villain in this story.

Pops points his finger toward Lee. "Your mama. She would be... disappointed in you, girl."

My heart stalls in my chest, Pops's words freezing the air. It's a low blow, and completely uncalled for. Especially since Ma *wouldn't* be disappointed in Lee. She'd be standing right next to her, begging me to come back home, demanding answers for why I didn't.

My anger drains away when I see tears lining Lee's lower lids, darkness swirling in her blue eyes. I recognize the hurt as it reaches out to touch my own.

We both have wounds from the same war, we just hide them in different ways.

Chase jumps from the table, hissing something low enough where I can't hear. I'm not listening anyway. My focus is busy, bouncing between Pops and my sister.

Lee looks down at the table, inhaling deep, while Chase moves in behind her, squeezing her shoulders. He's glaring at Pops like he's the dirt beneath his shoe. Something thick and putrid trickles through my veins as I watch how confident he is facing my father, shutting down his cutting words, and shielding my sister from the impact. I wonder what that's like —not feeling two feet tall under Pops's gaze.

Pops jerks to a stand and teeters, gripping the edge of the table to regain his balance. It happens fast, and I'm halfway out of my chair before my brain knows I've moved. My heart pounds against my chest, the visual of his inebriation filtering through my brain, tugging on thoughts I like to keep hidden.

How much did he have to drink?

"Pops, you okay?"

"Of course he's not fine. He's never fine," Lee snaps. "You would know that if you had spent more than ten minutes here in the past eight years."

I blow out a breath, my hands resting on my hips. *She's so damn dramatic.* "Sis—"

"Don't you 'sis,' me, Eli."

"I'm fine, dammit!" Pops's voice cuts through like a knife. "And I'm a goddamn adult. *I'm* the parent, and this—this is *my* house." He points to Chase and Lee. "You two, go on… get. I don't want you here."

"Pops," I breathe, my eyes wide, and my chest tight.

This situation is spinning out of control, and there's nothing I can do to stop it. I wouldn't even know where to start.

"Fine. I don't need this anyway." Lee's eyes are glossy, but her shoulders straighten and her jaw locks in place as she stands from her seat, facing me. "Have fun catchin' up on your missed years with Daddy. I'm sure he and this town will be thrilled to have you back. Sarah, it was nice to meet you. I'm so sorry you had to see this."

She grabs Chase's hand and they march out of the door.

They don't look back.

He kicked them out.

Regardless of the fact that Chase just spent all night cooking our meal. No matter that Lee's his daughter, and honestly has more right to be here than me.

Guilt prickles against my spine, and I wonder if coming home sooner would have made a difference. If I could have gotten over my shit and taken a second to just *listen*, maybe I'd be standing in something that's only broken, instead of what feels a lot like ruins.

I've spent a lot of time thinking on Lee's selfish ways, but this is the first time I've recognized the trait in myself. It settles heavy in my gut, cutting out a place for itself among the rest of my mangled pieces.

Pops doesn't say another word, just grumbles all the way to his brown recliner in the living room, promptly passing out.

Sarah's sitting next to me, quiet as ever. She hasn't said a word since dinner ended. I'm thankful for her silence, because right now, I don't think I'd care to hear whatever she has to say.

I imagined a lot of things for when I came back. Prepared myself for a hundred different scenarios. My shield, strong and sure, has been ready to combat all the emotions I'm not prepared to feel.

Embarrassment wasn't one of them.

That doesn't stop it from crashing through my defenses and sweeping away any hope that maybe there was something worth fighting for here in Sugarlake.

There isn't.

"I got that girl's number from your sister."

My body locks up tight at Sarah's words, my hand freezing on the open door of the fridge. "What girl?"

"Rebecca."

"Becca." I spin to face her.

Sarah cocks her head. "Huh?"

My heart thuds against my ribcage. "It's uh... it's just Becca. She doesn't like to be called by her full name."

Even as I say the words, I realize they aren't exactly true. Visions of how much she *loved* when the name rolled off my tongue flash behind my eyes. My gut clenches at the thought of her loving when someone else says it, too.

Sarah's nose scrunches. "Okay, then. *Becca.* She got us a meeting with her dad next Tuesday, said it was the best she could do."

I bite my cheek to keep the questions from pouring out. Questions I have no right to ask—ones I know better than to want the answers to. Because I shouldn't be *dying* to know what her tone of voice was as she talked about my wedding to another woman. My heart shouldn't be faltering in my chest, wondering if shards of glass are wedging in the divots of her soul, like they are for me, or if she's completely unaffected.

"You okay there, big guy?" Sarah giggles, waving a hand

in front of my face.

I snap out of my fog, swallowing around the burn of my throat. Wrapping my arms around Sarah's waist, I peck her lips. "I'm fine. Gonna run to the coffee shop and grab us some breakfast. There's not shit to eat in this house. Wanna go with me?"

"Nope. I'm gonna take a shower." She smiles, rubbing the bottom of my lip with her thumb. "Just hurry back. I don't really want to be left alone with your dad."

I glance toward his bedroom, grimacing at the fact it's almost ten a.m., and he hasn't woken up. I wonder briefly if he sleeps in this late every day, or if it's because his drinking got a little out of hand last night. Maybe he just needs the rest.

It's only two blocks to the coffee shop, and it's a perfect June day, so I decide to walk. It's early enough where the sun isn't blistering, and the fresh air will do me good. Clear my head. Hopefully, bring some clarity.

I think about showing Sarah around town, secure in the fact that it's a chance to start fresh. To make new memories here. Ones that don't sting as bad when I'm forced to look back.

Something makes me look up from the pavement as I step off the curb to cross the street, and once I do, I wish I never had.

Because there she is.

Fiery in her aura, and blinding in her beauty. I choke on my inhale, desire racing through my body. I had forgotten how she takes my breath away.

She's walking out of the very coffee shop I'm about to enter, and I'm a statue on the curb. My hand rubs my chest, trying to ease my double-crossing heart back into its natural rhythm. At the rate it's pounding, I'm afraid it might shatter. Like it's prone to do around her.

Becca's head is thrown back in laughter, her crazy curls cascading down her back. My hands tingle from the memory of those strands wrapped around my fist.

I told myself I was prepared for this moment. It's been five years. I've moved on.

But I'm transfixed at the sight of her.

Her hand grasps the arm of the man she's with, and he smiles down at her with a look I know well. A look I've worn a hundred times. One I've only ever felt when gazing at her.

My gut constricts, and I blow out a breath, moving toward the front door of the shop.

Fuck this.

She doesn't get to affect me anymore. Not when it's clear I *never* affected her.

She looks up just as I pass, her crooked smile dropping off her face. I watch from the corner of my eye as she sucks in a breath, hand flying to her chest, right where her heart would be, if she had one.

Her eyes widen, and as much as it fucking hurts to hold her gaze, I don't drop my stare. I couldn't even if I wanted to. Those emerald eyes are a vortex, sucking me in and twisting me up.

It's what she does to me.

It's what she's always done.

"Eli," she breathes.

My steps stutter, body jerking against the need to pause. I resist the pull, clenching my jaw and brushing by her without a word, treating her like the ghost she chose to be. If I try hard enough, maybe I can convince myself I don't really see her.

I walk in the store, ignoring the way my insides simmer and jump, ordering a coffee and a bagel. One for me. And one for Sarah.

When I walk back out the door, Becca's already gone.

But she haunts me, all the same.

BECCA

Dating app John has turned into a semi-regular thing. He's a little vanilla in bed, but he curbs the ache, and he's genuinely a good guy. He's a lawyer over in Chattanooga, so his hours are long and his time is precious.

He fucks with precision. Straight to the point. No forcing me out of my comfort zone or making me relinquish control. He's exactly what I need. Sometimes, the late nights turn into mornings, and I've found I'm okay with letting him stay. The loneliness dulls just a little when he's around.

I'm meeting up with him after leaving here—*here* being Papa's office at the church. Complete with that big, oak desk. The one currently taunting me from its place in the center of the room. It's lavish in its grandeur, much like the rest of the office. We're a small town, but religion is easy to profit from, and when it comes to Sugarlake, Papa's the number one salesman.

He wasn't always. Once upon a time, he believed in the words he preached. But real life doesn't have happy endings. It simply ends. And until it does, we're all floating aimlessly, trying like hell to find a purpose, hoping we outlast our demons in the game of hide and seek.

My own personal demon is currently staring at me, the memories seeping from the wood of this damn desk.

I hate it here.

The only thing worse than being stuck in here is being stuck *and* having to talk to my old man about Eli's marriage to another woman.

Papa's voice filters through the hallway, his boisterous laugh sending a shockwave of longing through my chest. It's been a long time since I've heard it, and the sound makes me want to jump out of my seat, rush into the hallway, and see what has the ability to break through his persona to draw out the man underneath.

I don't have to wonder for long, because in he walks, and behind him is the *true* whore of the town. Sally Sanderson, the youth leader of our church, and the woman who's been fucking my father for years like she has any right.

Bitch.

God, how dare she still work here. Thirteen years later, and she's still around, like a cockroach, infesting everything that used to matter.

I wonder if they're still bumping uglies, or if he's moved onto younger pastures.

Doesn't matter. I hate them both.

A scowl lines my face, stomach churning with disgust as I lean back in the chair and wait for them to acknowledge my presence.

They don't, too lost in each other to even notice I'm here. *Typical.*

I scoff, and Sally turns toward the noise, her dull brown hair swishing behind her.

"Oh! Hi, Rebecca Jean. It's nice to see you. Your daddy

didn't tell me you would be here." Her cheeks dust a light pink, and I want to smack the color off her stupid face.

My teeth grind together, jaw aching from the force. Crossing my arms, I turn my head to the side. She's not worth my attention.

Homewrecker.

Sally clears her throat, shifting on her feet and twisting back to Papa.

"Okay, Don, I'll um… see you later."

He nods, already moving around his desk to sit down, unbuttoning his suit jacket as he does.

Sally closes the door behind her. Papa lets the silence linger just long enough to make it uncomfortable. It's a power play, and one that he's perfected over the years, at least when it comes to me.

"Rebecca. There's no need to be so rude."

I shrug.

He steeples his fingers, resting his elbows on the desk. "What do you need?"

I twist a curl around my finger, ignoring the way my stomach revolts at what I'm about to say. "Lee's brother's gettin' hitched and wants to use the church." I rush through the words like they're on fire. If my dry, swollen throat is any indication, they singed me anyway.

Papa's eyebrow quirks. "He's not out in Florida?"

I sigh. "I don't know, Papa. I guess his *fiancée* wants to have it here." My voice breaks on the word 'fiancée' and I cough, hoping he doesn't notice. "I'm just the messenger."

He leans back, the desk chair creaking like it may collapse any second from his weight.

A metaphor for my fucking life.

Rubbing his chin, his eyes laser in on me. I'm not sure why, after all these years, he's still able to make me finicky, but he does, and I can't help but shift under his stare.

My hands grow clammy and I tuck a strand of hair behind my ear. "Anyway, they want to come check it all out on Tuesday, if that works."

He nods. "Well, make sure you're here for it then."

My heart stops. Actually stops in my chest, and it's a miracle I'm still breathing through the stall.

"What?" I gasp.

"They're your friends, so you can be the one in charge of makin' sure it goes off without a hitch. You need somethin' to do this summer, anyway."

My heart jolts to life, making up for the missed beats with the way it's thumping away in my chest. I think I may pass out. Or have a heart attack. Maybe both. I did *not* sign up for this.

"Papa, in case you forgot. I have a job. I work hard and I think I deserve to enjoy my summer break."

He chuckles. A short, sarcastic laugh that heats the blood in my veins, resentment spiraling through me.

"Idle hands are a devil's playground, Rebecca. This will keep you busy."

The universe is laughing at me. Proving what a cruel bitch it can be, because only a sadistic world would make me pay for my mistakes in such a brutal way. But no matter how bad I want to argue and rage, I don't. I don't remind him that I'm twenty-six and not sixteen. I don't tell him all of the things I *really* want to say. I spent most of my adolescence fighting against this man, and I've learned it's just wasted energy. My life has been prophesied. Written on the coattails of my mother, no matter how much I try to run from it.

I've accepted my fate.

For the rest of the night, all through my dinner date, I convince myself it won't be a big deal. It's been five years since I've even seen Elliot Carson, and if he can move on, then so can I. Maybe we can even be friends.

But still, when John sinks inside me, it's blue eyes and dark, honey-blond hair I see.

The next morning, when John and I stop by the coffee shop for breakfast, I'm feeling lighter than I have in days, content in my acceptance of the hand life has dealt me.

I feel him before I see him.

I pretend I don't, grasping John's arm, forcing a laugh at whatever he's saying. But I couldn't tell you whether it was funny.

There's a pull, and I know that if I give in, the glued together bits of my soul will shatter into a thousand pieces and blow away with the early morning breeze.

Still, I look. I've always been a glutton for punishment.

My heart stammers in my chest.

I knew this moment was coming, I just thought I'd have longer to prepare—build up the bricks to cover my self-inflicted pain, shielding it from his view.

"Eli," I breathe.

His jaw tightens as he holds me in his gaze, but his steps falter, pausing for the slightest moment. And that's all it takes, just one moment. One measly second for hope to explode inside every nerve, my heart bursting at the seams.

But my heart's a fool. Just like the rest of me.

Eli restarts his trek, breaking his gaze and breezing through the door, not giving me a second glance as he walks by.

I guess I can't blame him. Some days, when I'm weak and pathetic, remembering what I left, I want to walk past myself, too.

This is my purgatory.

And helping him marry another woman will be my penance.

35

ELI

It's Friday, the day I was *supposed* to be arriving in this hellhole of a town. Instead, I'm sitting on Pops's couch, wondering why I let Sarah talk me into coming at all. Because now I'm stuck, pretending like every day isn't slowly sucking away the tiny bits of life I've been able to grasp on to over the years.

Sarah seems to be enjoying her time. She's fascinated with the southern twangs and the fact everyone knows my name.

All the things I hate.

She's uncomfortable with Pops, though. He went out with his buddies tonight, so we're taking advantage, having a date night and finally relaxing. Pops hasn't been the most welcoming, and after his callous behavior toward Lee, I can't say I blame Sarah for being on edge when he's here.

Lee.

The thought of my baby sister makes my stomach fold in on itself. I should call her, but I have no clue what the hell to say.

The front door slams open, and I shoot to my feet when I see Lee storming into the room.

"Sis, what are you doing here?"

Her face is murderous—cheeks ruddy and lips turned down in a scowl. She surges forward, and before I can stop her, she's in my face and shoving me back. My legs hit the couch, and I reach an arm behind me to keep from toppling over.

I breathe deep, trying to shake off my anger. "What the hell, Lee?"

"When are you gonna get it, huh?" she hisses through clenched teeth. "I thought you bein' back would make you see. Get you to realize how bad things are, but here you are... sittin' pretty with your girl while Daddy's runnin' around town makin' a fool of himself."

I bristle at her tone, pressing back into her space. "I'm not his babysitter. Pops is a grown man."

"Do you know where we just came from, Eli?" she asks, her nostrils flaring.

Why the hell would I know that?

Sarah chokes in a breath from beside me, her arm tugging on the back of my shirt. I follow her gaze. Pops is standing in the doorway—if you can call being held up around the waist "standing." There's a sheen of sweat on his brow and his clothes are rumpled and skewed, his head lolling on Chase's shoulder.

They move toward the recliner and Chase plops him down. Pops hunches over, mumbling with his eyes closed.

My chest pinches so hard it hurts to breathe.

"What happened?" I manage to rasp.

Lee laughs. "What do you think happened, Eli? The same thing that always happens. If Daddy doesn't have a babysitter, he gets behind the wheel, drunk as a skunk, and ends up at his favorite bar. Only his favorite bar has *banned* him 'cause he always causes a scene."

She's talking to me like *I'm* supposed to be the babysitter, but how the hell was I supposed to know he was banned when she never said a word about it? I'm not a mind reader. "Lee, I didn't know…"

"I've told you a thousand times!" she screams, throwing her arms in the air. "Begged you a hundred more. You don't *listen*, Eli. You don't wanna hear it."

My stomach sinks like a cement block, my eyes bouncing between Lee and Pops. Heat infuses my cheeks at the thought of Pops pulling a fast one on me.

Am I that blind?

He told me he was going out with friends. Sure, he's been drinking, but he hasn't been belligerent. He hasn't seemed like he's needed anyone to *babysit* him.

Pops isn't that man. He never has been. But maybe I've been too lost in my own shit to pay attention. I glance at him again, taking in his features.

I swallow, peeling my dry tongue from the roof of my mouth. "I didn't think it was this bad," I whisper. "Pops said he was meeting up with his buddies. He said you just like to hover, like to control things ever since Ma die—since Ma's been gone."

I can't come to terms with the fact this man before me is the same one I've known all my life. The same one I've looked up to, admired, feared. How am I supposed to correlate the two? I've had years of being trained into thinking Pops's word is law, how can I flip that off like a switch?

If he tells me he's fine, then he's fine.

That's how it's always been.

But this—this doesn't seem *fine*.

Lee throws up her hands like she can't be bothered to try anymore. Like she's screaming into the void, even though she's staring at my face. "The only buddies Daddy has are Jim, Jack, and Johnny. Oh, and the cops that picked him up and booked him tonight."

My heart jolts. "He was *arrested*?"

Lee's eyes shimmer with the tears she won't let fall. "You gotta open your eyes. Daddy ain't the hero you've always seen him as." She presses her fingers to her cheeks. "I just need a minute."

She rushes from the room, and I collapse on the couch, Sarah rubbing my back with the palm of her hand. My head throbs, torn between what I want to believe, and what I know deep down is true.

I glance at Chase. His hands are in his pockets, and he's leaning against the far wall, his jaw locked tight as he stares me down.

Sarah stays quiet but steady in her support, as always.

I rub my temples. "Do you think she's overreacting a little?"

I don't know who I'm even asking. I guess I'm just praying for someone to tell me what I'm seeing isn't real.

Chase springs from his relaxed stance, moving to stand in front of me. "You know, you may not want to hear it, but fuck it." He shrugs. "Ignoring the problem won't make it go away, Eli. It won't make it stop. It'll just continue to spiral out of control, and then one day... one day, you'll wake up and wonder what the hell you were thinking. You'll wonder how you could have been so goddamn blind."

His voice hitches, and he rests a hand on top of his heart, clenching the fabric of his shirt. "Trust me, when that day comes? The regret will rot you from the fucking inside. Because you'll know—you'll *know* that you didn't do everything in your power to save them when you had the chance. You didn't do *anything*." He shakes his head. "I hope to God you wake up before then."

He sighs and storms out of the room, probably chasing after Lee, but his words linger, infusing the air around me.

My eyes jump back to Pops as he snores in his chair, his ghastly frame a whisper of the man who raised me.

My gut swims with unease. But there's nothing I can do about it tonight.

At least he's home.

I haven't eaten breakfast, my stomach is too jumbled to handle the calories. Sarah is *insisting* on going to Sunday service.

Kill me.

She wants to see the church and get a feel for Preacher Sanger. I'm having a hard enough time pretending his name doesn't send me into a blind rage. But I can't tell her that without her prying into *why* I have such a strong dislike for the man, and that's something I don't talk about with anyone.

Talking makes it real. Talking makes me remember. And I've done a damn good job of trying to forget.

I knock on Pops's bedroom door, but I doubt he's awake. He has a tendency to sleep in, and when he *does* wake up, he's a hungover asshole until he gets his coffee. I'm ashamed to say that yesterday was the first time I noticed the Jameson he pours at the bottom of every cup.

Still, I haven't brought it up, because what the hell am I supposed to say? Every time I open my mouth, something crawls up my throat and clamps my tongue. It's not easy talking to the man I've been raised to believe is beyond reproach.

"Pops." I knock again. "We're going to church, wanna go with?"

There's not a whisper of sound from the other side, and I'm not planning to wait, so we leave without him.

The church itself is beautiful, and one of Sugarlake's

historical landmarks. Stained glass lines the white exterior, and the steeple stands tall, casting shadows instead of bathing me in its light.

"Eli, this. Is. Perfect!" Sarah squeals, gripping my arm.

I smile, wishing I felt the joy I'm trying to project. My eyes soar past her to the church's cemetery a hundred yards away. I swear I can feel Ma's spirit calling out to mine. Or maybe it's just my guilt knowing I haven't been to see her grave. My throat swells, pain radiating into my ears when I think about how I wouldn't even know where to look.

"What's wrong?" Sarah asks.

I clear my throat, bringing my attention back to the moment. To Sarah. To a future I never asked for, but one that Ma did.

Marry in the church. A nice girl. A stable future. Take care of that lonely heart.

"Nothing's wrong. Being here just brings back a lot of memories."

"I bet."

I bring her into my side, and she presses kisses to my cheek, my insides humming from her warmth. It's nice, and I'm reminded of why I started wanting her around me in the first place. She brings me comfort.

But the comfort doesn't last.

A flash of red catches my eye and my heart gallops against my ribs, my body catching fire.

Becca's standing in the arched entry, staring at me, and once again, I can't fucking look away. Not even when another woman has her lips on my skin.

Why the hell can't I look away?

I clench my jaw, forcing myself to close my eyes, sick of this twisted feeling she's always given me. One that I'm ready to give back.

I don't want it anymore.

When I open my eyes, she's gone.

Sarah and I make our way inside, sitting in the back while Preacher Sanger drones on about spiritual growth through your service to God. Sarah's enraptured by the fraud, but I'm bored, my eyes wandering until I find Becca, her aura a beacon that draws me in, even though my heart is blaring a warning to stay the hell away.

It makes fury simmer in my veins, hatred for everything she's put me through filling me up until I'm choking on its filth.

The service ends, and I'm beyond ready to leave, but before we get to the exit, I see Becca standing next to her folks, saying goodbye to the congregation.

My rage boils hotter.

What a good little preacher's girl.

"Ah, the talk of the town." Preacher Sanger pats me on the back with an extra wide, bright smile lining his face.

The urge to strangle it off him is strong.

"This the lucky lady?"

I clear my throat. "It is. This is Sarah Whitson, my fiancée."

Becca's shoulders stiffen, and it takes everything in me not to give her my attention.

Sarah scoots in close, her arm linking mine, her other reaching out to shake Preacher Sanger's hand. "Soon to be Sarah Carson. Pleasure to meet you."

"Pleasure's all mine, Miss Whitson. I hear you're havin' your ceremony here. No better place to do it."

My eyes bounce to Mrs. Sanger. It's just like him to not even introduce her. It's even more like her to stand silently like the dutiful, obedient wife she is. My stomach rolls when my eyes gloss over Becca and realize she's doing the exact same thing.

Pathetic.

Sarah smiles. "Yes! We can't wait to meet with you on Tuesday."

Preacher Sanger chuckles. "You'll be meetin' with my daughter, Rebecca. She'll be the one handlin' anything you need."

An invisible fist slams into my gut, my breath racing out from the blow.

"Oh!" Sarah gasps. "*You're* Becca! We talked on the phone the other day, I'm so pleased to meet you. Thank you for setting all this up."

My heart pounds so hard it makes me dizzy. Becca's eyes glance at me before locking on to my fiancée, a beautiful smile gracing her perfect, freckled face.

"We've actually met. But it was a long time ago, back when I was at FCU... and only for a second."

Like a magnet, her eyes slide to meet mine again, only now, she doesn't look away. And just like every other time, neither do I.

She twists a curl through her fingers. "Anyway, I'll do my best to make sure your day is perfect. You deserve the best, and I'm happy to help you get it."

My nostrils flare against the sudden burn in my chest.

Becca dips her head, breaking our connection. "If you'll excuse me."

My stomach flips, hoping no one noticed the tension in the air.

Still, when I watch as she walks out the front door and down the steps, every fiber of my being wants to follow. Less than five minutes in her presence and my body craves her.

My mangled soul reminds me of the price.

So, I turn my attention from the woman who stole away my first chance at love, and to the man who will marry me to my second.

It's what Ma would have wanted.

36

BECCA

J ax has been back from California a little over a week. I haven't had an opportunity to pick his brain on everything Chase and Lee, so when he asked to meet for lunch, I jumped on the chance. Besides, I've been in a funk ever since Eli came back to town, and Jax is the perfect person to have around when you need to feel lighter.

I dip a fry in my ketchup and pop it in my mouth, smirking when I see the group of women peeking glances from the corner booth. "Your fan club is gettin' antsy."

Jax turns toward them and winks, dazzling them with his perfect smile.

I scoff.

"What?" He grins, tucking a strand of his shaggy, blond hair behind his ear.

"It's just disgustin' how easy it is for you."

"Don't be mad at this." His hand floats down the length of his body. "I can't help that the ladies like what they see. I don't wanna be rude."

He's cocky, but I can't really blame him. Jax might be the most beautiful specimen that's ever graced my eyeballs.

Similar to a Monet or Picasso, he's a masterpiece of art you're afraid to touch. Maybe that's why he's one of the only guys I didn't hook up with when I was in high school.

He snaps the hairband on his wrist, his green eyes dimming as he smirks across the table. We're similar souls, Jax and I, opting for meaningless hookups instead of grabbing hold of something real. The difference is I don't want to grasp mine, and his is out of reach.

I take a sip of my sweet tea, resting my elbows on the table. "So, how are you doin' with everything? Really?"

Sighing, he leans back, throwing his hair into a bun.

His knuckles tap the tabletop. "Did you know she was back with him?"

He's talking about Lee and Chase, of course. They're officially back together, and I know he's struggling with the news. Lee's the girl he's hopelessly in love with, and Chase is the man who broke both their hearts. I guess it's easier for some to forgive than others because I don't think Jax will ever let Chase back into his life.

I nod. "Not until after you did, I'm sure."

It's weird, but I feel closer to him in this moment than I ever have in the past. Maybe it's because for the first time, I see the torment he hides behind his carefree gaze. Or maybe it's my soul recognizing a kindred spirit, both of us left with nothing while the people we want give their everything to someone else.

I take one of the straws from the table and rip off the paper, putting an end to my mouth and blowing. The wrapper flies into his face.

He bats it away, chuckling, and I grin wide, some of the gloom slipping away with our laughter.

I point at him, squinting my eyes. "Chipper up, buttercup. You've got plenty of ladies waitin' for you out in Sunny California."

"Naw, not too much in Cali. Too busy kissing my boss's ass to find time to kiss any that are more to my liking." He shakes his head. "Hollywood producers are a different breed of asshole."

Jax works on movie sets, but even though he has movie-star looks, he's no actor. He's got a gift—always tinkering beneath the hood of something worn, and turning it into beauty. When he first moved to Sugarlake twelve years ago with his momma, he nabbed a job at the mechanics shop on the weekends. Over the years, his restorations gained notoriety, and California sets came calling. Now he's the go-to guy for the cars they use in blockbusters.

"When are you headin' back?" I ask.

"Next week. I'm staying in town until Sam's retirement party."

I grimace at the thought of that damn party. Sam's the owner of Sugarlake construction, and a beloved member of this community. He's done a lot for Sugarlake, so now that he's retiring, he's going out with a bang.

The thought of being stuck in a building with the whole town sounds like the worst kind of hell, but I wouldn't miss it. Sam is Chase's dad, and Lee would kill me if I wasn't there.

"I'm actually thinking of moving out there full time." Jax's eyebrows are raised, like he surprised himself by saying it.

I gasp. "What? To California? Does Lee know?"

He slides his fork through the leftover mayonnaise on his plate, shaking his head.

My chest pulls tight. "Are you movin' out there *because* of her?"

The muscle in his jaw jumps, his cheeks puffing with his breath of air. "No offense, Becs, but I'm not gonna talk about that with you when I haven't even told her."

"Fair enough." I sigh, imagining what her reaction will be. She'll blame herself, I'm sure. "Lee's gonna lose her shit."

He shrugs. "She has Chase now. And you."

My lips purse. I've been friends with Jax for a decade, and this is the first time he's seemed so beaten down. Moving away from this place will be good for him. My heart aches when I think of him leaving, but I can't ignore the gusts of jealousy that whip across my insides knowing he's freeing himself from his chains.

I stick out my bottom lip. "Wanna take me with you?"

He smiles. "You can always come with, Becs."

I huff. "I was jokin'. What would I do out in Cali? Cater to your every wish? Pass."

"You're right." He nods, rocking on the back two legs of his chair. "Better to stay here and cater to your father's."

I've never spoken about my family issues with Jax. That's not the type of friendship we have. The fact that it's so obvious—even to him—slams into me with the force of a battering ram.

I deflect his statement, throwing my balled-up napkin at him and scowling.

He bats it away, dropping the legs of his chair and leaning forward on the table. "Seriously, if you want to get away, Cali's always waiting for you. If you're ever like me and just… need to get some space from this place."

His swallow is thick, and he's fingering the chain around his neck.

My heart hurts for what I know he's feeling. Hell, I've only had to endure Eli being with someone else for five seconds, and I'm fixing to lose my mind. I can't imagine the wear and tear that's been taking place on Jax's soul for *years*.

He's never faltered in his love for Lee. Never pushed her for more or weakened in his support. He's just been there, molding himself into whatever she needs, allowing her to lean on him even when the weight is hard to bear.

"Jackson Rhoades, I think you're a much better human than me."

He cocks his head, the left side of his mouth quirking. "You just now figuring that out?"

I groan, throwing my head back. "God, your ego knows no bounds."

He laughs. "Becs, you're one of the best humans I know." He covers my hand with his. "And trust me, I know a lot."

"Yeah." I shrug.

"Okay, that's it. What's got you all twisted up? Is it John, 'The Becca Tamer?'"

I roll my eyes at the stupid nickname. I made the mistake of telling him and Lee during brunch that I was going on a date, and even though I'm not planning on seeing him again, neither one of them have let the idea go since. Probably because he's the first man they've seen me date. Ever.

"Honey, you should know by now I can't be tamed." I force a grin.

"That's right, baby. Don't you forget it." He taps the top of my hand with his finger. "I don't like seeing the Queen of the Jungle being kept in a cage."

My heart thunks at his words.

"I'm serious, Becs. If you want to come to Cali for a while, you're more than welcome to stay. You could take over babysitting duties for me." His hands come together in prayer.

I snort. "Is *that* what you've been doin' out there all this time? Here I was, thinkin' you were makin' it big."

"I'm a man of many traits." He smirks. "Really, it's just my boss's daughter. The kid never leaves me the hell alone. She's annoying as hell... bratty. Kind of like someone else I know." His eyes sparkle.

My eyes grow wide and I throw a hand to my heart. "Wow. She sounds *terrible*. Bratty *and* annoyin'? How will you survive?"

He doesn't smile, just shakes his head, running a hand over the top of his head. "That's the million-dollar question."

"I don't have the kind of money to come out there."

It's a weak excuse, one I'm using so I don't have to face the truth.

Just like Momma.

His brows jerk up. "There was a time you wouldn't have cared."

"Well, things change."

He hums, rubbing the scruff on his jaw. "And some things never do."

Pulling into the church parking lot, I take a deep breath. It's time to face what I've been dreading all weekend.

My meeting with Eli and his fiancée.

I have no idea what to expect. I know next to nothing about weddings, and even less about helping to plan one in our church. I'm not sure why Papa decided I'd be the best choice for this, but regardless, I'm going to put my personal feelings aside and try to give Eli the best damn wedding he can dream of.

Even if it *is* to the girl I've always known would come between us.

The moment I saw them on Sunday, embracing outside of the church, it clicked. I've seen the back of that head before— on national television while she hugged on *my* man.

Just friends, my ass.

A lick of anger flickers, but I tamp it down, knowing it has no right.

Walking into my old man's office, I'm surprised to see Papa sitting behind his desk, Eli and Sarah on the other side.

"Rebecca, you're late," Papa says.

Irritation grips my insides, making my jaw tense.

"Actually, Papa, I'm five minutes early." I smile wide.

Eli scoffs.

I spin toward him, my annoyance lasering in on a target. "Somethin' funny, big head?"

The nickname hurls out of me before I can catch it, my stomach jumping to my throat.

Eli stiffens, his eyes narrowing as they burn a hole through me. "You've never understood the importance of being punctual."

That tamped down anger flares, sizzling off my skin. "And *you* never understood the importance of not bein' a dick."

His eyes flash, sparking a fire in my stomach as I hold his gaze.

"Rebecca. That's enough," Papa chastises.

My cheeks heat as I snap back to myself. I had forgotten where we were. Who we were with. *Why we're here.*

Papa smiles. "I apologize for my daughter's behavior. Seems her momma didn't make those manners stick."

Sarah giggles, and my head snaps to her at the same time as Eli's. I'm sure I imagine the way his eyes narrow. Papa preens at her attention, his grin growing, and I brace myself for the hits I know he's about to rain down.

He holds eye contact with Sarah, but throws his jabs my way. "Must be all those high schoolers she's around all day long."

I roll my eyes. "Papa, you make it sound like I'm still a student and not the faculty."

"Oh, believe me, Rebecca Jean. I'm all too aware of your standin' in this town."

His words drill into the pit of my stomach, the shame of how this town sees me—how my *family* sees me—careening off my insides and blossoming on my cheeks.

My gaze drops, curls shadowing my face.

"Preacher Sanger." Eli's gripping his chair so tight his knuckles are white. My spirit soars, thinking he's about to put Papa in his place—that someone's going to defend me for once.

"I don't think this is a conversation to have in polite company. Do you need us to give you a few minutes?"

And just like that, my heart crashes, landing on its other broken pieces.

Of course he isn't defending me. *Why would he?*

I'm a stupid girl with stupid expectations.

"No, no." Papa waves him off. "I'm actually headin' out. I have a meetin' to get to."

On cue, there's a knock at the door.

Sally *fucking* Sanderson pops her head in. "Don, are you... Oh, I'm sorry to interrupt."

The irritation in my veins ratchets higher, threatening to explode out of me at any second.

A brash laugh bubbles out before I can stop it. "Have fun in your 'meetin'.' Hope it doesn't run late, so you can still make it home to your *wife*."

Something dark glimmers in Papa's eyes, but he simply jerks his head, and waltzes out of the room, his hand resting on the small of Sally's back.

The sound of the door clicking shut echoes off the tension in the air.

So much for professionalism.

I inhale a deep breath, trying to find my center, but it's too late. The scabs from my past have been picked open and left to bleed, and now they're impossible to ignore.

"So." I clap my hands, pasting a smile on my face. "Let's

talk weddin's. As you can see" —I wave my hand toward the door Papa just left— "marriage is somethin' to *celebrate*. Relationships last forever, even when you don't want them to. Let's get y'all hitched, shall we?"

I'm bitter and I know it, but screw this whole thing. This entire situation is a gigantic flashing sign, reminding me that *this* is the reason I left Eli all those years ago.

Because one day, he'd be having meetings with his mistress while I pine away, living in our memories. That fact is staring me directly in the face, in the form of a strawberry-blonde, prim and proper angel, wearing his ring and sitting by his side.

The one he works with.

Just like Papa.

I stand up straighter, a renewed determination spreading through my chest.

I did the right thing.

Small moments of happiness aren't worth a lifetime of misery. I won't forget that again.

"**R**elationships last forever."
"Not all relationships," I snark at Becca, unable to help the jab after what she just said.

Sarah cocks her head. "Honey, that's depressing. Why would you even say that?"

I grab her hand, kissing the back and placing it on my knee.

Forever.

The realization hits me like a freight train that once I marry Sarah, there is no going back. It will be us, every day of *forever*. It doesn't fill me with excitement. Not the way it should.

I care about her, though. She's been exactly what I've needed the past few years, and the type of woman Ma would have wanted for me. But for the first time, I feel selfish in asking her to be my wife.

Regardless, I wasn't talking about the relationship I have with *Sarah*. My words weren't meant for her.

Becca swallows and turns her face to the side, biting on her lips, I'm sure to keep that infuriating mouth of hers in check. Annoyance pricks my insides that I'm not getting the reaction I want.

She walks toward her father's desk, stepping behind it, her hands hovering over the top. Shaking her head, she glances up. Her eyes are swimming in something vulnerable —a way I've only seen one other time—the day we skipped our lesson after the phone call with her mom.

Just like then, I want to sweep away her sadness.

And *that* pisses me off more than her mouth ever has.

"Can y'all..." She clears her throat. "Do y'all mind if we move this to a different area?" She glances at the desk again and grimaces, stepping further away.

My eyes narrow, trying to figure out what her problem is.

Sarah smiles, jumping from her seat. "Lead the way."

She links their arms and Becca stiffens, her eyes growing round as she glances back at me, and then down at their criss-crossed elbows. I smirk, pleased with how uncomfortable she seems at Sarah's friendliness.

We walk to a conference room off the hall and settle in at one of the round tables in the corner.

"So, what are y'all thinkin'?" Becca tucks a strand of hair behind her ear, flipping open a notebook and picking up her pen.

I stay quiet because I'm not thinking *anything* other than getting this fiasco over with, and going back to Florida. I'm ready to start the next phase of my life. One that does *not* include anything here in Sugarlake. The only thing I'm taking with me is the memory of Ma, and knowing I'm giving her what she wants. I don't need any other reminders of this town.

Sarah sighs, patting my knee with her hand. "To be honest, I don't really have any clue, other than I want it here and I want it in a couple months."

Becca's pen stutters on the paper. She peers at me through

her lashes before angling her head back down. "A couple months?"

I bite the inside of my cheek to distract from the sting in my chest.

"Yeah, didn't I tell you that on the phone? We want to have the wedding in August. I want to start the next school year as Mrs. Elliot Carson." Sarah beams, her eyes tender as they meet mine.

I hold her gaze, but I feel the burn of Becca's stare. My hands grow clammy, and I shift in my chair.

Becca twirls a strand of hair around her fingers, the line between her brows creasing. "Oh, I must have missed that part. I thought y'all were just in town to scout the area."

Irritation spikes through my veins. We don't owe her any explanation for how we're doing things.

"Nope," I interject. "More of a wham, bam, thank you ma'am kind of thing. Being here once is more than enough. Too much, really. I'm surprised you don't agree."

Sarah's elbow nudges my side, and I lift my shoulders, my brows rising. "What? I'm just saying."

Becca's eyes laser into me. "Who says I don't agree?"

I huff out a laugh. "You tell me. You're the one living here."

"You don't have to love a place to live there."

"True." I rub my chin. "If you loved it, you'd probably leave."

Sarah's hand clamps down on my knee, and I jerk from the pressure, glancing at her. Her face is frozen in a pinched smile, her gaze full of questions. I don't bother pacifying her, my eyes already drawn back to Becca, needing to see her reaction.

Becca's nostrils flare, the fire I used to love about her raging on her cheeks.

Butterflies erupt in my stomach, the energy building until it spreads to my chest.

Becca's eyes become slits. "Mighty presumptuous of you to think you know anything about what I love."

Sarah laughs, her hand finally easing off my knee. "Jeez, you two fight like siblings."

My gut jolts from her words.

"Yeah, well that's what happens when you grow up with someone whose main purpose in life is to drive you insane." Becca smiles sweetly.

"Please." I scoff. "You weren't even a thought back then. Maybe if I *had* given you some attention, you wouldn't have a father who sees you as the town bicycle."

My heartache spews like vitriolic acid, hoping to eat away her cold exterior and show me the woman underneath. I *ache* to see her—to know if she still exists. To find out if she ever really did.

"Eli," Sarah gasps.

Becca's smile drops, her body hunching like my words are a physical blow against her chest.

The sour taste of what I said sits in the back of my throat, making me feel like I might puke. I suck my teeth to keep from apologizing.

This is why I need to leave here as soon as possible. She makes me lose complete control, and I don't want this shit in my life—all of these emotions I have no use for.

Becca clears her throat, blinking rapidly to stem the tears teasing the corner of her eyes. "Well, we all have our place in this town, I guess." She lifts a shoulder. "I'm the town bicycle, and you're the disgraced hero, too ashamed to show his face, even to the ghost of his momma."

The chasm in my chest widens, rupturing my heart, and leaving a throbbing pain in its absence.

Bitch.

Shame ignites my veins for the way I am. For the fear that keeps me from things I know I need to face. For the *failure* of not being the man I was raised to be.

The air grows thick, Becca's words mixing with my fucked-up emotions and sticking to my skin. How is it the girl who should mean nothing is the one to see through to my core, when the one I've promised my forever to hasn't even peeled a layer?

Sarah laughs, a light tinkling noise. "Well, this is awkward. I feel like putting you guys in time out or telling you to kiss and make up."

My stomach leaps at her words, my eyes searing into Becca's.

She looks away, focusing on Sarah, her eyes softening. "I'm sorry, Sarah. I'm bein' so unprofessional and it's not what you deserve. I really do want to give y'all a good cere- mony, even if your choice in husband is questionable, at best."

My muscles tense. "Nice. *Super* professional."

Sarah grabs my hand, linking our fingers. "To know him is to love him. You know, Becca... we were hoping you could be convinced to help with everything, not just the ceremony."

My stomach drops, my face flying to Sarah's. "We were?"

Her smile tightens as she peers at me. "Yep."

Becca's shaking her head, her eyes wide. "Oh, no I... I really don't know the first thing about weddin's."

"Oh, nonsense." Sarah waves her off. "I don't need you to know about weddings. As long as you know the town and where to go to get what we need. Please say you'll help. We'll pay you, of course."

I look at my lap to hide the way my teeth grind. I had no idea Sarah was planning this. There's no way I want Becca spending more time than necessary with my fiancée, plan- ning my wedding.

"How much?" Becca asks.

I snap my head up. *The hell?* My gut squeezes, shocked that she's actually considering this.

"However much you want." Sarah smiles. "You'd really be doing us a favor."

Becca's eyes are calculating, bouncing back and forth between us as she twists her curls in her fingers. She blows out a breath, nodding. "Yeah. Okay, I'll do it."

My heart catapults from my chest.

She never really cared, and that fact is more than obvious. Because even after all this time, after everything she's done, I could *never* stand by and watch her marry someone else. And I sure as shit wouldn't help make it happen.

My phone vibrates in my pocket, sending a tingle down my leg. I pull it out, planning to silence the call, but the number is one I recognize.

It's one I dialed this morning.

"Excuse me, ladies. I have to take this."

Becca doesn't even acknowledge me. Sarah gives me a weird look, but I'll explain it to her later, right after she tells me what the hell she's thinking, hiring Becca as our wedding planner.

I leave the room, walking down the hallway and pushing through the front doors.

Taking a deep breath, my heart ramming against my chest cavity, I answer.

"Hello?"

"Hi, is this Elliot Carson?"

My stomach clenches, my foot tapping against the cement. "Yep. This is he."

"Hi, Elliot. This is Mark, from Stepping Stones Rehabilitation Center. I'm returning your call from this morning. You're looking for some information?"

I sit on the front steps of the church, leg bouncing, and my heart thumping in time to my jitters. The sun beats down like a warning—do *not* pussy out of this call.

"Yeah." I blow out a breath. "I'm calling about my father. He uh…" I swipe my hand through my locks, tugging on the roots, searching for what to say.

How can I verbalize something I'm still attempting to understand?

"He drinks a lot. He's… not himself anymore." My teeth clench, a ball of anxiety lodging itself in my gut. "I don't even know why I called, I doubt he'll even go willingly, but—" The words stick in my throat. I grip the phone tighter. "He needs help. *I* need help. I don't… I don't know what to do."

My limbs feel shaky, fear trickling through my heart, afraid that this man, Mark, will brush me off. Terrified of a stranger telling me I'm on my own. That I'm overreacting.

That ball of anxiety breaks free, ricocheting against my insides, leaving holes from where it hits. Mark's voice is in my ear, but I don't hear his words, my mind bogged down by my sudden realization.

I've been ignoring Lee's pleas for years when she's been on the other end of the line, probably feeling terrified of me rejecting what she says. Every time.

Holy shit.

I *am* the villain in this story.

Turns out, Pops is human, prone to making mistakes just like the rest of us. He's not the man who raised me, and coming home has shattered any illusion I had left. The shame that's kept me away for years, the absolute terror of seeing the disappointment in his eyes—it's all a moot point.

There's nothing in his gaze except the fog of whiskey, and the shadow of Ma's absence.

I have no clue how to handle him. But I know my sister shouldn't have to. Not alone. Not anymore.

I pray I'm not too late.

"Are you there?" Mark's voice brings me back to the moment.

"Yeah, yes. I'm sorry, I just…" My stomach rolls.

He sighs. "Listen, Elliot. I know this is hard. The first step always is. But you're calling. You're *doing* it. You're taking that first step, and all we can do is hope your father does the same. You can't force someone to change if they aren't ready. The decision is always theirs."

My forehead drops to my hand, and I nod against my palm.

The decision is theirs.

I'm not very hopeful. It took me years to see the truth, and if I'm *still* struggling to face it, then I'm doubtful Pops ever will. After all, I modeled my stubbornness from him. A watered-down replica of the traits that live in his flaws.

It's hard to admit things about the people you love, the ones you've spent your entire life revering. Feels a lot like betrayal to the man who raised me.

It's even harder to admit things about yourself.

I've ignored a lot in my life—a master of avoidance. It's not a badge I wear with honor, but it's one I wear all the same. Coming home has loosened the stitching, warping the edges and letting them dangle off my soul. Maybe it's time to rip it clean off.

Pops is an alcoholic.

It's obvious in the pallor of his skin, and his liquor-soaked breath. Plain as day in Lee's shoulders as they slump under the weight of his addiction. It screams from the slur in his speech, and the defeat that pours from Lee's gaze.

Still, none of that is what made me open my eyes.

It was the look in Chase's stare as he pleaded with me to just fucking *see* before it was too late. I don't know what Chase went through, but I know what it looks like when regret lives inside you, and his was spilling on the floor with every word he spoke. He doused me in the icy water of truth, and woke me the hell up.

Now I'll never sleep again.

There's no hiding the handles of Jameson clinking in the trash after being emptied through the day—snuck into Pops's coffee cups and his Dr. Peppers. No ignoring the boxes of beer, broken down by the back door, slid behind the garbage can to keep out of sight.

I have no clue how he's kept it from the town for as long as he has. I will never be able to make up for the past. There's no magic button to reset all the ways I've failed the people around me, all the ways I've failed myself.

But I can keep from regretting my future.

I give Mark my email and hang up the phone, knowing I won't go back inside. I can't handle Becca, knowing she'll see the pain that's rubbed raw and exposed.

Instead, I study the church cemetery across the lot. My vision blurs the longer I stare, queasiness stirring in my stomach when I think about Ma's grave. I've only seen it once —the day she was buried—mounds of dirt coating my soul as it was shoveled on top of her remains. I remember the feel as it soaked into my skin, infusing every pore with grime that even the strongest soap can't wash away.

But more than that, I remember the feeling of complete and utter isolation in a sea of family and friends.

Lee had Jax and Becca. Pops had Sam. But I was just *there*, falling, with no one to catch me, dropping in the six-foot grave that was meant for Ma. I've laid there ever since, searching for a helping hand.

There was a time I reached for Becca's. Thought she'd be the one to help me climb. But she only pushed me further down, embedding my soles so deep, no one else could ever dig me up.

I'm tired of letting the past fester and rot in the deepest parts of me.

Tired of being afraid.

It's time to find my own way out.

It's after dinner when I decide to talk to Sarah. Shouldn't I be able to share the roughest parts of me with the woman I'm spending the rest of my life with?

Shouldn't she want to know?

She's sitting on the bed, fresh out of the shower, rubbing lotion on her legs.

I've just changed into basketball shorts and a white tank, and I'm gripping the edge of the dresser, watching her in the mirror.

"I think I'm gonna visit Ma tomorrow," I blurt.

"Hmm." She hums, rubbing the lotion on her skin.

I wait to see if she's going to say more. Maybe offer some support, and recognize that I'm vibrating from the effort to stay in one piece.

She doesn't.

I spin, the lip of the dresser biting into my skin as I rest against it. "Yeah. I haven't seen her grave since she's been buried there. I'm a little nervous, to be honest."

She stops, putting the lotion to the side and peering at me. "Why would you be nervous?"

Maybe her words are normal, but they feel like a thousand knives aimed directly at my chest. What does she mean *why* would I be nervous? I may not have opened up to her much, reveling in the surface level she provides, but isn't it obvious?

"I haven't been to see her since she's died." I repeat the words slowly, raising my eyebrows.

She smiles and lifts her shoulders. "You're here now. Better late than never."

Is she being obtuse on purpose?

Maybe she thinks she's helping, but she's not. She's just hammering home the fact that even though we're right next to each other, there's a rift that stretches wide, and maybe there isn't enough between us to fill it.

"Right." I sigh, shaking my head. "You're right. It's not even a big deal."

She grins, tilting her head. "Can I come with?"

"No." My response is sharp and swift.

She winces. "Oh, okay. That's fine, I ju—"

I grimace, swallowing the bitter pill of realizing she just doesn't get it.

I inhale deep, searching for some grace. "I'm sorry, it's... I need to do this alone. You understand, right?"

She bites her cheek and nods, but I see the tremble in her lips. I wish she would say what she wants to say, instead of keeping things so calm.

I've always been content in the fact we never fight. We've never had to douse the flames of a blaze we can't control.

Sarah's always been my Novocain, and I've bathed in the numb she provides.

But even the strongest drug wears off.

And I crave a hint of fire.

39

BECCA

"**Y**our brother is an asshole!" I burst into Lee's studio apartment, ripping the wine glass from her outstretched hand.

"I take it things didn't go well?" She smirks, sipping from her own glass.

"No. Things did not *go well*. Your brother is literally the worst person I've ever had the displeasure of knowin'." I guzzle my wine, rage heating my veins at the thought of Eli. The way he dug under my skin and scraped at my wounds, making them bleed.

Asshole.

"I mean, how did you survive growin' up with someone who's so... so... "

"Particular?" Lee suggests.

"Insane! Ugh!" I drain the last of my drink, knowing that I should be savoring instead of chugging, but I can't help myself. Eli is the actual worst. An arrogant, 'hit you while you're down' kind of man, who took all my tender spots and ripped them open, leaving me to suffocate in the hurt.

Literally. He just *left* like he couldn't be bothered to clean up his own mess. Like he expected his perfect, polished, future wife to do it.

The worst part is I actually like Sarah. She's so damn sweet she gives you a toothache, and that pisses me off even more. I *wish* I could hate her.

"You shouldn't let him get to you, Becca. He's doin' it on purpose. He loves gettin' a rise outta people."

"He'll get a rise out of my foot when I shove it up his ass." I reach for the bottle of wine, needing the red liquid to help drown out my memories.

Lee giggles. "Y'all have always been like oil and water. Remember how ticked he used to make you as a kid?"

Her words do nothing except fan the flames of my ire. I'm so damn angry at him for stirring up emotion I've worked for years to tamp down. I'm hurt at the things he said, and what I said back. The crater in my stomach threatens to swallow me whole at the sadness I see reflected in his eyes. Sadness that *I* caused. Sadness that turns him into a mean, vicious man.

I made the right choice.

That fact is more than obvious after this meeting today. How could I have ever thought we were compatible? Lee's right. We're oil and water. We don't mix.

My chest pulls tight at the thought. "Well, I don't know how Sarah puts up with him. I could *never*. Really, there's no way I could ever marry that man, let alone live with him. It woulda been a terrible decision."

The buzz from the wine filters through my bloodstream, my body humming with a fuzzy warmth. I sigh in relief, the throb in my heart finally dying down.

"Come again?" Lee's staring at me slack-jawed.

"Huh?" I yawn, suddenly exhausted from the drama of the day.

I can't believe I agreed to plan his weddin'.

But maybe this chunk of money will help me cut ties with

Papa once and for all. I can take Jax up on his offer and get out of this hellhole. How ironic it's Eli's marriage to another woman that ends up being my Hail Mary.

Lee's head is cocked, her brows pulled in. "You said it *would* have been a terrible decision. What exactly are you referrin' to in that statement? The marriage part, or the livin' together part?"

My heart stutters in my chest, my stomach free falling like I'm on a rollercoaster.

I straighten off the couch. "I didn't say that. You misheard me."

Shit. Shit. Shit.

"What'd you say, then?" Her gaze is locked on to mine, and I'm afraid to move. Scared that if I do *anything*, she'll see the truth. I can't believe I let my guard down and let that slip.

"Hmm?" I take another gulp of my wine. "Hey, how was your trip with Chase?"

Lee shakes her head. "Nope. Nope. No way. You don't get to change the subject like that, Becca."

I groan, throwing my head back. *Why can't she just drop it?* "I don't wanna talk about Eli anymore."

She throws up her hands. "That's the whole reason you came over!"

"Well, I just needed to vent. I did and now I'm done." My curls twist through my fingers, my stomach somersaulting to the beat of my heart.

"You know, you and Eli are really startin' to tick me off. I don't appreciate bein' the in-between for you two when neither of you will tell me what's goin' on."

Everything in me screams to just say it—push the words from the tip of my tongue, and let them settle in the space between us. But I can't. I'm terrified of losing her.

To this day, Jeremy tries to convince me to tell her, but I just can't risk it.

He wasn't here to witness the fallout when our best friend, Lily, found out about Chase and Lee.

Lily was already a mess, chasing a high none of us could provide, but realizing her big brother and her best friend fell in love behind her back? That was the push that launched her off the edge. I loved Lily, but my loyalty to Lee runs strong and true, so when she dropped Lee, I dropped her. And then she abandoned all of us when she ran away, never to be heard from again.

The absence of Lily hurts, but it's nothing compared to what it will feel like if I lose Lee.

She's been fragile as hell for eight years, and I will *not* be responsible for throwing her off that carefully balanced ledge.

Lee sits next to me, grabbing my hand. "You can tell me, you know? You're my best friend Becca. Nothin' will ever change that. Just *please*, tell me what's goin' on."

Guilt slides up my stomach and wraps around my chest, squeezing until my lungs constrict.

"Nothin' is goin' on, Lee," I whisper.

Omission is not a lie.

I wake up on Lee's couch to the smell of fresh brewed coffee and a note on my chest.

Hey Lush,
I love you, but some of us have to get up and go to work. You sleep like the dead. And don't think I forgot about our talk last night.
There's coffee, but if you eat the last of my Lucky Charms, I will end you, sister.
Xx
-Lee

I smile, crumpling the paper and stretching out my sore muscles. Her couch is super uncomfortable, and I'm a bit hungover from the wine I guzzled. I trudge my way into Lee's kitchen, grabbing one of her to-go mugs and pouring myself a hot cup of coffee. Glancing at the clock, I realize I barely have time to run home for a quick shower before I'm supposed to meet Sarah at the florist.

Something sinks in my stomach.

There's not much I want to do *less* than be the helping hand for Eli's marriage to another woman. But the money to leave town is a temptation I can't refuse.

Betsy's Secret Garden is the only floral shop in town, but Betsy's got the best green thumb in all of Tennessee. Too bad she can't tend to her idiot son, Jason, the way she does to her flowers.

Walking in the front door of the shop, I send up a quick prayer that Jason isn't here. We used to fool around in high school, but when he wanted to get serious, I cut him loose. He's never forgiven me, making it his personal mission to antagonize me, and every time I see him it's a little slice of hell.

The smell of fresh cut flowers tingles my nose as I walk by the register. Sarah's perusing a binder on the counter, and Eli's standing behind her, looking like he owns the whole damn town.

"You just gonna walk on by and ignore me like that, Rebecca Jean?"

I cringe, Jason's voice grating my eardrums. *Damn.* Just my luck he'd be here—icing on the cake to this already fucked-up situation. Eli straightens, his eyes hardening as he looks behind me. Sarah pops her head up, catching my gaze and offering me a small smile.

Sighing, I spin around. "Hiya, Jason. I honestly didn't even realize you were standin' there. How's the wife?"

He taps his short, stubby fingers on the Formica countertop. "Oh, she's just fine. You know how Amy is, happy to be
mine, and beggin' for a kid. She'll be pleased you asked."

I force a grin. "Happy to be of service, Jason."

"Just like you always have been." He smirks.

I'm no stranger to the things people in this town say about
me. I've been called worse by better, but still, my chest burns,
and I clench my fists to keep myself from punching that
disgusting smile off his slimy face.

Eli stiffens and Sarah glances up from the binder.

Jason's eyes flick to Eli before settling back on me. "You
here for Elliot Carson?" He rubs his chin. "Makes sense, he's
probably one of the only guys you haven't *serviced* yet."

I force a lazy smile, one side of my mouth pulling up.
"Oh, Jason. You afraid he'll be able to handle things you were
too much of a pussy to hold on to?"

Jason's lips flatten, his eyes narrowing into slits. "Please.
Ma would disown me. She'd never let me settle down with a
whore. You're lucky she ain't here… she wouldn't even let you
in the store with your filth."

The hole in my stomach grows. I'm not ashamed of who I
am, but when so many people see you as less than, it chips
away at even the strongest person's soul.

A whip of air brushes against my side, and before I can
turn, Eli has Jason's orange polo crushed in his fists, pulling
him until half his body hangs over the counter.

Jason's cheeks grow splotchy, his eyes big and round.
"What the hell, man?"

"If your momma were here," Eli starts. "I'd make sure to
show her the proper way to whoop some manners into your
disrespectful ass. You should be honored Becca's even graced
you with her attention." He stops, his fists clenching tighter,
the collar of Jason's polo wringing tight around his neck. "If
you ever talk to her like that again. If you ever *look* at her

again, I'll make sure you can never *service* anyone. You hear me, you piece of shit?"

Jason sputters and nods, clawing at Eli's hands.

Sarah is gripping my forearm, her nails indenting my skin. I wonder if it's Eli's outburst or his sudden accent that has her in shock?

My heart slams against my ribs so hard I'm convinced it's trying to break free, wanting to dive into Eli's chest and live there for a while.

All the beats belong to him, anyway.

Eli drags Jason completely over the counter until his feet scramble to find purchase on the ground. Letting go of his shirt, Eli pushes him forward until they're both standing in front of me.

My mouth parts, my stomach doing somersaults inside me.

He grips the back of Jason's neck. "Apologize."

Jason stares at the ground, mumbling.

Leaning in close, Eli's brows raise. "What's that?"

"I said, I'm sorry. Hell, man. Everyone knows Becca used to get around. She knows I'm just messin' with her."

Eli's eyes snap to me, his irises dark in their wrath. A throb spikes between my legs, shooting like lightning, electrifying every nerve.

"What in tarnation is goin' on in here?" Jason's momma, Betsy, stands in the back door, taking in the scene.

Eli doesn't move his gaze from me, and he doesn't relent his grip from the back of Jason's neck. "Just teachin' your boy some manners, Ms. Wallace."

Betsy tsks, walking over and smacking Jason on the back of the head. "Boy, what have you gone and done now? I ask you to watch the store for five minutes and I come back to you runnin' off my customers."

"Ma, it—"

She puts up a hand. "I don't wanna hear it. Go on now."

She shoos him away, and Eli *finally* releases his grasp, the deep red rings on the sides of Jason's neck making heat flare low in my abdomen.

It's disturbing how turned on I am by the evidence of Eli's violence.

Betsy puts a hand to her chest. "I'm awful sorry for anything he may have said. You know he's never quite gotten over you, Becca, but don't tell his wife I said it." She winks, turning to Sarah. "Now, let's talk weddin's!"

Bile rises in the back of my throat, because for a minute, I had forgotten that's why we were here. For just a split second, it was easy to pretend.

But Eli isn't mine.

Sarah smiles, sashaying toward Eli and standing on her tiptoes to kiss his cheek. "My man is always trying to be the white knight, riding in to save the day. Becca's a big girl, Eli. She can handle herself."

I suck on my teeth and nod my agreement, even though it's a lie. Because the truth is, I love the fact that *her man* defended me. Love how it seemed like his passion centered around me. And how, for that brief moment, *her man* still felt like mine.

The rest of the floral trip is uneventful—me staying back and not being much help, too lost in the teeter-totter of emotions sloshing around inside me.

After an hour and a half of debating whether the roses should be pink or white, Sarah finally makes a decision and we leave. I follow them out, silent and ready to get the hell out of here. I need to remind myself yet again why the decisions I've made are the right ones.

Right now, they feel a lot like a mistake.

I get to my car door, spinning the key ring around my

finger. "Well, y'all. This has been fun. I'll see you Saturday mornin' at the bakery?"

"Yes! Can't wait to taste all the yum." Sarah grins, patting her stomach.

I smile right as her phone rings. Her brows furrow as she glances at the screen, excusing herself and walking back toward the florist.

Before my gaze even falls on Eli, I already know he's looking. He's always looking. I wish he would *stop* looking.

The energy crackles between us. It's torture, being close enough to feel the pull, but too far to touch.

My stomach flips as I search for what to say. "Thank you."

His eyes spark. "For what?"

"You know for what. For defendin' me. You didn't have to do that. No one's ever—" I bite back the sudden sting in my throat. "Ever done that for me before."

The muscle in his jaw tightens. "Don't thank me for that shit, Becca. And don't let people talk to you that way."

"You talked to me that way." I tilt my head, wanting him to explain it away. To tell me *why* he likes to play with my emotions so much. I want to beg him to pick a damn lane and stay in it, so I can cast him as the villain or the hero. I don't know what to do when he's both.

He doesn't do any of those things, just swallows, his arms crossing over his broad chest.

I brush the hair from my eyes, shifting on my feet. "Besides, I can't control people's actions, Eli, I learned that a long time ago. I can only control my reaction."

"Believe me, I know."

His arms uncross and he takes a step forward. My heart batters against my sternum. I swear if I took a deep breath, our chests would touch.

"Tell me why, Becca." The deep timbre of his voice rumbles through every inch of my body.

I suck in a breath, my eyes closing against the fireflies lighting up my stomach.

Up until this point, I thought I had made peace with my decisions, but in this moment, I want to tell him I take it back. I want him to know how badly I didn't want to leave. How I broke my own heart in half and left the bigger piece with him.

But I don't. I can't. Rehashing the past won't change the present.

I glance behind him, reminding myself of all the reasons why my feelings don't matter. Namely, his fiancée. She's still on her phone, standing in front of the shop's front door. But her eyes are on us.

I move away until my back hits the side of my car, the metal frame hot against my skin.

"There's nothin' to tell, Eli. Just let it go." My heart revolts against the words. It's the same line I use on his sister, but it doesn't work as well on him.

He shakes his head, stepping into me. "Don't give me that bullshit. I deserve to know."

A hurricane of emotion rages in his blue eyes, promising to take me down in its storm.

My gut squeezes so tight, I'm afraid I'll faint. I bite my lip, shaking my head.

Let it go, Eli.

His hand flies out, smacking against the roof of the car. The sound makes me jump, but my body sizzles from the heat of his arm. My skin tingles as energy dances off my skin, flaring in its excitement.

I know his fiancée is watching. I *know* I should push him back—do something to break this moment, but I'm rooted to the ground. Unable to even breathe through the thickness of the air.

His head angles down, those dark, blond strands flopping

on his forehead, his breath tickling my cheek.

"Please," he whispers.

My stomach clenches, my heart lurching against the wall I've wrapped around it.

Elliot Carson doesn't beg. But he's begging for this.

And I know I'll give in—give him whatever he wants. Maybe if I do, it will appease the hands of fate and they'll stop tormenting me with his presence. Maybe they'll let me close the door and finally move on. To stay strong in my belief that I'm not the one for him, no matter how bad I crave to be.

I inhale, my lips parting.

"Hey, honey. Ready to go?" Sarah's voice shocks me out of the moment, my mouth snapping shut.

Eli's eyes clear, and he takes a step back, running a shaky hand through his hair.

I hold my breath, afraid that Sarah will notice the way my chest is heaving. The way my nerves are screaming from Eli's almost touch.

There's no way she missed what was happening.

Eli doesn't seem to care. His eyes are still on me, like they always are. Searching. Prying. Stripping me bare under his gaze.

I should look away.

I don't.

He sighs, finally turning to a frowning Sarah. I mutter a quick goodbye and jump in my car, desperate to escape this hell.

My shaking hands rest on the steering wheel, and I wait like a statue in my seat until they leave. Once they do, the rope binding me together slackens, my head falling against the wheel and my hand rubbing at the ache in my chest. I've gotten used to the hollow feeling, but right now it throbs, reminding me that I'm missing something vital. Something I left with Eli five years ago when I walked out the door.

Something I don't think I'll ever get back.

I don't think I can do this.

He's not mine. He never really was. And in two months, he never will be again.

40

ELI

The drive back to Pops's place is silent. Sarah doesn't say a word, just gazes out of the window as we make the quick five-minute trip from Main Street to the house. It doesn't take a rocket scientist to guess what she's thinking. Anyone who was in a ten-mile radius could have felt the forcefield of energy surrounding Becca and me. Like usual, she made me lose control.

I see her and it's this explosion of hurt slamming against raw, unbridled need, creating our own universe. My soul aches for answers. For the closure she never gave. To know what was so wrong with me that she wouldn't let me in. Couldn't let me love her.

Maybe once I know, I can finally move on and truly love someone else.

The second we pull in the driveway, Sarah's out of the car and up the walkway, slamming the screen door and rushing through the living room.

I blow out a breath, attempting to ease the knot forming in my stomach as I follow her in. I do a quick scan for Pops and find him snoring softly from his recliner, ESPN blaring from the TV.

Tentatively, I make my way to the guest room. Sarah's never given me the silent treatment before. I'm not sure what to expect.

Gripping the handle of the door—half expecting it to be locked—I walk in the room. Sarah's in front of the dresser, her frame tense as she grips the edge of the wood.

"Tell me what's going on with you and Becca." Her voice is low. Shaky.

I shove my hands in my pockets. "What do you mean?"

Her narrowed eyes meet mine through the mirror. "I'm not stupid, Eli. She looks at you like you killed her puppy. I ignored it because I figured it was some childhood crush she never got over."

My stomach twists.

"But you know what's worse?" Sarah moves, dropping onto the bed. "I feel invisible when she's around. I don't *like* feeling invisible, especially when you're *my* husband, not hers."

"Fiancé."

Her brows shoot to her hairline. "Excuse me?"

I clear my throat. "Fiancé. We aren't married yet."

Her lips turn down. "Yeah. I'm aware. And so is she, which is what concerns me."

I chuckle at the thought of Becca being a concern. As if she gives a damn about me or who I'm marrying. "Sarah, there's nothing to be worried about."

She taps her fingers to her head. "A woman always knows, Eli. You'd do well to remember that."

My heart ratchets up in speed, my ears deaf to everything except the sound of its beat.

I throw my hands in the air. "If you're so worried about it, why the hell did you ask her to plan our wedding?"

She stands up, her irises blazing, fists clenching at her sides.

My eyes widen. She's zealous in her rage, and my gut pinches, wondering why I've never seen her passion.

"Because like I said, I'm not *stupid*," she hisses. "Keep your friends close and your enemies closer."

A sadness settles in my chest, knowing my inability to control myself has turned Sarah into this mockery of who she truly is. Sarah isn't vindictive. She isn't mean.

But she is right. I should be putting her first.

My teeth clench, sending an ache up my jaw as I deliberate how much to tell her. I owe it to our relationship to make the effort, to continue the attempt at opening up and letting her in. But, I won't lie and say that part of me doesn't see this as an out—a way for me to wash my hands of the responsibility that comes with being back home.

I guess as many strides as a person takes forward, there's always temptation to walk it back.

"Sarah, listen. Being back here is hard for me, okay? It's got memories I'd like to forget and people who've already forgotten me. I'm trying to do this *for you*. But if it's gonna make us fight, maybe we should just go back to Florida. Forget having the wedding here. Your parents would love to have it closer to their home anyway, yeah?"

She shakes her head. "No, Eli. I want to have it where *you* grew up. It's perfect with the smoky mountain backdrop and the small-town charm. I love it here. Besides, everyone in town loves you."

My heart thunks and my gut tightens. People here don't *love* me. They love the idea of me—of who I used to be.

I sigh. "I guess, Sarah. Whatever you want."

"No. It's not whatever I want. I need to know what you want, too. Do you *want* to marry me? Really?"

Her question slams into my chest, my heart cowering against the attack. "I asked you, didn't I?"

"Well yeah, but... you've been different since we've been here, and then I see the way you are with Becca and..." She looks down at her hands.

"And what?"

"And you aren't that way with me." Her voice sinks to a whisper. "She knows you in a way I never have."

"Sarah." I stare at her, my mind racing as I struggle to separate the part of me that wants to shut this conversation down, and the part that wants to let her in.

I suck on my teeth. "I was with Becca back when she was a student."

Sarah gasps, her lower lip trembling. "I *knew* it. I knew there was something there. A student, Eli? Really?"

I rub my hands down my face, groaning. "I don't want to lie to you, okay? It was a long time ago, and things didn't end well." I cup her cheek in my hand. "I asked *you* to marry me. I'm here for *you*."

"Did you love her?"

"No." My soul rages against the lie, clawing at my body, etching truths into my skin.

I ignore it, leaning in to kiss her lips, sliding my tongue into her mouth.

Stripping her clothes off slowly, I pull her on top of me, needing to sink into her warmth.

Desperate for her to dull the pain.

Sarah's been hired to speak at a conference for physical therapy, and they're having Skype meetings all afternoon, so she's locked herself in the guest room, and told me I'm on my own for the rest of the day.

I'm thankful for it. I don't want her tagging along with where I'm planning to go.

Pops is still in his recliner. He hasn't moved all day, and my pulse ticks up when I think about the conversation that's long overdue. I pray I'll find the courage to have it.

But today, there's someone else I need to make amends with.

I park in the church's lot and sit in my car, staring at the rows of the deceased. For such a small town, there's a lot of people buried here. I have a vague memory of where Ma's plot is, but since I'm avoiding Lee, I can't exactly call and ask, and there's not a chance in hell I'll talk about it with Pops.

I've been wandering for a few minutes at a leisurely pace, taking in each name, half of me hoping the next one will be Ma's, and the other half praying I never find it.

The cemetery is pristine, hedges perfectly trimmed along the perimeter and the grass thick and green. My hand grazes over a dark gray tombstone and before I even look, I know it's her.

Ma.

My heart trips along with my feet, the paper wrapping the tulips I bought crinkling under my sweaty palm.

The pounding in my head rattles my bones as I squat in front of the marble slab. I slowly unbind my flowers, removing the wilted ones from the vases on either side. I brush away the fallen leaves, and take painstaking time removing every single speck of debris until her name shines as much as my memory.

Maybe if I wipe away the dirt and grime, it will cleanse the tarnish off my soul.

Sinking to the ground in front of her marker, my eyes devour the words inscribed, searching for a hint of her essence through the stone.

Gail Elizabeth Carson
Your life was a blessing, Your memory a treasure. You are loved beyond words, Missed without measure.

"Hey, Ma." My voice wedges in my throat, the words blasting me into a memory of the last time I spoke them. The last time I ever heard her voice. My chest splits open, eight years of grief escaping through the crater, raining down on my insides and crippling my composure.

"Ma, I..." My voice catches again, and I cup my mouth to stop the guttural sob that's scratching up my esophagus.

If I speak, I'll scream. So I stay quiet, instead. I already wrote down everything I needed to say anyway.

It could be minutes, or it could be hours that I sit in silence, but it's not until the setting sun dances across the marble that I finally stand to leave. My body feels heavy. The burden of my turmoil being pulled by gravity, trying to anchor me to the spot.

Somehow, I force my limbs to move.

With a kiss to her name, I slip an envelope under the vase of tulips and walk away.

Ma.

Hey Ma.

Dear, Ma.

I don't really know how I'm supposed to do this, or what it is I'm supposed to say. I'm sorry doesn't seem good enough, but it's all I've really got. And the truth is, if it weren't for Sarah, I probably wouldn't be here, so I'm not sure the apology even matters.

But I am, for what it's worth. Sorry, that is.

I'm sorry I was never the son you wanted me to be. Too

caught up in needing Pops's approval to realize I already had it in you.

I'm sorry I'm still not the son I need to be. I'm trying to do better. Think you can ask the big guy for some grace?

I didn't know, Ma. I didn't realize you were the glue holding our family together.

I'm sorry for not realizing how you were the center of every goddamn thing. You always told me to find my sun, but Ma, I already had it in you.

I didn't know true darkness until you were gone.

I'm sorry for not coming to see you sooner. More. At all. Even now, the thought of going to your plot makes my stomach turn and my chest cave in. If I stay away, I can pretend that you're still here... that I'm still just too busy to reach out, and nothing's really changed.

Visiting your grave is admitting reality isn't what I want it to be.

But can I tell you a secret? I already know it's not.

You know I dream of you? It's always the same memory. My last practice of high school. I was rushing out the door, and you were standing in the kitchen, that red and white cherry apron you always wore tied around your waist. You called my name and pulled me in your arms, telling me to enjoy the moment. To soak in every second of my last days with the team. I scoffed, patting your back and pulling out of your embrace, worried about Pops finding out I was running late.

But in my dreams... I grab on tight and squeeze you so hard I'm afraid I'll leave a bruise, trying to soak you in for as long as I can.

To bask in your glow.

You always slip away anyway, and I wake up with my fingers grasping air.

Not loving you enough when I had the chance is one of my biggest regrets.

I found someone. I think you'd like her. Someone who can marry me in the church you married Pops in. Someone who won't destroy the battered pieces of my soul if she decides to leave.

But she isn't the one who cures my "lonely heart."

... I don't know if I can go through with it.

So, I guess I'm sorry for that too.

I love you, Ma.

Forever.

-Eli

41

BECCA

This Saturday is Sam's retirement party, and it seems like everyone is talking about it. Personally, I just can't wait for it to be over. Ninety percent of the town will be there, and eighty percent of them think I'm lower than the scum on their shoes.

But none of that bothers me as much as knowing Eli will be there, cuddled up with his perfect fiancée. I already spend too much time with them as it is.

For the thousandth time, I consider how different my life would have turned out if I had made different choices. I was *this close* to freedom.

I need to talk to Jeremy. He's the only one who knows what happened with Eli and me all those years ago. But it's hard to find time to chat. Between him being the point guard for a team in California, and his secret life of loving dick, he's always busy, even on the off season, so we have to schedule times to talk. It's been a few months since I've even spoken to him, and I'm anxious to get the news of Eli's return off my chest.

My phone rings and I swipe up, grinning when I see Jeremy's boyish smile fill my screen.

"Hey, Jer."

"Hey, sweet cheeks. How ya doing down there in Hell's Pit?"

I fall back on my bed and hold the phone above my head, puffing out my bottom lip. "Shitty."

"Yeah." He grimaces. "I figured."

Over the years, I've opened up to Jeremy about what life was like growing up in Sugarlake. He's convinced my mind is warped, thanks to my dysfunctional family history. He's always trying to psychoanalyze me, even though *I'm* the one with the psychology degree.

I groan, dragging my hand down my face. "You've got no idea."

His brow arches as he takes a sip of his Coke. "No? Well lay it on me, girl."

I wrap a curl around my finger, tugging until it stings. "Eli's back."

Jeremy chokes, hunching forward and grabbing his chest. "I'm sorry, what?"

"Yeah." Tears burn my nose and choke my throat, but I bite them back. "He's gettin' married to that girl he worked with when we were students. *Sarah.*" I sigh. "Papa's makin' me plan their weddin'."

"You're kidding."

I shake my head. "I'm not."

"Holy shit, Becca. Are you... are you okay?"

"Yeah... no."

His cheeks puff out with his breath. "Tell me everything. Right now."

So I do. I rehash every painstaking moment of interaction. How it feels like I'm standing on a ledge, my mind pushing me forward and my heart pulling me back. How whenever I'm around Eli, it's easy to forget the reasons I left. I talk for what feels like hours, and Jeremy listens to it all, like he always does.

"I just don't know what to do, Jer."

He sighs. "You know what you need to do, Becca."

I don't want to hear what he's about to say, even though deep down, I already know what it is—I already know that it's *right*. The tears I've held back cling to my lashes, blurring my vision. I close my eyes, shaking my head.

"You do." His voice is stern. "Give that man his closure and then... you have to suck it the hell up and step back. Let him be happy."

My heart screams in protest. "But he doesn't *seem* happy."

Jeremy hums, nodding. "Maybe he doesn't seem happy because he's around *you*."

The words sucker punch my gut, making me wince. "I don't think—"

"That's just it, Becca. You *don't* think. You did this to yourself."

I scoff, my face flushing.

"Don't you huff at me. When have you ever known me to not keep it real with you?" His brows jump to his hairline. "We've been talking for twenty minutes now, and I haven't heard you shoulder the blame for any of what you're feeling. Everything's centered around Eli and how *he* makes you feel."

Bullshit.

What the hell is Jeremy's problem? He's supposed to be on my side.

"I do *not*."

"You do, Becca. Take a second and listen to what you're saying. That man didn't break your heart. You broke his. You have no right to him. You aren't owed anything from Elliot Carson."

Fire swirls up my chest, searing my cheeks. "I never said I was. Jesus, Jer."

My wall of defense raises high, but his words sneak through the gaps. Maybe he's right. Maybe everything he's saying is true, but it doesn't matter because all I can feel is the stinging lash of what feels like his betrayal. I came to him to feel better about my situation, not worse.

He shrugs. "Be mad at me all you want. Someone's gotta say it."

"Get fucked," I snap.

His head tosses back with his laughter. "Oh, honey. I plan to. Listen, calm down a bit and *think* about what I said. Call me back once you realize I'm right, so I can say I told you so." He winks. "I love you, sweet cheeks. Even when it doesn't feel like it."

He hangs up and I throw my phone across the room, screaming, trying to expel this fiery energy that's padding my stomach and making me fit to burst.

I pace my room for hours, until the song of the cicadas and the lull of the moon calms my nerves. And then, finally, I think about what Jeremy said. I focus on how it feels when he whips out his mirror and shows me the truth in my reflection.

The one I never want to see.

It's *so* damn tempting to close my eyes and turn away.

But maybe it's time I stop and take a closer look.

Tonight is my folks' thirtieth anniversary. I've never forgotten the date, but even if I had, it's obvious with the way Momma has taken extra care in getting ready for supper. She's even wearing her special pearls. The ones she says Papa gave her on their fourth anniversary, right before I was born.

I'm here because I know Papa won't be, and I just don't have it in me to let Momma suffer in her misery alone.

She's sitting in the dining room, ankles crossed, her peep-toed shoes hanging off her heel, tapping her foot rhythmically against the wood leg of the table. She's staring vacantly into the flames that are turning the beautiful cream candles from sticks to stubs—the melted wax a physical representation of how her marriage has diminished over the years.

I watch her from the hallway, my heart twisting because she looks so *empty*. So broken.

So alone.

I relate to her more in this moment than I ever have before, and it turns my stomach.

Taking a deep breath, I walk into the room, sliding into the chair next to her, reaching out and slipping my hand under her fingers.

"Why do you do this to yourself, Momma?" I whisper.

Her lips curl in, and she shakes her head. "He's just runnin' late."

"Momma." I sigh, my chest wringing tight. "He's not gonna show. He never does."

She flinches from my words, but that's the only break in her stillness.

We sit in silence, the ticking of the grandfather clock on the wall reminding us that Papa is shit at upholding his vows. At upholding his service to God. At upholding his respectability as a man.

"When summer ends, I'm gonna go to California," I blurt.

I don't know what makes me say it. Maybe it's a need to tell someone who understands what it's like to waste away under Papa's thumb, or possibly I'm just digging for a reaction. A break in that impenetrable mask she wears like a shield.

Her fingers squeeze mine tight before she moves her

hand, picking up her glass of vodka. She sips it slowly, her delicate throat bobbing with her swallow before she places it back down. Everything about her is proper. Pristine. Carefully crafted to put on a show. Even her sorrow.

"I always hoped you would, Rebecca Jean. You weren't meant for this life."

My heart stutters, and I couldn't be more shocked if she took out a knife and glided it down my middle, pulling out my insides and gutting me on the floor.

"Wh–what?" I gasp. "You've always told me I'm *doomed* for this life."

Her eyes flash, and *finally*, there's a chink in her frigid exterior. "When you got nothin' but time, you start to reflect. The years have turned me into a jealous, bitter woman. I'm not proud of it, but it's happened all the same."

I suck in a breath, sucker punched by what she's saying. Momma's word has always been my gospel, even when I didn't want it to be. She whispered in my ear and poisoned every decision of my life. I'm not sure what to do with this new information.

I'm not sure I believe it.

Anger, sharp and hot, percolates through my heart, dripping into my bloodstream. "You're really gonna sit there and tell me you didn't mean what you've said over the years? That it was all 'cause of *jealousy*?"

"Indeed, there is not a righteous man on Earth who does right and never sins." She swallows, her fingers trembling over mine. "I've let down God in a lot of ways, but the one I'll burn for the most is failin' at bein' your momma."

"No." I rip my hand from under hers. "No. You don't get to do this. You don't get to sit here, quote the Bible, and act like you've had some big revelation. For *years* you beat into my brain that I could trust *no man*, that I'd end up chained and shackled no matter what... you can't take that back."

Momma laughs, a sad, hollow sound. "Oh, child. Why would you listen to me? I'm an old lady who wastes all my days pinin' for a man who can't even remember that he married me twenty-six years ago."

I cock my head. "You mean thirty."

She frowns, taking another gulp of her vodka. "No, Rebecca Jean. I mean twenty-six."

My lips pull down, creasing my forehead. "But *I'm* twenty-six. Y'all were married long before you had me."

Momma sighs, patting the top of my hand. "Sometimes I forget the truth myself, we've been so good at lyin' all these years."

My heart stops.

"But I'm *sick* of lyin'," she says on an exhale. "I met your Papa when I was young, dumb and gullible. I knew he didn't love me. He never even took me on a date." She shakes her head, raggedness inscribed in the lines of her face. "I was so enamored with him I didn't mind much. But then I got pregnant."

My mind whirls, bile climbing up my throat. "But you said he loved you. That once upon a time, he would have moved mountains."

She shrugs. "I lied. Your papa moved many mountains, but they were never for me."

I gasp. "What? No, I... how did I not know this?"

Betrayal—dark and thick—trickles through my veins.

"How could you not tell me this?" I hiss.

"You think this is somethin' I'm proud of?" she snaps. "Gettin' knocked up like the town whore, and bein' shamed into movin' to a new town? One where no one would see the scarlet letter I ripped from my chest?" Her eyes blaze, and I'm stunned into silence. "You think it was *fun* to watch you go down that same path?" She pauses, her hand wiping a stray tear. The first one I've ever seen her shed. "Besides," she sniffs, "we have an image to uphold."

Revulsion pours over me, a sticky, black sludge that weighs me down and makes me want to puke.

Everything I've known—everything I've believed in has been a lie.

I shoot to my feet, suddenly unable to stand being here for a second longer. "You disgust me. You and Papa both."

I wait for an apology, but after a few moments I realize I'll be waiting forever.

The mask has dropped back down, her face a blank canvas, waiting for whatever she chooses to paint for the world.

I should know better than to hope.

I race out of the house, unable to breathe from the weight of the lies.

My entire life is a lie.

Ripping my phone from my purse, I pull up Jax's number and send him a text.

Me: Cali? I'm in. When do we leave?

I t's already been a long day and it's only twelve-thirty.
Sarah and I just arrived at the church to meet with
Becca about the wedding.

I don't think I want it to happen at all, which makes me a
piece of shit. Especially after using Sarah to fuck the feelings I
have for Becca away. It was an asshole thing to do, and I've been
nauseous over it ever since, but it also showed me clarity
because I know I need to let her go. She deserves someone who
can love her fully, and *goddamn* I wish that man were me.
Coming back here has pulled up the deepest parts of my longing, and I know I'll never feel for Sarah the things I do for Becca.

I don't *want* to feel them.

I would give anything not to feel them.

But five years ago they dug into my skin and settled into
my bones, becoming an integral part of me.

I don't think I'll ever forgive her for what she's done, for
the way she shattered me to pieces. Regardless, it wouldn't be
fair to live a lie with someone else even if it means I end up
alone.

The last time I saw Becca, we threw some hateful words, mine laced with hurt and hers laced in truth. I have no idea if she's upset, pissed, or indifferent. More than likely, she doesn't care at all, which just makes me wish I didn't either.

We get to Preacher Sanger's office and the door is open, so we walk in. He's nowhere in sight, but Becca is sitting behind his oak desk, hands resting lightly on the top, her gaze unfocused.

I expect her to startle when she sees us, but she's so lost in her thoughts she doesn't even acknowledge we've arrived. I tilt my head, the base of my spine tingling in warning. Usually, less than a second in her presence and I'm ready to explode, but right now there's no buzz. No electricity flowing off her skin and soaking into my soul.

Something's off.

"Rebecca." I use her full name for a reason. To see if there's a spark. A reaction. I'm searching for that fire. The one only Becca can provide. But I don't find it, and dread sneaks through my chest, pooling in my stomach.

She's always been my flame, bright with her glow, and dangerous in her beauty. But the closer the light, the bigger the shadow.

I was a fool to find comfort in her shade.

I'm desperate in its absence.

My voice jolts her out of her daze, and she musters up a small smile. "Hi, y'all. Come on in."

Even her voice is flat.

"Everything okay?" Sarah asks, walking forward and sitting.

I follow behind but hesitate, my hands wrapping around the top of the chair as I stand behind it. I angle my head trying to catch Becca's eyes.

She avoids my gaze.

"You okay doing it in here?" I remember the last time when she couldn't leave the room fast enough.

She lifts her shoulders. "Here is fine. This won't take long, anyway."

Sarah's eyebrow raises. "Oh? I'm excited to talk about what our options are—"

"I'm leavin'," Becca interrupts.

My heart slingshots against my ribs. "What do you mean you're *leaving?*"

She keeps her eyes firmly on Sarah, not sparing me a glance.

"I'm movin'. It's a spur of the moment thing, but since I won't be here after this weekend, obviously, I won't be able to help y'all with your weddin'." She wraps a strand of hair around her finger.

My gut clamps so tight it makes me nauseous.

Sarah smiles big and wide. "Oh, how exciting! Where are you moving to?"

Becca opens her mouth, but a man's voice interrupts.

"Don, I—oh, I'm sorry y'all, I'm lookin' for the preacher."

I twist in my seat, recognizing his auburn locks immediately. They're identical to his son's, who I played ball with in high school.

My stomach sinks. *Great.*

His brown eyes widen and he walks farther in the room, coming to stand beside my chair. "Elliot Carson. I heard you were back in town, but I didn't believe it for a second. Can't believe I'm seein' you right here, in the flesh. How ya doin', son?"

I nod. "Mr. Mazey, good to see you. I'm doing great, thanks. How's Pete?"

Mr. Mazey chuckles, running a hand down his face. "Petey's the same as he's always been... tryin' to put his mama in an early grave."

I smile. That was definitely the truth back in high school. It warms my insides to know that not everything has turned upside down over the years. That even though things have changed for me, other things are still the same.

"This is my fiancée, Sarah," I introduce. "Sarah, this is Mr. Mazey. I played ball with his son."

I feel Becca's stare on the back of my neck, and I grip the arms of the chair to resist turning around and trying to catch her eyes.

"Fiancée, huh? Y'all meet at that fancy college of yours? We follow all your games, you know. Lotta winnin' goin' on down there."

Sarah titters. "We sure did. I started working with him his very first year. Been there for almost all of his one-hundred and thirty-five wins." She grins at me, and I smile back, but there's a pinch in my gut at the way the conversation is heading. I don't want to talk about basketball. Not here. Not with Mr. Mazey. And *definitely* not with Becca.

"One-hundred-thirty-seven."

Becca's voice cuts through the air and slams into my chest, pushing the breath from my lungs in a whoosh. My head snaps in her direction so fast my neck pulls.

"I'm sorry?" Sarah asks.

Becca shakes her head, glancing at the desk. When she looks back up, her eyes collide with mine and lock on. That fire I was searching for roars to life, blistering me from the inside out.

She swallows, her throat bobbing with the motion. "You said he's won one-hundred-thirty-five games. It's one-hundred-thirty-seven."

"Oh?" Sarah looks to me.

I'm sure she wants me to defend her, and maybe if I was a better fiancé, I would.

But I can't.

Because Becca's right.

My ribs bruise from the pounding of my heart. I can hardly catch my breath, let alone voice a thought. My mind whirls at the insinuation of her knowing my record.

Of what that means.

"Well," Mr. Mazey shifts in place, clearly uncomfortable. "Alright then. It was nice to see you, Elliot." He looks to Becca. "Will you let your daddy know I stopped by?"

Becca nods, the red of her hair falling over her shoulders and highlighting the flush of her cheeks.

It's silent after he leaves. Sarah's hand claws into my thigh, her eyes narrowed on Becca.

"You know," Sarah says. "Since you won't be here to help with the wedding, I don't think there's any reason for us to stick around." She turns to me. "Ready to go, honey?"

No.

I want to stay. I want to lock Becca in this room and keep her hostage until I purge her from my fucking soul and finally gain some closure. I need it more now than I ever have before. But I don't think I'll get the answers I deserve, even if I ask. So I shake off my need, and let Sarah lead me out the door.

Driving home, I'm a nervous wreck, my hands tapping out an unsteady rhythm on the wheel.

"What's wrong?" Sarah peeks at me from the passenger seat.

I sigh, running my fingers through my hair. "Can we talk when we get to the house?"

She stiffens, her fingers twisting in her lap. "We can talk now."

I cringe. "I don't wanna do this in the car."

"Well, I don't think I want to stay in this car and wonder what has you so twisted up."

I glance at her before staring back at the road, clenching my jaw. My stomach tosses, but I breathe through the upheaval.

"Sarah, I really don't—"

"Just say it." She squeezes her eyes tight, her head angling toward the window.

My heart falters, and suddenly I'm not sure I can. Checking my rearview mirror, I pull to the side of the road, turning on the hazards and facing her.

"Why do you love me?"

Her nose scrunches. "What?"

"Why do you love me?" I repeat. "Because I'll tell you…" I pause, swallowing around the regret that's pouring from my heart and scratching up my throat. "I haven't been good to you. Not really."

She reaches out her hand, rubbing up and down my forearm. "Yes, you have."

I shake my head, briefly closing my eyes against the sting. *Fuck, this is hard.* "You know… I've been floating through life for as long as I can remember, only skimming the surface. Never delving deep, never wanting to. And then you came along. And you were this… balm to wounds I didn't even know were still aching."

She smiles, her eyes glassy.

My palm taps my chest. "You numbed my pain, and you never asked for more. And I'm so, *so* damn grateful for that, Sarah. I love you for that." The pit in my stomach grows. "But I've been wracking my brain, and I can't think of a single goddamn thing I've done that would make *you* love me."

She squeezes my arm. "I just do, Eli. Isn't that enough?"

My nostrils flare against the dip of my heart. "I don't know, Sarah. Don't you think that's an issue? The fact that you can't even say what it is you love? How do you know it's real? How do I?"

She sucks in a breath, her hand leaving my arm and covering her mouth. "Are you saying you don't know if you really love me?"

"I love you. I do, and I could watch you walk down that aisle, knowing I'd be content for the rest of my life."

She huffs out a laugh, a tear escaping from the corner of her eye. "*Content.* How romantic."

"I'm trying to be honest. Please, Sarah. *Please*, just be honest. To yourself and to me. Don't we owe each other that?"

She bites on her lips, staring out of the windshield. My leg bounces under the wheel.

"I guess..." She exhales through her nose, her jaw tight. "I guess you're safe to me."

My brows jump. I wasn't expecting her to say that.

"I've had that... *feeling.* That craziness that makes you feel like you'll die if you lose it. Like you'll never breathe again." She stops, blowing out a breath, tears dripping off her chin. "It's a drug, and it never ends well. It *hurts.* You don't make me hurt, Eli." Her eyes meet mine, and in this moment I know.

This is it.

We've been blanketing the hurts from our past with each other, settling for the warmth and pretending it's enough.

I breathe deeply, the lump in my chest growing until it clogs my throat. "I love you."

She hiccups, wiping her cheeks with the back of her hand. "I love you, too."

My nostrils flare, the salt of my tears teasing my lips. "But I'm not *in* love with you," I whisper.

Her eyes flutter closed, and she nods. "I know."

The second I say the words, there's a sense of peace. A

lightness from the relief of finally having an honest conversation. Of acknowledging what we've both always known, even when we chose to be blind.

When we pull into the driveway, she grips my arm. "Can we... Can I..." she huffs out a breath, tucking her hair behind her ear. "Will you wait to tell everyone? I'd still like to go to the party tonight, just... let me leave this place with a little dignity. I'll find a flight back home tomorrow. If you just give me a little time, I can be out of your house, I—"

She chokes on the words, tears cascading down her face, showing me more emotion than all the years we've been together. I realize in this moment that we've been living as acquaintances, accepting each other for the facade we portray, not loving each other for who we truly are.

I smile softly, the pads of my thumbs wiping under her eyes. I rest my forehead on hers, and her hands fly up, gripping the back of my neck.

"I'm so sorry, Sarah."

"I'm sorry, too," she rasps.

We stay locked in our embrace for long, tortured seconds, the air pregnant with sorrow of a fractured friendship that should never have been more.

Sarah is my drug, the one I use to blunt the pain.

But I'm ready to feel.

BECCA

It's an odd feeling realizing the way you've lived your life isn't how the world really is. They say perception is reality, and hell, I guess that's the truth because I've *perceived* my momma wrong all these years. I've placed her beside me as an innocent—a victim. A woman who fell short of the mothering aspect of life, but a bystander to the cruel and twisted man my papa is, nonetheless.

Too prideful to admit her pain, yet too weak to leave.

Just like me.

I've been so afraid of becoming her that I drank in her words and used them as my fuel, not realizing they were molding my cells into a perfect replica. Now when I look in the mirror, I see Momma staring back instead of my own reflection.

Thoughts become things.

Momma's an actress. A manipulator. And I've been her marionette, dangling from her lines for far too long. She played my strings so expertly, I didn't even realize I was her puppet.

Last night, particularly, was worthy of a standing ovation,

enough to fool even the harshest of critics. But it had the opposite effect on me.

I don't buy her sorrow.

My heart doesn't mend based off her empty apology. The only thing it does is show me that Momma is not the weak and innocent woman I thought she was.

Momma is a snake.

A viper, just like her husband.

Sickness spreads through my heart, poisoning my blood when I think about what that makes me.

Waiting on Eli and Sarah to show up to the church, I force my limbs to move until I sit behind Papa's desk—the one that represents the first crack in the foundation of my beliefs.

My folks are masters of deception. They prey on your trust and edge along the rim of honesty, until you don't know how to tell the truth from the lie.

Knowing that doesn't change the fact I saw Papa rutting on top of Sally Sanderson, and it doesn't take away the disappointment in knowing he made vows and broke them. But for the first time, I realize the image he shattered in that moment —that image never really existed.

It was a mirage. An illusion that's been propped up and executed beautifully for years.

My heart picks up speed when I think about what the motive was behind Momma finally telling me. I know as sure as the day is long, it wasn't from the goodness of her cold, dead heart.

I don't intend to stick around and find out.

My eyes glance over Papa's desk. Papers are strewn haphazardly, and there's a gaudy, gold cup in the corner, holding an assortment of pens. My gaze snags on the letter opener and I grit my teeth to keep from grabbing it, wanting to destroy everything on this desk and hope that somehow it will purge the years of Momma's words from my blood until my veins are free from her lies.

Words that Momma twisted into knots with her tongue and spit into my brain, knowing I'd leave them there to fester.

My hands shake as they hover above the desk's top, and I marvel at the deception in the oak's beauty.

Perception is reality, indeed.

I'm here to tell Eli and Sarah that I'm leaving and won't be planning their wedding, after all. And then I'm packing a suitcase and going with Jax to California. Like most of my decisions, it's sporadic, but it's the one part of myself that I *know* is really me. So even though I don't have money, I haven't quit my job, and I haven't even thought about breaking my rental agreement, I'm going. All those things pale in comparison to what's tearing at my insides and pushing me out the door.

If I don't go now, while my anger is hot and my betrayal is fresh, I may never leave.

The sound of a throat clearing snaps me out of my daze, and I snatch my hands back, placing them under my thighs to try and stem the tremble. I lock my gaze on Sarah, knowing if I look at Eli, I'll have to face the other lie I've been telling myself. That Jeremy was wrong. That it *isn't* me who makes the light dim in Eli's eyes.

If I look at Eli, I'll waver in every decision I've ever made, and while there's so much I'm coming to terms with, I'm not ready to face the truth about him and me.

Not yet.

Besides, it's not fair for me to stay around and muddle up his shot at happiness. This is what Mrs. Carson always wanted for him, and for once in my life, I'm going to step back and do the right thing. Not out of fear, but out of love.

So I won't look at Eli.

And I'll leave Sugarlake tomorrow, and never see him again.

I'll let him go, finally. Because until now, I never really did.

I drove myself to Sam's retirement party. I was tempted to skip it altogether, but it's important for me to be here for a variety of reasons. One being that I need to talk to Lee, tell her that I'm leaving, and the other is this *need* to show Momma her words don't affect me.

But I feel *sick.*

The rec hall's gymnasium is nearly unrecognizable. Long, white tables line the walls, filled to the brim with trays of hors d'oeuvres and platters. There's a bar set up in the corner, fully equipped with rows of bottles and a bartender ready to pour.

I head straight there, my mouth watering at the thought of a nice merlot, something to help me get through this night. I'm two steps away from my liquid courage when an arm settles heavy on my shoulders.

"Hey, sugar, what's a pretty thing like you doing all alone in a place like this?" Jax's eyes flash with mirth as he grins, his shaggy blond hair tied up in his signature bun.

I smirk, rolling my eyes. "Tryin' to find a gun to put a bullet in my head. This is tedious. You come to save me, Jax? Or you gonna let me find the good booze so I can make it through this hellhole night?" I gesture at the bar.

He laughs. "Jesus, Becs, it's a party. Lighten up. Let's go find Lee and then I'll get you your drink."

I grumble, but let him steer me through the throng of people. I see Lee first, her honey-blonde hair moving with the bob of her head as she talks. And then time slows down and my heart stutters when I see Eli standing across from her.

"Look at what the cat drug in," Jax says as we approach them.

I'm lost in Eli's gaze, unable to look away, trying to soak in every detail, knowing this is the last time I'll ever see him.

His jaw twitches, his arm wrapping around Sarah's waist, bringing her into his side. When his hand grips her hip, I feel the squeeze in my heart.

I force my eyes away, looking toward Lee. "What's up, girl? You find the good booze yet? My chaperone over here made me come find you first."

Lee gasps. "How dare he."

I grin, a little bit of warmth sneaking into the cracks of my soul. "I know, right? I told him you of all people would understand. Especially in situations like these."

I didn't mean to say the last part, and I hope she doesn't read into my words. Unfortunately, I've always had a shit poker face, and Lee's always been too perceptive for her own damn good.

My eyes trail back to Eli before I can control myself, locking on to where he's wrapped around his fiancée.

My gut jolts painfully and my throat burns. Suddenly, I'm desperate to explain why I left all those years ago. I ache to fix the breaks I caused from trusting the wrong woman my entire life. Apologize for believing her words when I should have listened to his. To my own.

But I'm not a homewrecker, and I made my bed years ago when it comes to him.

"Becca! Hi. Long time no see." Sarah waves.

"Hey, Sarah. You're lookin' just as pretty as you were this afternoon. *A true beauty.* Eli's a lucky man." My smile is slow, having to fight through the muck of my heart before it can grace my face.

"The prodigal son returns home," Jax snarks. His features

soften as he greets Sarah. "Hi, I'm Jax. You must be the lucky lady?" He reaches out to shake her hand.

Sarah's mouth is slightly parted, her eyes glazed as she stares at him. I bite down the chuckle that tries to escape.

Everyone who's anyone is charmed by Jackson Rhoades. There's just something about his aura—it reaches out and wraps around you, trying to pull you in.

"Nice to meet you," Jax says.

Sarah shakes her head slightly, her eyes regaining their focus as she places her hand in his. "Pleasure's all mine, and yes, I am. The lucky lady, that is."

My heart twists.

Eli tenses, his arm dropping from her waist.

"Are you Becca's boyfriend?" She nods toward me.

It's an innocent question, but my body locks in place, my eyes jetting to Eli, searching for a hint of envy. It's a sick, twisted game I'm playing, but for the life of me I'm not sure how to stop.

He doesn't react. *And why would he?*

"Ha! He wishes." I force a laugh, shrugging out from under Jax's arm, the air suddenly stifling. "I'm gonna go get some air."

My heart beats forcefully in my ears, my legs burning from how fast I push through the crowd, making my way outside.

What the hell is wrong with me?

I sit on the curb to collect myself, breathing in the fresh air. After a few moments, Lee plops down next to me, leaning back on her arms and heaving a sigh. She doesn't say anything, and neither do I.

"You wanna talk about it?" she finally asks.

My chest pulls tight. "How many times do I gotta tell you, there's nothin' to talk about?"

This is my moment. I should spill my secrets and beg for

her mercy. But pride is a foolish mistress, one that hangs on even when there's nothing left. So I don't.

"Oh, come off it, Becca. This ain't you. Anyone with two eyes can tell somethin' is wrong."

More like everything.

"Is it Eli?"

My heart jumps and the fear of her knowing trickles through my system. "No."

She chews on her lip, taking me in with a critical eye. "You know I don't believe you, right?"

I sigh, my eyes scanning the parking lot to avoid her stare. "Your brother has nothin' to do with me, Lee. That I can promise you." I squint, focusing on a figure leaning against a black truck. "Hey, ain't that your man?"

Lee follows my line of sight and nods, a smile growing on her face. "Yep, that's my man. I'm gonna go say hi."

I let out a breath of relief, thankful for the distraction. Lee stands, dusting off her knees and walking away. She only makes it a few steps before freezing in place.

My spidey senses tingle and I'm off the curb and by her side in a heartbeat, just in time to see Chase talking to a long-legged, black-haired woman.

"Who the hell is *that?*" I ask.

Lee shakes her head, her eyes wide, and I watch in real time as my best friend's heart breaks *again* because dickface of the century is letting some other woman shove her tongue down his throat.

Once a cheat, always a cheat.

My hand shoots out to grasp Lee's arm, holding her up in case she starts to crumble.

"Asshole!" I yell.

Chase breaks off the kiss and turns toward us, his eyes growing wide and panicked.

Rage boils in my veins. When he first came back to town, I

warned him to leave her alone—to stay away—knowing she wouldn't be strong enough to make the decision herself.

It's no surprise he didn't listen. She gave in like I knew she would and I accepted it. I'm not exactly in a place to judge her weakness. Glass houses and all.

Lee steps back, her face drained of color before she turns and runs. Chase yells after her, following quickly behind.

Meanwhile, I'm standing in the parking lot lost at what to do.

Do I go after her? Do I stop him from getting to her?

I don't do either. Not because I don't want to, but because I need to start trusting in Lee's strength. I'll be here for her at the end of the night when she needs someone to lean on.

I walk around the building, not quite ready to face the people inside.

There's a back entrance that leads to a hallway behind the gymnasium, filled with empty studios. Lee used to teach dance in one of them, and I know it will serve as a good hiding spot while I build the shield to face my folks, and the rest of Sugarlake, for one last night.

I grab the handle of the door and twist, when suddenly, heat slides across my back.

"Looking for somewhere to hide, Rebecca?"

My body spasms, the deep rumble of Eli's voice and my full name off his lips cascading over my body and infusing every pore with *need*.

His frame hovers against my back and I choke on my breath, my stomach somersaulting on the wings of butterflies. His hands skim my arms, fingertips teasing until he grips the outside of my shoulders. The feel of him is a thousand volts of electricity lancing off my skin.

It's the first time we've touched in years.

His breath ghosts along my neck, the ends of his hair tickling my cheek. My core contracts, a sharp ache slicing through my middle. My fingers grip the door handle so tight it hurts.

"Eli," I rasp.

"Tell me why," he whispers in my ear.

My heart pounds inside my chest to the beat of my thoughts.

Tell him.

My eyes flutter closed.

"Okay."

Becca spins, peering at me through her lashes. "What do you wanna know?"

I shake my head, irritation sparking in my gut. "Don't do that."

My arms cage her in, my hands pressing against the cold metal of the door behind her. I'm desperate to make her *feel* me, but I'm terrified that once she does I'll never recover. The whisper of a touch I've already given her is almost more than I can handle. "Stop pretending like you don't know exactly what I'm asking you."

She glances down and exhales a shaky breath. I grip under her chin without thinking, static running through my fingertips as I tilt her face back to mine. "I deserve to know."

"I just—" Her hand comes up, knotting in the curls on her head. She tries to duck under one of my arms. I slide it down so she can't.

She huffs. "Can I get some space?"

My jaw clenches. "No."

"I can't breathe with you this close, Eli. I need... I need some damn space, *please.*"

Funny. I haven't been able to breathe since she stole my breath five years ago. I'm still waiting to get it back.

"No," I repeat, my voice low.

She meets my eyes, the pull of her gaze hooking into my chest and tugging, trying to tether us together. "Why the hell not?"

Her question chafes the damaged pieces of my soul. I exhale slowly, my nostrils flaring. "Because I'm afraid you'll leave."

She sighs, her eyes turning glassy. I *hate* the way my heart pinches at the sight.

"I won't leave," she whispers. "I'll tell you whatever you wanna know." Her hands push against my chest, branding my skin through the fabric. "Please, I can't breathe with you so close. It's—"

"You think I *can?*" I snap, gripping her wrists and hauling her against me. "You think it's been easy for me to be around you all this time?"

I tighten my grip and step into her, pushing her body against the door with my torso. "You think it hasn't killed me to stand in your presence and remember the feel of having you in my arms? To realize that even after all these years..." My voice cracks and I grit my teeth, fighting the burn behind my eyes. "After all the *pain* you've inflicted, you still light my goddamn body on fire?"

A tear trails down her cheek, dripping off her chin. I watch as it falls, reveling in the show of emotion. My soul craves to dig deeper and draw out more. To prove that she actually gives a damn.

"I can't do this," she chokes.

My grip slackens, and she rips her wrists from my grasp, spinning around and flying through the door before I can stop her.

My heart pummels my chest.

I don't fucking think so.

I stalk after her, following her into the closest room off the hallway.

Grabbing the door before it closes, I step into the space and glance around. Other than a desk at the front and a few chairs pushed against the wall, it's empty.

Becca's standing in front of the desk, gripping the edge, her shoulders hunched and her breathing heavy.

"Still running, I see." My voice cuts through the air.

She shakes her head, her fingers flexing against the wood, making her knuckles turn white.

"Why did you leave, Rebecca?"

Silence.

Years of repressed anger rupture inside my chest and I twist, slamming the door closed. "God *dammit!* Stop bein' a selfish bitch and just *tell* me."

She spins to face me. "Because I loved you!"

My lungs collapse as her words slam into my chest, cracking it open and throttling my heart.

"What?" I gasp.

Her posture softens, her jade eyes glistening as they meet mine. "I loved you, alright? I *still* love you."

She moves forward and I step back.

I don't want her close.

I don't believe a word she says.

Bitterness rolls through me and I huff out a laugh. "You don't love me. You don't love anyone but yourself."

She tilts her face to the ceiling. "God, you have no idea how much I wish that were true. Do you think I like knowin' I lost you before I ever had the chance to really have you?"

"You didn't *lose* me." The audacity of her words pumps rage through my veins and propels me toward her. "You threw me away. I was *yours.*" My fist beats my chest. "Every inch of me was yours."

"Yeah. Well… now it's *Sarah's*," she hisses.

My brows shoot to my hairline, a spike of satisfaction worming its way in, mixing with my anger. Her jealousy makes me feel like she actually gives a damn. Like I'm not the only one who feels this goddamn *crazy*.

I shrug. "Yeah, well… one woman's trash is another woman's treasure, I guess."

"You're right." She nods. "I mean… you're right that I didn't treasure you. There's nothin' I can do to change that. But you're asking me *why* and that's the reason." She blows out a breath. "I love you, and that terrifies me, Eli. I don't know how to love. I don't know what it's supposed to be. I never have."

My heart kicks my sternum, and I step closer. "Bullshit. It was *supposed* to be us."

She stumbles at my advance, the back of her legs pressing against the desk. Her necklace jostles from under her shirt, catching my eye as it glimmers against her collarbone.

#1 Player.

My heart kicks into overdrive.

"I was scared," she whispers. "I don't know what else you want me to say."

I'm on her now, her breasts heaving against my chest with every inhale. My mind screams to back away. But I can't.

"You're a coward," I spit.

She nods, her eyes holding my gaze, causing heat to flare low in my gut.

Her tongue jets out to wet her lips and my eyes track the movement, my body coiling tighter with each passing second.

She sucks in a breath, her eyes dilating as she watches me war against my emotions.

I lose the battle.

My head drops, my nose skimming along the length of her throat, inhaling her scent. My tongue darts out because I can't be this close and *not* taste her, so I torture myself, my cock thickening from the tease of her flavor.

I rest my forehead in the junction of her neck, my teeth clenching against the urge to sink into her skin, my fingers coming up to tangle in the chain of the necklace I bought her when she was mine.

"If you loved me..." My voice breaks. "How could you leave?"

Her breath hitches. "I'm a fool."

My heart stutters, aching at the memory of how she broke me.

I lift my head, synapses firing from the heat of her gaze.

The silky fabric of her blouse bunches under my palm as I glide my hand up her side. My eyes trail over every single freckle until I finally meet her stare, searching for verity in her eyes.

I cup her face. "I don't believe you," I breathe.

And then I give in to the pull.

Fireworks burst in my chest when our lips collide. She moans, her hands gripping my shirt, dragging me into her. My cock jumps, straining against my zipper, desperate to dip into her after going so long without.

My hands leave her face, sliding back down her curves and pushing up her skirt, kneading the flesh of her ass.

I groan into her mouth. She feels so *fucking* good in my hands.

She nips at my bottom lip and I hoist her onto the desk, spreading her legs, and glancing at the thin scrap of lace between her thighs.

Goddamn.

My dick pulses, my mouth watering at the sight. I surge forward, trailing my tongue along her collarbone.

She leans on her elbows, her head falling back. Want spirals through my insides, making me dizzy.

Working my way back up, my tongue tangles with hers, trying to savor every moment, not knowing which one will be our last. I push her back with my body until she's splayed on top of the desk, my lips attached to hers and my cock weeping for the same.

She moans into my mouth when I dip my fingers inside her, pumping them twice.

"So wet for me, baby girl," I growl.

"Eli," she breathes.

A zing of anticipation shoots through me and I push my fingers farther, curling them forward until her back bows.

Working her hard, my thumb circles her clit. My palm is drenched from her juices, and I swear to God if I don't get inside her soon I think I might die.

I back away from our kiss, needing to see her come apart beneath me, needing to know if the reality is still as good as my dreams.

Her legs tremble as I finger fuck her into euphoria.

Christ, she's beautiful.

Suddenly, it's not enough to have her this way. I pull my fingers from her core and rip off my belt, frenzied in my need to dive deep inside her and drown in her crazy.

Becca bites her lip as she watches. "God, Eli, *hurry up.*"

I quirk a brow as I pull out my cock, stroking it from base to tip. Precum drips from the head and lands on her thigh. A sick, possessive pleasure flares in my chest at the sight.

Becca groans, her hands grappling to pull me back, her eyes wild. "Eli, please."

I smirk. "You know I love it when you beg."

She fists my shirt and pulls me close, rising up until her mouth brushes mine. "Shut up and *fuck* me already."

Her words blaze through me, capsizing my control in their fever.

My hand grips her jaw tightly. "That *fuckin'* mouth."

She grins. My fingers squeeze tighter as I bury myself inside her and steal her gasp with my tongue, my eyes rolling back at the sensation.

And then I hear another gasp.

One that *isn't* from Becca.

My head snaps up and my stomach drops to the floor.

45

BECCA

My heart hasn't beat since Eli snapped his head up, leaving space for me to lock eyes with my best friend.

"I'm sorry, I'm sorry, holy crap. I'm sorry." Lee's voice floats through the air, her hands covering her face. "I'm not leavin' this room, so y'all do what you need to do and get decent quick. Let me know when it's safe to uncover my eyes. Oh my *God*."

Eli's still inside me, his body pressed to mine so close I feel his heart beating against my chest. His hand comes up to touch my face, his mouth parting as if he's about to speak. But he doesn't. Instead, he just stares, his piercing blue gaze chipping away at what's left of my sanity.

I can't *think* with him looking at me like that.

I turn my head away, my eyes landing on Lee's back. Reason slices through the fog of my brain, banging against my skull.

What did I just do?

Eli slips out of me, his hands moving to my hips and I tense under the heat of his touch. His eyes are wide and cautious, cataloging every inch of my face, his jaw clenching.

I should move. I *should* be grappling to push him off me so I can try to salvage this completely screwed up situation, but I'm too busy being torn in two over my actions and it makes my movements sluggish. Half of me is desperate to keep Eli here, worried that once his weight isn't pressed against me, I'll unravel completely. The other part is disgusted at how easily I let go of my morals.

Less than fifteen minutes.

That's all it took to throw everything I thought I knew about myself out the window.

Eli lowers my skirt and straightens my top with one hand, the palm of his other caressing my hair, smoothing down the flyaways. He's touching me like I'm the finest jewel from the rarest treasure. Like now that he has me in his hands, he's afraid of having me stolen away.

I swallow around the swelling of my throat, my eyes stuck on his, wanting to prolong the moment even though I shouldn't. Even though his sister is standing less than five feet away.

The current of our connection sparks off his fingers, tingling my skin, and I want more than anything to lean into his touch. To breathe in his scent and wrap myself around his passion, letting it infuse me with its strength. I *want* to pretend he believes me.

That he'll teach me how to love him right.

That he still loves me too.

I jerk away from his touch instead.

His chin juts out and his eyes gain a sheen, but after a moment he nods his head and backs away, clearing his throat. With one last glance my way, he turns his attention to Lee. "Lee, it's all good."

She scoffs, spinning around and dropping her hands. "We

must have different definitions of that phrase, Eli."

The sharpness in her voice shoots through the air, piercing my chest and nailing my heart through the hole. *She'll hate me now.* Honestly, I can't blame her. I would hate me too.

My brain is confused. My soul is lost.

And I think I'm going to be *sick.*

I told Eli I loved him and this is where we end up. With me laid out on a desk, while my best friend watches from the doorway—Eli's fiancée none the wiser in a room down the hall.

Oh, God.

My hand curls around my stomach, pressing deeply, hoping the pressure is enough to keep me from spewing all over the tile floor.

What have I done?

Realization drops heavy in my gut and my stomach revolts, teasing the back of my throat with the tang of hypocrisy.

I am my father.

I move from the desk, toward Lee. I'm careful in my steps, afraid she's going to lash out and strike. She's radiating animosity, her stature cutting through my skin and bleeding my guilt into the space between us.

I should have told her.

I suppose hindsight is twenty-twenty.

"Lee, this isn't what it looks like." I'm not sure why I phrase it that way, because it *is* what it looks like. But it's also so much more.

"If I had a nickel for every time I've heard that phrase tonight." She laughs. "No. I think this is exactly what it looks like. And besides the fact Eli's engaged to be freakin' married, I probably wouldn't have cared. But I *asked* you, Becca." Her voice breaks.

Shame twists my stomach. It's always slinked around in

the background, but over the years I've been a master of repression—able to ignore the fact I've been keeping something gigantic from her.

Something that changes her perception of reality.

Just like my folks did with me.

My gut rolls with nausea.

Still, I have to try to salvage this. "I know, but—"

"Don't," she bites. "Don't try to excuse this away. I don't wanna hear it. I can't even begin to process this right now. All I know is how much it hurts that you thought I wouldn't understand."

What's left of my hope smashes into a thousand pieces, careening from my chest and mixing in the ruins of my soul.

Lee's eyes look through me even though I'm standing right in front of her. "I need to speak to my brother, Becca. *Alone.*"

My breathing stutters. The reality of losing Lee is much worse than the fear. It's an ache that penetrates my bones and settles in, spreading through every limb until it hurts to move. Even through the pain, it's a struggle to keep from looking back at Eli—to make sure he knows that I *meant* what I said. That through all of this, I have always, irrevocably loved him.

But the truth is, sometimes love digs in deep and draws out the darkest parts of your soul. The pieces you don't want to find, because of what you'll face when you do—the worst version of yourself.

Sometimes love is greed.

It's hurtful.

It's selfish.

So even though this might be the last time I ever see him, and every single fiber of my being is begging for one last glance, I don't turn around.

Instead, I walk out the door.

46

ELI

Perching on the desk, I watch my sister with wariness. The faint scent of Becca lingers, making my heart pound against my chest, begging with every beat to chase after her. We're nowhere near done with our conversation. Still too many things that are left unsaid.

She doesn't even know I broke off the engagement.

Lee's voice cuts through the air. "While you were busy gettin' your jollies with someone other than your fiancée, guess what you missed?"

I hate that she doesn't use Becca's name. Hate that she's reducing her to a non-entity. My stomach twists in realization that this may have ruined their friendship. The one thing Becca was worried about all these years, and even though we aren't together, it comes true.

I sigh. "What's that, Lee?"

"I'll tell you. Daddy gettin' in a fight with the man of the hour, Sam. Bein' a mess in front of the entire town and then stormin' off drunk as a skunk. That's what. Now he's out there, drivin', sloppy and upset."

I jump up, the back of my legs stinging from where the

desk pressed into them, but I'm too lost in visions of Pops behind the wheel to care. "What? Where'd he go?"

Before we left the house, I tried to talk him out of even coming to this party. It was a pathetic attempt, and I caved the second he raised his voice. I reasoned it wasn't worth the fight—that I'd have my eyes on him the whole time anyway.

"How should I know, Eli? Hopefully home." Lee shrugs.

My nerves are like ants, crawling through every cell, irritating me just enough to cause an itch. I pace back and forth, my jaw aching from the force of my gritted teeth. "Well, let's go. We've gotta find him."

Lee stiffens, her blue eyes piercing. "I'm not goin'. I just thought you should know."

My arms fly out to the sides. "What do you *mean* you're not going?"

She brushes a strand of hair from her face. "Look, if you wanna spend your time chasin' after Daddy and the devil on his shoulder, be my guest. He'll leave you in the dust, and all that'll be left is you chasin' your own tail."

I can see the resolution in her stance, the strength in her stature. Meanwhile, here I am, breaths coming quick and my chest caving in at the mere thought of standing up to Pops.

Lee's been taking care of him for years, shielding herself from weapons forged from the fire of his heartbreak.

Shame floods my chest and sticks to my bones, seeping through in every action.

When I've thought of Lee, I've always imagined the fresh-faced, naive girl she was before. But she's not. She's a phoenix, burning on a pyre and rising from the ashes. She's stronger than I'll ever be.

"I shouldn't have left you to deal with him alone," I whisper. "I should have come back. Should have done more."

Her nostrils flare. "Now's not the time, Eli. Literally any

other day you've been here would have worked. But tonight? I don't wanna hear it."

She turns to walk out the door and I rush after her, my stomach in knots from all the things I want to say. "Lee."

She spins, her eyes icy.

My fingers tap against the outside of my thigh. "You don't understand about Becca. It's not… we aren't… just go easy on her, okay? You're the best thing in her life, and she'd be devastated to lose you."

Lee cocks her head. "You sure seem to know an awful lot about my best friend, Eli."

I blow out a breath, grief coating my heart, heavy and thick, making it sluggish.

I *do* know things about Becca.

I know about the spot behind her ear. The one I'd always kiss because I loved the way it made her moan. I know she has twenty-seven freckles along the bridge of her nose, and that I would have spent the rest of my life tracing every single one while she slept, in awe of her beauty.

I know that I have loved her—every day—even in the darkest moments of my pain.

But I don't know this Becca. The one who's so afraid of her shine that she cowers in her parents' shade. I don't know how, after all this time, she can claim to love me, to have *always* loved me, but still run away when things get hard.

I don't know this woman, and maybe that means I never really did.

I shake my head. "No. I don't know her at all."

Lee's gaze pierces my chest with its intensity, but it doesn't last for long. She blinks once and turns, walking out the door.

I follow behind, replaying the memory of Becca's "I love yous" and licking her taste from my lips. My muscles strain with the need to run and find her. Finish whatever it is we started before it's too late and she leaves for good. But I tamp down the urge because even if I could forgive her, I'm not sure I should.

Becca isn't meant to be mine. I think she's meant to be a lesson.

I've learned we don't always get what we want—what we think we need. We just survive, trying like hell to be better than we were the day before, hoping to ignore the darkness that looms in our heart.

I spot Sarah and head that way, eager to leave quickly and hunt down Pops. My chest twinges when I reach her, guilt sneaking in through my cracks and reminding me that I left her alone while I fucked another woman.

Except Becca isn't another woman.

She's the goddamn sun.

I shake off the thought. "Hey, you ready to go?"

Sarah nods, the spark that flared earlier tonight when she claimed to still be the "lucky lady" dying from her eyes. When we walk out those doors, the curtain is pulled on our relationship for good, and even though we both know it's for the best, it still hurts.

I shouldn't have let us pretend tonight. It did nothing except muddy the waters. Truthfully, I didn't mean to put on such a show, but when Becca walked up with her body molded to the side of another man, I grabbed Sarah around the waist before I could think, pulling her into me and leaning on her like a crutch. Using her to keep me from tearing Jax's arms from his body for daring to touch Becca's skin.

"Is your sister okay?" Sarah asks.

My lips pull down. "Why would you ask that?"

She points behind me, and I twist to look. I find Lee in front of the bar, phone up to her ear and her face drained of color. Her hand shoots to Chase's arm and even from across the room I can see the tightness in her grasp.

Something's wrong.

My legs are taking me over there before I can think twice.

"Lee, what's wrong?"

She stares up at me, her bottom lip trembling. "Daddy was in an accident."

My organs shift from the punch to my gut, my lungs collapsing as I struggle for breath.

Not again.

"Is he... I mean..." I swallow. "Is he okay?"

She nods, blowing out a breath. "He's okay. Locked up for the night." She hesitates. "He hit a family, Eli." She stumbles over the last of her words and Chase is beside her quick, rubbing her back and whispering in her ear.

A pang of jealousy hits me as Chase supports her. I haven't been dealing with Pops for as long as Lee has, but the difference in timing doesn't mean I don't ache to have someone to lean on. Someone who will rub *my* back and whisper in *my* ear that everything will be okay.

I clear my throat. "Don't worry about Pops, Lee. I'll pick him up in the morning and we'll deal with it then." My eyes bounce back and forth between her and Chase. "You just enjoy the rest of your night."

Her breathing stutters and Chase's arms tighten around her waist, feeding her his strength so she doesn't have to search for her own.

"O... okay." She nods.

I open my mouth to speak again, but the words don't come. There's nothing really left to say right now, anyway. Nothing that can be fixed in a simple conversation, at least. So, instead I go back to Sarah.

Pulling into Pops's driveway, I feel a curdling in my stomach. Sarah's quiet, her fingers twisting in her lap as she stares out the window.

This is it.

She heads to the guest room for the night, and I'm left glaring at the worn, brown couch, dreading the kink in my back I'm sure to have when I wake up. But even through the lumps and springs, my eyes close the second my head hits the pillow.

When I wake up in the morning, Sarah's gone, but it's not her absence that causes the hollow ache in my chest. It's the memory of Becca's taste on my tongue, and her words in my ear.

I love you. I've always loved you.

47

ELI

The car ride home from the county detention center is silent. Pops is sober, his eyes bloodshot but clear, and I think it's the first time I've seen a hint of the man he keeps buried underneath the booze. There's an awareness in his gaze that's been missing since I've been back.

His lawyer says he'll need to pray to whatever God he believes in that the family he hit doesn't press charges.

He's lucky. And I think maybe Ma was watching over him —watching over that pregnant woman. That husband. That little girl.

Whatever the case, Pops is looking at some trouble.

The hands of fate have dealt too many blows for me to be convinced that it works in your favor, but maybe there's a reason I haven't talked with Pops yet. There's a tinge of hope expanding in my chest that he'll be more receptive to the idea of help today. Either way, my nerves are shot, too singed by the flame of Becca's touch and the ire of Lee's disappointment to give a damn about the heavy conversation that's ahead.

We make it to the house, and I follow as Pops walks

slowly toward the door. His back is hunched and his shoulders slumped, the bags under his eyes highlighting the soul-deep ache that he stifles with his drink.

He's just past the entryway when I say his name. "Pops."

He stops in his tracks, his head hanging low. "What is it, boy?"

I bite my cheek, pushing down the urge to say that it's nothing. To forget it. "Come into the kitchen. I'll brew us some coffee and we can talk."

"I've been up all damn night. I'm tired. Just wanna get some rest," he grunts.

"Pops." My voice is firm, the rumble vibrating my chest. He twists, his eyes clashing with mine. My natural instinct—what's been ingrained in me since I was a kid—is to lower my gaze, but I don't. Even through the tension in my muscles and the bite of anxiety suddenly eating my insides, I hold his stare. Finally, his back heaves with his sigh and he nods, his eyes breaking away to the floor as he walks into the kitchen.

My foot shakes while I start the coffee, pouring us both a cup and sitting at the kitchen table. Pops goes straight for the cabinet to the left of the sink—the one he *always* goes for—opening it and staring inside.

My fingers tap against the hot ceramic as I watch him, every second ramping up the knots in my stomach. "It's not there," I say.

His back straightens and he spins to face me. "And why the hell not?"

"Dumped it down the drain."

"You had no right," he hisses.

"I had *every* right. You're my father. And you're sick."

He scoffs. "I ain't sick, boy. I'm fine."

I sip my coffee, the heat scalding my tongue. I swallow the burn and nod. "You're right. Crushing your daughter's spirit day after day is *fine*. Killing yourself with every drop you pour down your throat is *fine*." I shrug. "Stupid me, for assuming otherwise. Make sure you tell the judge that same thing. I'm sure he'll realize you're just *fine* too, after almost killing that family."

He flinches and I grab on to his vulnerability before it disappears.

"Pops, there's no shame in admitting you have a problem. We've all got our shit. It's okay to need help after Ma."

He drops his coffee mug to the counter, his finger shaking as he points. "Don't—" His voice breaks. "Don't bring her up."

"Why not? Because you don't want to talk about her?"

"'Cause I don't think I *can*."

Pops's grief floods the room, cracking my chest wide open, my own agony rushing to fill the chasm.

My throat swells. "I get that it's hard, Pops... but you can't keep living this way. Ma wouldn't want this for you."

"Don't you tell me what she woulda wanted."

A little bit of anger seeps out at his words, flowing through my veins and pushing through my fingers until my hand slams on the table. "You think you're the only one who knew her? Who lost her? Guess what. You weren't." My fist beats against my solar plexus, the thunk screaming through the otherwise silent room. "I lost her too. I *miss* her too. And so does Lee."

"You don't think I *know* that?" he explodes. "Your mama was the best..." His chin quivers and he grips the counter behind him with both hands, clearing his throat. "Your mama... she was the best damn woman—person—I've ever known. I don't see how anyone could live in her shine and not lose themselves in the darkness after she..." Wetness lines his lids and my stomach clenches as he wipes away the tears.

"You can say it, Pops. Just because she's dead doesn't mean she's gone."

His eyes squeeze tight at my words, his knuckles tightening.

"But you've gotta get help," I continue. "Lie to me about it all you want, but at least stop lying to yourself."

His chest rises and falls rapidly but he doesn't respond. I trudge on, hanging on to my hope that something I'm saying will get through. That something will finally click. "There's a place."

His eyes snap open.

"It's about an hour away. I think you should go stay there for a while."

He stares at me, his chin lifting. "What kinda place?"

My heart beats so fast my fingers tremble. "A place that can help. They've got a spot for you, if you're willing."

He's quiet, his jaw working back and forth, his hands loosening their grasp on the counter. He walks to the table, the chair legs scraping against the wood floor as he collapses in the seat.

"When?" he rasps.

My stomach flips. "Today. Right now."

"Does your sister know?"

"Nope." I shake my head. "Not yet. But she's on her way and we can tell her. Together."

He nods, his hand dragging across his mouth. "I got some things to say to her anyway."

Relief flies through me, the tendrils of hope clinging on its wings. *He said yes.* I don't know what the future holds for Pops, but I know this is the best chance he has. It's a ninety-day program, and I want to stay close. Want to be able to support Lee—support them *both* in ways I've neglected until now.

Which is why, this morning, I called and resigned from my position at FCU.

I'm staying.

48

BECCA

I t's seven a.m. when a faint knocking wakes me. My eyes slowly open, my core throbbing from the sensation of Eli's tongue in my pussy and his fingers wrapped around my throat.

Too bad it was only a dream.

I groan, running my hands over my face, wondering who the hell is here this early in the morning. My thighs are still slick from arousal as I open the front door.

"I'm not leaving," Jax states immediately.

I blink, caught off guard from his tone and still hazy from sleep.

"Huh?" I yawn. "What'dya mean, you're not *leavin'*?"

It's not necessarily a game changer for me, either way. My ticket is bought, my suitcase is packed, and I can always call up Jeremy and stay with him if Jax is really changing his plans.

He pushes by me, his hand running through his wavy strands as he heads to my kitchen, rummaging through the cabinets and starting a pot of coffee.

My eyes track his movements and I cross my arms. "No, please. Make yourself at home."

He spins toward me, his back resting against the countertop. "You're gonna want coffee for what I'm about to tell you, Becs."

My lips turn down. Jax is not known for his broodiness, so the fact it's radiating off him in waves has unease prickling along my spine. "What happened?"

His jaw tics, his palms gripping the edge of the counter. "Let me ask you something." His eyes narrow. "Did you know about Lee's dad?"

My forehead creases. "You're gonna need to be more specific. What about him?"

"Yeah, that's what I thought. *Dammit, Sweetheart,*" he mutters.

A fist grips my stomach, squeezing. "What is it, Jax? Is he... is everything okay?"

"No. Things are *far* from okay with him." He fills two mugs and my eyes zone in on the steam as it spirals from the cups and disappears into the air.

"Where were you last night, anyway?" Jax asks.

The memory of Eli inside me makes my core spasm, sending a rush of blood to my cheeks. I walk over, grabbing the coffee cup and using it to hide my flush. "Don't change the subject, asshole. What's wrong with Lee's old man?"

"He's not good, Becs. Lost his shit last night at the party, and reeked of whiskey."

I shrug. "Find me a person in this town who *ain't* drinkin'."

His brows pull down. "Not like this, they aren't. I'm telling you, Becs. He's got a problem, and Lee's been dealing with it on her own for *who knows* how fucking long."

My brain races, confusion pulling my skin tight. "No, I...

Lee wouldn't keep somethin' like that from me. Besides, that's not really somethin' you can hide."

As soon as I say the words, I know they're bullshit. I think of Momma and how she's the picture-perfect wife always sipping on her "water." I think to all the times Lee couldn't have me over, all the reasons why they missed Sunday service. I think of all the things that *I* kept from *her*.

To believe she doesn't have her own secrets is naive.

My hand covers my mouth, my heart sinking in my chest. "Oh, God. Are you sure?"

He huffs a laugh. "Pretty fucking sure, Becs. He was a wreck last night. And if you could have seen Lee's face..." He pauses, running his fingers through his hair.

My stomach cramps at the thought of her holding this on her own. "How could I not know?"

Jax sighs. "I didn't know either. You know how Lee gets, always keeping everything close to the chest. Avoiding confrontation."

"Yeah," I breathe. "So, you're... stayin'? Just like that?" I snap my fingers.

He takes a sip of coffee. "How can I leave now, knowing what she's going through?"

"Don't you need to go back on set?"

He cringes. "Yeah, well... they'll just have to deal with it. They can fire me if they have to. It is what it is."

I gasp. "Jax, this is your dream. Lee would never forgive herself if you gave up on it because of her and you know it."

"I don't want to leave her alone." His eyes glisten and it hits me that he loves her enough to suffer, if it means he can support her when she needs it most.

"How do you do it?"

Jax's brows furrow. "Do what?"

"See them together and still be able to love her so selflessly."

He shrugs but I see the anguish in his eyes. "I just want her to be happy."

His words hit me hard, slugging my sternum and stealing my breath. I've always wanted Eli to be happy, but part of the reason I'm running so far and so fast is so I don't have to stick around and watch him pledge his love to someone else.

I sigh, resting my chin in my hand. "You're the best kinda man, Jackson Rhoades. You make the rest of 'em look bad."

He smiles softly, palming the back of his neck. "I hate when you use my full name like that."

I hum, taking a gulp of coffee and peering at him from over the rim. "Listen, you can't just *not* go back. Lee wouldn't want you to lose what you've worked so hard for."

The muscles in his jaw tense. "I won't leave her alone."

"She has Chase," I point out.

"And you trust him to stick around?"

Not really.

I blow out a breath, my stomach rolling. I glance at my packed suitcase, ready and waiting by the door, so close to the freedom I've always craved.

I guess it'll have to remain a dream for another day.

"I'll stay."

My plan was to show up to Sunday service, look my folks in the eyes, and tell them I was gone for good. Done with being their puppet. *Finally.*

Instead, I'm standing outside Lee's apartment.

She doesn't answer right away, but right before I turn to leave, the door cracks open and those baby blues peek out. They turn frigid when they meet mine, but still, she opens the door wider and cocks her hip against the frame.

My heart is heavy as I look at her. We've never fought before, not in our twenty-six years.

"Hey, sister." I force a small smile.

Her brow hikes. I wait for her to speak, but she doesn't, she just crosses her arms and stares me down.

I shuffle on my feet. "Can I come in or you gonna keep me out here all day, lookin' like an ass?"

The corner of her mouth twitches. "Well, if it looks like a duck and walks like a duck…"

I smile, a warm sensation teasing my chest, giving me hope that things aren't as broken as they seem. "Can't argue with you there."

She tilts her head, her eyes analyzing me from head to toe. "Well, come on in then."

The couch creaks as we sit next to one another, and I fidget in place. My heart palpitates against my breastbone, fingers twirling my curls.

She slaps her thighs. "Well?"

I sigh, dropping my hands. "I don't know what to say. I'm scared I'll just make it worse."

She scoffs. "Can't get much worse than what I saw last night."

I suck on my teeth, nodding.

Her lips purse. "I just wanna know why you never told me, Becca. I *asked* you. In a thousand different ways."

I blow out a breath, my heart clenching tight.

Emotion sticks to my throat but I push the words through the clog. "You're gonna hate me more than you already do."

"I don't *hate* you, Becca. I'm hurt by you. There's a difference."

Pushing down the fear of losing her, I search for a sliver of courage to say what I need to say. What she deserves to hear. "I worked with the basketball team when I was at FCU."

Lee's face scrunches. "You did? I didn't know that."

The root of my self-deprecation grows branches, rising through my stomach and into my chest. "I never told you."

She nods slowly, her nostrils flaring.

"At first, I didn't tell you 'cause if I did... I'd have to admit that I didn't hate your brother as much as I should, and that felt disloyal. And then, before I could take a breath, it was this gigantic, malleable thing that wrapped around me, makin' me lose sight of everything but him."

"Becca," Lee breathes. "You could have told me anything. Don't you know me at all? When have I *ever* made you think I'd judge you for that?"

I rub my hands on my thighs, the friction of my jeans against my palms almost enough to distract me from the nerves. "I was scared, okay? I remember what it was like with Lily when she found out about you and Chase. The thought of losin' you—" My voice cracks, tears warming my cheeks as they drip off my chin. "I *knew* it was wrong to keep it from you. It was on the tip of my tongue every time we talked. But how could I, Lee? How could I tell you that I was gettin' all his hours when you were beggin' for a minute?"

Lee bites her lip, her eyes glossing over.

"What you saw last night was a mistake. It wasn't..." My breath stutters and I shake my head. "No, It *was* what it looked like, and I *hate* myself for it, Lee. Can't stand the feel of bein' in my own skin after doin' what I did."

"You mean bein' with Eli?" Lee asks.

"Not for being with Eli. Maybe I should feel some type of way about that, but I don't." A sour sensation pangs in my gut, reverberating off my bones and making them ache. "But for bein' with Eli when he's supposed to be with someone else. Eli isn't mine to have, and instead of respectin' that, I ended up becomin' the thing I hate most. My father."

Lee's face drops and she's quiet, chewing on her bottom lip. She's the only person I've ever told about how I walked

302 BENEATH THE STANDS

in on Papa. How it dug deep inside me and latched on to the essence of my soul, suffusing it with betrayal.

She opens her mouth and closes it a few times. "You hurt me. Eli did too, but you... *you* are my person. I'm supposed to be able to trust you with anything and I thought you were the same way with me. But I..." She blows out a breath. "Do you love him?"

My heart clatters against my ribs, my stomach flipping at the question. "Yeah, Lee. I love him. I don't remember what it feels like *not* to love him."

Lee's eyes soften. "He's the reason you came back, ain't he?"

I nod, unable to speak around the sudden lump in my throat.

"Did he do somethin'?"

"No, I–I did."

Her breath whooshes out and she reaches over, tangling her fingers with mine. Her touch breaks the dam on my tears and they pour down my face, warming my cheeks and dripping of my chin.

"Ar–are you gonna forgive me?" I hiccup.

She cocks her head. "Do you think you can forgive yourself?"

Her question slams into my stomach.

Forgiveness.

I've heard Papa preach it a thousand times, and I've felt the weight of its absence as it crushes down on my soul, but I'm not sure I truly know what it means. "I don't think I know how to forgive."

Lee squeezes my hand. "I think before you worry about others, you should figure out yourself."

"Is that what you've done with your old man?"

Her eyes widen, her hand snapping back. "I shoulda known Jax would run and tell you." She breathes deep.

"Daddy is a work in progress for me. There's *a lot* to forgive." She glances at her lap. "But I've learned—very recently—that it's not about him… not really. It's about lettin' go of the hurt and the anger for *me*. So that I can find peace." She pauses, the palm of her hand rubbing against her chest.

"'Forgiveness is divine, Alina May.' That's what Mama always told me." Her eyes lock on mine. "Maybe you should try to find your faith."

49

ELI

I've lived most of my life living with certain proclivities. Beliefs that were projected like a bullhorn, blaring into my eardrums until I was deaf to anything else.

One: Pops's word is law.

Two: Success is the only thing that matters.

It's no coincidence the two molded together like play-dough. Different colors of the same thing mixing until I couldn't tell them apart. Pops's aspirations became my own. Still, through all the times Pops pushed me, all the critiques he gave instead of his pride, he was still my hero. In my eyes, he could do no wrong, and I was forever trying to appease him.

But yesterday, something shifted.

Something cataclysmic came loose, rattling around until it jumbled up my head and my heart, forming a new mold for my soul to fit into.

Now, I see things clear.

Pops *isn't* infallible. He's human. He makes mistakes. He'll have to pay his own penance for the things that he's done. For the people he's sucked into his vortex, whipping them through the tornado of his grief, and spitting them out damaged and torn.

My hope is he'll put in the work at Stepping Stones, which is where I dropped him off yesterday after Lee came over. He went without fanfare, solemn on the drive and quiet as he was checked in.

Now it's Monday morning, and even though I've been trying like hell to relax, my muscles are tense and my mind is a minefield.

Basketball lost its meaning once Becca left.

It hurt to look at the glossy maple floors and remember teaching her to own the paint. Too painful to reflect on the feel of her fingers under mine while I positioned her hands. But for the first time in five years, my fingers itch to hold a ball in my hands. To stand on the court and breathe it all in. Not because it's my job, but because my soul is yearning for solace.

It's that twinge of a spark which makes me head to Sugarlake High this morning. I'm not even sure the doors will be unlocked, but there's a pull between my stomach and my chest, tugging me in the direction of my memories.

For some reason, I know it's the only way to quiet my mind today.

A few cars are scattered through the lot and the doors are open, so I walk inside and head straight to the gymnasium. The squeak of my shoes rebound off the metal of the lockers, and the bittersweet taste of nostalgia fills me up as I remember what it was like to make this same trek eleven years ago.

Back when I was the next big thing. Before I became the town's biggest disappointment.

The thought doesn't sting like it once did. To assume we know our fate is futile, and when one path is stunted, another one is paved.

I stay quiet when I push open the double doors to the gym, not wanting to attract any attention. I'm not sure I'm technically *allowed* to be here.

A smile pulls at my lips as I make my way to the center of the court. If I strain my ears, I can almost hear the cheers ringing through the bleachers, chants of my name and thirty-three bouncing off the walls. My chest warms at the memory, but I don't ache to grasp the feeling like I once did.

My eyes take in my surroundings. Not much has changed in eleven years. The Sugarlake Bobcat is still painted in a gaudy blue, shining off the whitewashed bricks on the far wall. A rolling cart of basketballs are resting against its surface. I walk over and pick one up, staring at how the black lines cut through the dark orange surface.

This feeling right here—this *rightness*—has only happened with two things in my life.

The feel of a ball in my hands and the warmth of Becca in my arms.

I palm the leather, popping it up and spinning it on the tip of my finger as I make my way to the free-throw line.

Inhaling a deep breath, I dribble once. Twice. I take the shot at the exact moment a bang echoes off the walls, making my stance falter. The ball hits the backboard and bounces to the side, rolling toward the entrance to the gym.

My eyes follow.

Bright red heels.

Killer legs.

Hips that make my hands tingle with the memory of their curve.

Rebecca.

My stomach flips at the sight of her.

"You," she gasps.

I smirk, the first time we ran into each other at FCU flashing through my mind.

"Rebecca." I stride toward her, my cock jerking as she bends at the waist to grab the basketball. Those crazy curls fall over her shoulder, begging me to grip them in my palm, tug the silky strands as they tangle in my fingers.

She straightens, her cheeks flushed a gorgeous stain of pink. I stand close, peering down at her. Our gazes lock and heat simmers low in my gut.

She brushes a curl out of her face. "What are you doin' here?"

My eyebrow quirks. "What's it look like?"

She scoffs. "I meant at the school, big head."

My eyes narrow. "What are *you* doing? I thought you were gone. Running away to somewhere new."

She lifts a shoulder, chewing on her lip. "The people who matter most need me here."

Stale anger filters through my veins at the audacity of her statement. Once again, she'll stay when someone else needs her, but wouldn't stay for me.

It's the bitterness of that thought on my tongue which makes my voice sharp. "Never stopped you before."

She sucks on her teeth, nodding. "I know. And as much as I wish I could turn back time and change my choices, I can't." She sighs, her fingers brushing through her hair. "But I'm tryin' to learn. Tryin' to stand up straight for the first time in my life and see things from a different angle. To forgive myself for the mistakes I've made."

Old wounds throb inside me and the ache has me stepping in closer, my breath fanning the wisps of her hair away from her face. "Well what about my forgiveness, Becca? You give a damn about *that*?"

She licks her lips and my own lips tingle from envy.

"If I thought for one second it would make a lick of difference, I'd be on my knees beggin'."

Try it, baby girl. Just show me you give a damn.

Her eyes catalog my every action. She's holding the basketball against her sternum and she steps into me, the ball pressing uncomfortably against my abs.

My stomach jolts, my cock growing against my leg.

"I'm sorry, Eli. I'm *so* damn sorry for hurtin' you. I could go into all the reasons why, but they don't matter. Not really. They're nothin' more than excuses to try and keep my guilt at bay."

I grit my teeth, gulping around the lump in my throat. "What if I want your excuses?"

She shakes her head, a tear slipping from the corner of her eye and trailing down her cheek, her makeup melting away to showcase those perfect freckles underneath. "You deserve better. And even if I tried to give you reasons, they don't change a thing. I made a mistake. The worst..." She blows out a breath, her eyes squeezing shut as she swallows. "The worst mistake I think I've ever made in my life, and I'm still strugglin' to gather all my pieces and accept I was the one who broke them." She wipes her cheeks with the back of her hand. "I'm not the woman you deserve, Eli. I never was."

My heart slingshots off my ribs, my chest pulling tight at her admission. At her show of emotion.

At her heartbreak.

She backs up, the cool air slicing through my shirt, sending goose bumps scaling down my arms. My hand snaps forward and grips her wrist tight, yanking her back into me.

The basketball drops from her hands, the rhythmic bouncing an echo of the way my heart stutters in my chest.

"I broke it off with Sarah."

The words are gruff as they sail through the air. I'm not sure why I said it at this particular moment, other than the delicate thread holding me together is fraying at the seams, and all I can think about is how badly I *need* her to know.

"What?" she gasps, her eyes widening. "When? Was it after—"

"It was before the party," I interrupt. "Right after we left the meeting with you, actually."

"Oh," she whispers.

"Yeah. *Oh*. And do you know why, Rebecca?"

Her chest heaves against mine, the fabric of my shirt scratching against my skin with each of her breaths.

I lean in, my mouth grazing the shell of her ear. "Because it doesn't matter if she's the woman I deserve, when you're the only one I see."

She pants out a breath and I catch it with my lips, groaning at the explosion of her taste on my tongue.

Her moans vibrate through my body, her fingers diving in the strands of my hair and twisting, the sting just enough to make my cock pulse with want. I grip her arms and pull her closer, plastering her body to mine, lost in the blaze.

50

BECCA

I'm weak.

There's nothing I can say to defend how easily I give in, but when it comes to Eli, he demands my submission without saying a word.

When he tells me he's not with Sarah—that I'm the only one he sees—I'm lost in what he's offering. Drowning in everything he is and all the ways I crave him.

His tongue skims across my mouth, parting my lips, diving in and twisting with mine, sending sparks of his flavor across my taste buds. My fingers tangle in his hair and pull him closer. He slides his palms up from where they grip my shoulders until they wrap around my neck, his thumbs brushing my jaw, making my skin prickle with heat.

The kiss changes, his teeth pulling on my lower lip until it splits, the sting making me moan into his mouth. He growls, licking along the cut and diving back in, the tang of my blood mixing with the sweetness of his breath.

He walks us backward, his mouth never leaving mine. I stumble in my heels, but he doesn't miss a beat, gripping an ass cheek in each hand and lifting me, bunching my skirt until my legs are wrapped around him. His hip bones cut against my inner thighs, and my center presses against the rigid outline of his dick. I moan, grinding myself against him, my pussy clenching at the memory of what he felt like inside me.

"Goddamn, baby girl," he growls, slamming me against the end rails of the bleachers. The metal frame presses into my back. His fingers dig into the meat of my ass and he pulls my lower half into him, dragging me along the length of his cock. Even through his basketball shorts, I can feel it pulsing against my clit.

His mouth nips down my neck and my legs tremble from the torture of having him dangle me off the edge of euphoria.

"Eli, please. Do somethin'," I breathe.

He chuckles, his face skimming between my cleavage. "What exactly would you like me to do, Rebecca?"

His right hand moves from behind and trails up my thigh until he's cupping me through my soaked panties.

"Fuck, you're wet as hell. You miss me that bad?" He pushes the fabric to the side and spreads my pussy lips with his fingers. I'm so wet they glide easily along my slit, every stroke coiling me tighter until I could scream from how badly I need him to let me unravel.

My head smacks the railing and echoes off the walls, the rattle jarring in the otherwise silent gym. "Eli, *God*. Either finish what you started or get outta the way so I can do it my damn self."

His mouth curls up against my breast and he glances at me through his lashes. "Say please."

"No," I whisper with a smile. The fire surging through my veins mixes with the warmth filling up my chest from our banter.

The pressure leaves my clit and my legs tighten around his wrist, trying to keep him pressed against me. He dips in the top of my panties, twisting the fabric between his fingers, making my stomach flip.

He tugs slightly, making the lace pull against my hips and slide between my folds, creating a delicious friction. A slight sheen of sweat breaks against my brow from the exertion of being so close to relief yet constantly on the precipice of falling.

My stomach knots tighter with each jerk of his hand, my breaths coming quick as he manipulates the fabric against my core.

He leans in and kisses that spot. *That spot.* The one right behind my ear. Frissons of desire race down my spine and rocket through my body, spreading heat like lava, melting everything in its path.

"Eli, *please,*" I groan.

He smiles, his eyes meeting mine as he leans in for a kiss.

"You know I love it when you beg," he says against my mouth.

With a sharp pull, he rips the panties from my body, the sting of the fabric tearing against my skin causing a mix of pain and pleasure that has my eyes rolling.

I should probably care that we're at my place of employment—should give a damn about the fact he has me mewling like a schoolgirl against the bleachers of a high school gym, but I don't.

My need for him outweighs everything else. My control has been bent until it snapped, thousands of pieces scattering until there's no chance of being glued together again.

His fingers push inside me further, curling up and pressing against my inner walls, creating a deep ache in my womb. I moan, my body shaking.

"So many things I want to do with you," he rumbles in my ear.

"Like what?" I pant.

"We can start with your pussy sucking on my fingers until you're a puddle in my hands." His movement twists, making my walls quiver and my clit swell against his palm. "And then... I'm gonna fuck you, right here, beneath the stands. Bathe my cock in your juices, while that tight cunt milks me and has me filling you up with my cum."

My pussy spasms around his fingers, drawing them in deeper, desperate to give him what he's asking.

"Would you like that, baby girl?" he asks. "Want me to remind you who you belong to? Who you've *always* belonged to?"

His hand tangles in my curls, wrapping my strands around his fist and pulling sharply until my throat is exposed and my head is angled.

He laves kisses on the juncture between my neck and shoulder, my vision dotting from riding the ebb and flow of pleasure.

His fingers plunge deeper and I reach down, fumbling with the waistband of his shorts, desperate to feel him inside me. Clumsily, I push them off his hips, his thick erection bobbing against my heat. I stroke it once, from base to tip, relishing in the way his groan vibrates against my neck.

His palm pushes against my clit, and then he removes his hand, gripping the base of his dick and sinking inside me to the hilt. Pleasure skitters along my insides, my pussy walls clamping around his length as he starts a fast pace, driving in and out until I'm delirious in my need to come around his cock.

"This is gonna be fast, Rebecca. Come for me." His teeth sink into my skin, *hard*. The bite of pain sends me catapulting off the edge, breaking apart from the fall and hoping he'll pick up my shattered pieces. I'm vaguely aware of him spasming inside me, spurting so deep I'm not sure I'll ever be clean of him again.

His teeth stay lodged, tethering me to Earth until the fogginess subsides and my breathing regulates. He finally releases me, his lips kissing away the sting.

"Hmm," he hums.

My breath hitches, my hand reaching for my neck. "What do you—"

A voice filters through the door and my heart jumps into my throat. Hastily, I move to rearrange my skirt and put some space between Eli and me. We're hidden along the side of the bleachers, but barely.

Mr. Daniels, the principal, walks through the doors a moment later, his phone to his ear. I stare at Eli with wide eyes, urging him to back up a space or two. He smirks and reaches under my skirt, slipping his fingers between my folds, pushing the cum that's dripping out of me deeper inside as he pumps his fingers twice.

"Eli," I moan quietly. My pussy is sensitive from my orgasm, but his touch makes every nerve ending light up, begging for another one. He moves, backing up a space and bringing his hand to his mouth, slowly licking the wetness from his fingers. Butterflies erupt low in my abdomen.

"I understand that," Mr. Daniels huffs, "but I'm not interested in havin' someone come here, bond with these kids, only to leave after the year is up."

Eli leans in, palming my jaw and wiping his thumb across my lower lip, fixing my smudged lipstick.

I let him finish, my heart squeezing in my chest at the show of affection, my mind slotting the jigsaw pieces together, trying to make sense of what the hell is happening with us.

Mr. Daniels is going to have a fit over seeing me in here with someone, looking like I was rode hard and put away wet. My cheeks heat as I step around the side of the bleachers, determined to get this over with.

Eli follows and Mr. Daniel's eyes fly toward us, widening when they land on Eli. "Lemme call you back, Gene." He hangs up the phone, tapping it against his thigh while he stares.

"Mr. Daniels," I blurt. "Look who I found." My forced smile is splitting my face, and I pray to God he doesn't see my muscles twitching under the strain, or Eli's cum that I can feel dripping down the inside of my thighs.

"Elliot Carson. My goodness, if you ain't a sight for sore eyes, son."

Eli clears his throat. "Mr. Daniels."

When he speaks, I feel the rumble of his voice vibrating through my entire body. I rub my thighs together, trying to relieve the sudden tension.

"Nice to see you're still here keeping all the kids in line, sir."

Mr. Daniels chuckles, running a hand over his mouth. "Yeah, well, try as they might they just can't get ridda me. I heard you were in town, didn't expect to see you *here,* though."

"Didn't expect to be here, sir. Just found myself in a moment of nostalgia, wanting to relive the glory days." Eli's arm waves around the room and my eyes follow, snagging on the high school jersey hanging on the wall, the number thirty-three and last name Carson shining like a beacon. He really was the town golden boy. I don't blame him for not wanting to come home—to be slapped in the face with everything they wanted him to be.

"Yeah," I cut in. "I heard somethin' and came to check it out, found him shootin' hoops like he was still runnin' up the Bobcat scoreboard." I glance behind me, my eyes locking with Eli's until everything else dims—the air so thick it pulses in time with the pound of my heart. "You know, *ownin' the paint.*"

Eli's eyes flare. I turn back around, breathing deep through my nose, trying to tame the surge of electricity sparking through my middle.

Mr. Daniels whistles. "About time someone did. No one's been able to run this court quite like you in all the years I've been here." His eyes stray toward the jersey on the wall then back to Eli. "I've watched your career flourish, Elliot. You make this town proud, son. We're lucky to call ya our own."

"Th–Thank you, sir," Eli stutters.

"They're even more lucky to have ya down at FCU," Mr. Daniels continues.

Eli sighs, palming the back of his neck. "Yeah, well... I loved it there, but I won't be going back. Gonna stick around here for a while instead."

My heart stalls then kickstarts twice as fast until I'm sure I'll pass out.

"What?" I gasp, turning to face him fully.

"Yeah." The weight of his gaze pierces a hole in my chest, digging inside the cavity and making a home. "People who matter most need me here."

My throat swells like a sponge, siphoning moisture from my tongue until it sticks to the roof of my mouth. I hadn't even thought about how he's been doing being with Lee. With visiting his momma.

With his old man.

"Well, hot damn, son. You lookin' for a gig?" Mr. Daniels's voice is jumpy, the tone a pitch higher than it was when he first walked in.

My heart stutters at his question. I spin back around, my forehead creasing.

"Why, you got something for me, Mr. Daniels?" Eli grins.

"That depends on how much of a pay cut you're willin' to take." Mr. Daniels cringes. "I've found myself without a gym teacher. He up and left with his new wife and baby, barely givin' me any damn notice." Mr. Daniels shakes his head, dropping his gaze. "It's probably not somethin' you're interested in but—" His eyes raise back up. "He also coached the basketball team."

The air stills. Everything in me is locked in place—my breath frozen in my lungs—waiting for his response.

"I'll take it." Eli's words are quick and sharp.

My breath whooshes out as I twist to face him. His response surprises me. Eli's always been very controlled, overthinking every decision until he can dissect the pros and cons. "You will?"

He looks down at me, his eyes sparking with heat. "I will."

Eli focuses back on Mr. Daniel's, a thousand-dollar smile lighting up his face. "There's nothing that would make me happier than coaching these kids, sir. It's where everything really began for me." He pauses, his jaw ticking with the motion of his swallow. "I'd be honored to be part of where it begins for them too."

Shock surges through my veins.

Eli is staying in Sugarlake.

And so am I.

I'm not in a place where I deserve him. I know this and I think deep down, so does he. I can't be sure he'll forgive me for my mistakes. And I can't promise that I won't get spooked —won't run and hide from all the ways he makes me feel. But I'll work like hell to overcome the roadblocks and clear the path back to him.

He's here.

He's staying.

And one day soon, maybe...

He'll be mine.

51

ELI

I've lived most of my life striving for the spotlight and thinking it's what I needed to feel complete. Believing that one day, when I finally reached the top, the hole that drilled its way through my insides would close up and start to heal. That I'd finally get Pops's approval and he'd know all his energy hadn't been wasted on me over the years.

But living for other people's dreams is a bottomless pit. An emptiness that festers and rots in the deepest parts of you while your soul cripples from neglect.

It wasn't until I started coaching that I realized my true calling in life is to stand on the sidelines and help others shine. That maybe my career-ending injury happened, not because of bad fortune, but because I needed a push in the right direction.

My chest twinges when I think about my players at FCU. All the time and energy I've devoted to helping them achieve their greatness. I'll miss it there. Giving up the years of work I've put in to become the next head coach smarts at my insides, and it's hard to not pick up the phone and plead with them to take me back.

But then I think about my family. About building a relationship with Lee. Supporting Pops through his repressed grief and addiction. I imagine what it will feel like to help foster love of the game for kids who are just beginning to recognize their potential. And when I do that, an excited, nervous energy fills up my bones and settles in deep because I just *know* this is where I'm supposed to be.

Saying yes to Mr. Daniels just now may have been a rash decision, but it was the right one.

My eyes trail to Becca, and my heart palpitates, making my breath quicken.

The path I'm on now seems so clear, yet she's still the one thing that confuses the hell out of me. I spend hours of my day convincing myself I've moved on. That all I need is closure. But then I see her and all of it goes to shit. My precious control that's been fine-tuned over the years thrown to the wayside from less than twenty seconds in her presence.

I'm not sure if soul mates exist, but if they do, I'm sure she's mine. Not that it matters.

Becca has always been a raging inferno, and I've always been the moth to her flame. But where my soul used to call out for hers, now it cowers in fear, knowing she has the power to turn me to ash.

There's not much left from when she burned me the first time.

So I'm stuck in this limbo. One where I can't be with her but I can't be without her, and I don't really know what to do with that. And I damn sure don't know how to control myself when she's around.

Mr. Daniels's phone rings, pulling me out of my thoughts. Becca's cheeks are stained the most beautiful shade of pink. One I know for a fact goes all the way past her chest. My cock twitches, flaring back to life and I try to think of something, *anything* to keep the pathetic, lovesick fool inside me under control.

"Sorry, y'all. I've gotta take this," Mr. Daniels says. "Elliot, why don't you stop by here tomorrow afternoon and we can work out some more details."

"Sounds good to me."

He shakes his head, lip curling up on one side. "Whew, boy. I must have an angel lookin' out for me with the way you waltzed in here right when I needed ya." He glances at his phone one more time and answers, nodding at Becca as he leaves.

There's a tap, tap, tap against the court floor from the toe of Becca's heeled foot. Her arms are crossed and she's watching me.

Analyzing me.

"What?" My brow arches.

Her eyes narrow slightly. "I ain't sure yet."

"You aren't *sure* yet? About what?"

"I just told you, I ain't sure."

Annoyance pricks my chest. *Christ*, she's difficult. "Well, when you figure it out, be sure to let me know."

"What are we doin'?" she spouts.

My stomach twists. "What do you mean?"

She sighs, tugging on a curl. "Are we... ya know... you keep askin' me questions and then you go and fuck me stupid and I just don't know what that means."

I cross my arms. "Well, Rebecca, I'm pretty sure it means I want to fuck you and I want some damn answers. I think it's the least you can give me on both accounts."

Her eyes flare and it sparks a match low in my gut.

She scoffs. "It's not like you've been givin' me a chance to talk with the way you accost me after every question."

I take a step forward, that goddamn mouth of hers making my blood heat and my cock hard. "If the cum on your thighs and the smell of your pussy on my fingers is any indication, you liked the way I *accosted* you just fine."

"I never said I didn't." She smirks.

"So what's the problem?"

She shrugs. "You said I was yours. That I belonged to you."

My heart speeds up. She *is* mine, but I shouldn't want her to be. "I say a lot of things in the heat of the moment."

Her eyes dim and her body sways slightly, like my words are a physical blow to the chest. I resist the urge to grimace at their impact. Anger flickers through my veins at the fact she's making me feel guilty. "No, you don't get to do that."

Her eyes widen. "Do what?"

"Act like I'm hurting you. That's not how this works."

Her shoulders stiffen, her jaw locking in place.

My chest tightens with expectation. I *expect* to see what I've always seen—that wall of defense she builds up, one barb at a time until no one can break through to see the truth.

But it never comes.

Instead, she nods, biting on her lip. "Okay. I get that."

"Do you?" The surprise flowing through me shows itself in my question.

"Yeah, I do. But I'm entitled to my feelin's too, big head." Her hand presses against her chest. "I told you I loved you, then you try and dick me down every time we talk... and now you're actin' like it's no big deal." She waves her hand between us. "It's confusin'. You're like one big walkin' contradiction."

"Look." I sigh, dropping my head. "Clearly I can't control myself around you. I think that's been obvious for a while." I glance at her, our eyes locking. "But it has to stop. I can't... I can't *do this* with you, okay? I wish I could. Fuck, I wish more than anything that I had *something* capable of loving you again, but it's not there." I smack my chest. "You broke it, and it's been useless ever since."

She flinches and my heart jumps into my throat, trying to stifle my speech.

But I won't let my heart control my head.

Not again.

Her lower lip trembles and she closes her eyes, blowing out a breath. "I'm not askin' for anything."

Her words pack a punch, and I clench my fists to keep from taking her in my arms and telling her I didn't mean it. That the charred pieces of my heart still beat for her. That we can try to make it work. That I'll try to forgive and forget.

But I already know what will happen if I do. I'll lay down in her waves as they break on the shore and drown in her undertow.

"I get that I hurt you and I'm so, *so* damn sorry for that," she continues. "But we're about to be workin' at the same place. And now that I know what's goin' on with your old man, there's not a chance in hell I'm leavin' Lee to deal with you *and* him alone."

My stomach turns at the reminder of Pops.

"We're gonna be in each other's orbit, Eli. There's no way around it. So, I just want you to know that I'm gonna try."

"Try what?"

"To be the woman you deserve." She smiles and turns, walking away without another word.

My heart beats out of my chest, trying to follow.

"What the hell do you mean you're *staying* there?"

Connor's voice is incredulous and I roll my eyes, sipping my water while I lay back on my bed.

"Look, man. Pops is messed up. I gotta stay here and make sure my family is taken care of."

Connor scoffs. "You've never given a shit before."

Irritation slams into me. Maybe because it's the truth, or maybe because it isn't his fucking place to voice it even if it is. "Yeah, well I'm givin' a shit now."

"Is that why you broke it off with Sarah? Because of your family?"

I sigh, pinching the bridge of my nose. "No, man. I broke it off with Sarah because we weren't right for each other. We were just dragging each other down and that's not something I want to do anymore."

"Mmhm." He pauses. "I can't say I'm surprised."

"Really?" My hand drops to my side.

"Yeah. I wish you would have talked to me about it. Everything with Sarah, I mean. I'm here for you, ya know?"

Guilt slinks up through my stomach and into my chest. I've been a shit friend. Since coming back to Sugarlake I haven't even thought about Connor, let alone given him a call.

"Sucks you won't be around, though," he says. "What am I supposed to do without my wingman?"

I smirk. "Maybe you can take Annie."

He laughs. "Ah, hell. You were a shit one the past few years, anyway. You weren't supposed to let me get *married* to my Monday chick."

I chuckle. "You know damn well Annie had you by the balls before I ever walked in the room."

"Yeah." The line grows silent. "I'll miss you, man. Won't be the same down here without you."

My throat swells and I sit up, grabbing my water bottle to wash down the knot. I'll miss him too. He's been the closest thing to a brother I've ever had, and part of me worries that the distance will lessen the bond.

We talk for a few more minutes, catching up on things I've missed, until Annie calls him away for dinner.

I grab takeout for myself and plan to call it an early night when the urge to visit Ma hits me out of nowhere. Normally, the thought of going to her grave has nausea rolling through my gut, but after talking to Connor I feel anxious, and for some reason I feel like talking to Ma is what I need to calm the nerves.

Still, when I make it to the cemetery my legs are dead weight. Sickness swirls in my stomach and an ache cracks open my chest at the thought of being near the dead, rotted corpse that used to be my ma.

I force my heavy limbs to move, one step at a time. I physically count them as I walk to her marker.

One.

Two.

Three.

Four.

I'm at fifty-seven when I finally look up. A halo of honey hair, so similar to my own, is bowed in front of Ma's marble slab.

My heart kicks my chest, bruising me from the inside out.

Lee.

52

ELI

T
he grass crunches underneath my feet as I walk toward Lee, my throat swelling with all the things I want to say. And all the things I don't.

My nerves are so tangible I'm surprised she hasn't felt them. They expel from my body like fireworks, shooting through my fingertips and ricocheting off the ground.

I clear my throat as I sit beside her, ignoring the way the contents of my stomach whirl and tumble from sitting on top of Ma's remains.

Lee's body stiffens, but she stares straight ahead, not sparing me a glance.

Aesthetically, the cemetery is quite pleasing. But there's grief in the air. It's thick, and it sticks to your bones, until you feel the weight of a hundred broken souls bleeding out their sorrow.

There are pink tulips on both sides of the marble slab. They were her favorite, and my stomach tightens, wishing like hell I would have thought to pick some up on the way.

Stupid.

Even when she was alive, I always missed out on the things that made her smile.

Being here makes me reflect on the past, and maybe that's part of why it's so hard for me to come. Because when I show up, so do the memories.

"When I was about ten," I start.

Lee jumps, finally giving me her attention.

"Ma brought me to the basketball court that's on the side of the church... right over there." I twist and point across the lot where you can vaguely make out faded concrete and an old, torn up net. "I couldn't understand why she'd brought me here of all places, when we had a perfectly good hoop in our drive." I shake my head, chuckling slightly. "Even back then this cemetery freaked me out."

"It did?" Lee asks, her voice hoarse.

"Yeah, still does." I nod. "It wasn't until we were almost all the way back to the car when Ma dropped the real reason we were here. To visit MeeMee and Paw."

Both of our grandparents passed when we were young, and Lee doesn't remember them. I do, but barely. Just foggy smiles and stories told through Ma. She visited their graves weekly, but we rarely went with.

"I remember looking at each headstone as we passed, gripping my basketball tight while I imagined who each person was. The life they lived..." I swallow. "Whether they had a chance to grow into everything people expected, or if they died a disappointment."

"Dang, Eli. That's depressin'."

I shrug. "Doesn't mean it's not true. That's always been my biggest fear, you know?"

Lee faces me fully now, her head cocking. "What was? Dyin' a disappointment?"

"Just being one in general, I guess. Life was different for you growing up, Lee. *Pops* was different with you."

She scoffs. "Don't gimme that, Eli. I had the same childhood you did. We grew up in the same dang house."

Irritation cuts at old wounds. Lee never looks at things from my point of view. She never wants to. "I'm not surprised you think that."

"Was there a point to your morbid story?"

My defenses bristle, scaling along my skin like armor, bitterness that instead of asking *why* it was different, she brushes me off. Again. Like she always has. But I let it go because it isn't what's important, and despite her not realizing the ways she's wronged me over the years, I do realize the ways I've wronged *her*. And I'd like to try and rectify that.

"*Anyway*, we get to Paw's grave and after a few minutes, I ask Ma how he passed. I knew MeeMee had cancer, but for the life of me, I couldn't remember how he died."

"Huh," Lee murmurs. "I can't remember either."

I glance at the headstones across the way—where both my grandparents rest—the memory playing like a movie while the words slide off my tongue.

"Ma, how did Paw die?"

Ma's hand smooths over my hair, pushing it off my forehead. Her touch sends a blanket of comfort cascading through me and I smile as she looks down at me.

"He died of a broken heart, baby."

My face scrunches. "A broken heart? I ain't know you could die from that."

"Well, now ya do." She winks before her lips tug down in the corners. "Sometimes, when you lose the other half of your soul, you lose the will to live with it."

My brows draw in, trying to make sense of her words. I didn't know your soul was something you could lose. I wonder what it feels like. "That's sad."

The hand that was on my head trails down my arm, squeezing my fingers. "No, baby. Not sad. Your paw was one of the lucky ones. Instead of havin' to exist with half his heart, the Lord took mercy on his soul and let him live in Heaven."

"With MeeMee."

She grins. "That's right, sugar. With MeeMee."

I think about that for a moment, confusion twisting up my insides. "But what if he wasn't done?"

Her head tilts, eyes squinting against the sun. "What'dya mean, baby?"

"With livin'."

Ma squats down beside me, her hands framing my face. "Now you listen close. Just because he's dead, doesn't mean he's gone."

"Then how come we can't see him?"

"Because he's an angel now, baby. Him and MeeMee. They shine too bright for our eyes to see."

"Oh."

"But you can feel them," she says.

"You can?"

Ma nods, pressing her hand to the center of my chest. "They're right here. Always."

"How d'ya know?" I whisper.

"Because that's where we keep all the people we love." She taps her fingers against me. "In our hearts, so we can feel them with every beat."

She stands up, wiping a stray tear from the side of her face.

My chest pulls tight. I don't like it when Ma cries. It makes me want to do something to take away the sadness, but I don't know how.

"Hey, Ma. I'm gonna win the game on Friday. Just for you." I grin big and wide, expecting to see her frown disappear just like Pops's would—to see her eyes spark with expectation and distract her from her tears.

But she just smiles softly, interlocking our fingers as we walk back to the car.

"I'm sure you will, baby. But I'm proud of you either way."

"Paw died of a broken heart?" Lee asks.

I nod, my heart squeezing so tight I can barely get the words out. "So the story goes."

She looks down, picking at the blades of grass. "You think that's why Daddy is the way he is? 'Cause he's livin' with half his heart and God didn't show him mercy?"

My elbows rest on my knees, emotion rising into my throat and burning behind my nose. "I don't pretend to know the first thing about God, sis. But yeah." I blow out a breath. "I think when Ma ended up here in this grave, Pops stayed behind with her." I pause, looking over at her. "I'm sorry I never listened."

She sucks in a breath.

"I don't know that it woulda made a difference if I had, but..."

"Do you remember Lily?" she asks, suddenly.

My forehead creases, the abrupt shift in our conversation throwing me off-kilter. "Of course I do. Chase's sister, and your other sidekick."

"Yeah, the one you *didn't* go and fall in love with behind my back." She smirks.

"Lee, I—"

"It's okay, Eli." She waves me off. "My issue is with Becca lyin' to me, not with y'all two together. I mean... I think you're an absolute jerk for doin' Sarah dirty but that's between you, her, and the Almighty."

"But I'm not—"

"Lily overdosed, did you know that?"

The words die on my lips, because *no*, I didn't know that. It's just another reminder of how much I missed while I was trying like hell to stay away.

"No," I whisper.

Lee nods. "Yep. She was lost for a long time... probably longer than any of us realized. And by the time anyone did, it was too late." She shakes her head. "But *I* knew, Eli. I knew and I..." She closes her eyes and shakes her head. "I didn't speak up. I didn't try to help when there was still somethin' tangible to grab on to. And I can't help but feel like I did the same thing with Daddy."

A sob breaks free and both her hands come up to cover her mouth, her knees curling into her stomach as she rocks back and forth.

I'm frozen. I have absolutely zero clue how to make this better, and just like when I was ten years old and watching Ma cry, I don't know how to take away Lee's sadness. I only know that I *want* to.

Pulling her into my arms, I cradle her as she cries against my chest, her tears soaking through my shirt and seeping into my skin.

I hold her for who knows how long, absorbing her pain from the years I was gone, yearning for the right thing to say. But I don't have a clue what it is.

So instead of filling the air with worthless words, I sit at the foot of Ma's grave and rock my grieving sister, wishing I could bring back Lily and cure Pops myself, just to take away her pain.

53

BECCA

I t's been a week since Eli fucked me then flipped me upside down when he said it couldn't be more.

I don't know why I'm surprised.

Right now, I'm at Chase's place on the edge of town, getting ready for dinner with him and Lee. She's no longer mad at me—she's always been too forgiving for her own good—but this time, that forgiveness came with conditions. Number one being that I had to accept Chase in her life. Turns out he never really cheated on her in the first place. Not physically anyway, but that's a conversation for another day.

It's hard for me to trust him, especially after being the one who cradled Lee while he was destroying everything that mattered. But I can't deny it's been a long time since I've seen Lee look so *happy*.

There's something magical about watching them together. A magnetism between them, one where she moves, he follows. You can't see it, but it vibrates through the air so strong it's impossible not to feel. It's always been there, even when they were kids, but it's changed. Matured to the point where it's awe-inspiring to witness.

They aren't showcasing their love. They aren't putting on a show.

They simply are.

There's so much beauty in the way they effortlessly lift each other up, and that makes it impossible not to soften toward Chase, just a little.

"So." I smack my lips. "When are you gonna give up that tiny studio and move into this beauty?" I pivot from where I'm sitting at the island of the kitchen, waving my arm toward the spacious living room.

Lee's eyes widen, her knife pausing from where she is chopping vegetables.

Chase chuckles, wrapping his arms around her waist from behind and kissing her neck. "As soon as I convince her to."

She glares at me and I laugh. "My bad, Lee. Just an honest question."

She smiles, her eyes narrowing. "Since we're talkin' about honest things, let's talk about you, Eli, and Florida, hmm?"

I gasp into my wine, the liquid flowing down the wrong pipe, burning my esophagus as it chokes me.

My hand flies to my chest, eyes watering. "We've already talked about that."

"Well, *we've*" —she points the knife between her and Chase— "already talked about when I'm movin' in."

I throw my hands in the air. "Point taken."

She nods, her attention going back to her salad prep. I watch the slice of the knife as it slides through the tomatoes, the juice splattering on the cutting board. Chase grabs meat from the fridge and walks out back to grill.

"There is somethin' we wanted to tell you, though," Lee says without looking up.

"We?" I raise a brow, glancing at the back door.

"Okay, I did... but Chase *knows* I'm tellin' you."

"What is it?" I sit up straighter.

Her eyes flick to me, but she never stops chopping. "Chase hired someone to look for Lily."

My heart stutters from how fast my stomach drops.

Lily.

I haven't thought about her in a long time. Haven't let myself. She was a big part of my teenage years, and although she was closer to Lee than she ever was to me, I still felt her absence when she disappeared. Still dealt with the aftermath of her choices affecting everyone she decided to leave behind.

Fuck Lily.

She didn't care enough to stay so why the hell would I care about her?

Even as I think the words, anger brews beneath the surface when I hear her name.

I feel hurt. The kind that chomps at your very essence and punctures your lungs with its teeth.

And then those feelings flow out and slingshot back, punching through my chest and cracking my heart in half, because I realize that everything I'm feeling, all the ways I'm upset at how she could just leave without a word...

That's exactly how Eli must feel about me.

Oh my God.

No wonder he doesn't want to give us another chance. I'm surprised he can even stand the sight of me.

"Maybe he doesn't seem happy because he's around you." Jeremy's earlier words fly from my brain and sink to my stomach, making bile climb up the back of my throat.

"Hey, you okay, girlfriend?" Lee's voice shocks me out of my stupor.

I sip my wine again, trying to numb the agony in my chest from where I just split it open with my hypocrisy. "Yep. Just fine." I smile. "Hired someone? What's that even mean?"

She shrugs. "A private investigator. Big dude. Tattoos.

Lots of 'em." Her eyes grow wide. "I only saw him for a second, but dang, Becca. He was kinda scary."

"Was he hot?" I smirk.

She glances back at Chase before looking at me, her cheeks becoming splotchy and pink. "He was not *not* hot."

"That's a double negative." I point at her, my eyes squinting.

"You're missin' the point. What if he finds her?"

"I think…" *What do I think?* "I think if she wanted to come back here, she would have by now."

"Yeah. I'm just worried about what he'll find." She chews on her lip. "I don't want Chase to be disappointed."

I grimace, remembering the younger version of Chase. The one who had the best bravado and a fragile soul underneath. He fooled a lot of people, but I always saw the truth. It's easy to spot in someone what you try to hide yourself.

I reach across the island and cover her hand with mine. "Look, Lee. I've never been Chase's cheerleader, you know this."

She snorts. "That's an understatement."

I smile. "But even I can see he's changed. He's grown. He's… he's stronger. I don't think you need to worry about how he'll handle Lily and this investigator."

Her mouth twists, a line forming between her brows. "Yeah. He is strong. I just don't want him to go through more heartache, ya know? I want it to bring him peace."

"And what about you?"

"What about me?"

"Well… will findin' Lily give *you* peace?"

She lifts a shoulder. "I don't know. I feel like I let her down when I didn't speak up about my worries."

My stomach twists. "I didn't speak up either. We've all made mistakes. But Lily is responsible for her own actions, Lee. People have to wanna save themselves."

She sniffles. "You sound like Chase."

I cringe. "Yuck. Hard pass."

She points the knife at me. "Don't be a jerk."

I laugh. "I'm just playin'."

Chase waltzes back in with the steaks a few minutes later and we all sit down to eat. If you had bet me a million dollars, I wouldn't have guessed Chase knew how to entertain guests, especially ones who were hateful to him through most of our childhood. But he does it with grace, and I find myself in awe of the transformation.

Who is this man?

Lee's phone rings, and when she says it's Eli and excuses herself, the nausea I had pushed back down rolls to the surface. I take small sips of water to keep from throwing up my dinner.

Chase is silent, leaning back in his chair and crossing his hands over his stomach.

I squint my eyes at him from over the rim of my water. "I think I'm envious of you."

His dark brows shoot up. "I don't think anyone has ever said that to me before."

"Yeah, well, don't let it go to your head. I'm just sayin'." I cock my head to the side. "You were fucked-up before."

He smiles, making the dimples in his cheeks deepen. "We're all a little fucked-up, Becca."

"Yeah, but, you're so different now." I look down, weakness swimming in my veins and urging me to keep up the facade. Hit him with an insult instead of showing him the truth. But if he can work through all his issues and become a better man, maybe he's the key to helping me work through mine.

"How'd you do it?" I ask.

His lips turn down. "That's a vague as fuck question. Care to narrow it down?"

My curls knot through my fingers as I tug on the strands, the ends sticking to my clammy palms. "I just... there are some things I need to—some *issues* I'd like to tackle. To keep me from bein' so..."

"Fucked-up?" he guesses.

I nod, blowing out a breath. "Yeah. Fucked-up."

He sucks on his teeth, his chair creaking as he rocks back.

I shift in my seat, uncomfortable as the seconds tick by and he doesn't say a word. Just stares at me, letting me stew in my vulnerability.

Finally, he clicks his tongue, his chair snapping back into place as he rests his forearms on the table. "I know a guy who can help."

54

BECCA

"I want to be with him, Becca. He just... he drives me insane."

"So be with him, Jer." I cradle the phone between my shoulder and head, grabbing my popcorn from the microwave.

Jeremy is the only person I still talk to from Florida, but even with him, our conversations are far and few between. Over the years, both of our lives have pulled us down different paths—his in the direction of his dreams, and mine into the swirling vortex of everything I said I never wanted to be. Maybe Sabrina—someone I do *not* speak with—was right after all and you do think things into existence.

Either way, I'd be devastated to lose the little moments I'm able to grab, so even though they aren't frequent, I never miss our calls.

"I *can't* just be with him. I've worked so hard to get where I am. I can't risk that. I just wish he'd understand, it's not because I don't have feelings for him, it's just the way it has to be."

"Hmm." I pop some kernels in my mouth, chewing slowly while I think of the right thing to say.

Years later, and Jer still isn't out. I don't blame him, especially now with him being plastered on billboards, and companies begging for his face on their brand. People can pretend all they want that the world has progressed, but take a closer look and everyone is still busy hiding their truths in the shadows and pushing their lies in the light.

Funny how no matter where you go, big cities or small towns, people are the same at the core.

And people don't want their celebrity athletes to like other men. It doesn't fit the mold.

"I'm gonna tell you what you told me once, Jer, and I want you to listen close. Are you ready?"

"Hit me with it, sweet cheeks."

"If you can't love that man with all your heart, you need to let him go."

"Yeah." He sniffles.

"Don't be his disease, Jer."

He hums deep in his throat. "Damn, that's a good line. I said that?"

"You know you did." I laugh. "And you were right. Lovin' someone fully doesn't mean you aren't afraid. It just means you do it anyway, even with the fear, because they deserve all your pieces." I swallow, dropping the buttery popcorn from my hands, my appetite suddenly disappearing. "So if you can't give him every piece of you, then love him enough to let him go so he can find someone who will."

It's strange, switching places with Jeremy. Being the one who gives the advice instead of the one who needs to take it. I guess reflection makes you see your mistakes in a different light.

And maybe that's the difference between success and failure—whether you acknowledge your mistakes and learn from them, or choose to bury yourself in the debris of their destruction.

"Yeah, you're probably right." He heaves a deep breath down the line. "Shit, I don't wanna talk about me anymore, it's depressing. Tell me why I was gearing up for you to come out here but I still don't see that sweet ass anywhere in Cali?"

I sigh. "Runnin' away ain't gonna solve my issues, Jer."

He chuckles. "*Finally* you admit it."

"Honestly, I'm surprised you weren't the one to say it."

"Becca, I learned a long time ago that telling you something and having you really hear it are two totally different things. If you want to run away from your problems, there's nothing I can say to make you stop. There never has been... Plus, maybe I was willing to be a little bit selfish this time, wanting to have you close again."

My chest twinges when I think about how long it's been since we've seen each other. "I'll still come out and visit sometime. Just after I'm done tryin' to turn over a new leaf and all that." I hesitate, before spouting out the thing I've been dying to get off my chest. "I got this number from Lee's man. This... therapist guy. Apparently, he's the best."

"A *therapist?* Jesus, Becca. I never thought I'd see the day."

I cringe, throwing another kernel of popcorn in my mouth. "Yeah, well... I figure if he can fix Chase, he can do somethin' with lil' ol' me. He's in Nashville, though, so I don't know if it's gonna work out."

"Don't you hate him?"

"Who, Chase?" I stop mid-chew, thinking about what my feelings actually are toward Chase these days. "Hate's a strong word. I don't necessarily trust him. That's probably more 'cause of me than him, though." I purse my lips.

I've always believed that if you give a man long enough, they'll live to let you down. Watching Chase with Lee over the years only cemented my belief that he was just like Papa.

But I don't think that's the truth. I think Chase has a good soul, he's just been lost on how to show it.

I'm not sure Papa even has one, or if he does, he sold it for his sins a long time ago.

"Are you gonna set up an appointment?" Jeremy asks.

Honestly, I don't want to. I'm scared that if I start to dig up my issues, I'll end up ripping them out and nothing will be left.

Who am I if I'm not who raised me?

But I know I can't keep living this way. Not if I want to be healthy. Happy. Free of these demons that keep me chained to my folks and living in purgatory, blaming my decisions on other people with no way of knowing how to stop.

So yeah, I'll call him.

But it's the next morning before I actually get the nerve.

It's freeing not being at church on a Sunday. Still, there's an anxiety that trickles through my veins, making me feel like God may smite me down for missing service as much as I have.

I haven't been back since *the revelation* with my momma, but neither of my folks has so much as picked up the phone since. I expect they will soon. Small-town folk love to talk, and my absence won't go unnoticed for much longer.

I find it hard to care.

There's a cup of coffee growing cold in front of me while I sit at my dining table. My phone is in my hand, thumb poised over the green button as I stare at the ugly owl Lee bought me as a gag gift. I put it on the top shelf of my kitchen cabinet, swearing I would cherish it forever. But now, I can feel its wooden, buggy eyes staring at me. Judging me for not being able to make a damn phone call.

With a deep breath, I press call. It only rings twice before a voice comes over the line. "This is Dr. Andalor."

"Hi. Is this… is this Doc? I was given this number from a

friend and I'd like to make an appointment, I think?" I squeeze my eyes shut. *Stupid.*

"I believe I may be the *Doc* you're looking for. May I know who I'm speaking with?"

"Of course, yeah... I'm sorry, I'm Becca Sanger. Chase Adams gave me your number, said you helped him an awful lot and that I should call you if I needed someone to talk to."

He chuckles. "I assumed your friend was Chase. I'd love to talk, Becca. Let me just pull up my availability."

I'm not one-hundred percent confident that I'll see this through. It's embarrassing, admitting the things that I've let affect my decisions. The ways I've fallen for my family's lies and let them lead me around on a leash. It's shameful admitting out loud that I'm twenty-six years old and have never lived an independent day in my entire life.

"My earliest time is this Tuesday at two. Does that work for you?"

Panic seizes my throat when I think about having to talk to him face to face. "You know, I don't—I'm not sure when I'm free to drive to Nashville. Maybe I should figure that out first and call you back."

"Oh? Would a phone session work better for you?"

"A what?" I scrunch my nose.

"A phone session. I'll call at our dedicated time and we can talk, just like this."

"Oh, you can do that?"

"I can. There's no pressure either way, Becca. I'm here for you, not the other way around."

I nod even though he can't see.

I *like* that he can't see. It's knowing that I won't have to look him in the eyes as I spew all my secrets that has me agreeing to a Tuesday meeting.

Hanging up the phone, I blow out a relieved breath.

Then I'm back to staring at that ugly owl. Only this time,

the eyes don't bother me quite as much.

"So you called him?" Lee asks, sitting across from me on the couch, her hand on Chase's knee.

I nod, sipping from my water. "Yep."

Chase sits up straighter. "Good. Doc's fucking great."

"Well, if he can help with your shit, he should be able to handle a tortured preacher's daughter, no problem." I smile big and wide.

"Yeah, speakin' of your daddy," Lee says. "I saw them at the store the other day and they stopped me to ask about you." She cocks her head. "I didn't know you weren't speakin'."

I sigh, my gut rolling at the audacity of them to ask about me when they won't even pick up the phone. It's not like Sugarlake is a big town, if they wanted to find me, they know where I live.

The doorbell rings, interrupting our conversation, and Chase hops up, disappearing down the hall.

"Expectin' someone?" I ask Lee.

She grimaces. "Yeah, I didn't know how to tell you he was comin'."

My stomach jumps. "Who is *he*?"

"Eli."

The blood in my veins surge, rushing to my cheeks, my breath whooshing out of me. I'm surprised at the fact she would invite both of us to dinner. I'm also surprised she invited him at all. Last I knew, they weren't on good terms, and it makes sadness weigh down my heart when I realize she hasn't felt like she could share with me. Or maybe she just hasn't wanted to. I wonder when we'll get back to the way we used to be, before I ruined her trust.

She says things are okay, but I know just because you forgive doesn't mean you can forget. Even severed limbs ache with phantom pains.

I haven't seen Eli since he fucked me against the bleachers, and that was almost two weeks ago, so when his laughter floats into the room it sends heat swimming through my insides, my nerves dancing off the waves.

Chase walks through the door first but my eyes go straight to the man behind him.

When Eli's gaze finds mine, it wraps around my body and tugs, pulling me up off the couch before I know how to stop myself.

Lee says something, but her voice is muddled, every ounce of me focused on Eli and the way he commands my attention just by *existing*.

I stop when I'm right in front of him, close enough to reach out and touch, his energy snapping at my skin. "Hi."

"Rebecca." His voice is deep and husky, my full name off his lips making my entire body vibrate with the need to hear it again. "I didn't know you would be here," he continues.

"Ditto. Hope it's okay I am."

"It's more than okay."

"Good." My face stretches into a wide grin, my stare never leaving his.

The left side of his mouth pulls up, his eyes sparking. "Good."

Butterflies erupt in my stomach, making me giddy at the prospect of spending the evening around him. A chance for us to just *be* without all of the angst of our past.

So when Lee slips her arm around my shoulder and winks, saying it's time to sit down and eat, I follow them in, staring at Eli's back and letting hope for the future fill me up.

I damn sure like the way it feels.

55

ELI

There was a moment at Ma's grave where the world grew quiet. Nothing but Lee's tears soaking my shirt, and mine falling silently on her hair, the air heavy with all the ways we've never allowed each other to just *be* there, the way we should have been all along.

Both of us have been too stuck in our pride, expecting the other to give instead of take, not realizing that life is a balancing act.

Sitting in front of Ma's headstone with nothing but the whisper of the wind and our overdue confessions, Lee opened up about Lily and her fear of failing Pops. I told her how I used Sarah to numb the pain of Becca leaving, and to try and appease Ma's memory so the nightmares would stop.

It's hard being vulnerable, purging your deepest truths and laying them down to be judged. But it's also purifying to no longer hold it alone. And maybe if I had given Lee the support when she needed, she would have been more invested in supporting me. Maybe I wouldn't have felt the need to lock everything away—hide the burden of my missteps where no one could see them in the light.

But you can't grow in the dark. You'll shrivel and wilt until you're nothing but dried up remnants scattered along the ground.

Lee inviting me to dinner is just another step to our healing. I didn't expect Becca to be here, looking the way she does and making my heart scream with reminders of what we used to be. What we could be again, if only I'd let her in.

I realize it isn't fair to say one thing and mean another. And I wish, so damn bad, that I could dive inside her brain and learn all the reasons why she left. How she could say she loved me, but break me so easily. Maybe then I could reconcile the Becca from my past with the woman she is now and we could find some way to move forward.

"So." I set down my napkin, looking toward Lee. "Next week is the first family day at Stepping Stones."

Lee's fork pauses halfway to her mouth. "Mmhm. Mark mentioned it on the phone."

I nod, leaning back in my chair. "You wanna drive up there together?"

She sighs, dropping her fork to her plate. "I don't know, Eli. I guess I hadn't really thought about it. I mean, does Daddy even want me there?"

"I'm sorry, what exactly is family day?" Becca interrupts.

My eyes slide to her, surprise flowing through me that she doesn't already know. I guess I assumed Lee would have talked to her about it by now. "It's a day visit to the rehabilitation center. They have a group session for family members, and we have one-on-ones with Pops."

I'm nervous about what I'll find when I get there. Afraid that Pops will be even more pissed off at the world now that he doesn't have the drink to numb his senses. I don't really know what to expect, other than what Mark has told us. Not sure Pops will even want to see us.

Chase nods. "That's great. You gonna go?" he asks Lee.

Lee looks over to him. "I was gonna tell you, I just hadn't had the chance yet. I only found out today."

He smiles, leaning in and kissing her lips. Something yanks at my chest as I watch them love each other so completely. So openly. Envy lurks through me, knowing Lee was able to let her love overshadow the hurt and let Chase back in her life.

I wonder how she did it.

"That's okay, baby," Chase whispers. "Sounds like the meetings, you know?"

"What meetin's?" Becca chimes in, stealing the question from my lips.

Chase clears his throat. "Nar-Anon meetings. Recovery for family members who have someone struggling with addiction." He looks to me. "It's actually something I was planning to invite you to, Eli... if you want to go."

My stomach jolts. A recovery group? I've only experienced Pops's addiction for the past month, it hasn't had time to settle in and affect me. I feel *fine.*

I shake my head. "That's nice, man, but I don't feel like I really need it."

He bobs his head, his dimples showing with his smile. "Well, the offer's there. Maybe we'll talk again after 'family day.'"

"That group of yours like therapy or somethin'?" Becca asks.

Chase shrugs. "A little bit, I guess." His eyes flick to mine. "It's not as bad as it sounds."

I shift in my seat, suddenly uncomfortable with the way the conversation has headed. Becca's attention jumps to me at the movement, her head cocking to the side. And then she just *stares* with that green gaze of hers, watching me until I can't breathe.

"I don't know," she says slowly. "That doesn't sound so

bad." She shrugs, her gaze never leaving mine. "Not that I have experience with therapy. Not yet anyway."

My brow arches. "Not yet?"

"That's right. Got my first meetin' on Tuesday." She takes a bite of her food and smiles.

"You're seeing a therapist?" My stomach flips at the thought.

"Yeah, what about it?" Her shoulder lifts. "Everyone could use a little therapy."

"Especially you," Chase mutters.

Her head snaps over. "Watch your mouth, *dick*. Don't make me take back all the nice things I've been sayin' about you."

Chase chuckles, and my chest warms at her sass.

That damn mouth.

This is nice. I can almost convince myself it's a regular family dinner. That we haven't been estranged in all the ways that matter. I can almost pretend that being around Becca doesn't make me feel like a livewire on the verge of explosion —jumping between all the ways I want her, and all the reasons why I shouldn't.

But more than anything, this dinner gives me hope. And that's something I haven't felt in a long time.

Stepping Stones is in a beautiful area. Tucked away in the Smokies, it has the vibe of a retreat, more than a rehabilitation center. A tranquil setting, surrounded by blooming flowers and maple trees, hiding the struggles that exist inside its walls.

It's been a month since I dropped Pops off here. I haven't seen or spoken to him since, and neither has Lee. We've been relegated to getting general updates from Mark and even those are vague.

"Dang, this place is pretty," Lee says as we walk toward the front doors.

I hum my agreement. I would speak, but anxiety is making my tongue thick and my stomach jumbled. My mind is racing a hundred miles a minute, wondering where things are going to lead from this visit. If Pops is putting in the work to heal. If he's mad, I brought him here in the first place. If Lee is ready to deal with whatever happens once we walk inside.

Mark meets us at the front desk and steers us to his office.

Lee's chewing on her lip, her leg bouncing as soon as we sit down. Mark walks to the other side of his desk, his brown hair bobbing as he leans back in his office chair and smiles at Lee.

"You must be Alina. Your father's told me a lot about you."

She sucks in a breath. "He has?"

Mark smiles, nodding. "He has." He turns to look at me. "Eli, nice to see you again. You two ready for this?"

"Yep." My calf muscle burns from how fast my leg is bouncing. "What exactly should we expect?"

"I won't lie to you, it won't be easy. There's a lot that goes into family therapy, but it's good that you're here. It's important to show your father that you're willing to put in the work."

"And is he?" Lee interrupts. "Puttin' in the work, that is? So he can get better?"

"He is." Mark grins. "But there's no black and white, Alina. Recovery is one day at a time. Sometimes it's easy, and other times it leaves you broken and bruised. The important thing is that he wakes up, puts on his armor and fights like hell. He *chooses* to be the best version of himself, and every second he does is a win. He'll need your support, which is why your recovery is just as crucial to his success as his own."

A chuckle bursts out of me, even though nothing about what he's saying is funny. "What do you mean *our* recovery?"

"Exactly what I said. Addiction is a family disease, Eli. It affects all of you."

Why does everyone keep saying that?

Lee sniffles, and I see her nod from the corner of my eye. My heart wrenches against my ribs at her emotion. At her agreement with what he's saying.

"So, how will it all work?" Lee's hands wring together in her lap.

"Well, this morning we have a group session for all of the family members. Then this afternoon, you'll be with your dad during his session."

"*Just* during his session?" I thought we'd get to spend the day with him. Finding out we don't, makes the ball of anxiety mutate into a stinging irritation that pricks at my skin.

Mark's lips pull in a straight line. "It was his request to only see you both in that particular setting."

My stomach tangles and twists, worry pouring into every pore of my body over how Lee will handle knowing Pops doesn't want us here. I'm used to disappointment from him, but I'm not sure *what* their dynamic is these days.

"He doesn't wanna see us?" Lee's voice breaks, her words slow and thick.

Mark leans forward in his chair, settling his elbows on the desk. "This isn't a reflection on you. It's very common with people in the stage of recovery your father is in. It can be... overwhelming to face the people you love." He pauses, watching Lee's face carefully. "I know it's hard—trust me, I *know*. But it's a hell of a thing you're doing, showing up for him this way. Letting him set his own boundaries and then respecting them is what he needs from you right now."

She nods, wiping her tear-stained cheeks with the back of her hands. "Okay."

"Okay." Mark taps his knuckles on the desk. "Group starts in half an hour, I'll take you to the conference room and you can help yourself to refreshments until it's time. You two ready?"

I blow out a breath, the weight of his words settling heavy on my shoulders.

I thought Pops coming to rehab would cure him. That he'd work on his issues and come home where we could make sure he stays on the straight and narrow.

I didn't realize it would be like *this*.

But even if I don't understand it, I'll try like hell to learn, so I can be here by Lee's side, and by Pops's, every step of the way.

56

ELI

The past two hours opened my eyes, and I didn't even know they had been closed. The group session was unlike anything I've ever experienced. It was so different than what I was expecting—so much more.

I won't lie and say I can relate to others who showed up. But I see the same nervous shadow lurking in their eyes, the same anxious movements as I do with Lee. I sense the desperation oozing out of their pores, wanting to do something, *anything* to help, but not knowing where to start. At least that is something I can relate to. I have no clue how the hell to navigate what's to come. No clue what to do when Pops comes home. And maybe I haven't been here for his downward spiral, haven't felt the soul-crushing feeling of watching someone I love succumb to their weaknesses, but I feel the guilt that comes along with *not* having been there.

I feel the weight of responsibility from being here now and having no compass to direct me on the journey.

Today I learned that alcoholism is a family disease. It affects us all in different ways.

Codependency being one of the most common symptoms.

Denial being another. That's a sledgehammer to my psyche because fuck if I haven't been denying Pops's addiction for years. And I damn well know Lee's been codependent, adapting her life to fit his alcoholism, obsessively worrying about what was going to happen to him at the expense of her own self-care.

I'm not sure how to come to terms with the fact Pops's addiction has affected me more than I originally thought. Chase's invitation whispers in the back of my mind, and I file it away to bring up later, after I've processed the rest of my emotions from today.

They said a lot of things in the session. A dump of information, assisted by pamphlets and packets, showing us all the ways to support, and all the ways we shouldn't. It's a miracle I retained any of it. But one line stuck with me, and now, while Lee and I sit outside at a circular table waiting on Pops and Mark, I find myself repeating it over and over in my head.

You can't cure it. You didn't cause it. You can't control it.

I wonder if Lee's thinking the same thing. My gaze floats to her and I search for the right thing to say. She's right next to me but she feels *so* far away, and at this moment, I wish more than anything I could dive across the chasm and grab on to her—somehow heal the divide between us so we could truly support each other in the fragile moments.

"So… that was intense," I say.

Lee looks up at me from where she's reading one of the pamphlets they passed out. "Yeah," she sighs. "It makes a lotta sense though. I've been enablin' Daddy for years."

"And not taking care of yourself?" I phrase it as a question, not wanting to rile up her already frayed emotions, but by the way her eyes narrow I think I struck the nerve anyway.

"How do you know that, Eli? You ain't even been here to

know whether I was takin' care of myself or not. Too busy livin' your fancy life with your fancy people and their fancy dreams to give a damn."

My insides burn as her accusations sear into my skin. "Is that what you think? Really? That I was off living my *best* life?"

She shrugs, her arms crossing over her chest.

The restraint holding my anger snaps, my pent-up emotion barreling out of me, the taste bitter on my tongue. "Let me tell you somethin', Lee. Ma died and I lost the only family member who gave a damn about me beyond basketball. And then... I lost basketball too." I breathe deeply through my nose to keep the tears at bay, and ignore how my accent drips on the end of my words. "And I know I should have been around more. Should have made more of an effort. But you didn't even stop for *one* second and check in on me. You just sat here, wallowin' in your doom and gloom, not givin' a damn. Makin' assumptions about what you think of my life without takin' the time to see for yourself."

"I—"

"Well, guess what. You *don't* know. You have no clue what it was like for me."

"You never told me," she hisses.

"You never asked!" My arms shoot up, palms raised to the sky.

This isn't where I wanted to have this conversation. Not when we're here for Pops—when it's already an emotional day. But sometimes you don't control when things happen, and finally voicing it makes me feel better. Lighter.

Resentment sticks to your insides. Scraping it off may hurt, but at least it cleans the residue.

I tap the table with my fingers. "I wasn't here for you. I didn't listen when you needed me to, and I'm *sorry* for that. I'm sorry for the part I played in all the ways we've failed each other. But for once in your goddamn life will you just take a look in the mirror and accept some of the blame? *Christ.*" I huff out a breath, tugging on the ends of my hair.

Lee's staring at me, mouth flopping like a fish. "Eli, I—"

"You wanna know what my *fancy* life was like, Alina?" I cut her off again. "It was lonely. It was full of guilt that rotted me from the inside out because I didn't make time to come home. To hold on to Ma while I still had the chance." My voice breaks and I run my hand over my mouth, watching as Lee's eyes glaze over. "My *fancy* life was filled with people who loved to stand in my spotlight and run away from my darkness. My *fancy* life was tortured by the nightmare of livin' out your dream and then havin' it stolen away in front of millions of people." My fist pounds against my chest. "Thousands of moments were spent starin' at my *fancy* phone when it didn't ring from the only two people in my life who should have cared."

Lee's hand jumps to cover her mouth. "Eli, I didn't—"

"No," I snap. "You didn't." I take a deep breath, trying to regain some composure. "Do you know what it feels like to lose your purpose, Lee?"

"No," she whispers, her head shaking.

I suck on my teeth, choosing my words carefully. "It feels like... like you're floatin' in the middle of the ocean, surrounded by land. You can see your end game, but you can't *get* there." I break our stare, looking at the table, remembering how lost I felt before I went to Florida and coached those kids. Before I found Becca. "Eventually, your limbs get so damn tired you surrender to the pull of gravity." I frown. "You let the salty water fill your lungs and you accept your new reality. Dyin' a slow death, alone in the middle of the sea... all because you can't do the *one* thing that's expected." My voice breaks. "You can't fuckin' swim."

"I didn't think..." Lee trails off.

"When I lost ball, I lost my *reason*. My entire life was spent strivin' for greatness, and at the end of the day, none of it mattered. Every second was wasted."

Lee looks to the side, a tear streaking down her face and dripping off her chin. My heart twists at her sadness.

"I didn't tell you that to make you sad. Or to make you feel guilty. I just need you to understand. I stayed away because I *couldn't* come home. Couldn't face bein' the town disappointment. But none of that shit matters anymore. You can't go back and change the past—"

"But you can start where you are and change the endin'," Lee finishes, smiling through her tears. "That's my favorite quote."

My chest warms. "Mine too." I reach out, grabbing her fingers across the table. "I forgive you. Do you forgive me?"

She stares at our hands, sniffling. Finally, she nods and a fissure in my heart heals.

"Good, because we need to be a team to support Pops. And each other." I puff out a breath. "You ready for this?"

"No." She laughs. "But I'm as ready as I'm gonna be. Nice accent, by the way. Guess I just have to rile you up to make you sound like yourself again, huh." She smiles.

I look behind her and see Pops following Mark outside, his shoulders slumped and his head hanging down. Even from a distance, I can tell he's gained weight. It looks good on him. And when he looks up, for the first time since coming back home, a little bit of my long lost faith gets restored.

His eyes are clear and alert. And although he isn't smiling, there's an aura that isn't quite as dark around him. Like the grief he wore as a cloak has been stripped off his back.

Pops and Mark sit down in the two chairs opposite us. It's a circular table, but somehow Pops seems the farthest away, the feeling of how our relationships have eroded over the years manifesting in the space between us.

"Hi again, you two," Mark greets.

I attempt a smile, but it's all I can force, the heaviness of the day starting to wear on my shoulders until I feel the throbbing low in my spine.

"Today isn't going to be a 'session' per se," Mark continues. "Just a visit for everyone to catch up. I'm only here to moderate in case things veer into topics Craig doesn't feel comfortable handling."

"So, Pops," I start. "How ya doing? You look good."

Pops nods, resting his elbows on the table, causing it to shift slightly. "I'm doin' alright. But I won't lie, the urge to bust outta here and grab a drink is mighty strong today, knowin' I'd have to see y'all."

Lee scoffs. "Are you really blamin' *us*?"

Mark leans forward, cutting in. "Lee, Craig is just expressing his struggle today and that's something we should honor. It isn't easy facing the people you've hurt with your addiction."

My stomach squeezes. I don't understand much about what Pops is going through and what this process entails, but that feeling of facing people you feel like you've let down? That's a feeling I understand well.

"I'm not—I'm not blamin' you, Alina. I'm just bein' honest. Facin' you is hard. It was hard when I was two bottles of whiskey deep, and it's hard now that the shame is showin' its face. I look at you and I see your mama. It hurts." His palm rests over his heart, his gaze bouncing between us. "I look at both of you and see all the ways I failed you."

My heart stutters, waiting—*needing*—him to elaborate.

He doesn't.

Lee sucks in a breath through her teeth. "Okay, I'm sorry, Daddy. It's good you're here. I'm happy to see you."

Pops's lips lift just a smidge.

Mark clears his throat. "Craig, why don't you tell them about group two days ago."

At this, Pops does smile, reaching in his pocket and pulling out a coin, laying in on the table. I lean in to see.

"What's that?" Lee asks.

"That's my sobriety token. Thirty days." Pops's chest puffs, and my own chest swells at seeing a bit of the man who raised me filter through the cracks.

"That's incredible, Pops. Congratulations."

"Yeah, Daddy, thirty days is amazin'." Lee's eyes sparkle with unshed tears and she blinks them away. "I'm so dang proud." She looks down at the table, fingering the pile of pamphlets. "Mama would be proud, too."

Her words lodge themselves in my throat and my heart thumps out in pain at the mention of Ma.

Pops's face twists—the sorrow painting itself on his features—grief swirling through his irises. His hand snaps out and picks up the coin, his thumb rubbing one side, his fingers white-knuckling the other.

"You get one of those every month?" I change the subject back to something lighter, my eyes flickering to Mark who nods in encouragement.

The rest of our time is light. Surface level. But it's a nice visit, and it relieves some of the worry that was ruminating low in my gut at not knowing whether Pops was taking this seriously.

We'll have time to talk about the heavy. Time to figure out where we go from here, once he comes home and faces his recovery, and his punishment. He still has court for the accident, after all.

But for now, seeing that Pops is healing, that he's putting in the work... it's enough.

57

BECCA

I think I'll keep Doc. Virtually, of course. I'm not ready to meet face to face, not sure if I ever will be, but over the phone, talking is easier than expected. It's nice to vent my fears and frustrations. To word vomit everything and have no fear of retribution. No fear of being judged.

Doc actually listened. He told me my emotions were valid.

And then he gave me homework.

Write down three things I wish I could be, then say it on repeat until I believe them.

So here I am on a Wednesday afternoon, in the parking lot of church, repeating my newly formed affirmations.

I want to catch my folks before Wednesday evening service, and this is my best chance to corner them in a place where I know they can't leave. I have some things to say, and it's high time they listen.

I am strong. I am bold. I own my power.

With a deep breath, I stretch my legs out of my car and slam the door behind me, hoping the slight tremor in my hands doesn't show anywhere else on my body as I walk inside.

The office door is cracked, so I push it open the rest of the way and go in. My heart beats so fast I feel it slamming against the bones in my chest. Momma is hunched over the desk, Papa next to her, both of their attention on papers strewn across the desk.

"Hi, y'all."

Papa's head snaps up, his eyes narrowing as they land on me. "Rebecca, where've you been, young lady?"

My stomach jolts. *How dare he act like they care.* "It's not like I've been hidin', Papa. I just haven't been *here*."

His arms cross, his green stare slicing through me. "And why exactly is that?"

My eyes bounce to Momma. She's peering at me from where she's still bent at the edge of the desk.

"Momma didn't tell you?"

His eyes flicker toward her, his posture stiffening. "Tell me what?"

At this, Momma stands straight, her pearls bouncing slightly as they rest around her neck, the perfect accent to the facade she projects to the world. I wonder if I rip them off, would it strip her bare and show the world her ugliness?

She clears her throat. "We had a heart-to-heart the other night and she didn't take what I had to say very well. You wouldn't be interested, darlin', it's woman stuff."

There's a glint in her eyes as she levels her gaze at me. I'm not sure if it's a warning or a threat, but I don't care either way. I'm done subjecting myself to what she wants at the expense of what I need.

Doc says people won't give you power. You have to take it.

"No, Papa. It's *not* woman stuff. She told me how y'all lied for years."

Papa's brow quirks.

"How she *loved* you, but you never loved her. How you

got her pregnant, and had a shotgun weddin', then moved here so you could pretend to be somethin' you weren't."

"Rebecca Jean, that's *enough*," Momma hisses.

But I ignore her, my ire a tsunami, rising up to capsize everything in its path. Drowning the lies with truth.

"Is it, Momma?" I cock my head, locking eyes with Papa. "She told me how you've been lyin' to everyone in town for years, and lyin' to me my entire life."

Papa's eyes widen slightly as he sits down in the chair, his mouth parted, his gaze breaking away and landing on everything but me.

Momma stands stoic, her spine stiffening with every passing second that no one speaks.

"Well," I finally snap. "Don't you have anything to say for yourself? Either of you?"

Papa levels a glare at Momma. "Well, Rebecca, I'm not sure where you'd like me to start."

"Pick one," I bite back.

"Alright." He nods. "It's true your momma and I moved here after our weddin'... when we were pregnant with you."

I scoff. "And you didn't think you could be honest about that?" I raise my arms out to my sides. "Why? Were you so ashamed of me before I was even born that y'all had to hide it?" A pang hits my chest, making the last word come out choked.

"We weren't *ashamed* of you, girl. We were tryin' to make our own way. We planned to get married and move here long before we found out about you. You just sped up the process."

"What?" I shake my head, his words jumbling up the clear image I've formed of what happened. "But, Momma said—"

"I don't know what you think you heard from me, Rebecca Jean," Momma cuts in. "But clearly you're misrememberin' if you think I didn't tell you that same thing."

My jaw drops, nausea sloshing low in my stomach as I take in what she just said. "God Almighty, have you always been this manipulative?"

"Young lady, watch your mouth," Papa snaps.

I spin back toward him. "Are you tellin' me it's not true?"

He leans back in his chair, straightening his tie. "Depends on which part you're askin' about."

Frustration rips at my chest, my teeth grinding so hard my jaw aches. "Quit speakin' in riddles! For once, just tell me the truth. Treat me like an equal. I deserve to know." Tears break the dam and overflow, trickling down my face, the salty taste lingering on my dry lips as I wait for an answer I'm not even sure I'll get.

"We moved here, yes." Papa rests his elbows on the desk. "We were pregnant with you, yes. We didn't tell anyone the truth, *yes*. But I loved—" His voice cracks and he glances at Momma. Her jaw clenches, fingers clutching her pearls like they're the only thing tethering her to the ground. "I loved your momma. *She's* the one who didn't love me."

"What?" I gasp. "What are you talkin' about?" I look toward her. "Momma?"

She straightens, running her hand down the front of her silk blouse. "Honestly, this entire conversation is tirin'. We have a congregation to get ready for. Don, end this nonsense, hmm?"

She moves to walk around me but I step in front of the door before she can reach it. "No, Momma. Were you *lyin'* to me?"

"You are so naive," she hisses. "Of course I wasn't in love with him. My daddy *forced* me to marry him. I made a stupid mistake and the repercussions haunt me to this day."

My heart throbs in my chest, the lacerations from her calling me a mistake as painful as if she reached in and punctured the tissue herself.

"You think I wanted this for my life?" she continues, waving her arm around the room. "To be stuck in this small town, bein' the wife of a preacher and a mother to a daughter who can't keep her name outta everyone's mouth?"

I always knew Momma was unhappy, but I foolishly assumed it was because of Papa's actions. I never once considered it was because she didn't want to be here at all. "For years you made me believe Papa was the one who broke your heart. You made me feel *sorry* for you. Why would you lie about this?"

Disgust creeps through me at all the moments I wasted crying for her when she didn't deserve a tear.

Her lips curl. "To make sure you left. I know that boy is back. And I just *knew* you wouldn't stay away. Knew you'd be the talk of the town once again, and I won't stand for bein' the gossip, especially when it comes to you. Do you know how bad it makes me look? Like I can't even control my own daughter?" Her eyes scan me up and down. "Elliot Carson would do nothin' but break your heart, or worse, knock you up and trap you forever."

I shake my head, trying to make sense of things. "No, but, back in Florida... you made me think Papa broke your heart. That he fell out of love with you."

Momma lifts a shoulder, peering down at me. "I saw the way you two looked at each other in Florida, knew it was a scandal waitin' to happen. I was honest with what I told you that night. You'd have gotten stuck. Just like I did."

I stumble back a step, disbelief coloring my insides at the levels Momma has gone to be the mastermind behind my life. This whole time I thought it was Papa pulling the strings, but it's always been her.

A lone curl comes loose from her bun, falling on her forehead. She stops everything to fix it. *Of course she does.* Can't have an imperfection tarnishing her image.

"Lust is one of the seven deadly sins for a reason. I did what I had to do. Besides, you've always been so easy to mold with words, Rebecca Jean. It's one of your biggest flaws."

A burn starts in my chest, whipping through my insides and licking at my bones, torching through my veins and swelling my throat. I breathe deep to keep the ache under control.

I am strong. I am bold. I own my power.

I look toward Papa to see his reaction, but he's still as stone in his chair, his hand moving back and forth across his head like he can't be bothered with what's happening right in front of his face. Like he doesn't even care. Like it's just one big headache he's trying to rub away.

I've always looked at Papa as a strong man, but now, all I see is weakness. I don't know why I continue to let myself be surprised when they disappoint me.

I turn back to Momma. "Have you ever said a single truthful thing in your life, Momma?"

"You should be thankin' me. I've been tryin' to *save* you. I do what I have to do in order to protect my family."

I huff out a laugh because she's *still* trying to manipulate me. "No matter who you hurt."

She scoffs. "Please. You don't know what hurt is, Rebecca. Grow up."

Part of me wants to cower away. Lay down in my despair and let her words affect me the way I always have. It's comfortable to stick with what you know, even if it's unhealthy.

Another part of me wants to defend my emotions, because how dare she say I don't know what it means to be hurt, when she and Papa have hurt me the most. But if I do either of those things, she wins. So instead, I take a deep breath and repeat my affirmations.

I am strong. I am bold. I own my power.

I give her no reaction and give my attention to Papa. "So, what about Sally? You chose to make vows to Momma, and you break them like they mean nothin'."

"What are you goin' on about now, Rebecca? How do you know *anything* about me and Sally?" His voice is quiet and breathy, the way it gets after a long day.

"I saw you."

"You were sloppy, Don," Momma says. "How else would she know?"

Her voice sends a chill cascading over my body. She's speaking to him as if this is something normal, like it's something they've discussed a thousand times. And it hits me in this moment, that maybe Papa didn't sleep with Sally behind Momma's back.

Maybe he did it with her blessing.

I don't know for sure, and I don't *want* to know. It won't bring me peace. It won't help me stitch back together our relationships. I don't think there's anything there to mend anyway.

A weight lands in the center of my chest and spreads, sinking my stomach at the realization that in order to truly cut my chains, I have to cut *them*.

"Rebecca, Sally, and I—"

I raise my hand. "I don't wanna know, Papa. Truly, nothin' you say will make a difference." I close my eyes, trying to find ground in the center of this tornado. When I open them, Momma has moved back to stand by the desk, her hand on Papa's shoulder.

A picture-perfect moment, even behind closed doors. *They deserve each other.*

"I hate to be the bearer of bad news, Momma, but I'm stayin'."

Papa nods. "That's the right choice."

I shake my head. "No, you've misunderstood me. I'm stayin' in Sugarlake, but I'm not stayin' with this church. I'm not stayin' with this family."

Momma huffs. "Don't be ridiculous, Rebecca Jean. If you wanna stay, then *stay*, but don't pretend like you're not gonna be part of this family. The entire town will talk."

I shrug. "Let 'em talk."

"This is absurd," Papa huffs. "You will get over whatever issue you have with the choices your momma and I have made, and you'll do your duty to this family." His fist hits the top of the desk, bringing my eyes to the oak that's caused me so much discomfort over the years. Now when I look at it, I feel nothing.

It's not my problem anymore. It never really was.

"My *duty*?" I laugh. "My duty is to myself. I've given more than enough to this farce of a family. I'm choosin' to step away. You're lucky that's all I'm doin'."

"One word from me and you'll lose that precious job," Papa hisses. "That place you love to rent. Gone." He snaps his fingers. "You think my word doesn't hold weight in this town? If I say I need you here, they'll listen."

"Maybe." I suck on my teeth. "But I'd hate to see what happens when I tell everyone the truth."

"What *truth* is that?" Papa's brows raise.

"About how you preach purity and taint your soul with sins."

Momma's fingers tighten on his shoulder. "No one will believe you."

"You sure you wanna test that theory?"

Papa's jaw tenses, his eyes hardening.

Momma laughs. "So you're just gonna ignore us while we live in this town together? You're just gonna excommunicate us? We'll have to tell people *somethin'*."

"That's not my problem, Momma." I smile softly, even

though my heart twists in my chest. "I'd love to have both of you in my life. You're my folks and even if I shouldn't... I love you. I don't know how not to. I just wish you'd love me back." I shrug. "I'm not vengeful, I've accepted where we are, and I'll learn to be okay with that. But I won't let you manipulate me anymore."

Papa looks away, and Momma stares for a long moment before finally giving a brisk nod. Dismissing me.

I leave willingly, relief at the closure I feel pouring over me and soaking into my skin, washing away the questions.

But with clarity comes grief.

I'm not sure what I expected, but even after all this time, I long for them to apologize. For them to seek redemption and for me to be able to grant it. I guess in at least one thing, Momma is right.

Fairy tales don't exist.

Sometimes the villains continue on, thriving in their castles. And maybe happily ever after is finding peace in spite of that.

I am strong. I am bold. I own my power.

58

ELI

I've been redoing Pops's place for the past month. I wanted to give him somewhere new and fresh to come home to. Somewhere he wouldn't get lost in painful memories. I ran it by him in one of our weekly family sessions, and he seemed on board, so Lee and I have been working on it ever since. It's almost done, just his bedroom left, which is what we're tackling today.

He has one month left at Stepping Stones, and if it weren't for the court date looming above his head, I think we'd all be a bit more excited for his return home. His lawyer believes he'll be able to avoid actual jail time. The people he hit aren't pressing charges, and the fact he's already taken steps to better himself will work in his favor, but at the end of the day, he still drove under the influence and crashed into a family. He'll most likely be looking at house arrest and a long stint of probation. Normally, there would be alcohol courses but his lawyer thinks the ninety-day rehab will satisfy the judge, as long as he keeps going to meetings.

Meanwhile, here I am, trying to make moves to start this

new phase of my own life and also feeling responsibility for Pops's. I'm not sure whether to live here and keep him straight, or if I should find my own place. I've been wavering back and forth, the pressure grinding down on my chest whenever I think about making the wrong choice.

I called the realtor to start scouting the area, just in case.

It's been nice, having time with Lee. I never knew she was so *funny*. It makes me happy to get to know who she is in a way I never have before, even when we were kids. I'm grateful to be building the relationship I always envied in other families. One where we learn to appreciate each other for who we are, not who we want the other to be.

She's been asking about my time away from home, about what things were like for me with the injury. How things have been going with Becca since I've been back.

Which they haven't been. I've seen Becca a few times in passing, but even though every fiber of my being screams to stand next to her just to *be* in her presence, I've stopped myself.

I've heard the gossip around town, though. It's impossible to get away from the *scandal* of Preacher Sanger's ungrateful daughter disassociating from the church, leaving God—and her folks who raised her—behind.

I've been tempted to ask Lee, but something feels wrong about learning the details through anyone other than Becca.

I don't know how to approach her. Not sure how to bridge the gap from where we were to where I want us to be. But I'm so damn proud of her for finally breaking away and standing up for herself.

For not running.

I'm thinking about that very thing while Lee and I eat fast food she picked up on her way over. My phone vibrates across the kitchen table, and I glance down to see who it is, then reach out to silence it.

"You avoidin' someone?" she asks, taking a bite of her burger.

"Mind your business much?" I snark back, smiling.

She grins. "It's my sisterly duty to be nosy. I've got a lotta years to make up for." Her eyes widen. "There's a boatload of annoyin' left in me, just dyin' to break free."

"Now *that* I believe." I crunch up my foil wrapper, tossing it into the trash can. "It was Kim Bakerson."

Her nose scrunches. "The realtor?"

"The one and only." I nod.

"You two datin' or you lookin' for a place?"

I smirk. "I am definitely *not* dating Kim. I have her looking around to see if there's anything I'd be interested in. But..." I sigh, leaning back. "I don't know. Do you think maybe I should stay here? Make sure Pops has someone looking out for him?"

She scoffs. "No, I definitely do not think that. I know what it's like to spend every moment worryin' about Daddy. It'll suck the soul right outta ya. Don't fall into the codependency traits I've been learnin' how to overcome, Eli. It's a vicious cycle."

I grimace, picking at the napkin on the table. "You don't think I owe it to him?"

She shakes her head. "You're here. You're doin' every-thing you can. But you deserve to have a life you enjoy. Livin' life for others ain't no way to live." She pops a fry in her mouth. "What's your happy place?"

"My *happy* place?"

"Yeah... you know... it doesn't need to be an actual place. Just somethin' that makes you feel all warm and fuzzy inside."

I pick up my Coke and take a sip, thinking about what she asked. *My happy place.* I've never had too many moments of pure, unadulterated joy, not even when I went first in the draft. Everything's been tainted by the pressures of success or the sting of loneliness. The only time I've felt happy just *existing* was in Florida.

With Becca.

Which is maybe why it hurt so bad when she left. Why I've held on to so much anger. It wasn't because I hated *her*, it was that no one else could compare. No one else lit me up in all the ways she did.

"Becca," I mutter, setting my Coke back down.

Lee leans in, her brows shooting to her hairline. "Did you just say Becca?"

I nod once, my jaw tensing.

A knowing smile sprouts across her face, her blue eyes twinkling. "You two are really somethin' else."

"What's that supposed to mean?"

"You both are walkin' around town, tryin' like heck to be happy alone, when you could just get over it and be happy together."

I narrow my eyes. "Just *get over it*? Like that." I snap my fingers.

She shrugs. "Pretty much."

"Lee, she *left*. Without a word." My chest caves in with the sudden ache. "She made me love her and then she left me."

Lee crosses her arms. "And?"

My eyes widen. "And what?"

"We all make mistakes, Eli. Sometimes they're disastrous, life changin' mistakes." She reaches across the table and grabs my hand. "But eventually, we have to let go of the grudges that stunt our growth and keep us bitter."

"Easy for you to say," I scoff.

"It's not, actually. I know what it feels like to love someone so hard and then hate them for hurtin' you." Her hand comes up to rub at her chest. "But the thing is, Eli, it's easier to be angry than it is to forgive, because the anger gives you comfort. There's no risk. It might feel like crap, but at least you know what to expect when it hits."

"And what about forgiveness?" I ask.

"Forgiveness is…" She sighs. "Forgiveness is hard. Lettin' someone back in is harder. It's like takin' a leap of faith while bein' afraid of the heights."

My throat swells, the scar tissue forming the wall around my heart tearing at her words.

"Do you still love her?" She cocks her head.

My chest squeezes as I nod. "I think I'll always love her."

"Well, you'll do what you want. I won't push." Lee's eyes grow sad, a dark hue swirling through the icy blue. "I just hope you don't look back in five years and regret not takin' the leap. Especially if she's your happy place."

She drops the subject, but her words slide through the cracks of my heart, making it beat a different rhythm.

Normally Lee would be with me at Ma's grave. I've started visiting every Sunday with her, but she's in Nashville with Chase, so today I'm here alone.

My mind whirls the same way it has ever since my talk with Lee about what makes me happy.

I spent so much time after Becca left, blaming her for the hollowness that raged inside me. But she's not responsible for my emptiness, just as she's not responsible for my happiness. It's unfair to put your emotional well-being on someone else's shoulders, and I've spent the majority of my life doing just that.

Becca didn't cure me when she showed up in my life. She was the bandage to my loneliness, and once she was gone it

BENEATH THE STANDS

ripped the scab, making me bleed all over again, only this time it was worse because I knew what it felt like to love her and then lose her. So I channeled everything into my hurt, instead of working on healing the wounds that existed before her.

And then I used Sarah, hoping that appeasing Ma with a marriage after death would fill something within myself, some twisted sense of obligation for all the ways I didn't show up when she was still alive, not considering that all she ever wanted was my happiness.

There's no recovering from her death, no making up for the things I wish I had done differently. But Lee's right, you can either stay still, living in the mistakes, or you can take the leap and hope like hell you make it to the other side.

There's a sound behind me, like paper crinkling, and I spin toward the noise. As if I manifested her from my thoughts, Becca stands there with a bouquet of flowers clenched between her fingers.

My stomach flips, the way it always does when she's near.

"Hi," she breathes.

"Hi. What are you doing here?" I ask.

She lifts the bouquet and nods toward Ma's headstone. "Lee asked me to come by and drop these off since she couldn't make it." Her head tilts. "Surprised to see you here, though. She made it sound like no one else could do it."

I chuckle. *Of course she did.* "She knew I would be here. I've been coming here with her the past few Sundays."

"Oh. That's good. She said y'all were gettin' along better."

"Yeah."

She bobs her head, her gaze darting around the cemetery.

There are so many things on the tip of my tongue, but somehow, I still don't know what to say. So I'm silent—stuck in place—staring at her like a moron, the air spreading thin from the energy crackling between us.

She smiles softly and walks past me, her sweet scent floating on the breeze, making my nostrils flare when it hits.

Crouching down, she unwraps the bouquet, adding them to the flowers I already brought. Her hand reaches out and rests on top of Ma's name, her head bowing.

I stand back and watch her, emotion swelling in my chest at the sight of her having a moment with Ma. Sometimes, it's easy to forget how close they were. That she was affected by the loss too.

It isn't until she rises back up a few minutes later that I see the wetness on her cheeks. My heart thrums in my ears, my fists clenching to stop myself from reaching out to comfort her.

"So." She swipes a curl from her forehead. "How ya been?"

"Good. Really good."

She nods, shifting on her feet, her hands in her back pockets. "That's good." She blows out a breath, rocking back on her heels. "This is awkward, huh?"

A laugh bursts out of me. "Fuck... yes. I'm glad you said it."

She giggles. "You excited to start your new gig? Not long now."

My stomach clenches, my muscles locking tight. "Yeah. I can't wait."

She watches me, her gaze softening the longer she stares. "You nervous?"

"Yep."

She steps closer, and I can feel the heat of her body wrapping around me, offsetting the slight chill from the evening breeze.

"They're gonna love you," she whispers. "You're meant to lead, Eli. Don't forget it."

My chest splits at her words—at the fact she just *knows* what I need to hear.

"Yeah, hope so." I run my hand over my hair. "How about you? I heard about your parents."

"Yeah." She swallows thickly, glancing at her feet. "I've been lettin' them use me for a long time. Now I'm free of that, so I'll be alright. I'm a little sad though."

I nod, my hand scratching the scruff on my chin. "Takes a lot of guts to do what you did. You should be proud of yourself."

"Too bad it took me so long, huh?" She smiles.

I shrug. "Better late than never."

"Right." She scratches at her temple. "Listen, you." She reaches up, tangling her fingers through her hair. "You asked me *why*… and I never really gave you the answers you deserve. If you're still wantin' to know, I reckon it's far past time for me to tell you."

My gut clenches, the closure that I've been craving suddenly close enough to grasp. "You know I do," I rasp.

She nods. "I lived my whole childhood lookin' up to two men. My old man and the big guy up in the sky." She points above her head. "And then I experienced my first heartbreak when I caught Papa with Sally Sanderson when he shoulda been home with my momma."

My stomach sours at the thought of her finding him that way. Of all the repercussions that could have on any person, let alone a child.

Maybe I should be shocked, but I can't say I'm truly surprised. Preacher Sanger puts on a good facade but if you look close enough, it's easy to see through the mask.

"And from then on when I looked at my momma," she continues. "I saw a broken woman, tricked into a life by a man who spun pretty lies and trapped her in his web."

My chest squeezes. "So you're saying…"

"I'm sayin' I was afraid of what it meant to let myself love you. To let myself *be* loved." She swallows, glancing at the ground before meeting my eyes. "Have you ever let someone in, let someone else's words become your gospel?"

My heart stalls, images of all the times Pops's words gripped me tight and never let go, even after I had been gone for years.

I nod, my jaw clenching.

"Papa may be the preacher, but it's Momma who writes the scripture. And together they..." She blows out a breath. "Together they twisted me up so good I couldn't see the forest for the trees. It's not an excuse." She shakes her head. "But it is what it is. I loved you *so* much." Her eyes glisten, her tongue swiping along her lower lip. "And it terrified me." She smiles softly. "Still does if I'm honest."

My heart jolts, thumping against my chest at the thought of her loving me—of her never having stopped.

"I'm workin' on it, though. On *me*. I'm learnin' to separate who I've always been told to be with who I really am. Learnin' how to not let my fear of the future overpower my happiness in the now. That's all any of us can really do, right? Is try."

I swallow, my mouth sluggish while the missing puzzle pieces start to click into place. And while it doesn't make the past disappear, it does bring me peace. A blank hole that's been filled with a sense of understanding.

"Anyway." She sighs. "It was real nice to see you. I'll let you get back to time with your momma."

My heart stutters as she starts to leave. There's this *feeling* that's been flittering inside me for days. An anxious energy that bursts as she walks down the path back to the lot.

"Hey," I yell.

She turns, her eyebrow quirking.

"You hungry?"

A smile spreads across her face, highlighting the rosy hue that dusts across her cheeks.

She nods.

My heart leaps.

I follow.

EPILOGUE

BECCA

There's a sting in my back, but I wouldn't be able to tell you what it's from. Probably one of the random things on my desk that I'm currently laying on top of while Eli does delicious things in between my thighs.

"God, Eli, quit teasin' me. You're drivin' me *insane*."

"Good things come to those who wait, baby girl." He smirks up at me.

I quirk a brow. "Is that what you tell your players after you lose all those games?"

He chuckles, skimming my body with his hands as he rises back up, his lips meeting mine. "That fuckin' mouth of yours."

I grin against his lips, leaning in to nip at them. He catches my mouth before I can break away, his tongue tangling with mine. My eyes close while I savor his taste, a moan slipping out when I feel his cock nudging my center, then sliding inside me until we're hip to hip. He pulls out and repeats the action, my walls fluttering around him—his tongue having done most of the work to get me where I need to be. The heat spreads from my core through my body, my muscles seizing in anticipation.

"This is gonna be quick, we have places to be." He palms my ass, angling me so he can hit deeper.

"If you'd quit talkin' and just fuck me, we'd get there faster."

He smirks, pulling out and gripping his cock, his forearm flexing as he strokes himself. "Say please."

I shake my head, biting my lips to hide my smile.

He leans in, smearing his precum along my slit as he drags his tip between my folds. "Shame. What will my sister think when we're late to dinner?"

"I'll just tell her you couldn't satisfy my needs quick enough."

His hand comes up and wraps around my throat, his fingers squeezing just enough to cut off my air supply. Sparks fire, my pussy clenching against nothing, desperate to be filled.

"Keep it up, Rebecca, and I'll come on top of this pretty pussy instead of inside you." He emphasizes his words by sliding his length back and forth against my clit, making my legs shake with the tension that's pulling tight inside me.

He lessens his grip on my neck. "Tell me," he rasps.

"*Please.*"

"Good girl." He thrusts hard and fucks me fast, the motion causing the pens on the corner of my desk to shake. My legs come up to wrap around him, *needing* him deeper.

He trails kisses along my jaw until his head rests in the crook of my neck. His breaths are heavy on my skin, causing tingles to shoot down my spine and goose bumps to sprout over my body.

"I love being inside you."

"I love *you*," I moan back.

His hips jerk, pushing in so deep he hits my cervix, the

sharp stab of pain enough to send me spiraling off the edge. My fingers claw at his shoulders, pulling him close as I convulse around him, hoping to mold his body to mine until I can't tell us apart.

The sound of his groan vibrates against my skin as he explodes inside me, his cock pulsing against my walls, my pussy milking him of every drop.

"*Christ,*" he pants, collapsing against me.

I should be worried that someone heard, but the school day is already over and my office is in the very back hallway. I try to keep things professional while we're at work, but Eli likes to corner me in places I tell him not to and seduce me into submission.

I've always been a sucker for Eli's control.

It's been six months since we ran into each other at the cemetery. *Thanks, Lee.*

It was rough at first. There was a lot of hurt between us. But Doc says the best relationships start with friendship, and if the foundation is strong, even the strongest storm won't knock it down.

So, we took our time. Became *friends.* Built the trust on both sides. Learned how to communicate in a healthy way, and to keep from giving in to the voices that whisper we don't deserve the happiness.

And I've never been so damn happy.

Eli lifts off me and buckles up his pants, bending over to grab my panties off the floor. He winks as he slips them in his pocket.

I arch my brow. "You expect me to go to your sister's without panties?"

"Looks like it." He smirks.

"Okay, that's fine." I stand up and straighten my skirt, reaching for a tissue to clean his cum from where it's dripping out of me. "But don't come cryin' to me when you get jealous thinkin' Jax might accidentally see somethin' he shouldn't."

Jax came roaring back into town a few weeks ago, not willing to talk about the reason why. Just said he was done with California and everything that came with it. I'm not one to push, but he's crazy if he thinks we don't all see the change. There's a heaviness in his gaze that didn't used to be there.

The only person he'll talk to is Chase, which is ironic considering he couldn't stand him for years.

Men.

Eli's smile drops. "I forgot he was back."

I shrug. "Your choice, big head."

He rubs his jaw, walking over to me and grabbing my wrist before I can put the tissue between my thighs. "Leave it. I want to know I'm dripping out of you while you sit at the dinner table."

I roll my eyes, pretending I'm annoyed, even though his words send a spike of arousal through my body. I grasp his hips with my hands, dipping my fingers into his pocket. "Then give me back my panties."

Yanking the fabric from his pants, I push him back so I can slip them on and grab my purse.

When we get to the front entrance, there's a few kids by the doors, huddled around their phones, giggling.

"What's so funny?" I ask.

They straighten. "Oh, hi Miss Sanger. You'll never believe who we just saw!" Becky, one of our sophomores, says, her voice high and loud.

"Who's that?"

"Blakely Donahue!" she shrieks.

I widen my eyes and nod. "Oh, I see. Who's that?"

Sammi, another sophomore, giggles. "You don't know

who Blakely Donahue is? She's the freakin' best. My favorite influencer."

"Right?" Becky agrees. "She's so pretty. I heard she was datin' one of her daddy's employees. Some twenty-eight-year-old."

"She said it wasn't true, Becky," Sammi chastises. "Can you imagine, though? She's nineteen! That's fuckin' gross."

I put my hands on my hips. "Hey, watch your mouth, ladies. Where'd you see this Blakely Donahue?"

"She was just here!" Becky says.

I smile at their excitement. I don't spend time on social media so I have no idea who this girl is, but I'm surprised anyone would find themselves in Sugarlake by coincidence.

"Here as in Sugarlake?" Eli asks.

"Here as in *here*." Becky points out the windows toward the front of the school where a royal blue Maserati sits haphazardly along the curb—a girl with long legs and heels taller than mine stands next to it, talking on her phone.

My brows draw down as I glance back at the girls. "Alright, girls. Y'all don't stick around here too long."

"Bye, Miss Sanger!"

Eli squeezes my waist. "I'm gonna go grab the car and bring it around. You okay?"

"Yeah, I'm just gonna see if she needs help with anything." I nod toward the girl outside.

I follow Eli out the front doors just as the girl spins toward me, her shiny, brown hair whipping behind her. She doesn't look familiar, but Becky and Sammi were right. She is pretty. Stunning in fact. And *young*. If I didn't know every face in this high school, I'd confuse her for a student.

"Hi. Can I help you with somethin'? I ask, shielding my eyes against the setting sun.

Her amber gaze locks on mine as she slips her phone in

her back pocket. "Oh, hi." She chews on her lip. "I'm not sure."

"You new in town?"

She laughs. "I guess you could say that. I'm looking for someone, but now that I'm here I'm not quite sure where to look. I just stopped at the first place I saw." She gestures to the school behind us. "He doesn't exactly know I'm here."

"Surprise visit?" I smile.

"Something like that." She grimaces.

"Well, who ya lookin' for? Maybe I can help. Small town and all."

"Jackson Rhoades."

ALSO BY EMILY MCINTIRE

Sugarlake Series

Beneath the Stars, #1

Beneath the Hood (April 2021)

Title TBA (Coming Summer 2021)

ACKNOWLEDGMENTS

I never thought I'd be writing acknowledgments in the back of my own book, let alone a second one. The truth is that while I've always loved writing, it's all of you who have made me want to continue. Seeing you read and love my characters make every single second worth it. So thank YOU. For reading, for (hopefully) enjoying, for supporting an indie author. I'm so grateful that you picked up my book.

To my best friend and bufflehead, Sav. You are without a doubt my soul sister. I'm so thankful to have found you. I don't know that I'd be able to do this without you there to be my #1 hype woman and to talk me out of every single spiral that I go through. Love you! Cheers to the Smokies!

To my girls: Lee'Rain Jacquot, Greer Rivers, Kayleigh King. Thank you for your friendship and your motivation when I'm procrastinating. Y'all always push me to be the best and are the first ones to support when I need. I'm so lucky and thankful to have you in my corner.

To my beta readers: Thank you for being the ones who test run my stories—for always helping me work out the kinks, and for working with me on my ridiculously tight deadlines.

You are invaluable to me. My books would not be what they are without you.

Sav R. Miller, Lee'Rain Jacquot, Greer Rivers, Kayleigh King, Garnet Christie, Michelle Chamberland, AV Asher, Clara Elroy, Ariel Mareroa, Melissa Whitman, Ashley Adams, Alison Butler

To my editor, Ellie and fairy proof mother, Rosa at My Brother's Editor: Y'all already know. I promise to try and stop putting an s on the end of toward. (But I'll probably forget.)

To my amazing cover designer, Clarise at CT Cover Creations: You are without a doubt one of the most talented people I've ever met. I'm so glad I found you!

To my Glammers: Where would I be without you? You guys are my #1 Hype Team and my internet family. The place where I can go to vent, laugh, cry, and talk about our favorite books. I'm so thankful for y'all to be on this crazy ride with me.

To the Bloggers and Bookstagrammers: Thank you for reading, reviewing, shouting out, making edits, spending your time on anything that has to do with my books. Indie authors would be lost without you.

To my family: Thank you for your constant support and cheerleading even though we all live so far away from each other. Again, #sorrynotsorry for the sex scenes. You know what you're getting into at this point if you decide to read it.

To my husband Mike, Thank you for being my soulmate. For being my rock. For bringing home flowers and Sephora gift cards just because. And for bringing home champagne to toast with every success big or small. There's nobody I'd rather experience life with than you. I love you and Melody more than anything.

To my daughter, Melody. You are the reason for everything.

ABOUT EMILY

Emily McIntire is an emerging author of New Adult, Contemporary Romance. A long time songwriter and an avid reader, Emily has always had a passion for the written word, and a penchant for painful, messy, beautiful romance. After all, what's a happily ever after without a dose of angst?

When she's not writing, you can find her chasing her crazy toddler around laying by the pool with a good book. She lives in Florida with her husband, daughter and dog.